REDEMPTION

GOVERNED BY INDEPENDENCE

OLEN BAKER

DEFIANCE PRESS
& PUBLISHING

Redemption: Governed by Independence

First Edition: April 2023

Printed in the United States of America

10 9 8 7 6 5 4 3 2 1

ISBN-13: 978-1-959677-28-4 (Paperback)
ISBN-13: 978-1-959677-27-7 (eBook)

Published by Defiance Press and Publishing, LLC

Bulk orders of this book may be obtained by contacting Defiance Press and Publishing, LLC. www.defiancepress.com.

Public Relations Dept. – Defiance Press & Publishing, LLC
281-581-9300
pr@defiancepress.com

Defiance Press & Publishing, LLC
281-581-9300
info@defiancepress.com

CHAPTER 1

Day 7

*"It is better to have less thunder in the mouth
and more lightning in the hand."*

– Apache proverb

So, there I was, as we all are at the start of the worst part of our lives: either hoping things will get better or, for some, using the experience as a learning tool to twist against others.

My friends call me Bodhi, but I don't have many friends here in this prison on the western side of "God Blessed Texas." I tend to get called a lot of other names, but as long as they smile when they do it, I tend to let it slide.

Let's just say this ain't the first time I had to work the hard way to earn my keep and save my ass to have a plate at a table while I chose my battles with care. These days, as some would say, I would be happy with the crumbs from the floor if it got me out of here.

My spirit is nearly broke, and as one of my distant cousins or ancestors said, I am sick and sad for it.

You'll have to excuse me—sometimes I get philosophical and ramble in my own head.

It gets worse, though, when I'm trapped behind concrete and bars instead of under open skies. Or even riding shotgun in an ambulance, charging into war against death itself for the people in my care.

You see, I was an EMT before I found myself here … but that was another life that I will never return back to.

"Hey, watch what you're doing, asshole!" said one offender at another. In fact, it was my celly, Spike from the Diamondback Motorcycle Club. I went into guard mode to watch his back and scanned the faces I saw, only to catch the sound of a grunt and cough from Spike.

"HEY!" I cried with the thunder of a buffalo and charged at the shanking sumbitch. I didn't know him well, but his tats and skin put him with *Las Hermanas del Muertos.*

We called them every derogatory name you could think of, and we didn't give anything like a friendly smile, either. Not that they were offended in the least, since they worked that image to their sick advantage to isolate and "turn out" young and dumb fish new to the market. The silly sissies even claimed to have witches and were a coven with major outside juice, not a local prison gang of deranged fruity fairies.

Now, understand that I'm not thinking all this as it happens; I'm just telling you how it is and keeping you up with current events, such as my shin crashing into his knee as I stepped up with a sucker-ing feint that flowed into a crippling roundhouse.

Shin beats shiv. I won.

Oh yeah, I was raised in the shadow of an army base, and my grandad was a close-quarter combat instructor during the Korean and early Vietnam Wars. I liked Muay Thai the most of what he taught, so I went behind his back and learned from his students when I got old enough to decide not to grow up as a victim who had wasted his life playing video games. When I wasn't eating up martial arts and working, I would lift weights to relax.

Then I got to prison and learned what work really is.

There was a snap, crackle, pop, and squeal before I kicked the shiv across the floor through the chaos of the bedlam happening around us. I stood over my brother and tried to keep my eyes every-where at once.

Another brother from the Diamondbacks came up to stand with me, and I looked down to see blood coming from Spike's lips.

"Spider, get some others over here to look out! I got work to do!" I didn't think to ask or beg—I just said it, because it looked like Spike had a punctured lung.

I ripped his shirt open and confirmed it: bubble, bubble, toil and trouble from his wounds. I slapped the palm of my hand down be-cause I had nothing else. I let the air slip out and none go back as I let good thoughts flow through my hands the way Grandma had taught when we made bread, something that I took with me into the field of emergency medicine.

Back when I was a warrior fighting death, and not here … not here. I nearly cried when my mind started going back there, think-ing of the failures I made … but I was raised better, stronger than to weep and wail unless it was in victory with blood on my hands. "Get the medics in here!" became my war cry, and I used it now for my brother.

I got shoved out of the way by coarse uniform-wearing bodies and ballistic shields and came back into myself as thunder clapped in the room and the roar of the war happening throughout the building began to quiet and still.

I went with the shove, scooting on my feet and butt until I was against a wall with blood on my hands, but not from my enemies. I turned my gaze at the one screaming loudest—he was hurt least. I eyeballed the ones nearest him and waited to see how they wanted to move, but they were backing up and taking their little boy with them like a kitten mewling for momma.

Yes, there were hard feelings between me and them, and them and mine.

The Diamondbacks claimed me first in this prison, but they were never cruel to me. I earned from them, and they earned whatever I'm worth here in return. I went through worse going to grade school, to be honest, with bullies on both sides telling me I was too white to be red and should be dead, and military brats who said I was too red to be trusted. Seems we take those first lessons of emotional pain into the world to inflict on others, and no one wants to stop the pain but the healers. My grandmother would often argue and fight with my grandad over that ... before his heart and lungs gave out.

I looked up and faked a cake-eating grin at the guard in front of me. The times I had split skin and bruised bone in here came from this guy more often than not. "Howdy, boss," I greeted Guard Carls as friendly as I could.

"Bodhi, I see you are at the middle of a shitstorm again."

"You know me ... wrong time for the right thing to get in trouble over."

"Get off your ass! I got to make a report to the warden about what you did. I should kick you in the face and scalp you for all this!"

I slapped my hand to the side of my face, eyes wide in mock shock, and streaked my bloodied fingers toward my mouth. "Me, boss? I was only trying to help my brother and avoid trouble."

The big beefy guard turned his face from me in disgust.

"Let's go get you cleaned up, stupid. There's blood on your hands, blood on your face—all of it from your *brother,* who I am sure will claim you saved his life rather than tried to kill him and blame it on those other pukebags."

"Well, when truth is on your side, ride with the wind."

"More like speak with a forked tongue holding an apple."

That's Carls. Give him an excuse and he gets preachy, and I try to shut up about beliefs that I learned should be respected growing up. Even if my own were not.

CHAPTER 2

"He was straddling the body of his cellmate with blood all over him, proving means and opportunity better than anyone else." Carls was in the middle of giving a play-by-play that would do justice to any TV police forensic sitcom—with probably more drama here in reality than in the land of fiction—after we made it into the warden's office.

"Inmate Benavides looks like he has a shattered knee," Carls continued with a finger pointed at me. "And no one saw anything or can find the shiv that was used."

Gotta hate it when the sitcom leaves plot holes. One minute, he had means and opportunity; the next, no weapon and I'm breaking someone else's leg when I'm supposed to be shiving someone else, like I'm Superman and can take on two at once. Ok, yeah, I could probably handle two, but I would rather not tempt fate.

"I think Goody Two-Shoes here got into it with his cellmate and shanked him, then laid out the nearest fink for us to gobble up like a fatted calf."

"Bodhi, what do you have to say about what happened?" Warden Hardcastle asked me.

"I say that what I say does not matter to someone that does not want peace," I said after pausing to gather the million fragmented thoughts in my head. "Especially since we are under surveillance and watched by the guards. You have your truth all ready to use against me."

"You were actually standing at the precise angle to cut the view off from Spike's stabbing, and all of my guards say they were looking at someone else when it happened. I ain't asking you to rat someone—I am asking you to speak for yourself and tell me how to treat you from here."

"Ok, I will tell you what you know." Hand me a problem, and I'll make a solution. Whether anyone likes it or not is another matter. "You know I came here for manslaughter charges because a family claimed I killed their son by overmedicating them with meds that also were expired. I was proven guilty and served most of my time at another prison before coming here a few months ago, and I've been around here when a lot of trouble started. I get the fact you don't know me, and there is some history from the other place making a big elephant in the room here because of what I was forced to do by the other warden—"

"Allegedly," Carls interrupted. I'm not sure "alleged" meant what he thinks it means. Clearly we were on different sitcom scripts since he was wearing the cool Oakley flea market sunglasses … indoors. *Dork.*

"Spike is going to go to the hospital for a while. Probably a week, depending on how they treat that lung and any infection … " I paused before hitting them with my best shot at staying out of trouble. "Why don't you put me to work where I work best, in the infirmary? And you can see if I'm worth staying there until Spike shows up. After he comes back, I would like to be kept as close as you feel safe and care for him until he is back on his feet. If anything happens while I do what I am tasked with—to the equipment, to the people, to the patients, and to Spike there—while I'm there … you are welcome to hold me accountable for it."

"Well, part of that idea appeals to me. I miss the day when we had a man run for office that promised he would make convicts make big rocks smaller. I don't go that far, but I do believe in restitution, rehabilitation, and most importantly, redemption … and we are here to help people pay or work it off according to their means. Carls, what say you?"

"Put him in the same room with the inmate he tried to murder in front of everyone, when nobody is watching? Sounds like a safe bet to me," he sarcastically added.

"Ok, then don't. But you guys already proved you have nothing on me. So, I'll go back to life in the big house, y'all worry about this, and when I'm not around him and something happens, at least I know who you can't blame for it." I turned to leave only to catch one right where it drove all the air from my lungs.

"Hang on, boy, the warden ain't done speaking to you yet!" Carls said as he chopped a hand down on the nerve cluster at my neck and shoulder. He roughly put me back in my seat to catch my breath from the sharp jab.

"He makes a good point, though. I think it is better we put him where we can keep an eye on him, and the man someone around here wants dead." The warden turned to look at me. I was just trying to breathe and be upright while looking like the sweet innocent boy my granny always accused me of being.

"Or we could stick him in solitary, keep watch over Spike, and everyone walks away breathing."

"Or, hey, stick Spike in solitary the rest of his stay, even!" I said in mock excitement as I tried to stand up to leave over the brilliant inspiration Carls had. What a shmuck.

"Have a seat, inmate." Carls slapped a hand on my shoulder and did a Spock move, his fingers digging into my nerves.

I was sitting before I even knew my ass had hit the chair. No one could accuse Carls of not knowing how to fight and put people on the ground ... just that he lacked any brains.

"Yes, let's all sit down, chill out, and figure out the best solution for this problem."

The warden had made himself a fresh pot of coffee that had just stopped dribbling into the pot. I bet it tasted way better than what we had. Then he surprised me. "Bodhi, would you like a cup while we talk?"

"Yes, sir, I would." My manners cut through the bullshit my mouth was nearly walking me out of. The warden got me a thick enameled cup with a gold sheriff's star on it and handed it to me. All black, the way I normally took it ... but I sure wanted sugar the way my grandad had liked his. Then he threw a few sugar packets down on the desk in front of me with a plastic stir stick thinger-doo. Heaven, here I come, I thought. I mixed, he mixed, Carls even mixed—we were having a mixer.

I took a sip and burned my tongue. I was so wrong; it tasted exactly like what we got. Plus, it was scalding hot and seared my taste buds. But I did have more respect for the warden now that I knew he drank what we were given.

"Seems to me, both of you have good points. And yeah, your skills are being squandered a little working the showers and toilets, but from what I've heard, you kept them cleaner than just about anyone else. So let's see what you both think of this: You go to work in the infirmary for now. Carls watches over you and reports to me in the meantime before Spike comes. If he tells me you haven't killed anyone between now and then, we will revisit the idea of you taking any part over being Spike's service tech for the medics and the nurse down there. And that will also come with reports from what they tell me about your performance. If either of you want to tell me I'm wrong in my suggestion, let's hear it."

For the first time, Carls and I agreed exactly the same way with the same two words.

"Good, the yays have it. Now finish your coffee, and Carls, throw your fish back in the tank before we have too much democracy in here. God knows I didn't vote for that guy we got as president."

"More like a snake, but as you order."

"Actually, let someone else do it. I got another errand for you when you pass him along."

"Yes, sir."

As we left, I was feeling a little better. I would be spending more time away from walls and the crap of the world that was getting on my mind, going back toward the light, so to speak, by getting into the infirmary. My second home from the time I'd spent working in the ER and working in the back of ambulances ... which I did not want to think about right now. But I knew my craft. I would be running the show for those people in no time.

I was relayed from guard to guard, door to gate until I got to my cell, where I finally got to relax.

The warden had ordered some years ago that they put Christian religious quotes for peace on the walls, and they gave us all a New Testament Bible when we came in with a pocket Constitution of our country attached to it. At first I had rebelled against this, for some not-so-obvious reasons I won't get into.

But here I am in hell, and they want me to respect the laws used against me?

But the discipline of my grandad and my granny won out somewhat. I could not make the Bible of the forefathers of my grandad defeat the Bible of my grandmother. She even often reminded me that the Great Chief Geronimo became a Christian while still having his wives.

We all have two dogs to feed inside us, and I will close the mouth of the yappy one spewing philosophy for now.

I sat back in my bunk and closed my eyes to try to settle my raging thoughts when I heard someone put their hand on my cell bars. I opened my eyes and saw the tatted face and chrome grill of a scrawny punk looking at me.

"We saw what you did to our brother, homes. There will be a day for us."

"Your mouth is bigger than your eyes. I wonder what your ass will show me when you turn tail the other way. Big and juicy, or skinny from being worked over by your little sisters? Find me when you can do more than talk. We both know you won't reach into a snake den."

The fish flipped his gang signs and spewed cuss words at me.

"Oh, and I hate kicking boney ass. It hurts my feet, so make sure if yours is being worked over, you send someone that will please my feet better than you!" I called after him and let out a war yelp.

Now, you may think I am all full-blooded Native. Not so, and I will never claim to be more than one just raised on the rez for a short time. But the blood from my grandfather had rubbed off on me out there, even as it was falling in the dirt of some of the playgrounds. My mother had been there. My own father, well, we'd tried to have a relationship when I was young, but he loved rodeos and buckle bunnies while playing cattleman more than the idea of loving a wife and son and learning to be a father.

Too little of one blood to be much of another family. I claim what I am: a mutt of everything all mixed up and best left alone.

After I calmed down, then got pumped up by the *Hermana*, I got up and started doing body weight exercises that I had learned to make a habit of in prison every time I found myself awake with nothing to do.

Not to toot my own horn, but a prison diet, discipline, and lack of anything else to do will either break you or make you. My mind may have been a mess, but my body and social skills were a whole other matter. I was learning a lot of the nuances of socializing from the cons here. A lot of what I learned was just the temptation to use it as a weapon against anyone in front of me.

Talk about playing with fire, especially for someone involved in a Central to West Texas biker-slash-prison gang. In here, I was just one of the gophers—as in a gopher snake? Get it? Hahaha. Barrel of laughs, since I had to fetch and carry anything and get whatever done whenever I could while acting as muscle when needed and watching the backs of the Diamond … Backs.

Insert internal cough at pseudo pun.

King himself came by and slapped his hands on the bars to get my attention while my world was upside down at this point. Literally. Handstand pushups, see? Bet you are all kinds of impressed.

"Hey, King. I'm guessing the warden wants to speak to you next since you're here first," I took a shot to get the ball rolling the right way.

"Don't get too smart for yourself, Bodhi. They took my rat first, but good try. Tell me what happened."

"I was looking at the wrong place at the right time for them . . . or the right way of putting it, for us, would be that I dropped the ball and wasn't alert enough to keep Spike safe when I was closest to him. One of the little homos we can now call Wounded Knee," I said with a heartless chuckle, which also made King grin while his eyes narrowed. "Got in the way of my leg for what he did. I slapped my palm on the wound and tried to get help and heal and guard all at once after that."

Oh yeah, and ladies and gents, we tend to cuss in prison and say the meanest words. We ain't saints, and if you thought we were, God bless your little heart! I will pray to the Big Spirit in the sky for you when I see Him! But I will do my best to spare you from the mean words. That's the least I can do since I can't spare you from my nightmares while we travel this same journey in spirit together.

"Not much different from what I heard. You did well and did what you were supposed to. I know you're still deciding where to go when you get out of here, but we're saving a spot for you if you decide you want to wear our colors when you get out."

"Thank you for the choice, but yeah, I am still hoping to hear something from some of my family before I have to decide. Those twisted sisters are getting out of hand. You want me to let this go?"

"Be strong for yourself first." He came close and hissed that out at me through gritted teeth and constricted facial muscles. "That is your first law here for us."

"Then I know what to do. Anything else?" I asked as I came close enough that he could whisper his command.

"Only take advantage of the right opportunity, if it presents itself, to teach others the same lesson."

And there it was, just like that: a hit without orders. A strike with no rattle. No puns this time—just dead serious reality.

CHAPTER 3

DAY 6

"No man in the wrong can stand up against a fellow that's in the right and keeps on a-comin'."

– Captain Bill McDonald, Texas Ranger

"Hey, boo!" Cherry called to me when I walked into the infirmary. Cherry was … what's the best word? Polyamorous? A fellow inmate that belonged to the prison gang Tribal.

She—or he, depending on which way you faced—was a good friend and someone I could unload on about my outside personal problems. If I didn't have someone to help take that steam off, I would've been running mad in here by now, no doubt. Bad medicine on the brain destroys the body and spirit.

What? You thought I was a bigot? Get real. Only thing I have enmity for is anyone that wants to make me their whipping boy the way *Las Hermanas* tried with me on day one.

"Hey, Cher." I knew Cherry was a huge fan of the diva singer and liked it when I called him that.

"How did you get down here? Does this have anything to do with that shanking I heard about yesterday?"

"Well, in a manner of speaking, the boss wants me where they can watch me mess up easier than where I was."

"Well, you are supposed to get out soon, right? How much trouble can a booty Bodhi body get into with your Cher on your shoulder?"

Flamboyant in manner, style, and charm, that Cher had me nearly smiling. I didn't have it in my mind that I'd be out in a little less than a week. It had been a busy day or so for me in the big house, and that had messed up my internal calendar. I wondered if it had slipped the warden's mind too. Was this was a favor, or a curse?

"Can't be soon enough. But when Spike gets in here, I need to be as close as I can. Looks like someone put a hit on him over a sideways deal a while back. I don't know what happened, so it's not worth guessing more."

"I hear ya, better to stay stupid around here than be dead and smart. So, whatcha gonna do when you get out? You never told me if you got families to turn to."

"I can go back to my grandmother and mom's … but I would turn into a burden there. No job opportunities for me, and I would end up sucking her government checks more than the other cousins I have. The Diamondbacks are my home here, but they haven't told me if anything waits outside. I don't know what else I could do."

"Oh, Bodhi baby, don't be down! You get out, you will find something that fits if you look in the right place and take off like that wild stallion I can tell you are."

I blushed. No, I am not that dark at all, and yes, even though I'm straight and proud, the compliment was nice, no matter that it came from someone whom I bore no physical attraction to and had to look past a social norm or two with as long as boundaries were respected. Besides, five years is a long time without even a visit from anything female to be attracted to.

"Thanks for the sweet nothings. You ready to show me around and introduce me to everyone?"

"Every time I think I get to keep you all to myself, you have to go be with everyone else," Cher whined—no, really whined. Sometimes I couldn't tell where the drama ended and began with Cherry.

But I suppose it wouldn't be fair to judge if you didn't know "Cher" was short for Cherry Bomb.

OK, backstory time. I know you're thinking, "When will you tell us what's in your closet?"

Well, how about never? I know. Good luck—we are stuck together in this journey, so you get to wait until I am ready. In the meantime, let me formally introduce you to the firebug known locally by the Tribe as Cherry Bomb, aka Terrell Jefferson in another life. His family here in prison was an all-Black street gang that called itself Tribal for short. The story behind the name went along the lines of saying "Try it, baller" to anyone who crossed their streets. Those who are Tribal reach across the southeastern states and are trying to reach across Texas.

The sob story I had worked out of Cher was that when he was around four, he got into the Christmas decorations and decided to help his mom by decorating when she was sleeping in their two-bedroom apartment that was also home to his dad and three other siblings. I never asked the age ranges or other details; I try not to pry where it isn't my business ... and yeah, none of it technically was. But Cher was unloading on me last Christmas while decorating the clinic, and I was there accepting delivery of ... umm ... some presents for someone from Santa. Don't ask.

So apparently, little Terrell went overboard enough with the lights, the floor heater, and no telling what else, to the point that the sparks flying out of the wall quickly ignited the dry Christmas tree that had been donated to the family and torched all the presents.

Luckily, his mom had heard the screams and came out and used a fire extinguisher to put everything out. Unluckily, Mom had grabbed a work utility belt that belonged to his dad and gave him a beating with the leather and buckles. She tore him up so bad, he nearly had to go to the hospital and probably should have, even though that would have left them without a mom for Christmas and added to the trauma the children were going through.

And in my opinion, it sounded like—and was confirmed by the emotional scars—that he would have received transport and children's services being reported had I come along something like that on the job. Yes, I had been in emergency services and my job was saving people's lives, prior to being incarcerated for manslaughter.

That is what it means to be an ambulance-riding EMT. Well, not the manslaughter part, of course, but as one of my instructors taught us, when you play with the drugs we do to start life, sometimes life stops too. And you better be ready to have that one death knock you down under every life you ever save.

What level EMT was I, you ask? I've always hated that question, because it's paramedics who save lives and basics that save paramedics, as I was taught and learned firsthand as my skills progressed. Granted, a basic didn't save me, and I didn't save a life to wind up here.

There, you got something out of me. Happy?

So, anyway, back to the important person here. Cherry's dad got home from his job at construction about the time the proverbial dust cleared and had quite a mess on his hands. Apparently the old man was former army engineer and knew a thing or two about first aid, as well as repairing all the scorched walls and ceiling with surplus and scrap supplies from work. But Christmas was ruined; no one got any gifts except cuts and welts and tears all around.

When young Terrell grew old enough to work, his dad got him a job at the company he worked for and made sure he showed up for every shift.

Yeah, I almost didn't believe it either until I heard what Cherry Bomb was arrested for. Let's say what I heard could be done with an MRE was just a firecracker compared to the stick of dynamite that Cherry had cooked up after spending a few bucks at a dollar store and applied to a police car ... and the city hall building it was parked beside. The charges were dropped down to basically criminal mischief and destruction of public property ... and assaulting a public servant, and disturbing the peace ... and contempt of court got added during arraignment and trial. Apparently, the courts had decided three to five would do Cherry Bomb some good.

Oh, yeah, what did Terrell's dad specialize in while serving as army engineer? Demolitions. Dad was also the demolition man for the company and could bring down a house of cards into a single stack with a firecracker by placing it at the right stress point. No lie, according to Cherry.

And he could do the same trick in reverse and send the entire house of cards flying through the room with the same firecracker.

The finer details of how Cherry had made such an explosion, and really the why of it, were never disclosed publicly. Needless to say, the squad car had actually belonged to a man that Cherry had found out was married when they were, uh, having an *extramarital* relationship.

I did not feel the need to know any more details than that, so let's stop there, shall we?

Yeah, Cherry had some issues, but then who doesn't here in the big house?

We can boil our issues down to two types: those we inflict upon ourselves, like my own, and those that others have inflicted upon us. We internalize those issues, and they become malignant tumors we use to destroy ourselves until we externalize them. Then we destroy others.

If you think I figured that out through on-the-job training, you would be wrong. That's firsthand experience, right there. Want to tell me I am wrong? Say it to my face. I know what I did to myself and how I did it. Now, I externalize my issues through training my body and mind using the self-defense techniques I learned in the shadow of my grandfather. I would apply my tribal survival training, too, but that's kind of impossible under my current circumstances.

Bars, walls, no sky, no earth. Just concrete, artificial lighting, and social etiquette from gen pop. The sound of rain and thunder were the closest I had been to freedom while here, and it only broke my heart to hear what I could neither see, smell, nor feel on my skin.

Boy, that rabbit took us for a ride to Albuquerque. We better take a left here and get where we're going.

"This is Miss Nancy," Cherry said, adding a syllable more than necessary to say the name of the RN in charge of the clinic.

"Hey, Bodhi, good to see you again. I've been hoping you would find a way in here to work with us. Looks like it's just in time, huh?"

"Hey, stop acting like you know the cons, Miss Nancy! It's my job to show him around and show him how everything operates around here, and if he already knows anything, I'll have nothing to do for the rest of this detail except count the bandages again."

"Cher, you better start over and do it again, besides I don't think you did it right. You shouldn't be that friendly with the staff here," I helpfully offered.

Nancy was the basic picture of a favorite auburn-haired aunt who always treated everyone that came in with kid gloves and open, honest smiles. She had earned the protection of nearly all of the gang bosses and was regarded as a treasure. She was neutral in the prison. And as far as I could tell, she had done so by showing that simple Texas hospitality and friendliness that was becoming increasingly rare these days.

"Oh, good lord, you two. I can tell y'all are going to be running this circus and keeping me in stitches," she said between eye rolls and giggles.

"Now y'all are ganging up on me!" Cherry said in a pouting whine with his hands on his hips. "And I like it a lot!"

For the rest of the night, I was pretty much led by the nose, introduced to everyone, and familiarized with all of the menial chores I would be doing, which I already knew how to do from the world I'd left behind. When I would not be spending the night folding fitted cot sheets for the patient beds, I would be cleaning the beds as inmates were released back to their cells, mopping, taking out trash, and being an extra set of hands any time any of the medics or nurses needed help when directly supervised. The prison did not staff a doctor on-site, or even a physician's assistant. They were only called in for exams if needed. If anything happened that was bad enough to warrant a trip out, a county sheriff would pick up the inmate, or ride escort with the county EMS, and take them to the ER. If it was *really* bad, then 911 services would be called in to pick the inmate up, and he would be transported under guard with sheriff's deputies giving escort.

Ok, I hear you already—way too many details on what isn't important. What is important to know, however, is that working in the infirmary is considered the cake job for the most trusted of inmates. Was that me? Probably not, since I'd sent more than my fair share here. But I had less than a week before I was released on parole, so between that and what had happened with Spike, and my background as an EMT, I had gotten real lucky. In fact, since the clinic was already fully staffed, I didn't think luck or coincidence had anything to do with it. Someone wanted me here.

Oh, does that sound paranoid, or even like I might be foreshadowing the obvious trouble that was coming my way? Well, duh. If you expected this to be one of those story sagas where I'm the hero and everything goes my way, welcome to the suck that is my life and learn to love it for me, then tell me the trick to make me love it too. In the meantime, I have learned that things could always be a lot worse.

How, you ask? Let me introduce you to Reggie. Now, I didn't know his last name; I didn't want to know anything else about him than I already knew, which was too much. The reason Reggie was restrained, both hands and feet, and laid belly-down on the bed was because he was waiting for ambulance transport and had two guards as babysitters making sure he didn't fight the restraints or help more than he already had. No, he was not having a psychological emergency. How do I put this delicately … he was having a proctological emergency? Ok, maybe considering the circumstances Reggie was going through, that might be too cruel in humor.

You see, Reggie was here in the land of the "freed from freedom" because he was found guilty of child rape. Now, before you bring out the pitchforks and torches, you may want to know first that Reggie claimed he didn't do it.

I had to say that first so we could all laugh, because here is where it gets murky. According to Reggie, his ex-wife was actually a prostitute and addicted to a number of street drugs, including the big *H*. Reggie claimed that he noticed a sudden and drastic change in his daughter's behavior and went over for a surprise visit. The surprise was on him, because according to Reggie, his wife had been entertaining a John—after she had claimed to be cleaned up and reformed by the church—and they had doped his daughter up with a date rape cocktail. The biggest surprise? The John was also a cop who was using Reggie's ex as an informant with perks.

Now, I said all that to let you know that some cons have very elaborate-sounding true stories. Because seriously, the last place you want to be as a child predator is in prison. It's enough to turn you into a jailhouse "Hemingway," forcing you to tell a story to get you out of the karmic payback that becomes an endless cycle of destruction on your body and soul by other inmates turning you into a human toilet.

Since I had no way to verify if his story was true or not to know if I should even bother offering a sympathetic shake of my head, I tried to avoid him as much as I could and develop short-term memory problems. Yes, I hate and used to preach against apathy. But the last thing you want to be is emotionally invested in someone who is just … running a con.

That happened to me more than a few times, well before I was incarcerated, with eye candy yanking at my heartstrings. Compared to those games, what happened in here was more like a psycho circus version of *The Young and the Restless* with an all-male … ish … cast. And unlike soap operas, when someone died here, they always stayed dead. None of that bad Hollywood writing "coming back from the dead" crap.

Long story short? Yeah, things could be worse for me.

CHAPTER 4

Sometime well after midnight—I had learned a long time ago not to watch the clock to make time go faster around here—I was mopping the floors, walking backwards as I covered the entire area, even under each bed and around their wheels, when I felt the air dramatically drop in temperature.

Now, most people know healthcare professionals keep the work and patient areas pretty chilly, and there is a critical health reason for this. We hate to sweat around patients. And considering the fact in emergency situations, we often lean way over patients, you should be thankful that we try to avoid dripping sweat onto their faces.

But this wasn't just cold air from the vents overhead. One minute I was nice and comfy while working and moving around and the next I felt chill down to my bones, without even a goose bump or shiver to show for it. But the skin at the back of my neck sure felt tight.

I turned around to find both the guards at the side of Reggie's bed where all three of them were out, well … cold. In fact, Nancy and Cherry and the medic were all out cold, too. I was just about to wake Nancy, Cherry, and the medic first and then bust on the guards for falling asleep on the job when there was a click of the doors unlocking. As in the secured doors that couldn't be opened without the passkey that only one guard here had access to …

I turned to see who was coming and got a real sick feeling as I recognized the Hermana walking in—in fact, the same one that had recently visited my cell.

"Hey, dummy, this isn't the place to settle beef with me. You better carry your bony ass where it came from or you will get heat on all of us."

"I'm no here for you, *cabrón*. You are just a cherry for me to pop if you interfere, *pinche.*"

"Now, my granny always called me sweet and innocent, but if you think I am a cherry you can pop, you are going to be in for a miserable letdown. If you aren't here for me, then who did you think you could get with two guards and a full staff awake and alert to keep you from doing anything?" See, the last thing I really wanted was to be involved in—and let me emphasize the first word—*ANY* incident or slightest hint of trouble.

"There is no one here but you to get in my way, *Hombre*. Our *brujo* has put these ones into la-la land. They will no trouble us."

"Well your brujo is on crack—I'm still awake. I think your Hermanas put some gas in the vents. Magic is for fairies. You better get back to where you belong. If it didn't knock me out, it won't keep everyone here down that long."

"*Pinche gringo.* You know nothing, *ese.* We give you a choice: You can stand aside while I take care of business, and you live. You don't, then I cut your heart out first and we will eat it when I finish killing everyone in here."

Now, let me tell you something that is probably being lost in translation. This little punk was moving to a rhythm only he could hear playing. He was moving from one foot to the other while pointing at me with a bladed shiv. In short, not only was he full of himself—he was believing it, too, and we were about to dance. We were just waiting to see who was going to call the tune. Hell, I was a head-banging heavy metal freak when I was working.

"Well, your first problem is, the only way I would find you scary is if you wore a pink tutu and clown paint. Clowns are pretty scary. You are just funny." I started walking toward him, dragging the mop behind me, careful of the slippery floor I had just mopped. In fact, I stopped after a few steps when I decided to let him come to me and try to avoid busting my ass. That would have just been humiliating.

"You got more problems than that, ese! I'm gonna cut off your *cajones* and feed them to Reggie before I do him and everyone else in here!"

And that is just what he said *after* saying a bunch of mean-sounding Spanish words that I couldn't quite follow. But he sounded confident in spite of the language barrier.

"Your second problem," I continued after being rudely interrupted, "is that you and ten others like you can't handle me in a fight."

I then raised my voice and spoke fast to cut him off from interrupting again, pointing my open hand his way for an invitation to the dance, "And if you don't scamper your bony butt back to your gang of little sisters, I am going to stick the end of this mop somewhere that will brighten your day. Guess which end?"

Now, here I would love to tell you how I defeated my opponent with my superior martial prowess and dominated him while imposing my will and all that other crap you see in MMA fight announcers and Chinese soap opera dialogue. But that wouldn't be honest, and sometimes the truth liberates ... with hilarity.

Apparently, calling Las Hermanas "little sisters" got the little feller agitated ... that, or the idea of having one end or another of a mop stuck into him got him real excited.

Either way, I got charged at. A full-on sprint by Speedy Gonzales, minus the whiskers and tail.

Something I did not mention earlier was that this was my second turn of mopping this evening. The first was round was with bleach water, which evaporates pretty quick. But no one had given the floors a good polish waxing in ages, and I was trying to make everything shiny to impress people on the need to have me around.

So here came Speedy, and I went on guard with the mop, ready to sling or trip as the opportunity was handed to me—but my preparation was not needed. His feet ran away from the rest of him and he slammed the back of his head on the floor with a sick crack, which resulted in those chromed teeth chomping down on his tongue.

I winced and stepped to the side as Speedy slid by. I couldn't help it—I snorted and started laughing. If you think that is mildly funny, you should have seen the sight of Speedy sliding right by me like he'd run across a banana peel. But I had to hand it to him, he held on to his shiv and started climbing back up to his feet.

"Are you done beating yourself up because I won't let you get to first base with me?" Dude! That was so clever, I should write for sitcoms. Where did that smart mouth of mine come up with that!

I got nothing but more rapid-fire mean-sounding words in reply, which were even harder to understand through the bloody spit. But I swear now he had a lisp.

"Look, this is embarrassing. Why don't we call it a home run before I knock you out of the park and you just go back to your dugout?" I don't even care for baseball, but the metaphors were just too easy to come by.

I kid you not, he charged again. No, for reals, he totally went full Speedy Gonzales on me again. This time, I saved him from himself.

My foot stepped on the head of the mop as I dropped the handle and let him catch it somewhere below the belly button.

I didn't move, and he went from sixty to zero real fast. The mop handle was pretty heavy-duty … aluminum? Or something? Hey, I'm no expert on the construction of mops, but had it been wood, I could have snapped it and staked him like a vampire. 'Course, that would have earned me more time on my prison sentence.

As it was, Speedy probably had his spine tickled in a bad way, judging by the color he was turning. *Oh, I've seen that look before.*

I stepped back and out of the way as Speedy projectile vomited across my freshly mopped floors.

"Aww, crap. Now I got to clean everything again!" Yes, people, my good humor was gone now.

Speedy wiped his mouth, still hunched over, and began a lumbering shuffle over to me, still hanging onto his shiv. Seriously, was it glued to his hand?

I let him get close enough to bring the head of the mop up and around in a reverse swing against the side of his head. Now, that mop head was still pretty saturated; don't ask me how much it weighed, but it was enough to knock Speedy off his feet—again—and send him down to crack his head—also again—on the floor.

This time, he stayed down and was out—you guessed it—cold. *Must be a theme in this infirmary.*

I quickly evaluated who to wake up first, decided I'd better get witnesses for me before the ones against me, and went over to Nancy to try to "shake and wake" her. I thought to slap the insides of her wrists after shaking her didn't work. Don't ask me why, but ever since I saw a seasoned medic do it, I always gave it a try, and it usually worked pretty good before we broke out the ammonia pellets. Which totally gave me an idea.

While Nancy was waking up, I shook the medic awake, too, and went over to inventory and found said ammonia pellets. Insert snarky giggle.

"Miss Nancy, you awake yet or still groggy?" I called while fishing through the first aid supplies with evil intent.

"What happened? I have never fallen asleep on my shift! I always make sure to come to work rested and caffeinated."

The medic was getting up and moving, too, both of them rubbing their faces and trying to sort through the cobwebs.

"Well, from what I got out of Slippery Gonzales on the floor there, I think we were gassed. He was going to kill all of us, except he slipped on my mopped floors and knocked himself sillier than when he came."

I went over to the guards, both of them slumped on each other's shoulders. I broke open the pellets and waved them under their noses. Did I giggle? Of course not! I was too busy biting my tongue while they acted like their butts had caught on fire.

"Come on, guys, wakey, wakey! There's been a situation while you were both asleep."

I could hear Nancy on the phone in the background. Oh, she didn't mess around either—she was talking to Warden Hardcastle at three a.m. She hung up about the time I had to start answering silly questions from the guards. Reggie was still asleep.

Things got increasingly stupid as the guards woke up. I wound up in cuffs belly-down next to Slippy, as I had named him. Didn't matter what name he had before; after this got out across the block, Slippy was going to be his new name as long as he lived. Better than Pokey, right?

One of the guards justified cuffing me by saying I should have woken them up before taking matters into my own hands. Needless to say, he didn't like my excuse of thinking he needed the beauty rest.

Alarms and flashing lights started going off about that time. The whole place was on high alert, and of course Slippy Gonzales was awake and lisping sweet nothings in my ear. You know, the whole "I gonna keel jew, *ethe!*" and other lisped, accented mean-sounding words. Took me a minute to control the giggles when "*ese*" came out lisped. Totally takes the menace out of the words. I couldn't remember the last time I'd laughed so much since coming to prison.

"Your first night here and already you blew it by trying to murder a fellow inmate, Bodhi?" I heard the voice of Guard Carls behind me.

"As long as little things like honesty and honor mean nothing to you, then yeah, you can make that claim." What can I say? I'd never learned to shut up when someone said something outrageously stupid at me. It was one of the reasons my grandad had strongly advised me against trying to enlist in the military and why, instead, I went into EMS. Not that smart-asses were welcome in EMS ... but yeah, we pretty much were.

My retort earned me a light kick in the kidney from Carls. I say "light" because I didn't curl up in a ball from the pain, just breathed through it. Yeah, I am tough and can take a hit, or else I would have been broken a long time ago.

"You trying to say I have no honor, jackass?"

"No, boss, just saying you are way too smart to believe cheap lies. Especially since y'all have surveillance cameras going here."

"Well, that is a funny thing. Apparently those cameras, and only them, were all offline during the time all this happened. So I got two convicts, one beat to hell, and a bunch of people who were asleep that should have all been awake."

"That's too bad, you would have missed comedy hour the way Slippy here slipped and busted his head and tried to impale himself on a mop handle. Swear to God. Ask him if I beat on him and see if he admits it."

Of course Slippy alibied for me, bragging that I could never beat him in a fight, half of which was lisped "cuth" words in Spanish.

"Slippy? You mean Jaime?" There was a silent *J* on Slippy's old name. "Stop baiting the inmates, Bodhi."

"Hey, he worked hard to earn that name. Don't belittle his effort!"

"Fine, so what was *Slippy* doing in here?" Carls asked in an exasperated tone.

"Ensuring OSHA regulations for safe working conditions were

being maintained?" Ok, seriously, I am not normally this witty, but it's like they were handing me the obvious lines. And the last thing I would do is rat someone out, even a member of Las Hermanas, but the fact that one was lying right next to me made Carls either insane or stupid for thinking I would tell him anything useful. "Why don't you ask him?"

"Ok, Slippy Jaime." Why didn't Carls rules apply to him like they did me? "How the hell did you get in here, and what did you think you were going to do?"

"Es like he says, I'm inspecting the OSHA." The lisps were killing me. Seriously, just hold your tongue and say what he says—you'll get the idea. "Es all good."

"Did you bite off your tongue, Jaimie?" Carls asked after picking up the extreme lisp.

"All right, Mr. Carls, tell me what happened here to get me out of my home with my family at nearly three in the morning." Hardcastle made his appearance in a black wind suit with purple race stripes with flashy reflective silver pinstripes, the legs of which were crammed into orange ostrich skin cowboy boots, and he had a silver Stetson on. Classy.

For the record, older gentlemen that dressed like that probably drove late-model corvettes, too, and should neither drive corvettes nor wear wind suits.

"Well, of course I can't get a straight story from either of these two jackasses. Bare facts are that thirty minutes ago, the cameras to the clinic all went offline, and sometime after that Jaime Hernandez, aka Slippy here—"

"Man, your parents really didn't like you, huh?" I whispered to Slippy, earning a thump in the kidney from Carls again.

"Slippy here," Carls started again from where he'd left off after reminding me to follow my grandad's advice to be seen and not heard, "somehow got access in here with only Bodhi somehow awake and able to let him in. Whatever happened after that, Jaime got the crap drummed out of his skull, puked everywhere, and was found knocked out with a shiv in his hand by the guards when they woke up, and is now talking like a retard."

He got a perturbed look from the warden.

"I know it looks ridiculous, but that is where I'm at right now."

"It isn't your findings that bother me; it's your choice of words that demean the mentally impaired by comparing them to Slippy here. Any reason to think that things are not as they appear?"

"Someone on the inside had to knock out everyone in here with something. We are giving everyone drug tests now and doing blood work to see what they were given. Only one that wasn't drugged was Bodhi."

"Hmm," the warden grunted and nodded his head. "Go ahead and put them both in solitary, clean this mess up, and get all the paperwork done, reports filed and on my desk by morning. Get this place running back to normal ASAP. I will have to notify the county sheriff and likely the Texas Rangers what nearly happened as far as we know and see if they want to stick their noses in while we run our investigation too."

I was lifted to my feet and marched ahead of Slippy out the door and down the halls. No good deed goes unpunished here. I was shoved into my cell and it was locked behind me while I was still in restraints. Ok, now *this* sucked. *Hopefully they'll be right back to take these things off.*

In the movies, escape artists would shimmy their butt over the cuffs and over a leg. Let me tell you, that is something only a professional contortionist is able to do without the help of a very sloppy application of cuffs. These cuffs were on high and nearly too tight, and I am no contortionist.

So, I waited a minute or so while glaring at the door, giving serious thought to taking my anger out on it. Just about the time I stepped up to launch my attack at the helpless victim, there was a clatter of keys in the lock.

CHAPTER 5

I restrained myself, without getting any further head trauma, as the warden walked in and, before I could say anything, beckoned me with one wagging finger and turned and walked out in front of me.

No guards.

Say what? Yeah, you heard me, no guards. I was open-mouthed, speechless between wanting to complain about the cuffs still on me and doing a quick jog to catch up as he led me back the way I had come, past the clinic and into his office.

"Mr. Carls, would you kindly remove the restraints from Mr. Bodhi and then leave us alone?"

I expected a loud and vocal protest from the head guard and was disappointed. He did what was asked without a word of objection and left the office.

"Mr. Bodhi, that is twice in a few days that you have managed to get yourself in the spotlight with gang members of Las Hermanas Del Muerte. Can't you stay out of trouble?"

"Not trying to be a smart-ass, but if I knew that trick, I wouldn't be here in the first place."

"Be that as it may, you have five days left before you are due for release for probation. Those five days are going to be mighty long once word gets around what you did in that clinic. And frankly, that is something I would like to see you avoid and would like to help with."

"You want to let me go now?" I asked, trying to hide the sarcasm from my voice but not the skepticism from my face.

"Don't be dumb. You were sentenced to seven years for manslaughter, and you are getting out in five because you are a well-behaved inmate. Hell, I don't even want to use the word 'offender' on you. Plus, we have crowding concerns with seriously violent offenders that need three hots and a cot. No, whether you know it or not, you just put one foot in hell tonight. Let me show you how before you say anything else."

He went around his desk and turned the monitor of the computer around so I could see. It was security footage of the clinic. He clicked a button under his desk and the playback with sound hit where Slippy was bragging about having a brujo knock everyone out.

"There have been a lot of unexplained, borderline supernatural, things happening around here. From people totally disappearing to suddenly acting against their natural behavior with no explanation, and the worst was when a guard vomited out his own intestine and died from organ failure before medics could figure out what to do."

"So you think some Mexican hoodoo is going to come after me?" Ok, I couldn't keep the sarcasm or skepticism out that time. Being closely related to Native lore through my grandfather's Lipan Apache tribe, yeah, I knew a little about the supernatural. And even if I did not binge-read everything from Westerns to sci-fi, these days sparkly vampires and ghosts were half of what appeared in the movie theaters.

"Whether this is legit shit, as Carls would say, or just a cult of deeply organized psychos, I would say you better pay attention and look out for yourself first and your friends sometime after."

"Ok, you have my attention. Now what do you want from me?"

"Bait," the warden said simply. He stared at me and watched my wheels turn.

"I'm no damn rat," I said after putting one and one together.

"I don't need a rat for this. I need a snake that can take care of business."

"That sounds like a rat to me, but I'm listening."

"We are going to turn you loose, but we are going to expose the truth of what happened in that clinic to a point. That Slippy there came to kill, and you were the hero of the day." I groaned at that and rolled my eyes, but he continued. "Las Hermanas are going to be pissed when they hear how inept their boy was; they are going to lose face. You know that. You know what they are going to do to get it back and who they will come for."

"Son of a bitch. You don't want a snake, you want a worm." I know, I promised no bad words, but I was pissed.

"Worm—yeah, that is a good way of looking at it from your point of view, I guess. But we do not intend on letting them have you. We just want to see what swims up to the surface for a look at you. See, there is something you may not know about Las Hermanas. Not many do because the name throws them off the wrong way, and they play into it with their MO. They take their name from the leaders of a satanic cult somewhere down in South America. We are talking serious ritual sacrifice and followers that try to traffic in slavery and demonic stuff. If they are playing those games in here, we need to break their spine or this could get very bad for everyone not playing on their team."

"I'm not seeing your big picture. So far, I see me being your rat against Las Hermanas. Granted, I would normally agree to helping you take people like that out, but where I live right now is anything but normal. We have our own laws, our own rules."

"And if you think I don't know those laws and rules better than you, you better grow a brain in a hurry, because it's going to get real deep in Satanists and snakes around here. I am not asking you to do anything but obey two laws that you haven't been caught breaking here yet."

"Which two?" I asked, eyeballing him, very displeased with the situation he was putting me in.

"What is your first rule of medicine?"

"Do no harm," I said automatically without hesitation.

"And what is the first law of the Diamondbacks?"

"Be strong for yourself." My eyes narrowed as my alarm lowered to suspicion.

"I can't promise you gratis treatment at all. In fact, expect things to remain as they are. For now, I have a decent bed in the back of this office that is yours for the rest of the morning through afternoon while we clean up the mess and go through all the formalities of an investigation. I don't know if I can keep a lid on the secret surveillance cameras, but we are going to try. That means that the truth is going to leak out about how you made Slippy your little bitch in the clinic and stopped him from doing his job. And that means as far as the prison grapevine goes, either you or Slippy squealed and told us what happened.

"My suggestion to you is to own it and turn it to use against Las Hermanas before they use it against you to make you a rat. Tell the world you couldn't keep your mouth shut about how clumsy Jaime was and we put two and two together, and you couldn't deny it because you don't owe Las Hermanas a damn thing after what they did to your boy Spike. Just understand one thing: only Carls and myself know the truth about Las Hermanas and what we are asking of you. And don't expect any favors from Carls. He is my pit bull here, and his main job is keeping all of you in line and reminding you there is a higher authority you all answer to. Give him an excuse, and he will put you in a world of hurt."

I resisted the urge to roll my eyes. "Other than talking my ass off to the world out there, I don't see how this really does anything for you to warrant bringing me in here and giving me the kid glove treatment. What is it you expect from me?"

"Two things. First is the easy one: You will find a new celly when you are put back where you belong. I want you to keep him under your wing as much as you can while you're here. He is a good man, too good to be here, but he beat a member of his church nearly to death, and there was no real proof to back up his story as to why to even make it excusable."

"His church?" I asked the obvious.

"Apparently, he was an interim priest and was counseling a couple and felt it necessary to counsel the husband, nearly three times his size and weight, with his fists. I suspect he is going to be as prone to trouble here as you are, if not more so."

"Great, a babysitting gig. What's the other thing you're holding back?"

"Whoever it is that is calling the shots in Las Hermanas is not Ascencion, or Topaz as he likes to be called. He may be their *jefe,* but he isn't the brujo that Slippy was talking about. I need to know who that is, and I don't care how you do it or how I find out. Do that for me, and when you are out of here, I will use any influence I have to make sure you stay out as long as you don't go outlaw and deserve to be locked up."

"So, babysit a priest, and do the dirty work for the law? Something about all this makes me think I should be talking to my lawyer and the press."

"Go ahead. I will deny, of course, and leave you holding the bag that's already in your hands. In short, you have no leverage on me and even if you did, what would you ask for that I'm not already trying to give you? A get-out-of-jail card and possibly easy street to becoming righteous again in the eyes of the law."

"Oh, you are all heart. You or Carls blab about what you want me to do for you and it gets around, and I'm dead before I even get out of here."

"Well, that won't happen from me. Carls, on the other hand, he isn't above pulling something like that if you aren't in my graces. But hell, sometimes he goes off on his own and does things against my wishes anyway to see what hits the fan."

"Boy, you sure know how to give a man peace of mind, huh?"

"Bodhi, I think we're done here. I'm not someone that begs people to do the right thing; I am the man that makes sure they serve their time and rehabilitate for not doing the right thing. I suggest you sleep on it in my bunk while I work, and wake up determined to always do right. Because I believe a man is at his best when he is doing what he knows is right."

"Funny, my grandad said something along those lines."

"Sounds like a good man. Go to bed, Bodhi. I will have coffee waiting on you in a few hours when we wake you up to send you back to your cell in time for chow. Meantime, treat everything as if it is all business as usual."

"One thing bothers me about all this, Hardcastle," I said as I stood up and half turned to follow his orders.

"At least we have it narrowed down to one thing?" he replied with a questioning tone. "What is it that troubles your peace of mind?"

"The fact that you should turn this over to the FBI, or the Texas Rangers, or just about anyone but a convict known for being dumb muscle." I aimed a thumb at my chest.

"Yeah, but you are obviously not as dumb as you want everyone to think," Warden Hardcastle answered as he dismissed me with a hook of his thumb over his shoulder at a door that was open into a dorm-style bedroom. I had never noticed the door before because first of all, I rarely saw the warden in his office. Second, the door handle and seam were hidden by the construction of the wall and shelf space, and an innocent-looking coat rack. Not totally invisible, but pretty close to camouflaged amid the wood paneling so that a passing glance wouldn't notice the semi-hidden room.

The room itself was a wall-to-wall library of law books, writings, and biographies of the Founding Fathers, and just about everything I could see at a glance had to do with the foundation of America.

"Guess everyone needs a hobby," I muttered. Historical books weren't really my thing. I used to love history in grade school, and I had read Westerns passed down from my grandfather until I tried to have a relationship with my dad. That hadn't worked out, so I had started escaping reality by reading science fiction. Give me a good Robert E. Howard or Lovecraft tale any day over some dusty wig giving their version of reality they wanted everyone else to believe.

I didn't see anything that looked like it would hold my interest longer than five seconds, so I stripped out of my shoes and socks and crawled in bed after turning out the lights.

CHAPTER 6

DAY 5

"Soft is hard, hard is soft. Be as contrary as you have to be to get where you want in life. Keep repeating the same technique if you are where you want to be."

–Caedmon Murphy

I was actually led to a new cell rather than put back in my old one, and at first glance, my celly looked like a twelve-year-old. He did not help my first impression when he hopped up, extending his hand with a smile too sunny for this prison to lock up.

"Caedmon Murphy!" he proudly boasted and vigorously clenched my hand in an iron grip as he pumped my arm.

"Oh dear lord," I moaned as I realized this was not going to be just any fresh fish. The stories I'd heard of sport fishermen going after bluefin tuna worth hundreds of thousands of dollars made a metaphor of Caedmon in my imagination when the rest of the block saw what was in the water.

"Oh, goodness, no!" Caedmon's accent was thick with an Irish lilt. "I only work for our Savior; I am no impressionist. So instead of callin' me Lord, Caed, as you Yanks say, will do fine for short for me friends and family."

"Ah, well ok … Caed," I replied as I glanced around, seeing my belongings had been all laid out on the bunk Caed wasn't using against the far wall. No, we didn't have top and bottom bunks like you see in movies. Some prisons did that, but not where we were. Those accommodations tended to start fights over who would be climbing to their bunk every night. I also noticed that the first two knuckles of each hand of Caed's were covered in scar tissue and larger than normal. His nose also had no discernable ridge. Time to test his upbringing. "So, what are you in here for?"

"Oh, I nearly killed a wifebeater to death. What about you?"

"None of your damn business, Caed." It took a second for my brain to catch up to what he had said since my first thought was a sleeveless shirt. Either he had a very subtle sense of humor, or I was going to get a lot of laughs at the way he stated certain phrases. Killed to death—I was going to have fun with that one. "You need to learn you can't ask someone questions like that, and when someone asks you, you damn sure better stand up for yourself and not take that from them or you will be chum in the water. Catch what I am saying?"

"Oh, dear." He looked actually and sincerely grief-stricken. "I did not consider that you would be so ashamed and scared of what you did that it would pain you to get it off yer chest."

"No, that's not what—look, Caed, I am trying to rub some of that shine off of you so you won't start a riot the first time we go for chow. You are a walking filet mignon, the way you act and talk to people. I can tell you been in a few fights, but you are so new here, the only person you have to look out for you is me. And if you think I am going to stick my neck out for you against the wrong people, you don't know how things work here."

"So what you are essentially telling me is that if someone asks me what I've done, I should lie to them or feign aggression to make them back off?"

"That is closer to the idea," I sighed as I started unrolling my gear and putting things away so I could sit back, get to know Caedmon, and try to school him on what little prison smarts I had.

"I prefer to feign weakness when strong. I have nothing to fear from any man in here. I have a secret weapon."

"Well, you impressed me with Sun Tzu reference. I am a fan of The Art of War, too, but can you share what that weapon is?"

"Well, sure, I can share, and I'm glad to because that is the only way I can keep it." He said stepped closed to me, looked around, and whispered, "See, I walk around with a God inside me."

I groaned. Of course. I'd walked into that one, unless this Irish fighter was also more than a little crazy, and that jury was seriously out. It was looking like my prison smarts weren't smart enough to handle this job.

"Look, Caed, I don't want to start off on the wrong foot with you since we are going to be cellmates, but you need to slow your roll down a little and work on keeping low-key."

"That seems a mighty hard thing to do, mate, but I am listening to you and willing to take any well-intentioned advice to heart that I can. So, go on and tell me what you think I need to hear, then?"

"For starters, you are built like a twelve-year-old girl. You need to find people you can be cool with and start hanging around them before some bad people out there single you out and make your life into a living hell."

"So far, sounds like good advice that I would do well to follow. Anythin' else, then?"

"Yeah, when someone asks you what you did to get here, assert your boundaries and for Christ's sake"—yeah, I took the Lord's name in vain, something I generally tried to avoid just out of respect and good manners, but I needed to push a button or two to see how he would handle it—"whatever you do, don't tell them you were a priest. I believe you that you're in here for assaulting a man, but there are a lot in here that are going to accuse you of assaulting a child, if you catch my meaning, and handle you accordingly."

"Well, the pity will be on them for speaking falsely of me, then, but none will I give. Don't you be frettin', Mr. Bodhi, if there be a donnybrook, I can handle me own and keep you safe to boot."

I noticed his accent got a little thicker at that statement, but I put my palms to my eyes and wiped my face of the frustration I was feeling. How the hell was I supposed to keep this guy out of harm's way like the warden wanted and do his dirty work at the same time?

Caed patted me on the shoulder and I looked at him through narrowed eyes.

"Now, look, I can tell you may be feeling a touch frustrated, but there is no need. I am my own man, and I was not always a priest. I have a lot of sin to atone for, things only my maker knows of because I repented of them. But what I will say is that I still on occasion enjoy a prize fight against anyone above my weight class that thinks I make a merry dancing partner."

"Yeah, I am betting all of gen pop will want a two-step with you. Doesn't your God want you to be a peacemaker and meek as a lamb and all that?"

"Oh, give me a freckin' break. You know how many times I heard da?" The accent was thick with this one.

"Turn the other cheek … ? Isn't that in there?"

"Let me tell you about the Lord I serve. From the lips of the same Messiah that you carelessly blaspheme who died for you and called you a friend and loves you, he said this to us, allow me to quote loosely from memory: 'Behold, I send you forth as sheep in the midst of wolves: be you therefore wise as serpents, and harmless as doves. But beware of men: for they will deliver you up to their councils, and they will scourge you in their synagogues. And you shall be brought before governors and kings for my sake, for a testimony against them and the Gentiles. But when they deliver you up, take no thought how or what you shall speak: for it shall be given you in that same hour what you shall speak. For it is not you that speak, but the Spirit of your Father which speaketh in you. And the brother shall deliver up the brother to death, and the father the child: and the children shall rise up against their parents, and cause them to be put to death. And you shall be hated of all men for my name's sake: but he that endureth to the end shall be saved. But when they persecute you in this city, flee you into another.'"

"You have the whole Bible memorized?"

"Oh, hell no. I've only been reading it for about a year. That bit just impressed me because it could have been me own testimony. Probably yours, too, I'm betting. That was in Matthew chapter ten. Point is, though, that here we be, men that want to be good and innocent, but put in a place where we have to have the mind of a snake, where brothers and fathers turn on their own, where men will make their own courts and put us on trial. And way I read the Constitution of this country, not only do I have a right to defend myself and face my accuser, but I don't have to testify against myself. Yet neither am I a liar, nor have I anything to be ashamed of that put me here. In fact, I think a lot of people could learn from me experience."

"Well, you say it in a way I never heard from any other preacher, but you skipped the 'turn the other cheek' part."

"Jesus told his disciples to pack a sword, too. Thing is, every time Jesus spoke of the laws the Jews lived under—which were being used by their law enforcement to make them all guilty, which should remind you of the coming times of the day?—he always raised the bar above where they tried to set it to make people live under. He wanted to prove to them how impossible their standards that they were trying to live under were and prove how pious and perfect they thought themselves to be. Hence why he ran around calling everyone hypocrites."

"I'll have to take your word for it. I haven't been to a church in over ten years, and I barely read the Bible at all."

"Well, you are welcome to call me a liar if you can prove it. Iffen you can't, though, and call me one, I am liable to give yer brain a message with me knuckles to see if it needs some circulation restored."

That made me laugh, and not in a mocking way, either, since he was smiling when he said it.

"I probably need a good message anyway. But it's nearly chow time, and I missed breakfast."

"That sounds fine by me, but tell me a bit about yourself, Mr. Bodhi. What are you in here for?"

My eyes rolled. This guy wasn't listening. "Going past my boundaries. Let's go eat. If you survive the cooking you might be able to handle my testimony, as you call it."

"Sounds good. Maybe you can introduce me to those people you mentioned would be good for me to hang around, yeah?"

"All we can do is see how things go, and don't stick your neck out far enough for someone to rip it out," I said as I stood up and led the way out of our cell.

"Funny how the geography changes, but not the challenges or interactions people face, isn't it? Scatter everyone here across a city, or country, and we would still have to handle them the same way as we do here in a closer community."

"Never gave it that much thought, but I can't argue with your point."

"Well, as you Texans say, this ain't my first rodeo." The Irishman even threw in a drawl. "I noticed the fact a long time ago that faces and names change; personalities and egos, not so much."

"Yeah, I think I know what you mean."

CHAPTER 7

I was mindful of the fact that the warden had tasked me with watching out for this little Irishman, but I could tell a whole army would have their hands full keeping him out of trouble in this place. Guess it was a good thing I was in the pocket of the Diamondbacks, but that didn't mean the club would watch out for this fighting preacher, or that he would even associate with them.

I kept my eyes busy observing who was already in the chow hall and who was coming in behind me as casually as I could, letting Caed go ahead of me in line for the food trays. Some kind of enchilada slop with cornbread and pinto beans. *Yum* ...

We went over where a few of my compadres in the DB had a table, among them King himself, and took a few of the seats at the end. I made sure Caed sat closer to the middle and left myself with my back to the crowd.

I know, very Hickok of me, right? Maybe one day I will share with you why I get to be the one keeping my back to the danger while everyone else is looking at it over my shoulder.

"Bodhi, who's your new buddy?" asked King.

"Yeah, who's your new buddy, Booty?"

Even King rolled his eyes at that. I cut my eyes at Copper, our resident smart-ass, and fought not to grin. It was actually funny, and his humor was starting to rub off on me in all the ways to keep me in trouble if I wasn't careful.

"You better stop trying to steal the thunder from King before he tells me to thump your skull with a table. And keep your mouth shut with food in it until I have had a chance to eat!" And before I could introduce my new celly ... of course, I should have expected this.

"Caedmon Murphy, and pleased to meet ya!" he said with enough enthusiasm, you'd think he won the lottery just to introduce himself and shake hands.

I groaned to myself and winced. I decided the best thing for me to do was to pretend nothing happened and start mixing up my food to make it edible. I glanced at King and was surprised to find the man smiling through his thick beard.

Funny, King reminded me of a grizzled Viking more than

anything, and I'd never seen him smile before. Then King glanced at me, and I raised a brow while putting another spoonful in my mouth.

"So what is your story, Mr. Murphy?" King asked. I waited to see how Caed handled himself.

"Well, like I am sure at least one other at this table would say, no one told me there were limits to what I can do, so I am here to see if this institutional rehabilitation can teach me my limits."

"Oh, now *that* is funny. Well, if you didn't know your limits out there, I'm not sure what may happen to you here, except something will bend or break—you or everyone else." King cut his eyes over my shoulder as he finished that statement. I stood and turned to see the head honcho of Las Hermanas threading this way.

That he was coming without any of his enforcers was just for show. We were watched by guards, and his crew all over the place. No one was going to lay a finger on him, and he knew coming to our table with his little sisters in tow would just show us his real weakness.

"Booty! My favorite sugar baby of the Diamondbacks," Ascension, aka Topaz, greeted me and made my skin crawl. It didn't help that Topaz had almost no voice left from being on a ventilator after surviving a shanking sometime during his twenty-year incarceration for multiple murder, prostitution, and drug-dealing charges across international borders along with a litany of other felonies.

"Don't we all wish flattery could get you anywhere? Just remember, look but don't touch. What do you want, Topaz?"

"Oh, we can get to that in a minute—let me have a look at you! I hear you have been causing quite a stir with my homies. One will be walking funny for years after what you did to him, and another came to you last night and apparently has not recovered from his exertions to give us the nitty-gritty details of what happened!"

Topaz walked and talked like a flaming homo, but he was still one of the deadliest people in the block to tangle with. Standing this close to him, if we threw down, odds would likely be in his favor of leaving me dead and him surviving.

"Oh, that guy? What was his name … Hiney? Hernandez! I call him Slippy. I didn't know you had anyone so clumsy and stupid in your hen house. That guy came running into the clinic across my freshly mopped floors and slipped and busted his head. He got up and slipped again, but landed on my mop handle and puked everywhere before he got himself knocked out cold. Funniest thing me and the guards ever saw. I'm surprised you didn't hear about it already since they asked me what happened, and I couldn't cover his stupid ass while laughing my butt off."

It was real quiet around us all of a sudden, but I was laughing while retelling the event, even if the laughter was just a little forced.

"I heard no guards saw anything," said Topaz.

"Oh? There were guards assigned one of the prisoners right where I was working, watching me, too. I don't know who told you there were no guards, but you might want to get your information from a more honest source in the future. Did they tell you anything different about Slippy than I did?"

"Oh, look what we have here—someone new and fresh. Who is this pretty thing?" Topaz switched topics, obviously dismissing me and stepping around to invade Caedmon's personal space.

"Caedmon Murphy! How are you this morn?" Naturally, Caedmon reacted with his over-the-top greeting and didn't seem to pick up at all on the tension in the entire chow hall, as we had become the center of attention. I glanced at King, who returned the glance without any expression or signal to do anything.

"Well, I see we woke up on the right side of our bed this morning? It gives me such a warm fuzzy to see such excitement bubbling to greet me on such a pretty face." Topaz reached up to lay the backs of his manicured fingernails across Caedmon's cheek. I cringed and wanted to step in but refrained, hoping Caed would assert his authority without causing a riot. Yeah, high expectations that I did *not* see happening, no matter which way the cards landed.

"Tell me, what did you do to get in here with deplorables like us?"

"I was challenged by someone that was born to be a man and decided he would rather be something less. I attempted to turn him from such sinful ways and show him the path to God through our Savior. His rejection of the way, the truth, and the light to become a true man is what took him to a hospital for treatment of the injuries his iniquities brought onto him, and what brought me here."

"Oh, you sound like a child-raping priest. You all talk of your faith in your sky faerie god, but when it comes down to it you are all hypocrites that only turn a cheek when you are bending over for your own pleasure."

"Aye, I have heard much the same before from people that judge others from their own experiences. You should get out more, you know, or open your eyes when you see a real man of faith, rather than open that arse of a mouth that fills the air with the crap in your brain."

I was in the process of just thinking the words *'Oh, hell'* and before I could think of completing the thought, three things happened at nearly the same time. Topaz tried to throw a punch at the little Irishman and before he could, there was a tray in his face, put there by Caed with one hand as the other brought a straight left cross through the tray and into the forehead of the leader of one of the smallest and most vicious, bloodthirsty prison gangs in this part of the Southwest

I wasn't sure who was more stunned—me or everyone else in the hall as Topaz was knocked on his butt. However, Caedmon was not finished yet. Before anyone even had a chance to flinch, he jumped on top of the table he had been sitting at and aimed a finger at the guards, some of whom were open-mouthed and wide-eyed at the riot that was sure to happen in the next heartbeat.

"I'll have me say before you take me out of here!" His words ripped across the room like a buzz saw. I'd never seen or heard of anything like this, but I was as frozen as just about everyone. Caed may have been pointing at the guards when he said that, but his eyes roamed over all of us that stood in front of him.

"Let him speak," King made the decree. And as high-ranked as King was with verbal judo, being no slouch myself when the need called for it, I honestly wasn't sure if Caed needed backup to calm the crowd from breaking out into a riot.

"Like everyone here, I did'na come to be in this place of me own choosin'. But here I am, and because of that, I will serve me callin' to be a brother to them that claim me as theirs, and a friend to any in need of one such as me self. But the rest of yas hear me, and hear me well. Iffen we can't be friends, you better come at me where I am weakest, find me blind side, and give it your best shot, because that is what you are made of when you toe the line against me. Come at me where I can see you and I will not back down, and I will bring the weight of truth with me on my side and let it leave its mark on you where all will see what you are truly made of! Alright, boys, let's go do me penance for not having the patience to suffer fools," he said at last as he hopped down from the table and walked nonchalantly toward the guards, leading them out of the chow hall without waiting for them to catch up.

And then two things happened. Topaz sat up and pulled the tray off his face, leaving behind two bloody marks where Caed's knuckles had punched two holes through the aluminum and gouged Topaz's skin, and King started laughing. If I had heard him ever laugh before, it was never with this level of amusement behind it. Let me emphasize what he did: his two first knuckles … punched holes … through an *aluminum* tray. Good luck trying that on someone's forehead, much less a hyper-fast psycho killer.

"Oh, not just a Bible thumper, but a skull thumper, too! I like that man." I wasn't sure if King was drunk on his blend of hooch. "He has the mind of a snake."

"Funny, that's pretty much what he said to me before we came to try to have breakfast," I replied before trying to reclaim my seat.

"Well I don't think it's funny," Topaz said as he got up to his feet again and was surrounded by his Hermanas. "I have one of my crew in the hospital that will never walk right again, another missing in action after having a late night date with your Booty Boy here"—I'd heard that so many times since grade school that I only let it bother me when I wanted to let it bother me—"and now this insult! What do you plan to do about it, King?"

"First of all, you should wipe your forehead. You're leaking from what that Irish runt did to your face. Second, you have two boys that tried to dance with my snake and paid the price for it—after one of them tried to gank one of my men. Now you're bitching to me to protect you from yourself?"

I was starting to see what had the warden worried, and what he meant by Topaz being a puppet. This was pretty insane behavior for a prison gang leader and did nothing but project weakness and liability. As it was, I did not see a way for Topaz to save face, which was going to do nothing but embarrass Las Hermanas below the image they had cultivated to appear like a bunch of twisted sisters off psycho meds.

"If you won't give, then we will take what is ours."

"We just gave you everything that is yours to have. Don't bite at what you can't chew, or in your case, swallow." Yep, King had a way with words when he spoke, so let me spare you some of the more vulgar details of the conversation. That was pretty much it; Topaz scurried back to his pack, and I sat back down to finish my now cold meal of … stuff and waited for King to say something to me before I opened my mouth for more than a bite of what we called "lunch." It didn't take long.

"Ok, Bodhi, what do you know about your celly?"

"Not much more than you. He's from Ireland, he knows how to throw a punch, he's got fighter's hands. Claims he hospitalized a man for spousal abuse in front of him when he was trying to give them marriage counseling, and he says he wasn't always a priest. And I would say Las Hermanas will be killing him before we get to know much more."

"Yeah, well, do what you can to watch his back until we can bring him into the fold. I like him and want to have a chat with him when there's time, before his time is up."

"You gonna make us all be choir boys, King?" Copper volunteered to be the next punching dummy.

"Slap him, Bodhi," King ordered, and I did, up the back of his skull.

"You might remember that our president down in San Antonio was a chaplain after he was awarded the Silver Star in Nam and still runs a rehab program for cons. We're only One Percenters when we're locked up with our backs to the wall, dufus."

"King, not that I don't like the guy, but I think we should name him Snowflake for his chances of getting out of here alive."

"Nah, I like Whip better. We call him The Whip and we'll keep him front and center, where those queer sisters can look but not touch and break themselves apart trying to get at him. I can't wait to see how long that damage stays on Topaz's forehead. The prez would want us to watch out for that man, whether he is one of us or not. So do what you can to save him from himself."

That put King and the warden on the same page, and made my job a lot easier as far as the warden was concerned. In fact, as far as covering my butt over the news about Slippy and watching out for

Caed, the only thing I really had to work on was drawing out this brujo running Las Hermanas. And I had a feeling this morning's drama would put me on the radar of the Hermanas brighter than if I wore a tutu covered in neon lights. And let me tell you, with my hairy legs, that is a scary thought.

"Any news on Spike?" I asked, trying to get the subject off Caed and my mind off the bad medicine being brewed by Las Hermanas.

"Word I got is another day in the ICU at the hospital, then a day or two more before they bring him back here and let him finish healing up in the clinic before turning him back loose, the way he is healing up. You did good that day, Bodhi. Fighting back is one thing, but knowing how to stop him from dying until help got to him is another."

"Topaz already tipped his hand. I expect him to try to finish the job when Spike gets back, and probably go after Caed and Bodhi while he's at it," Copper put in his two cents. See what I did there?

Copper's given name was Jacob Penny. I bet you thought the club names were just clichéd, or whatever we wanted to call ourselves. Not hardly; I still wasn't up on calling myself anything but my given name. The only way you get named is by getting "blessed" by the chapter president. Granted, they tend to be names worth fighting over, and seldom ever had anything to do with snakes. Of course, we could call ourselves whatever the hell we wanted if we didn't want Joe Public to know more than we wanted them to know.

"Well, that would be obvious," I replied, giving King a look.

"Wouldn't it? Tell me what I don't know that happened in the clinic last night," King said without asking.

"They sent a dumb punk in to gank either that molester, Reggie, and or everyone except me if I didn't go along with his plan. And somehow they made sure everyone was asleep before he walked in the front door like he owned the place."

"That's a lot of juice to use up on a waste of skin like Reggie. Did Slippy run his mouth about how they knocked everyone out?"

"Not really. He said they had a brujo take care of that for them. I think they got a guard to roofie everyone's drinks."

"Are they running a nightclub or a clinic in there?" Copper. Remember when I said his humor was rubbing off on me?

"Copper, shut up. It's too damn early for a smart-ass to crack wise. All right, I would tell everyone to be on high alert or some crap, but if you aren't already, then you deserve to let one of those faerie sisters make you their wife. Now, I am going back to my bunk to finish sleeping before they let us go into the yard. Try to make sure their bad luck is permanent."

That sounded like the best plan anyone had suggested since things started getting crazier.

CHAPTER 8

I headed to my cell after turning my tray in. I even ate all my meal. The real surprise came when I got to my cell. As if I needed more surprises, right? 'Least no one was dead yet. Caed was there waiting on me, licking his fingers and munching on a gooey-looking cinnamon roll.

"What the hell, Caed? Seriously?" No solitary, no riot act from Carls and a lecture from the warden, or even a slap on the wrist?! There was no justice. I sat down and Caed lifted his plate with one roll left, for … me?

"Warden Hardcastle told me you were feeling a little stressed about your release soon and asked me to help you be prepared to be a man again, rather than a caged animal."

"These things will make you soft in here. You know that, right?" I said as I grabbed the roll and tried not to scarf it down. The little Irishman made it into my will when he tossed me a little carton of milk to wash it down with.

"Soft is hard, hard is soft. Be as contrary as you have to be to get where you want in life. Keep repeating the same technique if you are where you want to be. So, what did I miss?"

"Where did that come from?" I wasn't much of a philosopher, but I'd never run across that little proverb before.

"Something I picked up in Bartitsu training."

Now, some people might be a little familiar with this nearly deceased martial art, but my grandad actually knew a little about it from some cross training he had with SAS vets that applied it against the Nazis. Not exactly the Fairbairn-Sykes curriculum most people know about, either. Picture a Golden Gloves boxer marrying a karate expert that had a Greco-Roman wrestling child, and you might have a glimpse of the nightmare of vague idea that never took root. It was MMA before there was MMA.

"Well, for starters, you are on King's good side. As long as the Hermanas let you live to enjoy it, anyway," I said before draining the milk and getting up to throw away the trash and wash my hands at the sink.

"Ok, well first of all, you promised if I lived through breakfast, you would tell me what you got yerself locked up for. After that, I have some questions that need answerin' if you want me to be of any use around here."

Seriously, Caed's accent was way thicker than I could keep up with half the time. It's almost like hanging around a bunch of Mexicans speaking Tex-Mex at each other and including you when all you speak is Texan. If you haven't been there, done that, you are missing out on a bastardization of culturalization. Sometimes Caed's accent smoothed out enough to barely hear it, but if he was wound up, look out!

"After breakfast, I'm not sure your idea of 'being of use' is the same as mine. But yeah, I guess you earned it. I was an EMT for about five years. I didn't make it to paramedic level, though, just right below it. Never had the money to stay in school and get the gold patch and afford to make a living. But the level I was at, intermediate, let me provide essentially the same care and same skills, just not earn the same pay and same recognition. With me so far?"

"A little. I know some about medics across the pond. So how many levels are there?"

"Well, nationally there are essentially three levels—basic, intermediate, paramedic. But states tend to add another level or two at the basic and intermediate levels and throw more confusion into the mix. At my level, I was teaching essential critical skills to all health care providers. Not just EMTs, but anyone that needed to give CPR and push drugs to bring the dead back to life."

"Oh, wow, yer a hero then!"

"No, I'm no hero." That was not the first time someone had tried pinning that on me. Some first responders among the police, fire, and EMS community were there for that kind of thing. I got into it first of all because I needed a job and it was there, and second of all, I stuck around because I found out I was good at it and liked what I did. "I wasn't then when I was working, and I'm damn sure not now. I was just someone with a skill set, like a mechanic or carpenter."

"Be humble all you like, but you had the weight of a person's life in yer hands depending on yer judgement and actions. Not many can say that and say what they did made a difference. So, now that I know what you did, tell me what you done."

"Manslaughter of a ten-year-old boy," I said simply. I'd had dreams that kept me restless for over two years after that. The dreams I had now weren't always about that, but I still hated to sleep. I had no peace about what had happened during the entire series of investigations, arrest, arraignment, trial, and incarceration.

"You murdered a boy?"

"By the letter of the law, not necessarily. I just bear responsibility. By the eyes of the family, the community, and just about everyone else that heard anything about what happened? Yeah, I may as well have put a gun against the head of that kid and pulled the trigger."

"Well, I wasn't born yesterday. I know you didn't do that, and I can tell there is a weight of guilt on you that wasn't put on you by the court system. Speak honest and lay yer cards out, as you Yanks say."

I gathered my thoughts while taking a deep breath, preparing to retell this part of my life yet again. This was what I hated the most, and there was no escape but to relive it over and over again every time I let someone crack open the book of my life to bare my soul and face their judgement or acceptance.

"I was working two jobs basically. Part-time for a county rescue, and I'd just started a full-time gig with a private ambulance service. Way I had things scheduled was to work a twelve-hour shift with the county, evening to morning, and then go straight to the other job and work another twelve with them."

"Wait, you would work twenty-four hours straight?"

"Oh, counting drive time and hours between shifts, it was usually closer to thirty hours before I saw my own bed again."

"Is that common for medics? That sounds insane."

"Some companies have forty-eight-hour shifts. It just depends on your stamina, sanity, and call volume. My county job had good bunks and low call volume, so I got to sleep a little before the other job."

"Sounds like stories I hear about doctors that work insane hours and sleep at the hospital."

"Pretty much the same concept. It sounds insane to people outside the healthcare field because they don't think about death not waiting for shift change and partners arriving on time. So, our employers and taskmasters would rather keep us running around the clock and keep our wages low than pay us enough to make it worth working a two- or three-day work week with sane hours. Anyway, don't get me going on the politics and policies—it may all be behind me, but I will still bitch about it."

"You're right, and I am puttin' you on a rabbit trail, so back to what happened to bring ya here."

"I got to work at the private ambulance company. I was a little behind the clock because of a late emergency run and when I got to the other office, a call was pending: take the kid to his doctor appointment. So we took off as soon as I clocked in, without checking off the ambulance to make sure it was fully stocked. Properly checking off their ambulance would have taken at least thirty minutes and made us way late for the appointment, and that was the kind of thing that got people removed from scheduled shifts as punishment, or straight up fired."

"I feel like I see where this may be heading, but there wasn't any way for them to make sure you had a fully stocked ambulance?"

"Not really. The last crew is supposed to leave it fully stocked, but sometimes they get off late or are just dog-tired and leave things for the next fresh crew to clean up after. So yeah, long story short, we pick the kid up, a ten-year-old boy with history of diabetes. What I did not know until we picked him up was what a train wreck of health history he had, and how serious he really was. He was bed-bound, on a Foley catheter to drain his bladder into a bag, and his organs were already shutting down on him. He was waiting for multiple organ transplants. The mom met us and had his history and told us everything going on, said she was concerned about a low fever he was running, but explained his home health nurse was going with us because Mom had to go to her day job."

Caed was doing a great job of just listening and letting me get this off my chest. Problem was, this was the umpteen thousandth time I had retold this story, and it only made it harder on me each time. Each time I went through it seeing all the mistakes I made and what I could have done different every time the inevitable question gets asked: "What could you have done that would have changed it?"

"We got the kid loaded up, and I noticed his urine was very brown. I was thinking urinary tract infection, and going through his medical history while asking his nurse questions on his recent history, I asked her if they knew anything about him having a UTI, or was this normal for his urine to be so dark? She told me she didn't know if it was normal but thought so because of his renal failure and kidneys shutting down. I took a temp. Fever was a little over one hundred. Kid was breathing a little too fast, blood pressure was a little on the low side. I started getting a bad feeling, and this is all before we even got out of the parking lot. I got a glucose reading and it read in the low fifties, which isn't the worst. At least it was reading.

"My judgement was telling me this kid needed to go to the ER, but we were there to take him to a doctor's appointment. I told his nurse I needed to give him oral glucose to bring his sugar level up and told her that with his history and symptoms, I believed he really needed to go to the ER, not to a doctor's office. She told me it was his endocrinologist and if we missed the appointment, he might not get seen for at least another month. So, here I am in a situation where if I was working 911, I would override her, take the boy to the ER, and not worry about my job because I did the right thing by the patient. However, since I'm working for a private company, it's more customer satisfaction than care based. So, since Mom and the nurse are essentially my customers, I have to make sure they want to keep using us again or be blamed to my boss and get fired for anything happening they did not like."

"I thought an EMT was an EMT. How come it's so different when you work at different places?" Caed asked, shifting my gears and giving me a chance to come up for air.

"Some of that is over my head, but a large part of it depends on the medical director overseeing the treatment we give by the protocols he authorizes us to use. A private company working in the same area as a 911 system is probably using totally different medical directors. Different medical directors means different protocols, different means of treating patients. 911 systems are run under a government or municipality, whereas a private ambulance service is just run by whoever has enough money to be stupid with. They generally only handle doctor's visits and transports out of the hospital to nursing homes and don't usually handle emergencies like 911 systems do. But the irony is that enough people abuse 911 to go to the ER just to see a doctor and get their coughs and boo-boos 'checked out' that the chances of having a true emergency for a private ambulance crew are nearly as likely as a 911 crew. Only real difference between the two is one is better trained and rested than the other."

"So how come all ambulance companies aren't swallowed up by 911?"

"Short answer, politics and insurance payouts. Long answer, some places actually are. It always comes down to money. If the local government can suck it out of the taxpayers while collecting from insurance, then they will muscle private companies out and take over. But I never worked in an area that did that.

"So anyway, we went ahead and took the boy to the doctors, but we didn't even make it there. I was checking the kid's vital signs every ten minutes; his sugar level wasn't going up. I told the nurse what was going on and told her it looked like I was going to have to start an IV and give the kid dextrose straight into his bloodstream to get his sugar up if it wouldn't go up from the oral glucose I was giving him. She told us that we had to make this appointment—that it was more important than going to the ER, just to give him sugar and he would be fine; he was just slow to react to it. So, I gave him another mouth full of glucose.

"We got about five minutes from the doctor's office and I checked again on everything. The kid wouldn't wake up, his breathing was slower, and his glucose was so low, the machine wasn't reading it. I told my partner we had to go to the ER, and that started an argument with the nurse. But I was busy starting an IV on the kid. In the background, I could hear my partner trying to explain to the nurse, but she demanded to speak to our supervisor. So he called up our dispatcher, and I was digging through the supplies we had to get everything I needed for an IV and then trying to start an IV on this kid, who really did not have any veins. I tried once in the big vein in each arm, got nothing, stopped playing around, and looked for what we call an EZ-IO. It's a drill we have been using in emergency settings for a while to start an IV by going straight into the shin bone. Problem was, I couldn't find it.

"My partner was dealing with the nurse and dispatch at the same time, and I went back to trying to start an IV, and we weren't going anywhere closer to the ER. Then my partner wanted me to talk on the phone to the supervisor. I don't think I have ever been so stressed out before. I told him before he said anything that I had a kid going critical that should have been taken straight to the ER, and I was about to have to start CPR on him if I didn't get some meds in him. He was smart enough to shut up and ask to talk to the nurse. I don't know exactly what was said, but my partner got us turned around and put us on the way to the ER about the time I got real lucky and found a vein to start a line in. I remember thinking how cool that kid was. He had a Mohawk, and his eyebrow was pierced. I have been wearing a Mohawk ever since I was found guilty and put out of sight and out of mind of the family." I took a breath and clamped my eyes shut, breathing shallow. *I will not lose it remembering his face. I will not lose it again.*

"Yeah, he was real young for that look, but I learned later that people born with his condition of diabetes seldom live to see twenty. With his organs going out the way they were, it was a constant battle, and I dropped the ball on him. Before that, I was letting him listen to my music before he went out. Found out we both loved Black Label Society."

I stood up and filled my paper cup at the sink. I took a drink and started pacing while I continued, uninterrupted, wishing I would get interrupted before it all went to shit.

"I got the dextrose vial and started giving him a dose, since he was bottomed out according to the machine. I gave him about a third at first to start because I wasn't sure how he was going to handle that plus the oral glucose I had already given him. I kept a close watch on his vital signs—understand, though, this company did not have any fancy equipment other than the machine we use to monitor blood oxygenation. Just an old-fashioned blood pressure cuff, stethoscope, thermometer, and the glucometer for his blood sugar, all of it telling me this kid was going down for the count. I told my partner to go lights and sirens.

"I went through that first vial, got nothing back from the kid. We were about ten minutes away from the ER and I called them to let them know what we were coming there for. Kid was still breathing on his own at this time, and I asked if they wanted me to give a second vial of dextrose since I was getting no reading. They denied since I was less than ten minutes out and told me to continue monitoring and let them know if status changed. Well, five minutes later, it changed. The kid stopped breathing, and I had no pulse. He had coded on me. I told my partner to call the ER and let them know I was doing CPR, but he had his hands full. I had my hands full. We got to the ER, and by then the shit had already hit the fan."

"Shite, I need a smoke already. How the hell do you medics manage the stress?"

"Some of us smoke," I said with a laugh. "But smoking is expensive. Some go to drug use and wash out. We just suck it up and learn to love the pain, until we break. They are just now starting to call that PTSD for us, but when I started, we all called it just 'burnout.' We never put it together that what we were going through and breaking down from was the same thing that has been happening to soldiers in the military since the Second World War, and there's no telling how far back into history we could go before people started putting labels on everything to treat without curing."

"You can't manage that kind of stress like that. Trying will only drive you crazy. So, I am guessing the kid never made it after that? How is any of that yer fault to wind up here?"

"No, he didn't make it. First of all, the charge nurse wanted someone to blame for the kid not making it. I made an easy and obvious target, starting with the fact that the glucometer we were using was not calibrated and probably never tested and no doubt giving us false readings. The bloodwork showed the kid had a blood sugar level over twelve hundred. I've never heard of a patient that had one so high. The vial of dextrose still on the IV line showed an expired expiration date. I did not have the times documented of when the dose was given on the paperwork at the time the nurse asked to see it. She called the state Department of Health in to inspect our truck, and it failed miserably for so many missing and expired items, it wouldn't pass inspection as a clown car.

"The boy's nurse threw me under the bus, my partner threw me under the bus, the company threw me under the bus. I wasn't just fired. When the mother came looking for blood after that charge nurse got her wound up, there were civil and criminal charges piling up. It all came down to the fact that I did not check off the truck. I was the medic in charge, I had the highest cert on the truck, and I had used expired medication. I was found guilty of manslaughter and the judge, a stiff-necked Republican in election season in 'tough on criminals' mode, served me up and sliced me to pieces, then threw the book at me for taking life for granted and playing God. And they were all correct—the kid was dead, and it was all because I broke too many rules."

"Seems you had more than a helping hand from the company you were working for."

"Yeah, well, they don't exist under that name anymore. Of course, the same owners are still operating a private ambulance service—just with different licenses and branding."

"And I thought I got the raw end for stomping a mudhole in a jackass, as you Texans are found of sayin'!"

"Yeah, that is pretty easy to brag about. What happened with me forces everyone to play judge and give me either pity or judgement every time I tell the story."

"Right, well, let's get off that subject. Tell me about the Hermanas and King and anything else I need to know to make it through the day."

"Aww, don't you want to offer to pray for me and heal my soul?"

"Bodhi, me being here means people are already prayin' for ya. I can pray *with* you if you would like. But it is up to you to put Band-Aids on your soul and stand on your own feet if you don't like lying there, making yourself miserable. No one else has the power to hurt your spirit like you do."

"You don't talk like any preacher I know. What denomination are you?"

"Denominations cause wars. I have enough to fight as it is without starting more over dummies that want to divide themselves over labels and issues such as whether or not Adam had a belly button."

"Ok, that made my head hurt," I said, trying to figure out if that was a serious debate in churches. "I do need to tell you about King and the Hermanas, since it looks like you earned your death sentence by knocking Topaz on his ass."

"Oh, is Topaz important to them?"

"He's their big chief. There are close to twenty Las Hermanas Del Muerte, or Sisters of the Dead, running around here. There are bigger Mexican drug gangs running around, but everyone leaves the Hermanas alone. Mainly because they are freaks, but mostly because they are vindictive and sneaky as hell. When they want someone dead, they usually always get what they want—until lately."

"What's been happening lately?"

"Me being in the way. The other day they tried murdering my celly during lunch, right in front of the guards and everyone. Then last night, one of them came into the clinic while I was mopping floors and tried to take out one of the inmates and all the witnesses except me."

"So, if I'm gonna get it for just knocking Top Ass on his arse, they certainly won't like you any better for spoiling their plans." Caed was a quick study and made me nearly grin at him using our nickname for Topaz. That, or maybe we all had the imagination of a playground bully when it came to making fun of people's names.

"That's what we think, too. 'We' being the Diamondbacks. We are a prison chapter for a biker club run out of San Antonio. HMFIC here is King."

"Ah, I have heard a lot about American biker gangs. We have some across the pond, too. Never been around any that came off like that TV show you Yanks had."

"Ok, first of all, you are in Texas, and we are part of the South— don't call us Yanks. We reserve that for people from the Northern states that act like asshats and come down here to try to teach us how to be like them. And second, yeah, that show sucked donkey nuts after the first season, in my opinion. But I have never been a part of any biker club or gang before coming to prison. They tell me I have a home if I want it when I get out, and they operate differently out of prison than here, but we'll see if I live that long and can't go home. "

"So what are the Diamondbacks all about? How do they recruit and get by? Same with Topaz's bunch."

"I don't know a lot about how the club operates outside of prison.

Not really any of my business, and I have already learned too many hard-earned lessons about sticking my neck out. What I pick up is basically, the club doesn't really operate like a classic one-percenter biker gang. No organized crime to speak of. I was told the president is a marine vet and basically uses the club as a place for vets and rejects like me to get back on their feet. Inside, we do what has to be done to get by, and get out in one piece to the land of the free. Though King has a recipe for prison hooch that makes everyone want to be on our nice side."

"You make the Diamondbacks sound like a cupcake gang. Don't tell me you're all saints?"

"More like we aren't ambitious to be career criminals," I said, not taking offence to Caed's light-hearted remark. "That would describe Las Hermanas Del Muerte. We call them sisters, herms, and just about any queer name you want to sling at them. And they feed into it all and vomit it back. You want dirty deeds dirt cheap? That's where you go. From prostitution to drugs, and now it looks like murder for hire inside. They were always a sadistic bunch. When they decide they want to make an example of someone, they have done things that would make a buzzard puke."

"Well, at least I pissed off the nicest people here. I think I've given you enough of an interrogation for now. Is there anything you wanna know about me, since we're gonna be sharing the same cell for a while?"

"Important thing right now is, where did you pick up the Bartitsu? And have you ever been in any kind of ambush environment where someone will likely murder you for what you did to Topaz?"

"Ah, well me granda was a Scottish Commando in the Second War. After he finished killing Nazis for the British, he moved to Dublin, got married, and had some kids. We all learned from him how to fight. I took to the pugilism and used to prizefight before I went into seminary. Almost all of our family was involved with the Republican Army. I was getting sucked into it until I got sick of us killing ourselves to hate the Brits and stopped having a priest read the Bible at me and started reading it for meself. Now, I have Catholics *and* Protestants hating at me, and I travel around to any church that invites me to fellowship with them."

"That's good, but prizefighting isn't the same as prison fighting.

I hope if you get into trouble, you won't plan on inheriting the earth by being meek and turning the other cheek."

"No, I do not read the Bible the way a lot of others do. If I lived under those laws, then yeah, I would turn the other cheek. But here it seems we live by another set of laws, and those I will respect, while also inviting anyone to live by the laws Jesus wanted us to live under with me. The book of Psalms comes to mind, sayin', 'Praise be to the Lord my rock, who prepares my hands for war, my fingers for battle.' Donae be worryin' for me, Mr. Bodhi, for I am well loved, as are you. For if you weren't, then you would not be so blessed as to have me watching over you."

That made me laugh.

"Well, that makes me feel better. If you don't mind, I'm going to take a nap until we go out into the yard before lunch."

"No worries, I got some reading to do and could use the quiet time, too."

Normally, I would have used this time to work out in the cell. Yeah, you are probably used to seeing movie scenes where we go into a yard and pump iron and get all hulked up. Only problem with that idea is that there is one area where we have gym equipment, and if you don't feel a little vulnerable laid out on a bench under several hundred pounds of weight, you won't last long in a prison with a bunch of violent thugs around you. It wasn't like I was hanging out at the club with Martha Stewart for a celly and hanging with the girls from *The View*. Although, Cherry did kinda look like a scrawny Whoopi Goldberg.

In case you haven't caught on, I was doing everything I could not to think about my life prior to prison. But those things kinda sneak up on you, even when you don't tell a stranger your inner demons. It wasn't like the only time I'd ever delivered a dead person to the hospital was the time that landed me in here. Hell, that was only half the stress of the job.

The politics of healthcare, the good ol' boys clubs that play favorites with who gets hired and promoted and who gets the hose. Nothing was worse than working under someone that had never matured past grade school drama cliques. At least here, that behavior was expected. The different angles that stress came from seldom had anything to do with the actual performance of giving care to a patient.

For me, that was when it was the most pure, the most stress-free. There was no going back to that life now, but that felt somewhat liberating. I just had the challenge of trying to figure out what was going to happen with the next chapter of my life and where it would begin.

Even if my own family had been writing letters and visiting me while I was in prison, I would have considered them a last desperate option. But no visits, and only a few letters. Some of that was my own doing, though. The family that cared about me enough to write, I had stopped accepting from. Those letters made it harder on me, made me softer than I could afford to be. As for the other family that did not write, did not try to see me? Well, I am sure Dad and my half-sister were too busy pretending I did not exist to remember.

Ugh, if I kept thinking about all that mess, I was bound to turn into a sullen angsty teenager that sparkles whenever he reveals himself to stRangers. Let's not put me in a position to take advantage of teenaged girls now, mmkay?

Now, trying to work something out with the Diamondbacks and moving to San Antonio? It was the smart move, considering my options, but the drawback was that it would take me further from my family and any chance of reconciling with my dad. And likely closer to becoming a true outlaw, the way things were shaping up.

A South American satanic drug gang operating in this prison no doubt would chase me all the way down to San Antonio if I kept sticking my nose in their business. And if I did what Hardcastle wanted of me, I would probably never fall off their radar.

A brujo? Guess it was a good thing I had a priest for a celly, but I wasn't sure that was even worth mentioning except as a joke.

CHAPTER 9

Next thing I remember feeling was someone tapping my foot. My eyes popped open and the remains of my dreams were drifting away, but not before they left me with all the guilt I'd thought I was finished tormenting myself with.

I thought I was finished having those dreams. No such luck. I glanced up at Caed. "Time to go see fences and sun, huh?"

"Aye, plus you were looking like you were resting too peaceful and pretty there."

"Heh, wish that was true." I stood up, stretched, and went to the sink to scrub my face, trying to wash off the sleep and the memories of the tormented dreams of doing my damndest not to let a child die in my hands. *By* my hands.

"Ok, let's go. Besides, I'm curious if anyone is gossiping about what you did to Topaz."

"How likely am I to get shanked out there?"

"Well, this isn't the yacht club, but compared with the last prison I got transferred from, this isn't bad either. Just stick with your own, try not to have any blind spots, and you will be ok. When you start mingling or playing with the equipment, that's when trouble can happen quick. But pretty much everyone is keeping an eye on the Hermanas, expecting them to be the troublemakers, and it's getting harder for them to surprise anyone."

"I can't imagine why they're using that name in prison. Seems like it's just asking for trouble to call yerself a sister in a men's prison, don't it?"

"Ever listened to that song by Johnny Cash, 'A Boy Named Sue'? Some names make you tougher. But in their case, I think it made them stupid." My earlier jovial mood was totally gone, and it wouldn't hurt my feelings to make someone else pay for it, either.

We were walking out into the yard and toward King, Copper, and a few others who were enjoying smokes and jokes. I stretched my arms, chest, shoulders, and neck before accepting an offered smoke. I was down to one a day—as in one cig, not a pack. That first hit, straight into the lungs and out through my nose, took a load of stress away with it as I leaned with my butt against the edge of the table we were parked at. Two of our crew were enjoying a chessboard, while others were playing the card game spades. I had half an ear on the talk from the table as Caed made his thunderous introductions and nearly laughed while keeping my eyes and focus out on the yard.

Las Hermanas were playing at the exercise equipment. The Tribe was around, and so were a few other gangs with a lot more juice and notoriety across the state, and even the nation. Names you did not mention casually, and players you did not glance at without giving respect to. Those gangs had documentaries made after them; the FBI had profiled and studied them. They had paid their dues and were still around, and Joe Public thought they were just harmless TV stars.

And then came Reggie.

I couldn't keep my eyes off him, and neither could everyone else in the yard. Then the catcalls started, one of the Hermanas promising him a good time tonight. He shuffled slowly, gingerly, but steadily and with determination as he came to our table. And since his eyes were on me, I figured I was the reason for this rare public appearance by the man of the hour.

"Mr. Bodhi, I heard about what happened in the clinic last night. I just wanted to say thank you in case I didn't get another chance," he said after stopping several feet away. He turned to leave, but Copper's voice stopped him.

"Why are you thanking him, Reggie? I heard you put a hit on yourself to get out early."

Reggie turned and looked at Copper. He squared his shoulders and lifted his chin just a little off the ground.

"No one has ever given a damn for the facts about what happened to me, except my lawyer. He was working on getting me an appeal and having the charges overturned. Yesterday, he was run off the road, his skull caved in. Did you know there was never a rape kit collected on my daughter? But the officer that arrested me, the same officer that is pimping my wife as a drug informant, made sure she was examined and made sure I knew she was raped. I'm the only one that knows he is her rapist now, and if I die, who will bother to try to get her out of that hell?"

"See, Caed, this is what we call a child rapist," Copper offered. "Around here, they're free game for anyone that wants to make a name for themselves. What Reggie isn't telling you is, the court system found him guilty of drugging and raping his daughter when she was at his house for a visit. So, we can take his word, or we can go with the State of Texas and a jury of his peers and all the evidence they went through and convicted him for in thirty minutes."

"Aye, but the interesting thing is, he isn't lying," Caed said before snatching Copper's pack of smokes and taking one for himself.

"Are you a human truth detector, Caed?" This was from King. I was busy watching the yard and looking past Reggie, who was still standing in front of me. Topaz had made it into the yard and was walking toward his crew at the workout area.

"I know liars well enough when I see and hear 'em. I hear no lies from this man."

"Bodhi, was that punk in there to kill Reggie last night?"

"I wasn't too sure, King, but he sure was biting off more than he could chew. He only said he was going to kill everyone and make me watch."

"Just a big coincidence his lawyer gets his head crushed in the same day that a lone punk tries to take out over half a dozen people and hang that on one of our boys. All right, Reggie, what's your game?"

"Whatever it takes to get my daughter somewhere safe. I don't even care if that pig cop and my ex get theirs for what they did right now."

Caed stood up and walked over to offer Reggie one of Copper's smokes. The little Irishman was sure being generous with them. "Mind if I ask you a personal question?"

"I got nothing personal left to me anymore. Ask away." Reggie took the smoke and lit up.

"Do you have any relationship with Jesus?"

I glanced at Caed and back at the others, who all shrugged and left it in my lap. I just shook my head and kept an eye out while Caed did what Caed does.

"I don't know anymore. I tried praying, I tried reading the Bible, talking to the chaplains. I got nothing back from it but pain and misery. I still pray for my daughter, every day. But it's more of a habit than belief."

"While I am here, and you are with me, you will be safe. As for what happens outside, they have to take care of themselves for now."

"How are you going to keep me safe?"

"Oh, that's easy. I walk around with a God in me."

Reggie laughed—probably the first time I'd ever seen him so much as smile before. I glanced over at Las Hermanas and sure enough, every single one of them, including and especially Topaz, was eyeballing us.

"Besides, the Diamondbacks are in love with me, and as long as

I keep stealing Copper's smokes, he is going to keep me around until I pay him back. Ain't that right, Copper?"

King came up and stood beside me, whispering in my ear while Caed and Copper went back and forth.

"If they are really after Reggie like he said, and we know they want the priest and you, we are putting a huge bullseye on everyone here if we give any protection to Reggie."

"I know you aren't asking my advice, King. And since you do the thinking and shot calling, you tell me what you want."

"I want to know you can handle how fast this is getting out of control before I grow a gray hair over the idea of one of those queer sisters giving me a kiss when I'm not looking."

"No other choice, is there?"

"You could crack and go begging the warden for favors to save your hide since you are out of here in about a week."

"Is it me or humanity you have no faith in?" I said before rolling my eyes at him.

"Humanity. Don't let it bother you, I am naturally pessimistic. Helps me prepare for the worst."

"Yeah, but when you enjoy the worst, your pessimism is just really another form of optimism. Relax, I haven't cracked yet. And now I got an angel on my shoulder," I said with a twisted grin. "When I leave, y'all are going to have your hands full with him."

"You gonna take Pappa Gun's offer and go to San Antonio when you're out?"

"Doesn't look like I'm welcome anywhere else."

"Yeah, I heard your family doesn't speak to you much. Last thing you want to do is try to go back home with no game plan for taking care of yourself. You'll end up back here again that way."

"'Least it's three hots and a cot. I guess Topaz didn't get enough love off Caed this morning ... here he comes again for round two."

"Never a dull minute lately," King muttered before he walked over to reclaim his seat. Letting himself get baited into a prison fight causing a block riot was a good way to wind up in solitary.

Topaz came with a full entourage. As he got closer, I could see that where Caed's earlier lesson in manners had been covered up with a hasty tattoo. *For real? A tattoo?* Wait till you find out what it is—you will never guess!

"Better let me handle this, Mr. Bodhi. 'Tis me they have come for," Caed said, stepping up beside my shoulder.

"Nah, you might be their cherry, but we're the ice cream sundae for them. If they wanted you by yourself, they wouldn't come at us to get you, so just hang loose and don't smite anyone else, ok?"

"Who, me? I am as innocent as the driven snow itself! 'Tis the angels protecting me that are the troublemakers!"

"So, a priest, a child rapist, and a rat walk into a bar," Topaz said as he came near.

"The joke never ends, huh, Topaz?" I asked.

"Did you come over to apologize to me, Mr. Topaz? Or perhaps you want me to pray for you after showing you the light of truth?" Caed made it a challenge for me not to laugh. I couldn't tell if he was honestly sincere or just yanking Topaz's chain … or perhaps he was sincerely yanking on that chain?

"Not at all. I came over to show off the new ink work I had done. How do you like it?"

"Makes me think of my grandad," Caed said. I turned and cut a glance at him.

"Oh, was he a fan of Hector James?"

"Not at all. I am not sure who this Hector James character of yours is. Me Grandfather was a commando in the Second War and had a trunk full of war trophies he took from Nazi officers that he assassinated."

"Hector is a prophet of the apocalypse, a great leader who was born with a vision of what is to come."

"So you decided to make sure that every time you look in the mirror at yerself, you would always be reminded of the two greatest people you have known. I am touched!"

"Hector is a gibbering loon that found people stupid enough to brainwash themselves on shrooms and kiss his ass." I couldn't resist putting my two cents in. "Topaz, you're making the guards nervous. If you don't slow your roll out here, they're going to cut our time in the yard short."

"Hey, I just came to wish you well when you get out, Bodhi, and to let you know we will be taking good care of your two friends, the priest and the baby rapist."

"Well, you are going to have to find your own priest to play with.

We have been talking about Caed, and we like the sermons he gives and have adopted him as our spiritual adviser." Now you should know that while I'm talking at Topaz, I'm not focusing on him or even looking him in the eye. I'm watching his shifty-eyed, twitchy-handed crew.

"Oh, we have our spiritual needs getting fondled. In fact, we will be holding church services any time you would like to come and bow over the altar, your pretty face would be welcome while we make you sing for the angels."

My skin was crawling, and it was taking everything in me not to put my foot in Topaz's ass and break it off. Not my foot—his ass, that is. Because breaking my foot in his ass would be ... you know what? You get it.

"Why don't you tell your priest to come see me? We can share notes and give him a good sermon for you on being delivered into insanity for walking a twisted path," Caed offered.

"The last thing we need is to hear the lies of an impotent god that abandons his meek little lambs to be slaughtered by wolves like me."

"I speak no lies. Look in the mirror—you tested me, and now you will wear the mark of failure from your attempt for the rest of your life. Where is your victory in the direction you have strayed? Do you need me to blow a trumpet for you to heed the warnings you have heard your whole life? Read Ezekiel's fourth verse in chapter thirty-three and see what awaits you at the end of this road."

"What are you doing here, Topaz? You're making King bored." We were getting nowhere, and I had an itchy feeling that Topaz was keeping our focus while something else was going on.

"Just a social visit. I wanted to get a whiff of rat, so I came over to tell you we know all about your new relationship with Hardcastle."

"Topaz, did they switch your mouth for your bunghole when you got tattooed? I hear a lot of sloppy wet sounds and nothing worth remembering," King spoke out while moving a chess piece behind me. I knew he moved because he said, "Check," after a short pause.

"Hardcastle got your boy into his private room and made him promises if your boy gave him good service. That's why poor Jaime is still in solitary and Bodhi here is enjoying the sunshine and free air with the rest of us."

"So you're trying to call me a rat? Gee, if only I could think of a name that you wouldn't find flattering and probably tattoo my name on your ass for leaving such an impression. Oh, I know, how about dummy?" I had to walk on eggshells. First of all, I had no idea how Topaz had gotten that intel, but it would make me a marked convict if he could prove it.

"There are no secrets from us in this prison, Bodhi. We know what you are willing to do to get out of here."

"Yup, I'm pretty cool with doing anything that displeases you at the moment. I may even talk our priest here into having church services here in the yard so you can attend! Bet you would love getting some religion in you."

"Oh, he could put his religion in me without any resistance. In fact, I doubt I would even know it's there and would have to ask if it's in yet!" Topaz said before leering at Caed.

See what I mean about making my skin crawl? Who says crap like that and actually means it?

"I don't know about church and worship services, but I think a Bible study here in the yard would be a grand idea now that you mention it, Mr. Bodhi. In fact, tomorrow I think the first lesson should be in the rewards for overcoming the temptation of a reprobate mind. You should attend and bring your amigos."

Now, let me say, watching Topaz turn bright red and grit his teeth the way he was doing while Caed spoke was something you would laugh at if you saw how dramatic he was being. Except when you were face-to-face with him and nearly a dozen of his shiv-loving homies, you tended to stay pretty sober.

"Ambitious, since you haven't even made it through your first night here. Now you are going to make saints of all the sinners here with lies and fairy tales of hope and miracles. It won't save them or you from the tender hand of death as she wraps you in her embrace and teaches you to love what you fear."

"And just what is it you think I'm afraid of?" Caed's words lilted softly and he took a step toward Topaz, getting an instant reaction from his entire crew. "'Tis obvious, isn't it? It isn't you or anything you can have done to me from behind or below since you cannot face me from above or before me."

"We will see about that, *padre*. *Vamanos!*" And with that, he turned and shoved his way through his crew and stalked back to their corner.

"Topaz is getting himself worked up for you two, looks like. Are you serious about starting a Bible study, Whip?" Copper asked.

"Are you callin' me Whip?"

"Yeah, King says that's the nickname we're giving you after you put the stinger on Topaz earlier."

"Wonder what me ma would say about that? She said, 'Get me the switch!' to me brothers and sisters so much, it got confusing if she meant that for me name or something to hit me with when I was growing up. But aye, I would enjoy being able to share what I have learned with people that are willing to listen and challenge me with questions. Looks like you might be a wee bit more of a challenge than I can handle, though, Mr. Copper."

"Ha! You got that right. I was born Heathen and will stay that way till Odin sends a Valkyrie to claim me from battle. That didn't happen when I was fighting hajjis in the sandbox, and I keep waiting to find someone worthy to kill me, but it hasn't happened yet. Till then, I'll be too busy chasing women and getting drunk to worry about your Jesus telling me what an awful sinner I am for not going to church."

"Oh! A fighting man, are ye? I just got me citizenship earlier this year, so please let me tell ya how grateful I am to you for yer service to God's country, the USA. Now give me another smoke or I will preach at you for being daft and thinking tithes and church make you a Christian."

"Seriously, King, how the hell are we going to come off to the gangs around here when we are doing altar calls and acting like choir boys?" Copper said after he tossed his dwindling pack to Caed.

"Well, if they hear you whining they will call us choir girls, not boys, first of all. Secondly, Pappa Gun acted as chaplain when he was in Nam with the marines. And after seeing Caed lay out Topaz this morning, do you want to tell either of them what a sissy they are for being Christian? Stick a tampon in it and stay in your cell if words make you bleed, Copper."

"Oh, man, that's harsh right there," Spider finally chimed in. Spider never said much, just sat back and watched more than anything. Right now, he was watching King take his rook off the chessboard.

"Caed has my vote. I don't mind hearing a little good word. Besides, it will keep a fly in Topaz's ointment and make it easier for us to socialize and conversate without being disturbed. They won't be coming near us without their ears and whatnots bleeding. And it will make us look good to the warden, too."

"Ok, I can already see this is a battle I won't win, but that leaves us with Reggie here," Copper brought up the elephant in the room. I glanced over my shoulder at Reggie, who was looking like a deer in headlights, not knowing which way to run.

"I was giving that some thought while Topaz was sweet-talking our little Bodhi. Topaz seems to have an itch for Reggie all of a sudden. Only two reasons I can see is, Reggie put a hit out on himself because he is too much of a coward to kill himself, or someone wants Reggie out of the picture. His lawyer turning up dead at the same time sure makes it convenient if any of Reggie's story is true and some pig cop is trying to make his problems go away."

"Mr. King, let me ask you a question. If I am telling the truth and my daughter has been getting raped and used by a scumbag cop and her mother, what fate do you see for her if I were to kill myself in prison on top of that? Would it be any better for her mentally if I was murdered, even?"

"On the other hand, you are a lying sack of dung that did what your jacket says, and your daughter would be better off knowing you're dead than living every day worried you'll come back into her life again."

"Good grief, Copper, are you always this cheerful? For a man that would do evil to his own daughter wouldn't care about doing what's right by anyone but himself for his own comfort." Caed made a good point. "But he claims her well-being and mental health are the first priorities with his very life itself, and the fact he came here to thank Bodhi for saving his life says a lot about what's inside him. I see a lot of good, and after everything he has been through, if he was a sociopath to try to con us with that story, he would be over with Topaz and his boys and not here."

"Well, for now, Reggie is welcome to hang around us as Caed's guest as long as Caed wants to hang around us as Bodhi's guest," King decreed.

If there was a God, someone lied to Him that I made a good

babysitter. To make matters worse, I watched Carls coming our way about that time. *Great, the riff leaves and the raff floats in.*

"Bodhi, the clinic staff is requesting you for a special duty shift," Carls said as he came near. "You need to carry your butt with me and have a chat with the warden about it since it will affect your rest and nourishment schedule."

"Brother Carls, we were just about to start our first Bible study. You should stay and join in our fellowship before taking me to see the warden!" Yeah, that was me. Converted on the spot, and if you believe that, ha! But it was fun watching Guard Carls squirm, trying to figure out if I was full of it.

"Oh, don't worry, Brother Bodhi. If the good guard wishes to join us for Bible study, we will postpone so we can fellowship when you can both attend!" Of course, Caed had to take my fun seriously.

"Yeah, sure wouldn't miss that. Oh, if only I wasn't working! You know, holding down a job and being an honest citizen! Maybe when I'm not. Meantime, *Brother* Bodhi, let's go." The way he said "brother" reminded me of that cheesy TV wrestler. Come to think of it, they had the same male-pattern baldness issue.

CHAPTER 10

I was led into the warden's office yet again. This was becoming a habit lately that happened more in the last few days than in the last several years.

"Bodhi, did you get much rest since last night?" the warden asked as I stepped into the room in front of Carls.

"I'm good. Carls said you guys needed me to put in some odd hours?"

"Well, an opportunity is open for you to do that, yes. Normally, we want inmates on a set routine and running like clockwork so nothing can happen through the night hours. We let that cat out of the bag letting you in the clinic and having you stay later than usual, but you came in handy when the proverbial shit hit the fan. Would you like some water or coffee to drink?"

"No thanks."

"Ok. Have a seat and tell me about what happened this morning with Topaz and Caedmon Murphy and what just happened in the yard."

I took a seat and a deep breath before recounting the events as they transpired the best I remembered. I added extra emphasis that Topaz was bragging about knowing I was dealmaking with the warden while I was at it, giving him a pointed look.

"Oh, yeah, you can thank me for that, Bodhi," Carls confessed. "I figured it would make it easier for you to get yourself into trouble."

"I got a hunch you got the training for being a prison guard by getting beat on in grade school all the time," I muttered.

"What the hell's that supposed to mean?"

"Both of you quit your bitchin'." Now, folks outside of Texas probably don't know that when we say it here, it sounds like just one word to tell someone "quityerbitchin'." But it also almost always works when the source is a parental figure. Hardcastle was the dad everyone had that would put a knot on your head for misbehaving in public.

"Well, between Reggie, Bodhi, and Caed, looks like we got a stew pot coming to a boil. I'm asking you to work in the clinic during the night hours that we've seen the most activity from the direction of Las Hermanas gang members. This is going to seriously break your sleep pattern into pieces, and we need to know if you can manage that for the days remaining in your sentence without any complaints so we can keep it off the … official records. And before you ask, we are already giving you just about everything we can and then some, so don't expect anything more."

"My 'give a damn' button is too broke to think of asking for something that amounts to a peck on the cheek while you have me where you want me. I still don't get why you're coming to me for help instead of asking the FBI or the Texas Rangers to deal with these guys if they're this much of a problem for you."

"Bodhi, I know what you went through at your last prison seems worse to you than what you've seen going on here. I know some of what happened at that place, and I wouldn't be surprised if you weren't forced into some of the cage fights the guards were organizing there."

"I took care of business and did my best to keep my nose clean and stay under the radar. Three rules I have tried to live by since I got into prison and came here, too."

"And I appreciate that in inmates that try to work and rehabilitate."

My eyes nearly rolled into the back of my head at that. What was there for me to rehabilitate from except to learn not to try to help anyone unless I was in a perfectly controlled environment, as in totally not emergent?

"But there have been things happening here I don't know how to explain enough to get the special attention we need. So far, Las Hermanas has been covering their tracks exceedingly well. As it is, they nearly had you take the fall for killing a child rapist and three clinic personnel without anything to connect to them. That is means, motive, and opportunity for any sloppy prosecutor to lock you away for life, and maybe even earn you a needle."

Ok … put that way, combined with the fact I was already on the hit parade for Las Hermanas, I needed to get on board and be more proactive.

"All right, Mr. Hardcastle, I'm your man. What do you want out of me?"

"Your previous cellmate, Spence, is coming back this evening and will be in the clinic under observation while he finishes his recovery for at least the next three to four days. I would be very surprised if Las Hermanas doesn't make another go at him. The question is if they are going to play a waiting game and let the climate de-escalate, then hit when we've let ourselves relax, or if they are going to keep the heat up and keep making things worse around here for everyone. And that is an answer we aren't going to know until we find out if they are organized and have a plan of action or if this is random chaos, just a seek-and-destroy mission whenever and wherever given the opportunity to strike."

"Sounds like I just got promoted from cage rattler to fixer. I can sit and twiddle my fingers in the clinic, keep playing the same day-to-day game during our meals and yard time, and we let Topaz and whoever his witch doctor is call the shots, if that's how you want to play it," I said as I stood up.

"If you have a workable plan, I'm all ears, Bodhi."

"One of the toughest lessons I had to learn when I got incarcerated was what it means to be an operator. To not just control my mind, my environment, but the outcome of the situation by controlling the environment I operated inside of. I am no master at it; that's the job of some of the gang bosses you see around here. But I understand enough to know right now, you are being played like a mark, and this whole prison is not under your control."

"And what would you have us do about it?"

"Take me off the hook, off your fishing line, and let me swim. Or the way I look at it, take this muzzle and leash off of me. You need me to roam around freely and unchecked by your people to accomplish what you want."

"That'll be the damn day! Warden, we let this jackass have too much slack as it is. He's way too big for his britches, and there's no reason to trust him not to get in bed with Topaz to screw us all over."

"Carls, if you had given yourself another thirty seconds to think, you might have pulled something scarier-sounding from your ass. I am out of this place in a week unless Las Hermanas kills me or sets me up for some other cheap frame job and keeps me here a day longer than I wanted to ever be here in the first place. Stop hurting your brain."

"Bodhi, I'm still listening, but you are wearing out my patience bickering with my guard. If you got an idea, spit it out. If not, you either play ball with us, or we put you back where we found you."

"You already designated me as your hunter—now you need to declare open season on the Hermanas and let me go to work. *Unfettered.* I go where I want, when I want, unchecked by your people and without any consequences for what I will be forced to do to Las Hermanas."

"You are out of your damn mind to even think we would consider doing that," Carls growled in my ear.

"What's the difference if it's them doing it without your consent or me doing it? Y'all are all wound up over the idea they have some supernatural witch doctor giving them an edge. Since when has any prison needed angels and demons in it to get past sloppy security and greedy guards?"

"It isn't that I think Las Hermanas is using any kind of black magic, Bodhi, and I wouldn't appreciate you trying to spread a lie like that around. But it is important that their people believe it enough to become more creative, and more careful about how they accomplish what they are getting away with scot-free. Prisoners mutilated to death, yet no one hears a sound? Ok, I get it no one rats. But our security footage shows nothing? I have little doubt you're right to imply we may have some corruption to blame for that, but it looks like the inmates would be concerned enough to lift a hand in objection, doesn't it?"

"You've never watched a buzzard peck out the eyes of sheep before."

"How's that apply?"

"Buzzards don't go after anything with any fight in them. That's why they eat the dead. Some sheep and goats are domesticated to the point that when they feel threatened, they lie down and play dead. I have seen sheep with their eyes pecked out and heard ranchers talk about it. Sheep lies there and does nothing while a buzzard just pecks, pecks, and pecks and gets full and flies away."

"What's that got to do with anything, Bodhi?" Carls demanded. But I was looking at Hardcastle, who was thinking beyond what I said and considering the situation we were all in.

"Who are the sheep in here for the buzzards, Carls? Me, or you for wanting to keep still, keep doing what you are doing, and not strike back?"

"All right, Bodhi, you said enough and gave me more to think about and work with. But for now, let's get through this evening and see what tomorrow looks like."

"No problem. Like I said, few days from now, I'm history. Whether you have the same problems or not when I am gone ain't my worry."

"Warden, no way could you even think about that. The corruption charges you would be guilty of could bring everything down!"

"Yeah, how many of those charges are we breaking already?" I had to point out the obvious.

"Bodhi, I like the idea, but it just can't happen. And there's no reason to explain the why of it and argue. For now, you're stuck on a short leash. Let's hope it's good enough, because if it isn't, we'll be relying on the proper authorities to give enough of a damn about inmates murdering each other to send undercover agents in to start where you leave off."

"Man, you guys are just too fun." I moved to leave, tired of this waste of time. It reminded me of being stuck in administration meetings that resulted in being told to keep doing what you were doing but with less mistakes and more enthusiasm. I kid you not.

I always figure some people need to be told the obvious, or maybe administrators just need to justify their roles in life by pointing out the obvious and expanding on it with a presentation. Don't get me wrong—Hardcastle seemed like a good man, but good intentions don't last long when the job gets nasty.

"Well, that's the whole point of being in prison, isn't it? Bodhi, just keep your eyes and ears open for something I can actually use, something that makes all this look more organized than random acts of prison mayhem, and look out for my people. You do that, and like I said, I will take care of you, too. Carls, go ahead and toss him back."

CHAPTER 11

Luckily for me, Carls brought me back to my empty cell. I needed the downtime to think about everything and process what had happened since Spike got shived.

Explaining my existence to Caed had seriously drained me, on top of getting into the confrontations with Las Hermanas. *This may be my last chance to prepare mentally for what's coming.*

Good thing my life and my future were being endangered again—that distracted me from worrying about my next five-year plan. Ever been asked in a job interview where you see yourself in five years? I didn't have any good answers for that these days. Further from family and anything I called home is what it looked like.

That cheerful thought brought me to my present problems. Excuse me for a minute while I internally whine about it.

I was a week from release, and it looked like Las Hermanas were eating crack and drinking PCP to make everyone's life more miserable than it already was. Granted, the last prison I was at in East

Texas we fondly called "Thunderdome" because of all the corruption, and especially because of the gladiator-style fights the guards used us for. Trust me, if I was making that up, I would invent a way better name than Thunderdome, but guards have zero imagination.

So, here we are with Las Hermanas Del La Yada Yada running around murdering pretty much anyone they wanted in the prison with little resistance from the authorities. Unless you counted me as the authority since so far I was the only one that had stopped their murder streak the last two attempts, giving me a bullseye for a trophy.

Now, just about everyone that knows anything about prison gangs and Mexican cartels probably knows or has heard about this Santa Muerte crap riding on the themes and coattails of such holidays as "Day of the Dead."

But that was just superstition, right?

Nearly every Mexican gang I ran across had that superstition hocus pocus tainting them, with nothing making it exclusive to any one gang. So why was this so special that a warden was crossing lines to get help from an inmate? Hence my internal crisis alarms going off.

How did I wind up being the champion chosen to single-handedly go head on against a South American hoodoo cartel? This was either something or nothing, and I did not have enough information to see the big picture. All I could do was run blind and treat this like nothing, stamp out a brush fire, and not worry about the unintended consequences down the road. Right?

Or option B: I sit in my cell, stay under the radar, ride out my time … which had been my original plan and got me where I was now. All other options were self-destructive for me and not worth considering or mentioning.

I rolled out of bed and started doing my workout routine with push-ups. I stopped thinking and worrying and let my body take the punishment instead of my mind for a while.

Caed came in and caught me planking. I said nothing, but he tilted his head one way, then stepped into the cell and asked, "Are you stuck?"

"No, it's called planking. It works on your core muscle region, which is where I am weakest."

"Well, I can see why. You aren't doin' nothin' and thinkin' you are doin' somethin'!"

"Well, first of all, it's doing something, or I wouldn't feel any burn from it. Second, if you know anything better, let me know. Besides, I thought Christians were supposed to be patient?"

I looked up to see Caed make himself into a human flag hanging off the cell bars. "Can you do this, then?"

"Aren't Christians supposed to not be smart-asses?"

"I learned to be what me Father in heaven wants me to be, not what the world wants," he said casually as he held his body perfectly horizontal from the cell bars. He then started walking with one hand above the next, climbing up to the next level of bars.

"Ok, wiseacre," I said, giving him the same term of endearment my grandad had saved for me before I graduated into being "wise ass." "If you are in a mood to teach, I am in a mood to learn."

"Oh, are you now? Then tell me this: Do you know one truth, or do you know truth in everythin'?"

"Questions like that make my brain hurt." I narrowed my eyes at him. "Seems like there is always truth to be found if you want to find it bad enough to make it yours. But it sure seems like everyone else has their own version to tell you that what you believe isn't their truth."

"Aye, I like that answer. May not have been what I was reaching for, but it is … true. Now take your plankin'. You can do that, you can sit there and wait for somethin' to happen. I know about plankin', and I was just givin' you fits. But there are more fun ways to get where you are goin' that I can show ye."

"Ok, I want you to show me, but first I have a question for you. Do you know anything about South American satanic cults?"

"Enough to make a good horror movie or two from. Why are you askin'?"

"Las Hermanas have taken credit for some killings around here, and they are bragging about some hoodoo voodoo crap. I'm not religious, or that superstitious, even, but I do want to know if you have any idea what they are playing with—if it's real shit or real bullshit."

"Why are you worried about it, Bodhi? Forgive me for being blunt, but whether 'tis or 'tisn't makes no never mind, does it? You're askin' questions that take you into a battle of the spirit, and that is not a battle you will do well in unarmed."

"Caed, I don't know if you've caught on yet, but you and I have the direct attention of the leader of the most sadistic and perverted gang in this prison. I doubt I'm getting out of this prison without at least one more confrontation, but I still want to know if they can make things go bump in the night while I try to sleep."

"You know I can only give you a biased opinion on the issue here, Bodhi. In the Bible in the book of Ephesians, you may have heard talk of the armor of God, the shield of faith, the sword that is the Word of God, neither of which you appear to have to protect and defend yourself with. For we wrestle not against flesh and blood, but against principalities, against powers, against the rulers of the darkness of this world, against spiritual wickedness in high *places.*"

"Metaphors and parables don't seem to be moving mountains these days, Caed. So you believe there is a spirit world, with demons, angels, ghosts, and stuff?"

"My belief is in things even more awesome than that. I believe in the power of forgiveness, of redemption, of healing. Can things not of this world come and make us miserable? No doubt. I come from a very superstitious culture that has legends and fables they make movies about every year. But I think the greatest harm comes from our own beliefs, and it can also be our greatest strength and protection."

"So what made you a Christian and not something else?"

"I can't ignore that everywhere I look, everywhere I go, I see and experience an intended purpose. Fate, destiny … whatever you want to call it. We walk through life, and I see little, if anything, that happens for random accidents. There are no coincidences that I can see, just me blindness missing where things connect. Even having met you has been a blessing. You seem to have introduced me with good people in a place such as this where we are all carrying the guilt of trespassing against the laws of man. If there is a design in this, and a purpose, there is Someone who is in control of things. And there is only one story I've heard that shares a God with the world to go through the suffering and judgement of being a man, and dying in our place because that God loves us. If you ever cared enough for someone that you might lay down your life for them, how hard is it to believe that we are created by a God in that same image? That proved He did the same for us?"

"Love? See, that's the thing I have a hard time with. This God of love, and here we are robbing, murdering, raping each other to death. Where is the love in that? I've had children die in my hands, and by my hands. I can't let go of that, and I will always pay for it wherever I go. This God of yours and his dead Son never were a part of my life that mattered. I never saw any angels with flaming swords defending abused wives and kids from their husbands, and the only dead I saw brought back to life were saved with my own hands and no help from God. I can't believe in something I know is a lie."

"Bodhi, there is simply not a short answer for the issue you brought up. And it is one that is constantly raised by unbelievers and absolute nonbelievers all the time. To get the real answer, you have to seek God and read the Bible. The short answer, I can give you, though, if you want to hear my thoughts on it."

"As contradictory as the Bible is, it's probably better you leave it out with me, but I would sure like to have a visit with the Man Above. So, what's your short answer?"

"Simple. Look around you at this prison. What if I said this is paradise, and we should name it Eden? We are clothed, sheltered, fed, and cared for here, not much different from how Adam and Eve were in their garden. And elsewhere in this world, I have been places firsthand and experienced misery in the conditions people had to live by that would make this a true Eden to them, somewhere they would give anything to live in."

"Last I checked, Eden didn't have psycho queers running around trying to rip your guts through your nostrils, though."

"Obviously not, but my point is still there if you want to accept it. Funny how truth is like that, ain't it? Have yours or a part of mine, but Adam and Eve were essentially imprisoned and told basic rules of 'Do this, don't do that' no different than what we are told, no different than how we tell our children 'Don't eat that, it will be bad for you if you do,' and of course we break rules and rebel anyway to learn for ourselves if the consequences were really that bad. Did your parents ever warn you not to do something, and you went against them until they let you have your way?"

"This is the short answer? Ugh. Let's get back on track about Satanism."

"Ahh haha!"

Glad I could make someone laugh. I was getting worried.

Caed went on, "The temptation of rewards for turning against our maker. It always comes at a price and only delivers destruction of ourselves and others, just like when we ignore the rules of our parents. Practitioners of the dark arts call it the 'left-handed path,' and half a dozen other names. I will give you a modern-day example of it that maybe you can latch on to as a history lesson: Hitler and the Nazi government took it serious enough to create a not-so-secret society for it. You can look up 'Thule Society' on the internet, of all places, and learn everything you need to know about how they dabbled with it. Explains a lot about some of their experiments and atrocities. I would say to you, as a person trying to pierce through this present darkness, that if a first-world government takes it serious, maybe you better as well. And if you are going to deal with it, you must pick a side."

"I wouldn't even know how to start," I said, trying to dismiss the recruitment drive. "Right now, my first priority is getting through the next week without getting you or me killed, or worse."

"It starts when you are hungry for what you don't have that you can't get nowhere else, Bodhi. Then you ask, then you seek until you find. I can tell, for whatever reason, you ain't hungry yet. And I can tell you've had enough of me preachin' for today, so I will be lettin' ya surrender in defeat until you are ready to battle for your poor sufferin' soul some more."

"It ain't you, Caed. It's your God that beat me."

"Well, then, I am glad to hear it. Maybe we can get serious and have you brought to Him."

"Maybe one day. So, in the meantime, you say not to worry about being hexed or cursed or having demons come to murder me through my sleep, huh?"

"No more than getting shanked around here, anyway."

"Ok … you win for now. Let's get back to serious business. How about you show me better exercises to train my body? You already wore out my brain, and it's nearly dinnertime."

"Your loss is no gain of mine, Bodhi. Just let me know when you have any questions I can answer, and seriously, make them simple ones, like 'What is the meaning of life?'" He finished with a laugh, and I loosened back up to where I was before we got started.

CHAPTER 12

DAY 4

"I cannot think that we are useless or God would not have created us. There is one God looking down on us all. We are all the children of one God. The sun, the darkness, the winds are all listening to what we have to say."

–Geronimo

"How did your day go, Booty baby?" Cherry asked me when I got into the clinic.

"It made me miss getting bored, Cher. For starters, I got a new celly."

"Oh, that's good!"

How would he know? Why would he think that is good? "Yeah, he's from Ireland. If you got a thing for Irish crème, you'll love his accent." *Maybe I could play matchmaker for Caed?*

"Oh, is he anything like Liam Neeson? I heard he has the biggest—"

"No, he's smaller than you. Think more like that guy that was with Samuel Jackson in that movie *Formula 51?*"

"Oh, the one that was in *The Full Monty*! YUM!"

"I never saw that one, but I can't think of the guy's name. Anyway, him and Topaz hit it off this morning. I bet you heard something about that already, though."

"Oh, that was him? Booty, y'all better be careful. I seen some of what was left after Las Hermanas was done."

"Well, dead is dead. They can only kill me once, and so far they haven't been able to do more than get in the way of my knuckles."

"You wouldn't say that if you seen what I seen, though," Cher warned as he started walking toward the front of the clinic to sign out for the day.

"Hey, all I heard was they killed a few people and had a little too much fun with the corpses after. Granted, that is pretty sick, but I won't be around for the party if they get me."

"Bodhi." He turned and looked at me eyeball to eyeball. "You sound like you think you bad. But you don't know, man. I didn't see anything official, but those bodies was too bloody for everything they did to be done after they died."

"Oh?" Now that brought me up short. "I was in the same block when one of those murders happened, and I didn't hear a thing."

"Nobody did, Bodhi—that was what was so freaky! Everyone slept all peaceful-like while those men visited hell before they died!"

"Or at least no one wanted to hear anything. But I figure they were probably knocked out somehow if they were still alive."

"Speaking of knocked out, your boy Spike made it in today. They are keeping him on pain meds, so he's loopy when he wakes up."

"Oh, glad to hear he's on the road to recovering. I'll go bug him after I finish doing all of your chores," I popped off with a laugh.

"Ha! Be ready to stay bored tonight—I didn't leave anything for you to do!"

"Well, I guess I can mop and polish the floors again. That cured the boredom last time."

"Bodhi, you better not cause any trouble tonight. I was told by Carls to keep an eye on this one," Nurse Nancy said with a chuckle as she walked up.

"Carls would never say that. He knows I'm sweet and innocent," I deadpanned, which caused Cherry to snort while laughing.

"You crack me up, Bodhi. You gonna do stand-up when you get out in a week?" Cherry asked.

"Nah, I'll do stand-up here, where I'm appreciated, till I get out and crack up from the lack of emotional support."

"Ok, Bodhi, we finished restocking supplies and folding linens. Not much else to keep you busy other than keeping an eye on Mr. Spence."

"No worries, Miss Nancy, I will find stuff to keep me busy."

"Don't worry about it; I don't believe in making work harder than it has to be. That only adds to stress and stress brings drama. We don't want no drama, do we, Cherry?"

"We don't want none, no!" Cherry agreed before cackling.

"Ok, I'll keep things chill tonight. I'm gonna look in on Spike and see if he's awake."

I left Nancy and Cherry behind and walked over to Spike's bed. Looking at the label on the IV bag, he was on antibiotics strong enough to cure a horse. He was still on a heart monitor and getting his blood pressure checked every four hours. The machine kicked in and inflated the BP cuff just as I finished looking at his vital signs and made sure everything was within normal limits, considering what he'd been through and now being on pain meds.

"Well, I see you haven't had a shave or a bath since you been gone. Didn't they give you a pretty nurse?" I asked, getting an instant response from Spike as his eyes popped open.

"Bodhi, don't you dare make me laugh, you bastard. Waking up to your face is bad enough!"

I laughed for him and took his hand in mine, giving him a bro hug.

"They told me I nearly bought it. Sons of bitches smeared that shiv in caca. How messed up is that?"

"I'm passed fed up with them. Did you do something that put you on their hit list I don't know about?"

"Yeah," Spike said in a slow, drugged, tired voice. "During breakfast that morning, I overheard that Topaz really isn't their boss here. He's just their puppet. The real juice is that freak they call Annie, with the red curly hair. I didn't get a chance to tell King before they got me. But when Annie tells them to jump, they turn into a bunch of frogs."

"Is that guy even Mexican? I thought he was just a punk they grabbed and pimped out."

"I don't know what he is—I never gave enough of a damn to find out or ask around. That's the only thing I can think of that would make them come after me like that, if there was any reason behind it to make it personal."

"Well, for now, you are out of this mess. I doubt you'll be out of here before I'm gone, and at the rate Las Hermanas are going, I expect the proverbial shit to hit the fan and splatter down on them pretty soon. They're getting too big for their britches." I filled him in on everything he had missed out over the last few days.

"Sounds like your new celly is crazier than I am," Spike chuckled as his eyelids drooped lower.

"He is a distant second. Get some rest, bubba. I got your back." Poor guy was out before I finished speaking.

I stood up and walked around the clinic, looking for any trash lying around to throw away and any trash cans to empty before

inspecting the work on the linens and restocking. I cast an inscru-
table glance with an arched brow at Nurse Nancy while making a
show of counting the stock and got a quick grin as my reward.

I went to each bed and made sure everything was put up and
nearly organized, all cords and hoses to vital sign machines un-
tangled and placed where they would be easy to grab. Cherry and
Nancy hadn't been kidding when they said there wasn't much to
do. I debated over mopping the floors now or waiting till the end
of my shift but decided to be proactive, betting that whoever came
through in the morning would start off by mopping. Biggest difference, though, was that the trustee that would come through and clean
wouldn't be allowed to meddle as much as I was getting away with.

I was about halfway finished when the radios started squawking.
Now, I was kind of in my own world, daydreaming about being a kid
riding horses at my dad's ranch during one of my sparse visitation
days, so I kinda missed the first part. But it sounded like big emergency—lots of yelling … "inmate," "hand," "amputate"?

I went on alert, even though I was not supposed to be involved
in any plan of care actions or activities, and put away the mop and
bucket while Nancy and her medic got gloves on and waited near
the doors.

I snuck a pair of gloves for myself, just in case this was bad. And
if not, well, believe it or not, inmates have uses for rubber gloves
that make them a solid barter item. Don't ask—you probably don't
want to know if you don't already.

It sounds cliché, but when you are waiting and not much else,
time seems to stretch out and makes you think they're taking longer
to get there than they really are. But the truth is, yes, they are really
taking that much time to get there. Of course, I was also watching
the clock while hearing the chatter on the radios. About five minutes
after the alarms began, my floor had nearly dried and I could finally
hear them coming down the hall, yelling at each other and through
the radio.

Two guards showed up dragging a bloodied and diaphoretic little
friend of mine. You may remember him fondly from times past as
Slippy, aka Jaime. *This guy always interrupts my mopping!*

"He won't tell us how this happened, and we didn't see his hand
in his cell."

"Eddy, elevation and pressure! I'll get bandages and see what we have for a tourniquet."

Eddy the medic stepped up as the guards all stepped back, and I snorted. Yes, I really snorted. Not to sound like a cop hater or anything—I would have done it if they were firemen too … but probably while making fun of them at the same time. It's a responder thing, not a convict thing.

I gloved up and helped Eddy, which made the guards nervous.

"Relax, guys, Eddy needs a second pair of hands to help Nancy. This guy needs an IV and some fluids and another set of hands to help with the bleeding," I explained while reaching high up Slippy's slippery arm to find the brachial artery between the bicep and tricep muscles on the inside of his arm. I dug my fingers in deep to help pinch off the flow of blood going through the arm.

"Hey, Slippy, let me give you a hand, since yours seems lost." Oh, the things I could never say to my patients when I was doing this for a living!

Now, you might think amputations should send blood spewing through the air like a fire hose. Not so much, especially at the extremities and with a clean cut, which this seemed to be somewhat. Blood loss is still a major concern, but the body tends to compensate by pulling the veins and arteries deeper into the body. Between that and a little thing called shock, you won't die from blood loss immediately, and you have more than a few minutes to do something to turn things around. Which explains why my first priority was to raise the arm above the heart—makes it harder for blood to go uphill and clamp down on an artery. If I had a third hand, it would be holding any kind of bandaging down on the stump.

Could the patient do that? Normally they are the perfect ones to do that, but in this case, Slippy was in pretty sad shape and wasn't dealing too well. The fact that he was starting to giggle and laugh while his eyes tried to roll back was really worrying me.

"We have bandages but no tourniquets. I didn't remember ever seeing them in inventory, but I couldn't find anything that would work to make one with, either," Nancy said as she ran up, red-faced and sweating.

The AC kept this place at near meat locker temperature, but when your nervous system's sympathetic response kicks in, firing off your adrenaline and fight-or-flight responses, you tend to leak here and there. You can also develop tunnel vision.

"Give me the roller gauze and a pen and swap places with me! I can get him bandaged down so you can keep fluids in him," I volunteered. She handed me the package of gauze and I let her fingers take the place of mine over Slippy's brachial artery, then I stepped around her to grab a pen out of the shirt of one of the guards, who was doing a great job keeping the forces of evil at bay and not much else.

Roller gauze has a lot of great uses besides being just a wraparound Band-Aid. I unrolled an arm's length, doubled, and tripled the wispy thin cotton over itself, then twisted it into a cord and wrapped it around Slippy's arm and back around the pen before tying it down. Next I used the pen for a windlass—don't try this with a cheap pen. I would have used trauma shears if I could have gotten my hands on them.

We laid him down on the bed and Eddy went to work finding a vein just as a guard went flying through the air, landing with a horrific crash against the wall on the other side of the room.

I looked up as another guard went flying the other way, thrown one-handed by Spider. I was so confused. Spider didn't have any clothes on and everything below his waist was a bloody ruin. He was also holding a severed hand. I looked up at Spider's expressionless face and couldn't miss the new tattoo he had on the middle of his forehead, identical to the swastika Topaz just got.

"The hand that needs ... is the hand that bleeds ... will give service for the hand that feeds."

Ok, looks like Spider, talks like Dr. Seuss ... sounds like nothing I've heard this side of hell. Eddy spun around and was thrown across the room, while Nancy did the girl thing and started screaming. I did the hero thing—not smart.

"Spider, what the hell?!" I stepped up to him ready to do whatever was needed to put him down and get him help. No doubt, Slippy and his crew had tried to make him their latest victim. *Damn, damn, damn, this is bad.*

Spider stopped and looked at me, then he grinned. "Bound to hell for your sin ... no loyalty to win ... will you keep your skin?"

Nancy's screams got choked off. I looked over and Slippy had his one good arm across her throat and his legs wrapped around her, trapping her in place.

"Bodhi, we have one final offer for you. More sweet than the last one. Join Las Hermanas, or we will send you to hell." Slippy nodded at Spider, and Spider slumped down to the floor like a string-cut puppet.

"What we seek is but a thrill … join with us, you will … or else blood, we spill." That same exact voice and cadence, but now coming from my favorite punching bag, Slippy.

I was stunned motionless as Slippy snapped Nancy's neck and cast her aside. I didn't know where everyone else was, why the place wasn't flooding with guards, but from my peripheral vision I saw movement where Spider was, drawing my attention to him getting back to his feet. Only his color was off so bad … his lips and face reminded me of pictures I had seen of people suffering from frostbite.

Yes, pictures. No, I did not have firsthand experience with frostbite; this is Texas.

"A spirit so blind … your life has been unkind … power with us, you will find."

"Do you know how lame you sound?" I said, backing up and moving to the side. I wasn't sure who was more dangerous of the two I now faced, but Spider seemed to be moving slower and stiffer than before. A zombie came to mind—Spider was definitely not Spider right now. Movies made zombies look ridiculously easy to take down. Just snap the neck or crush the head of the shuffling dead, right? Trying to figure out my course of action, I watched Slippy move backwards to the wall and start climbing up it like a crab.

"In fear, you cannot mask … in your eternal torment, we will bask … your submission is all we ask."

I rushed to Spider and shot a left roundhouse kick to the outside of his right leg. He sent his right arm swinging in a looping arc that hit my left forearm and sent me flying. The back corner of my skull cracked against the floor and sent pain from my nose to my toes. Good news, I wasn't knocked out and wasn't any more senseless than usual, but I knew I was going to have a hell of a knot there when this was over. Bad news, my whole left arm and shoulder was tingling and numb and did not want to move.

Spider was down with his right leg going in multiple directions—my kicks tended to have that effect when I hit the sweet spot.

Spider started crawling my way, showing zero pain, emotion, or recognition. I scrambled to my feet, shaking my arm and finding nothing broken, just cold to the bone. Time to get an equalizer, as my grandad would say. I raced over to the nearest guard and hit pay dirt when I patted the hip pockets of his slacks. I whipped out a pocket folder—which guards shouldn't be keeping on them in case some pickpocket gets lucky enough to grab it—and flicked it open just as Spider crawled into reaching distance and grabbed for my lower legs. I skipped back and reversed the grip on the folder. Oh, man, I loved this knife. Had a good hilt, the lower part of the blade had huge serrated teeth, and it had a nice long, fat blade.

Spider reached and I danced to the side, kicked a supporting arm from under him, and came down with a hammer blow, knifepoint first, and rammed the blade to the hilt through the bone. I regained my center of balance and danced back out of reach, trying to keep Slippy the demon crab in my peripheral vision as he crab-crawled along the corner of the wall and ceiling. Luckily, he was content to watch, because if that lobotomy operation I performed on Spider worked, it didn't show. Spider was already climbing back to his feet, knife buried to the hilt from the top of his head, making him a macabre version of a unicorn. Ignoring the broken leg and putting his weight on a shattered knee, he was coming back for more. I obliged by racing to the other side, sending a right roundhouse to his left leg. Snap, crackle, pop, and down he went, with me learning from earlier and not taking a hit for my effort.

"Oh, come on! It's not just a flesh wound!" I yelled at the ridiculous tableau unfolding in front of me. I was feeling my awareness trying to detach to observe what I was dealing with.

I snatched the handle of the mop bucket and brought it down in an overhand swing as I stepped into range of Spider, aiming for his head. The heavy-duty bucket was full of bleach water. Spider reached for my legs as the bucket crashed over the back of his skull, slamming him face-first down into the hard floor.

I started curb-stomping Spider's skull until everything was a crunchy mess, the way all spiders die under someone's shoe.

I looked up at Slippy looking down at me. He was perched and hanging from the freaking ceiling like a … well, a spider. His head cocked to one side, then the other as he glared at me. I fought to control my breathing and clear the panic from my mind while I was being scrutinized.

"Another time, we will meet … then you will know defeat … a fate you will not—"

"Shut the hell up and dance or run!!" Today was as good a day to die as any for one of us.

Slippy fell to the floor and crashed off the side of Spike's bed, then started screaming, "HELP! HE'S KILLING EVERYONE!" exactly when a mob of guards came running in and spotted me standing with one foot in the crushed remains of Spider's skull, surrounded by dead guards and a dead Nurse Nancy. Guess what happened next?

I got beat on, stomped, tased, cuffed, and nearly stuffed before Carls came in and started shoving and peeling guards off me. Weirdly enough, he was my new friend. *Not the strangest thing that has happened to me tonight.*

"Bodhi, if you got a good story, let's hear it before I put a hole through your head and line you up beside my men and tell their families we got the bastard that did this."

"Slippy killed Nancy" was all I could wheeze out. I was a hurt pup all over. It hurt to breathe, hurt to move. I was curled up in a ball. Most of the licks I'd caught were on my back near my kidneys and on my arms and shins. It was my kidneys that made every other pain receptor sing out. I'd never peed blood before, but I bet I would be from this.

"That pipsqueak is nearly dead from having his hand cut off! You better come up with something else fast."

"Check the video." I was learning to breathe again, yay me. I sat up, gritted my teeth, and faced my accuser, looking him right in the eye. "Are you one of the good guys, Carls?"

"He is a liar! His boy cut off my hand and came in here to finish me off, and all the guards were trying to protect me!"

"Is he telling the truth, Bodhi?" Carls asked.

"Uh … that much might be true, I don't know what happened to Spider." What the hell was I supposed to say to that?

"You killed him so he would stop screaming like the bitch we made him!" Slippy yelled in laughter. Moving faster than my thoughts, I tried to shoot to my feet to go after him and rip his throat out. First problem, pain; second problem, cuffed hands; third problem, a foot crashing in my face sending me down again.

"Carls, my boy didn't do it. He asked you to look at the videos—why aren't you?" Spike was awake and backing me up. Carls wasn't my friend no more.

"Because there is no surveillance in the clinic since prisoners get privacy and protection, thanks to the new prison regulations we are now under. Which means if you don't shut your hole, Spike, you will get what Bodhi's got coming, too!"

"Las Hermanas will be glad to take care of Bodhi and his bitch Spike for you guys. We aren't afraid to get bloody."

I smiled my hate at Slippy. "No kidding, every time your punk ass comes at me, you get bloody." I turned and looked at Carls. "If you aren't going to be a good man, then I see no reason why I should be, either. You know I would not and could not do the crap that lying punk claims."

"Then you better tell us exactly who did what here, Bodhi, and it better sound half straight or you aren't walking out of here."

Gee, officer, let's see. A body snatcher turned my friend into a zombie after he murdered everyone but me. Yeah, that sounds legit, right?

Someone wake me up from this nightmare. I want to be home with my family on the rez, see the storms sweeping across the plains, smell the rain and feel the sun on my face, and swim in the creek at Medicine Park with the army brats from Fort Sill when I was a kid, before I tried to play hero and do something important with my life.

"I talk no more." If I could've said it with less words, I would have. I sought solace in my mind and went to another place and time only to catch a boot in the face, sending my head crashing back into the wall behind me. I was out cold before I felt any pain.

CHAPTER 13

S truggling to swallow woke me up … or maybe it was the pain from being stomped by a herd of braying jackasses. I was awake, but only because I couldn't sleep like this. I struggled to open my eyes and get a sense of up from down, and which direction a threat would come from. After the fog drifted away, leaving me in a gray room under an irritating florescent light that buzzed overhead, I started trying to assess my body from head to toe. Or, to be exact, to assess what hurt the most to the least. Good news, nothing on the left side of my upper body hurt, from shoulder to fingertips. Bad news, it didn't hurt because it was totally numb. My hands were still cuffed behind my back, and I must have been lying on it wrong.

I had no sense of time and no idea how long I'd been in this room. Hell, even solitary had a cot in it; this wasn't any better than a barren storage closet. That might be good news, if I were an optimist. As it was, after recalling the events prior to my nap, Carls likely wanted to stash me out of the way until he could have some alone time with me later.

I rolled to my knees and climbed to my feet, using the wall to push off from, and promptly spewed. I got so dizzy while puking I had to go back down to my knees again. And ... I had to pee.

"*So, dear, how did your day go today?*" I laughed as I imitated my granny's voice. "All the kids hate me at school, Granny." She told me that would either make me stronger than all of them or weaker, and the choice was mine to make. It didn't feel true then, but it does today.

I sat there glaring, in pain, dizzy, nauseated, and kneeling with my hands bound behind me. Glaring at the door, waiting for it to open, hoping it would before I let go and unloaded my bladder in my pants. Along with the smell of vomit, it should be a great scent for mating season for some species, I was sure.

"I'm pert as a ruttin' buck!"

About the time I was just about to let go and end one pain, the door opened. *Damn thing wasn't even locked.*

"Hardcastle and Carls, my two favorite jackasses. Thanks for keeping me safe and in a controlled environment. I have to give this resort a downgrade, though, for no mint on the pillow." You might think I was cracking jokes and ready to get hugs and forgiveness. But inside, I was ready to go Native and take hair. Ok, maybe I wouldn't scalp them, but their shoes would not be safe from my pee ... if I could get my hands free.

"You sound upset. Did a bump on the head hurt your feelings?"

Carls was such an asshole.

"Carls, don't open your mouth again until you apologize to Bo-dhi." Hardcastle just became my new friend. But then again, I wasn't on much of a winning streak for making new friends lately.

"What happened after Carls gave me a concussion?"

"Uncuff him, Carls. You sure you have a concussion, Bodhi?"

"All the classic symptoms without a CT scan and x-rays to rule out bleeds and breaks. Yeah, I know I do. Thanks, shithead." I know, I have a potty mouth, but I only cuss when I mean it.

"Aww, I am sorry, Bodhi. If I hit you again, will it make it bet-ter?"

"You were the stupid stepchild of your family everyone abused, weren't you?" I accused and rubbed my wrists.

"Well, we have some good news for you, Bodhi. Even though you may have tipped everyone off about questionably legal video surveillance being used, we know you didn't kill anyone except Spi-der. But we got a hell of a mess to figure out and no time to really do it in."

"Don't see how any of this is my problem. I nearly got killed back there by that thing, and by your dummy here." Calling Carls a dummy was childish, but it was funny to watch him turn red, cuss me out with everything I'd heard a million times before, and be held back by Hardcastle. I took my guilty pleasures where I could.

"Go stand outside, Carls, and cool off."

"I am about to piss all over your shoes," I said while trying to lean against a wall and keep the world from spinning out from under me.

"Carls, never mind, get back in here and carry Bodhi to my office and help him to the bathroom." Carls cussed, while I grinned and started singing.

"It's a beautiful day in the neighborhood, a beautiful day to be a neighbor! Won't you be my neighbor?" I asked and was rewarded by Carls making faces of displeasure at my puke breath.

"Bodhi, do we need to send you out to the hospital? You're act-ing drunk, and that is worrying me."

"You guys got any idea what they did to Spider to make him do those things?" I ignored his question for now. Getting out for a while sounded like a spectacular idea, but I had obligations to get word to King about what was going on and try to get this shitstorm settled before more people got hurt like Spider. Besides, I knew the routine the doctors would give me and could take care of it as good myself. Not that I would ever suggest someone without a medical background consider that.

"What we can put together is somehow, Spider attacked Jaime in his cell and chopped off Jaime's hand. Jaime and his celly retaliated and Spider got clear. During the searches, members of Las Hermanas got out of their cells and started a minor riot with the guards while Jaime was brought to the clinic. Spider got through all the guards without getting caught, came into the clinic, and started killing everyone and stopped when he faced you. We saw Jaime kill Nancy and somehow climb up the wall until he was out of camera range, but we have no audio feed, so we don't know what Jaime said to you."

"So you didn't hear what Spider said, either," I stated the obvious.

"Bodhi, they cut his throat vertically up and down. I can't confirm it, but I am betting they did it to sever his vocal cords. I don't think there is any way he could have spoken through what they did to him."

"Oh, he was talking. But not in his voice. He made me an offer to join him, but in rhymes like a psycho poet. Then he stopped talking, dropped to the ground, and Jaime started, same voice, same way of rhyming. Scared me worse than anything I ever faced." I can admit it, I was freaked enough that part of my brain was shut down from trying to process what had happened. It sounded like something out of a Hollywood horror movie, and that thought made me stop and remember Caed saying almost exactly that phrase. We were definitely going to have to talk. Had Hardcastle not confirmed what had happened, I would be taking them on that offer to go to the ER and get a psych eval to go with it.

"He made you an offer you couldn't refuse, in rhymes? What did you do?" Carls asked as we got to Hardcastle's office. He started the water running in the sink for me—guess he didn't want bloody prints all over the place. Priorities: first, I had to pee.

"Ahhhhhhhhhhhh." Relief! "Well, he scared me so bad that I had to kill Spider, because whatever Spider had in him became Slippy.

Then Slippy ran his mouth a little more, same voice and rhymes that used Spider, and after that he fell from the ceiling when the cavalry arrived to capture this redskin that killed all the whites," I said sarcastically before flushing, stripping out of my shirt and pants, and giving myself a whore bath with hand soap.

"How the hell am I supposed to report all this on that? I got video that can't be used, a dead gangbanger that was tortured and mutilated that could not have killed the guards he killed, and another gangbanger that did it all after his hand was cut off. I'm open to ideas."

"Well first of all, Jaime and Topaz are just puppets. The juice in their gang is their brujo. Spike overheard them talking and caught who it is. We call him Orphan Annie—he's that new inmate with red hair and freckles they pimp out and spit on in the yard."

"Rudolph Vera. He was brought in for check fraud and child support delinquency and kiddy porn. History of dealing pot and scamming people with tarot cards. He is no leader, he's just a punk."

"Yeah, easy to ignore him, huh?" I mentioned. "If he could do those things to Spider, would you jump when he said 'boo'?"

"Ok, so why is he letting them use him for a toilet?"

"Either he likes that treatment, or it's an act," Hardcastle pointed out. "He fits the puzzle. This mess came from South America somewhere, and didn't start till after Vera was here."

"Great, now I can go to my cell and scrub my brain of this ever happening. Get me some jammies with footies in them and hot chocolate and we'll call it squaresies, ok?"

"Bodhi, we got nothing but what a lawyer would claim is conjecture. Yeah, it makes sense. But you killing everyone makes even more sense than what we saw and only *think* happened. It's nearly breakfast … time to wake everyone up and get them ready to do their work jobs. First shift will be coming in and noticing dead bodies, especially Nancy, and wanting answers and investigations and blame assigned. I'm all about the guilty parties paying for their crimes, but this is beyond me. I'm going to have to make a call I tried to avoid making."

"Well, Slippy had a good idea."

"Let them take care of you?" Carls asked.

"Something like that. Turn me loose to report to King. If Annie is dealt with, the snake's head and all that. Put everything on a riot in the clinic by Las Hermanas trying take over the prison and them killing everyone. Guards came in, and me and Spike got saved?"

"Too many of our guards were involved. There's no way to keep a lid on that many lies. Too thin," Carls said, frustrated.

"Well, you're going to have to excuse me—kicking my head in didn't make it easier for me to play criminal mastermind and come up with a cover story for you. You got a prison full of shot-callers that can do that, and a few of them are in the Diamondbacks. But I do know this: You can't sweep it under the rug and let it go away by putting it all on me. Las Hermanas owns you and this prison by the end of the day over what happened if you do that, and both of you with it. So you two better learn to cheat if you want to win, break some rules for the right reasons, and get your hands dirty."

"What do you mean they own us?" Carls asked the silly question.

"It's pretty obvious they're already getting help from the guards to move around when the rest of us are locked down. Either of you two want to try to claim you won't bend over to help them if they say you do or die like Spider? Maybe use you like they did Spider and turn you on your families when you go home?"

"What makes you think they can do that?" Hardcastle asked.

"I was trained to prepare for the worst and hope for the best. What I saw in that clinic was scarier than any Hollywood horror movie—monsters or demons or whatever. Spider could not have done those things as torn up as he was, and no one climbs up walls like a … " I tried to think of something other than "a spider, man." I give up—who was the idiot that had designated me as the smart one in the room? "Especially after having a hand cut off and being in shock from blood loss. And what they said to me … that was from another world in itself. I don't know the how of it, or exactly the why. But we got a what, and the 'what' is total evil, and it isn't slowing down for any law or cage made for man."

"Get him dressed and send him out to breakfast. Our worm on a hook better land us a whale for breakfast, looks like," Hardcastle said in a resigned tone. "And God help us."

CHAPTER 14

I was put back in my cell just a few minutes before the lights would be coming on to wake everyone up for breakfast. Caed was on his knees, hands together and bowing over his Bible, obviously in prayer.

"Glad you're awake," I stated as I crossed over to my bunk and started climbing into a fresh onesie. No footies, though. *I should lodge a complaint for the abuse to my rights.*

"I have been in prayer all night, Bodhi. Never have I experienced so much dread as I'm feeling now that something is … wrong."

"Las Hermanas tortured Spider. He's dead. They killed everyone except me and Spike in the clinic. I hope you are ready for a war, because hell is coming to breakfast."

"Surely the authorities will come in and stop all this?" he asked after a shocked pause. "Why is there going to be more fighting?"

"I think it's time you told me about what you could put in a horror movie. I saw things last night that were … " I had to think how to word my statement so I wouldn't sound psychotic, yet rational and reasonable. "Not natural."

"That would take some time. First of all, what I know about and what I know firsthand aren't the same thing. I was raised in a land that makes superstition into a religion in and of itself. Me first crush was on a Wiccan, and we both went to church where the priest was also an exorcist. I read books, played games about all of it. But generally, what I've seen—strange noises, sounds, things that move—is nothing that really can hurt you more than what you believe. And what you believe can do more damage than a thousand stories of the worst demons. So, tell me what happened, and I will tell you what I know that you can use."

The lights turned on and Caed got a look at me.

"You look like ten pounds of shite stuffed in a five-pound bag. Didn't anyone tell you to duck with your head and not block with it?"

"You're the first one, smart-ass. Maybe you can give me lessons if we live to see the sun come up. I'm not going to get into all of it with you now, except that the warden here and some authorities in charge have been worried about occult activity, and a while ago I saw what looked like an evil spirit jump from one person and into another while killing the prison staff, and Spider."

"Aye, well, demonic possession is well-documented and centuries old, going back to the Bible age and beyond. Only way I know how to fight against it is with faith. Anything else, you might as well put out a house fire with gasoline, because you are just playing their game."

"Have you ever confronted one and beat it?"

"I do not know they can be beaten, as you would understand it. But cast out, oh yes. But they can be invited back in, or even summoned into someone else. The people I've seen fighting demonic possession are in a very bad state. Mind and body, tormented near to death. You have to understand, being possessed by the demonic is mentally and physically destructive. But never have I seen a willing host—someone that wants this and invited it into themselves and wants to stay that way. The stories I hear, though, these are tales that make the fables of the werewolves and monsters of old."

"Let's get to breakfast. Maybe you'll get the chance to show me how to duck a werewolf. I have to tell King what's going on and then, people are going to die if we want to live."

"Bodhi, don't ask me to kill anyone. And don't you be tryin' to murder someone in front of me, either."

"Oh, a Goody Two-Shoes, too, huh?" *Takes one to know one.* But just because I wanted to do good didn't mean I always got to. And I was not going to run around with a sign stuck to my head telling a bunch of prisoners what a nice guy I was, and that included letting Caed know. He could either figure it out for himself or judge me as guilty like everyone else in my life. "Think of it more like premeditated self-defense. Now let's go see what we can do to stop this war from being lost."

We were among the first to get to the chow hall. The trays had not yet been put out, but coffee was available. I grabbed a cup and a fistful of sugar packets and claimed a table with Caed following my lead. 'Course, he took creamer and not as much sugar in his. I wondered if the bit of caffeine would help fight the pain and fuzzy thinking in the wake of getting my butt stomped earlier enough to help me stay alive. I had no doubt this dance would get started soon after Las Hermanas walked in. If not, maybe I could get a bite in before I started the dance.

"I still don't understand why the warden is going to let this escalate into a block riot."

"Frankly, Caed, you really don't have to. If any demons pop up, I will let you cast them out and keep a look out for werewolves so you can teach me how to duck. I got an idea how to make this easy to resolve, but only if I get some help from the Diamondbacks and hopefully some cooperation from the other gangs here. Otherwise, it looks like I am going to be falling on my sword here in a while."

"You seem to be handling the situation pretty well."

"I kinda got used to the idea of not making it out of here. I'm less than a week from being released—at least I'm not going to be disappointed. And I would rather fall on my sword than be pushed on it or get it in the back."

"Maybe I can help you become disappointed, then. I don't plan to let Las Hermanas get by with murdering people while taking the path of the left hand."

"Left hand?"

"Aye, that is how occultists refer to their dark arts. Their phrasing, not mine. I guess it's their PC way of saying they want to fornicate evil."

"Yeah, someone should keep those people out of prison."

"Generally, they wind up in insane asylums, strapped down and drugged up."

"I feel like that's where I need to be after what I saw last night." My grandad would call that whining. But seriously, wall-crawling demons and walking dead ... Spider, whatever he was, was not something I had been trained to handle by anyone, from my grandad to anyone he taught or any volunteer fire department EMS class.

"Bodhi, you look like you got your ass beat," King said as he and Copper took a seat. Had I dozed off? I was doing my best to keep an eye on who was coming in. Obviously I needed to mainline the coffee to get anything from it.

"It's a fashion statement. It's part of the theme for the riot that happened last night."

"What riot?" Copper asked.

"Did y'all sleep through it?" Seriously, how could anyone sleep through what had happened?

"Must not have been much. Anyone seen Spider? He wasn't in his cot when I woke up this morning. I thought he was already here."

"Spider's dead. Las Hermanas got their hands on him and tortured him." I let the cussing and anger build up before laying the rest out.

"How the hell did they get him from our cell with me there the whole time and the door locked?" Copper asked the million-dollar question at me.

"I don't know," I responded with a shake of my head. "They sent one of their punks into the clinic last night with a hand cut off, and while we were busy working on him, they came in with what was left of Spider. Killed all the prison staff in there, from what I saw, and left me holding the bag when the cavalry showed up to save the day." Ok, so that wasn't exactly the truth, but I'd gotten kicked in the head a lot, and I'd heard somewhere that it was my right to not incriminate myself. Especially when the guilty were trying to set me up.

"They kill Nancy, too?"

"Yeah. King, this has gotten out of hand. The warden believes me, for now, but there's no proof they can use to pin this on Hermanas. No guards saw anything." I tightened my hand around my cup of coffee. "No explanation for how Spider got out of his cell and into a Las Hermanas cell to chop off a punk's hand and get himself castrated, throat cut, and dragged into the clinic, all while we were working on the one-handed punk who was somehow found before Spider. And in the middle of all that, Spider shows up to kill the guards and staff in the clinic and leaves me standing in the middle of it waiting for the response team to kick my face in."

"Ok, so how the hell are they doing this?" King asked after taking a bit to process all that.

"I say we're getting drugged somehow. But there are sketchy rumors they're using witchcraft or Satanism. Right now, the how doesn't seem important. They obviously have guards working for them, and probably will have a lot more after this crap splatters over us from hitting the fan."

"It's way too early to be dealing with all this. What are you going to do, shank one or two now? That won't make any of this go away, and you're going to get yourself stuck in here for years if you do."

"King, you tell me to face them on my own because y'all don't have my back, and I will. My back is against the wall here."

The table got deathly quiet at that. I knew I was pushing buttons, but I was too damned tired and hurt to find a crap to give at the moment. Do or die was coming before the bacon and eggs would get served.

"Every man at this table, even Caed and Reggie, is going to have your back. But someone better come up with something solid, because I don't see how this goes away just by shiving one or two little punks in Las Hermanas. We need to put all this on their shot-caller, Topaz."

"Oh, I nearly forgot. Spike is back and he didn't get killed last night, either. He said reason they shanked him was because he overheard that Topaz ain't their *el jefita, la jefito,* whatever. The redheaded punk they pimp out that we call Annie is their top bitch."

"You gotta be shitting me, that little fairy fart?" Copper nearly got a smile from me at the imagery.

"Spike said the doctors told him the shiv they used was smeared in dung when they stabbed him. Yeah, these guys dance to their own tune."

"Ok, Bodhi, you got anything else we need to know?"

"I think the warden will be in our corner for just about whatever it takes to resolve this if we can do it before they finish their shift change and start having to answer for the bodies on the ground. He didn't look thrilled with the idea of this prison being run by Las Hermanas and being on their leash."

King sat up a bit straighter, resolute. "Copper, you get G-dog and Hoodwink and fan out to the gangs. Ask them to pass word to their shot-callers for an emergency meeting with me right now. Tell them Las Hermanas murdered Nancy and we are all getting heat for it and I want to discuss politics. Rest of you, leave me this table and find another."

If you think it's a small deal for a shot-caller to empty a table and sit by himself with no apparent backup, think again. But as King decrees, we do.

Reggie, Caed, and I were able to claim a corner of a table to ourselves. I got another cup of coffee on the way and looked around, counting heads and faces.

"I don't see a single member of Las Hermanas in here yet. And just about everyone else is here."

As all the gang bosses congregated at one table, the lunch room grew silent as a tomb. Nearly five years in prison, and I had never saw this. Maybe others had in other places. Boy, wasn't I lucky?

Coffee and trays were brought to their table. Two of them were major Black gangs, three were old-school Mexican gangs, and one was a white power gang. None of them got along on the streets at all, and in prison none of them usually got within a hundred feet of each other. Getting one or two of the groups to cooperate at times was rare, and usually catastrophic for whomever they aligned against. If it was Las Hermanas, great! If it went south and came at little ol' me, I wouldn't have to worry about my five-year plan for the future.

I stood up to get another coffee and felt my gut twist into a hundred knots. Las Hermanas walked in en masse, with Carls leading them and a response team behind them. Why did this worry me? Because they were dog whistling and throwing gang signs and attitude. The response team fanned out around the room.

Me? I decided to finish what I'd started and went to get another cup of coffee.

I saw Topaz, taller and heavier built than the others. He had fresh ink done on his head and had shaved all his hair off. On my way back to the table, King caught my attention and waved me over.

"Word is already going around that the guards and Las Hermanas are all blaming you for the deaths, Bodhi. Said had you been a model prisoner and in your cell, none of this would have happened."

I took a sip of coffee and glanced at each boss, eye to eye, getting a mixed reception of animosity and curiosity in return.

"So, I should have stayed out of their way and been their prison bitch? They made that offer to me twice already—now there are bodies on the ground. I made my choice. I may be locked up, but no one owns me."

"You talk tough, little man, but that is what it is. Looks like your mouth is what escalated this mess, and it goes away when you go away." I was being addressed by a prison boss in charge of every member of a Black gang that stretched north to Detroit and west to California, a hulking brute that was still in charge of a cocaine and prostitution ring on the outside.

"Spoken like a model inmate that will go along to get along with Las Hermanas at any cost." Being defended by a skin-headed fan of Aryan principles nearly made my head swim.

"No joke, some people wake up and should stay in their cell and write letters to their parents." A *vato* from a … "syndicate" founded in Texas during the fifties laughed.

I have to point out something before you get the wrong idea. Using a language filter makes it way easier to tell you what was said without the air turning blue from profane filler words that became common in our everyday life in the big house. If you think you're missing something, just add n F-bomb every other word or two and you'll be caught up.

"Can't do that when you don't know which daddy is yours and your momma doesn't know which child you is," the other Black leader joined in with at least twice as many wirty dords.

And to really spoil the party, Topaz and his crew came sashaying up. Ok, maybe it was more of a strut, but seriously, half of them walked like their hips were broke. I was also puzzled at what Topaz had tattooed on his head. It took me a minute, but I figured out it was meant to be an upside-down skull, with the eyes being the actual eyes of Topaz. The nose was inverted and surrounding the swastika he'd done the day before, but instead of a mouth, it was a nest of octopus tentacles reaching up his head and down the back to wrap around his neck.

"Topaz, this is not a meeting to organize a dance-off. You aren't welcome." I squared up against them. The enforcers for each gang started crowding up to face off against Las Hermanas.

"Bodhi, I've heard you are telling lies, trying to cover your ass. But don't worry, we aren't here for you. That's why all the guards are here—to take you away to answer for the murders that happened last night. Killing a member of your own crew? I am surprised at you. Don't worry, though, we have a special place in our family for someone just like you for being such a spirited fighter." And Carls just stood there next to him, watching me and giving me nothing.

"I told you, Carls, if you won't be the good guy, don't think I will, either."

"See, Bodhi, if it was comfort and privileges you wanted, you should have come to us. We are the ones with all the power around

REDEMPTION: GOVERNED BY INDEPENDENCE

here. You didn't have to turn into a rat and bend over the warden's desk."

"Come along, Bodhi, this doesn't have to be worse than it already is for you," Carls finally spoke. Now I was really mad. I could feel my pulse jumping into my throat and my face getting hot from the rush that made me nearly mindless and robbed me of any clear thought I had.

"So you're saying Bodhi killed Spider?" Caed asked and started walking through everyone.

"Yes, he was standing over Spider when my guards pulled him off and had to subdue him."

"Topaz said 'murders.' Meaning he killed others. Now what others is he talking about?" King added.

"When the response team got into the clinic, two of my guards had been killed along with the RN, Nurse Nancy."

"Who witnessed this, and what proof do you have Bodhi did it?" King pressed.

"Security footage is logged showing video that began with two cell doors malfunctioning and opening. Inmate Michael Perez is shown on video leaving his cell and walking straight to the cell of inmates Rudolph and Jamie. A short time later, footage shows Jaime leaving his cell with his hand chopped off and yelling for help. Jaime is brought to the clinic and a response team is deployed to his cell in response. Before they arrive, inmate Michael walks out and follows Jaime to the clinic. At no time did anyone else go into the clinic until the response team arrived and found Bodhi standing over Michael's body. Bodhi's lower body was covered in blood and remains of the skull of Michael, and the two guards and the nurse were obviously dead."

"There was a medic named Eddy, and Spike was also there, too, Carls. Did Eddy die?" I asked. My anger was cooling and allowing me to focus. Maybe it was the caffeine kicking in, but I was ready to kick someone's ass before I got taken down. Carls was first on my list at this point.

"Eddy was unconscious, unresponsive when medics arrived and took him and inmates Jaime and Spence to the local hospital. Now, Bodhi, come with me so this doesn't have to go up another level."

"See, all your lying didn't accomplish anything, Bodhi. And I can absolutely be totally honest and tell the truth, and no one can lay a finger of blame or punish me for it," Topaz taunted. "That's why Carls and every guard here is on my side and why you are going to be made an example, and no one here will lift a finger to help you."

I take it back—Topaz was back at the top of my list ahead of Carls. Or better yet …

"Bodhi, why don't you be honest and tell everyone here everything that really happened? Let the truth set you free. No one is going to be blamed for what happened to Spider, and you are only making it worse for yourself by trying to manipulate everyone here with your twisted stories. We'll even kindly ask the guards to back off and let you say what you truly witnessed if you give the whole, gospel truth." I had never spoken to Annie, aka Rudolph, but there the little red-headed punk stepped up to me like he had the biggest balls in the whole prison. And man, did he stink, like he never washed and had a diaper on full of old poop.

I was pretty certain Rudolph would be dead before I was put in cuffs. I looked from him to Topaz, smiling like a creep in a rusty van to chase little kids around with. I glanced around at no one else stepping up and felt every bruise from every fist and foot that had hammered me from my toes to my nose and just felt … tired. The easy way out here was to give everyone what they wanted: a scapegoat to blame and make all their problems go away. *My fate is the same whether I murder this punk or not.* The only difference was whether I had it in me to do a solid for everyone that turned their back on me.

"Would telling another version of the events change who's responsible for the killings?" Caed asked.

"I've heard of you, Christian. You should want the whole unvarnished truth to be said."

"More than the truth, it is justice that I want done. The guilty to be punished. I ask you this: Who has the blood of the innocent on their hands? The blood shed on the ground cries for vengeance against whom?" Caed stepped up and was eye to eye with Rudolph. Funny that they were both in the same weight class … in more than one way, it seemed.

"Justice? This man is an obvious liar! The things he has accused us of doing—rioting in the clinic and killing everyone, but leaving him standing until guards beat him? He may as well try to claim the man we used to teach a lesson made it in there and killed everyone without any balls to fight with! For his lies, your dead and powerless God has abandoned him and left him in our hands, damned as all of us here are, except we're honest about it and accepting of those who aren't perfect and admit it while living as our nature demands for us to enjoy life. Look at this man before us—found guilty of manslaughter for the crime and sin of killing a child! Here, he is a liar, unsaved and unredeemed and bound for hell for eternity for his crimes by the church. Who would have him like this, accepting him for all his faults and calling him 'brother'?"

"Only a hypocrite would damn someone for not being perfect." Caed's words quietly offered dropped a bomb across the room, leaving a reverberating tone that rocked my world. "We are all imperfect in our own ways. But we will not be judged eternally by our mistakes and flaws, but by our hearts and intentions. Actions speak louder than words. I asked ye, who shed the blood of the innocent in the night? You did not answer, and you condemned Bodhi for the crime of not confessing your truth. So why don't you confess your truth for him, since you will not point the finger of blame of murder at him?"

"I will say this," I butted in. "Carls knows what really happened in that clinic. So does the warden. They installed hidden cameras in there, showed me the footage of the first time Las Hermanas tried to green-light Reggie the other night, and let me off if I would help maintain the calm in the clinic if Las Hermanas tried again. But they won't admit they have cameras rolling in the clinic because it violates our privacy rights. I ain't a saint, but I ain't no snitch, and I got no love for Las Hermanas and what they have done to people around here, including my people. What they know is that Las Hermanas did not stop at castrating and cutting Spider's throat last night—I had to put him down because of what they did and end his suffering. More blood on my hands, but the blood of the guards and Nancy … you own that, Annie," I said jabbing, a finger at his face. "Not me."

"Carved him up, put a curse on him, and let a demon ride his corpse to the clinic. Now that you've come close to the truth, I'll say the rest for you: we even had a hand from our boy," he finished with a laugh. "Go ahead, Carls, tell everyone the truth now that it's out there."

"They made Spider into a zombie, damned his soul, and sent him into the clinic. But it doesn't matter, because all of it can't be proved. Someone is going to pay for this, and Bodhi, it's you. But do this quiet and willing, and we will make this as easy as we can and everyone will get along."

I got pulled back like I weighed nothing. Everyone was stunned into silence except Caed, who stepped up. "I won't let him or you fall to evil."

"You can't stop this." Annie and Topaz stepped up, Topaz eye-balling me and breathing hard and heavy. "The authorities of man are blind to the truth. What are they going to convict us for? Trafficking demons and zombies? Right, and we will ride out of courts on unicorns. Everyone knows such things don't exist. And in retaliation, we will do the same to any that stand in our way. But why would you resist us? We only want the same as anyone—to exist and enjoy ourselves without bringing harm to anyone we love. Why the hell should we subject ourselves to moral laws and be damned on earth by hypocrites when the power of death is in our grasp and we own man's law?"

Oh, this was going to be good, I was going to get to go *mano a mano* with the scariest fighter in the prison. It wasn't just that Topaz was fast—and he was super-fast, and strong, at least as strong as me—but he always found ways to rip and tear flesh with fingers that gouged and ripped tendons and soft tissue like paper. I had witnessed him tear an arm tendon and rip through a cheek before the poor bastard even had a chance to flinch. The fight was over, but Topaz didn't stop until the man was crippled and barely left alive.

"Not everyone in here is evil. I doubt there are even a few that are," Caed's voice carried through the hall. Even though it did not seem he raised his volume, he became … intense. "Maybe you have the mind of a reprobate—that is not for me to judge. But I know in virtually all of us is a sense of good. We love, we learn, we grow to become better than we were. Some of us get trapped in the guilt and judgement of our own bad choices, but that does not mean we have to be damned by them and face the hopelessness of not learning from our mistakes.

"Every one of us is in here for the same reason: to be redeemed by the laws of man and go back into the world and have relationships with the people we care for. Some of us have only ourselves and no friends or family to belong to, but I think we all remember the ones we grew up with that we loved. Whether it was the mother that nursed us as babies, fathers who took us fishing, grandparents, siblings we tried to protect. Many of us know the feeling of earning an honest living by the sweat of our brow and the taste of ash from stealing from others what is not ours to take. And many of us know the shame we feel when we abuse others when we cannot control our own emotions. Fury, greed, lust … these are things rob us of honor and dignity, and we are more than capable of learning to control and tame the beast that rages inside of us and become the good men our loved ones see in us. To reclaim our lost honor and reap the rewards of a life of virtue.

"Words like 'honor' mean nothing to the reprobate who has none and gives no damn about it. But to nearly every man in here, honor means a lot, and so does loyalty. These are virtues that we can reclaim and be redeemed by. Love means nothing to you, but you will deny it. You love the things that give you pleasure, but will you sacrifice for who you love? Can you give love back and love someone for their own sake, the way you have been loved by others that you took advantage of for your gain? The reprobate-minded cannot do this, won't do this, will scoff at it. And now, I am done talking. If you want to damn Bodhi, you will have to get to him through me first. And frankly, dear, you aren't man enough."

CHAPTER 15

"Oh, I wouldn't dream of handling you—not my taste. Topaz, on the other hand?" Annie stepped back and unleashed his dog. "He's all yours, daddy!"

Maybe I was loopy from the kicks to the head—or, more likely, too busy mentally barfing at Orphan Annie calling Topaz "daddy."

"Ugh, what a sick little bastar—" I started to say when faster than a blink, a slap landed in front of my face before I registered Topaz had thrown a punch. Well, tried to anyway; Caed had intercepted it cold, and he appeared totally relaxed before he turned his head and put his focus on Topaz—and then he tensed his body. I'd never seen anything like it. It was like a shockwave exploded out from the center of Caed's being and extended itself to the tips of his fingers.

Topaz began to turn a little red as his fist was pushed back slowly, and it turned into an exhibition of strength. Topaz was nearly a head taller, and around a hundred pounds heavier. Like I said, Caed was a little guy in stature, but things began to pop. Topaz's eyes turned from anger to worry, then to horror as the bones in his fist began to snap under Caed's iron grip. Topaz went to his knees and began to cry out in agony.

"Carls! You have no authority for this—what are you doing?!" Hardcastle's rough voice cracked across the room like a marine drill instructor.

All eyes in the room went to Hardcastle as he walked into the chow hall, and before I could put my attention back on the players and the haters, Annie stepped up and shived Caed once in the belly, twice in the chest in the blink of an eye before I reacted.

I tackled Annie down to the ground and rose above him with his left arm pinned over his right shoulder. My fist came down with the force of a charging buffalo as the thunder from my heart pounded in my ears. I aimed for the center of his face and hammered straight at the floor, but his upper face and nose kept getting in the way of nearly all of my weight combined with the mountain of rage behind my fist. I didn't know how many hits I got in before I was tackled from the side—I just knew every time my fist landed, things broke. Topaz was now on top of me and reaching with one hand for my throat. Before I could register that much, he ate a foot from King and went flying off of me from the field goal attempt.

Alarms, bells, and whistles went off along with bangs from sting-ball grenades.

The block riot started and stopped in just a few seconds, but there were already bodies on the ground bleeding out. Caed was one of them.

I crawled over to him and ripped his shirt down the middle to expose his torso. I wasn't too worried about the belly wound, just the two in the chest. The rule of thumb for medicine in general is blood goes round and round, air goes in and out—not the other way around—and I was seeing blood going in and out and air going where it shouldn't. I put both my hands over the wounds and looked down into his eyes. "Don't you go nowhere on me, brother."

"Sorry, Bodhi, not our call. So much I wanted to say to you … I wish I had the time," he weakly offered with short gasping breaths, just a word or two at a time. He was losing the fight and all the air to speak with it. I had seen that look and knew in my gut he was going fast. "Oh, me poor family is going to miss me something fierce. I hate to leave them," he said as his eyes watered up.

"I ain't letting you go without a fight!" I said as a member of the response team trotted up.

"Get out of the way, I'm a medic!" he said to me.

"Yeah? I am, too, and I ain't moving until you pull out chest seals and get him into an ambulance. And you better get ready to intubate, too."

"Oh, hell, I don't have my jump bag with that stuff in it."

"Then you better get it, Sparky, and give me your rubber gloves, too!"

"I only have the set I'm wearing!" he said in exasperation.

"Take them off and give them to me, and your trauma shears and tape, and get moving!"

Of course he had a roll of duct tape he pulled from his … somewhere. He handed me everything, including a package of roller gauze, and ran off. I got busy making chest seals and got ready for him to try to quit.

"If you could grant me one dying request," Caed whispered as his eyes started to glaze over, "it would be to use … " His eyes didn't close, and he went still as death.

I felt for a pulse.

None. I didn't bother to check for breathing.

I went to work and placed my hands on the center of his chest and began working to crush the life back into him. "One and two and three and four … " On and on through the cycles of compressions, my mantra against death controlled my rhythm and focus until I became more machine than man in action, energy, and thoughtless production, no different from the involuntary muscle contractions of a normally functioning heartbeat driving blood through the body to the brain to keep the signal alive. I hesitated for a split second on giving him a rescue breath, but just then another response member came up with a pocket mask and took that role from me. Yes, I am squeamish when it comes to mouth to mouth—not just because I am a raging hetero, but the belly tends to fill with gas when the head is not maintained properly, and those gases will come back to … haunt you. Food for thought, so to speak.

With the guard helping with rescue breaths, I went to town. I felt bones crack, but this was normal; I was certain some probably did break. Before the two-minute cycle was up, Skippy came running back, jump bag slung over one shoulder, and he had a LIFEPAK with him, too, the doodad that shocks people and shows us the heart rhythm.

"I got compressions—just tube him then run your arrest algorithm."

He didn't argue, and I nearly thanked God that he pulled out a King Airway and had Caed tubed within a couple of seconds. A geyser of bloody pulmonary fluid shot out of the tube with every push on his chest. We suctioned what we could, then turned Caed as far over onto his side as we could to try to let more drain out. It didn't help much, but if I could have turned Caed on his head and shook him clear, I would have. Then Skippy pulled out an IO gun and inserted a needle into Caed's shin to start an IV line and deliver cardiac drugs while I switched out with a guard and took over respirations, trying to squeeze life into Caed's lungs with the ambu bag. After that, the code ran itself pretty much. Everyone knew their roles—it was all down to training and response based on recognition.

Medics from the outside world showed up and took turns with compressions. I didn't know how long had passed exactly. Once you get airway established, chest compressions become a nonstop thing that we had to take turns with after every two minutes when we checked for a heart rhythm and then gave a shock if it was shockable. And eventually we got to that point, which was better than seeing a flat line. A heart has to have rhythm and a beat to sustain itself—Caed had no beat, and as much rhythm as an old rich white Republican trying to look cool dancing to hip-hop. Yeah, someone had to put an end to this herky-jerky crap. We got clear, he got shocked.

And a heartbeat got established.

I sat back and watched that monitor. I was beyond thought, beyond anything, in a trance within my own world. I felt a hand on my shoulder tug me back away from the scene and looked up at Hardcastle. He was pulling me away to make a path for the local EMS crew to come in and take Caed away.

I was spent, emotionally and physically. King put a hand on my shoulder and gave me a bro hug when I turned to him. I felt a hand on the back of my head, heard "You did good, son," and felt a kiss on my forehead.

I looked around, taking in what responders identify as "the scene." A solid ring had been made of an audience of the prisoners that watched what we were trying to do for Caed. Annie was where I had left him, eyes closed, face hammered and bloody with his nose and no telling what else smashed. I didn't see Topaz anywhere, but I did see enough blood on the ground to know that there were more dead or injured.

I watched them load Caed onto the stretcher and take him away. I didn't give him very good odds of walking out of the hospital, and I wasn't sure I had done him any favors. But it wasn't in me to turn my back on someone in need. I was wracking my brain, trying to remember if there was anything that could be done to evacuate fluid from the lungs in a hemopneumothorax emergency, when I felt a hand on my shoulder and turned to see Hardcastle.

"I'd like to speak to you in—"

"No!" I said, letting what anger I thought was dead in me begin to rise. "No, I am not your pawn, your worm on a hook anymore. I did right by everyone I could, and when it came time for them to do right by me, only one man did, and I may never see him again. So go choke yourself!" I finished and walked away.

The guards were all hands on deck in the chow hall. It was a little pathetic how easy it was for me to just sashay by the doors and go to my cell with hardly any notice. Not that Hardcastle had missed me; he probably had his hands full dealing with an irate King and Carls yelling at each other.

I sat down on my bunk and looked at the Caed's bunk. His Bible was left in the center where I had seen him earlier, praying with his face against its cover. No, I was not moved to tears, honest. My grandmother would have probably called my mood "melancholy."

No doubt, I was down and feeling pretty alone in this world and had not a soul to reach out to. What Caed had said in his speech to all of us hit me pretty hard. I tried recalling one phrase that really went deep. "We love, we learn, we grow to become better than we were."

Caed also had a notebook in his bunk. I reached over and thumbed through it. Some of it was notes, but there were some prayers, some poetry, and references to scripture. And there were pages and pages in a language I didn't know, because it was in gibberish. Maybe Gaelic? I put it with his Bible and placed both on the shelf by my bunk, then stretched out to try to ease my state of mind.

I was pretty confident after all that drama that I was in the clear as far as the murders were concerned. *No way they could try to pin it on me after the confessions from Las Hermanas with Carls validating them ... right?* The question was if there would be retaliation and ramifications. From both the law, and the gangs. Was it too much to ask and expect this would end in a kumbaya campfire moment with beers and s'mores? *I would even let you have all the s'mores for a beer, and maybe a smoke.*

I reached out to Caed's Bible and put it over the center of my chest. No, I was not a praying man, and I was not defensive about it. While I accepted there was definite evil in a supernatural sense, I had little, if anything, to go on that there was an active good working against it ... or working at all, for that matter. But holding the Bible felt good, and I sent my good out to Caed and the battle he was now in. Yes, I actually believed in energy and the ability we had to harness that energy to our will. Mothers rolling cars off their babies is one "common" example. Or people having premonitions, as my grandfather often did. I come from a people and culture where sweat lodges drive out the bad in us and we seek visions on quests of higher enlightenment and abilities. Now that I considered all of that in the backdrop of apparently dealing with a zombie and a malevolent spirit, maybe a good sweat and a trip down the "Red Road" would be good for me.

While I nodded, nearly napping, suddenly there came a tapping, as of someone gently rapping, rapping at my chamber door. "'Tis some visitor," I muttered, "tapping at my chamber door. Only this and nothing more."

CHAPTER 16

Aand then there actually was a tapping at the bars of my cell. I had dozed off, apparently, and woke up to the love of my life, Carls, and his porn star copstache facing me behind a pair of dark aviator sunglasses. There was a reason for the stereotypes, and that was why I had a hard time ever taking the dork seriously.

"You know wearing sunglasses inside went out with the mullet, right?"

"Ok, Bodhi, the warden says I have to apologize, but I guess I really do owe you one."

"An apology, right?" I said, filling in the absence of apology or further explanation. "Because according to the prison rape intervention policies, you can't offer me what you should."

"Ha, yeah, funny," he said with a lack of laughter. That was fine; I wasn't laughing either. "Look, I'm not going to say you would have done the same, but I will say this. There was a number of people and their families that were being held hostage for my cooperation. I made a judgement call to de-escalate the situation by serving you up and to try to retaliate later."

"Carls, I'm not mad, not even the littlest bit. I would have to have something left to give a shit about. As it is, I should probably thank you, right? If it wasn't for you striking out on your goals to serve me up and save justice for later, and getting people killed in the process, I would have a hard time remembering I am a lowlife that belongs behind bars for someone dying over my bad judgement." Ok, so I'd probably lied a little about not being the littlest bit mad.

"Yeah, I can see why you would feel that way. Apologies don't mean anything, especially around here. But I can tell you if I could've seen a way to play it straight and keep you out of it and make them pay, that would've been the way I wanted it."

"Anything else? I'm fresh out of hugs." I didn't have anything for him. If he wanted a turn the other cheek, forgive and forget . . . that was Caed, and Caed was probably dead from the choices he made.

"Yes, the warden wants to talk to you. He also has an update on Caedmon. Or you can stay here, sulk, and cry by yourself if it makes you feel better."

"Let's go." I put the Bible to the side and stood to face him.

I was in my own funky haze as he led me to the warden's office. I stepped in and didn't wait to be invited to sit. I just sat and watched the warden typing away at his computer for a brief moment before he stopped stood up and told Carls, "Thanks. You can go make sure every cigarette butt is picked up in the yard before the inmates are released for their break, and then don't forget the parking lot when you think you're done. After that, you make sure that the remaining days Bodhi has are spent doing whatever he wants within the limits of his incarceration here as our guest."

I raised a brow. Hell, I would have smiled, but between a busted lip, busted head, and busted temper, that wasn't happening.

"Don't smirk unless you can convince me you wouldn't have thrown Carls under the bus had the situation been the other way around. And good luck trying." I made no comment as the warden threw the remains of a coffee cup down the sink in his private restroom and rinsed it out before coming back and refilling from the carafe on his desk.

"First thing you probably want to know is about Caed. I got a report that he coded again en route to the ER. They worked on him and got him back after they arrived at the hospital. Last word I had was they're still in surgery with him."

"I'm not sure they did him any favors bringing him back. I don't know how long I worked on him—around eight minutes, give or take—but people seldom make a full recovery from being down that long."

"Well, he is Irish, and while he was here, he stepped up to be your guardian angel. Hopefully that earned him some brownie points."

"Good deeds is why I'm in your office, right?" I said with just a touch of sarcasm. I'll admit, I was in a funk just then.

"Damn, Bodhi, would you like a razor blade to cut on yourself a little since you won't cut yourself some slack? I get it, you had it rough and you probably shouldn't have been here in the first place, but—"

I tried not to snort.

"First of all, my job is not in finding guilt, but finding good and releasing that back into the world." Wasn't that what I wanted, too? "You have just a few days left in my hands before you'll be out of here like the wind … but for how long?"

Never was an eternity. I didn't care what the cost might be. I took a deep breath and let it out and tried to give the warden my attention.

"You did good, Bodhi. I don't know what would have happened had you not been able to expose Rudolph as the Las Hermanas 'spiritual leader,'" he said, hooking his fingers for quotation marks. "I went into his cell with a forensics man that actually used to be a convict. Trust me, he knows all the secrets that inmates use, and then some. We found Rudolph's secret journals. I only glanced through one of them—pretty sick shit. Some of it in a language I don't recognize, all of it obviously occult."

"Anything explaining what I had to deal with in the clinic?" I was reminded of Caed's Bible and prayer book when he said that.

"I saw a lot about mutilations, sacrifices … but I didn't go past the surface. There was a shank made out of chipped glass and covered in blood that was probably used last night. If you knew what you were doing, you could take someone's hand off with it, maybe … but I don't know how all this happened without anyone hearing anything. Your boy Spider might not have been able to scream, but Jaime sure would have while someone used glass to hack through his wrist."

"Same question I had, but hell, it looks like he summoned a demon and turned Spider into a zombie. If I nitpicked over someone not screaming, I would never sit through a sci-fi horror flick without being one of those people harping on accuracy in the movie."

"Oh, God, I am so guilty of that. I grew up watching Westerns with the cowboys shooting dozens of rounds through a six-gun, but let me hear someone call a magazine a 'clip,' or see a finger on the trigger in a gun bunny poster, and I flip out. And hell, don't even get me going on movies that have anything to do with prison life," he said with a laugh, and it made me laugh too.

"Yeah, I couldn't watch any more TV shows about doctors. Great, this is going to make me one of those people screaming at the screen in a movie theater that the zombies aren't real enough." I covered my face with a moan, trying not to lose my ever-loving mind.

"But I like a story where the good guys win and at least one guy does the right thing when it would've been easier to tell everyone to kiss his ass."

"Yeah ... " I trailed off before completing my thought. "But it sure seems this world will teach you it's best to mind your own business."

"From what you told me about your grandad, I think he would say you're wrong. I looked him up after you mentioned that he said something along the lines of what I told you a few days ago—that a man is at his best when he does what is right."

Yeah, that man would probably give me a slap up the back of the head if he heard me talking about sitting out a good fight. I nodded my head at the warden, saying nothing of what I felt.

"I admire men like him. Awarded the Silver Star, action report cites he was surrounded and defending against a dozen commies and could've run. But he covered the retreat of his men and got captured. Unloaded his Garand and 1911 and used his rifle and bayonet to stab and club six more to death. Sounded like he would've picked up rocks to throw if he had to, and wouldn't have run."

"He never talked about what he went through. I never asked. When it came time for me to think about enlisting, I talked to him about it, and he told me not to. Said he didn't want to see me change the way he did and become an asshole to his family. He wanted me to stay close to home and be the one to take care of them."

"Are you planning to go back when you're released?"

"I don't know." I wiped the sleep from my face. "They are pretty bad off. I don't want to make my problems getting on my feet their problems. Only other option I have is an offer from friends to move down to San Antonio, but that will get me lectures and good advice not to associate with ex-cons."

"Not from me. I've seen too many walking the streets without convictions that should be behind bars. Hell, this country tends to elect them to office. Oh, sure, you can do things that most people get arrested and imprisoned for, but ain't it funny how a president can laugh off smoking pot and accusations of rape and worse?"

"Oh, I try not to get into politics. It's bad enough what I had to deal with when jackasses in office decided to make health care more affordable by forcing everyone to have it that can't afford it, and fining them if they were too broke, while the rules they forced hospitals and doctors to treat their patients with were getting people killed. Reminded me of the new rules of engagement our military had to operate under, walking around in combat zones with unloaded weapons and disarmed on their own bases, basically just sitting ducks waiting to be shot at by traitors screaming how great their god is."

"Amen!" he said and raised his coffee cup, getting a mirthless chuckle from me.

"Oh, great, I went from having a preacher for a celly to a political pundit for a warden. Can we go back to talking about science fiction? I could use a good vampire story."

"You want one that glitters and chases around psycho teen girls that need therapy for codependence? Gotta love a story where the predator turns into the victim."

"That would be a curse, alright. So what is a man your age doing seeing movies like that, anyway?"

"I have a wife and two daughters. I was an unwilling participant."

"Hopefully they don't make you watch those channels with reality TV housewives fighting each other."

"Put it that way, it would be interesting to see one of those shows where they stripped down and got into a cage and fought it out. But yeah, we get to watch the drama on TV. It's almost all you see these days." He took a slurp of his coffee before getting serious again. "Bodhi, I wanted you to know there is justice still alive in this world. Carls is going to keep his job and his position. I don't want you letting people know I'm punishing him, though. He made the same mistake everyone in here has made: bad judgement. Big difference in this case is that he was cornered, and people he cared about were put in harm's way. If that had not happened, I have no doubts that he would not have colluded with Las Hermanas' attempt to enslave all of us."

"So, what will happen to Topaz and Slippy and anyone else that was involved?"

"I don't know. What is lifetime times lifetime? They were already at the start of fifty-plus-year sentences. Most we can really do to them now is move them to a higher security prison. The problem I'm having is how the hell to deal with what they tapped into. For the most part, a lot of it can be explained away to the authorities when they come in to investigate as long as we suppress truth and evidence. If it can't, then I'll likely be on the front page of one of those newspapers you see at the checkout line with the two-headed bat boy and UFOs dancing around my head and no job to pay the bills with. Spider, unfortunately, is going to be remembered for being a murderer by his family and friends."

"They might prefer being told it was demonic possession. His wife and mom never missed a visit."

"Well, I can't do much but try to make sure *someone* is released when they've served their time, and let them try to explain if they want to."

"Yeah, I am heading that direction anyway," I said after wiping my face with my hands and letting out a long sigh. I was starting to feel a little weird. *Lack of sleep and my head being dribbled like a basketball wouldn't have anything to do with that, right?*

"So ... how does that conversation go? 'Your son was tortured, and a dark satanic ritual left his body possessed and turned him into a mindless monster'? They put people in mental asylums for saying things like that! And I have a hard time believing there is a God, but I guess I need to rethink that if there is obviously an evil counterpart to Him running amok."

"Well, Bodhi, I'm not sure what to tell you if you do decide to talk to the family. But out of curiosity, how come you don't believe there is a god?"

"Well, maybe that isn't totally true. I guess maybe agnostic, or even deist would be more accurate? That worked for the Founders of the government, right? It isn't that I don't think there was something bigger than us that made everything and pushed the first domino over. But a being of love and kindness that protects us and takes us away to the land of milk and honey seems absent from the table here."

"Well, as far as the Founders go, there is a lot of BS flying around about all that thanks to Hollywood and public education. There was maybe one who could rightfully claim to have been a deist, but even he believed there was a God and acknowledged Jesus as the Christ. But every one of them you could name all believed in the God of Abraham that created this universe. And they absolutely believed in defying evil, while defending the good of the human soul."

The warden stood up and stretched a little while talking and refilling his coffee cup, offering a cup to me with a gesture. I was tempted, but I really just wanted to sleep if I could find a place to take a nap. He stepped into his little sleep room and came out with a pamphlet.

"Probably the only one of the Founders that could honestly claim to have been a deist was Thomas Paine. And I can't find where or how an atheist would have been elected to office in those days at all. Thomas Paine died broke and was buried in a pauper's field with no country to call his home after he alienated himself to his peers for what he wrote in his *The Age of Reason*. But, as I mentioned, even he acknowledged there is a God and the teachings of Jesus. But kinda like you, and a lot of us, it's easier to tell ourselves no one is watching or will catch us doing what we know in our hearts is wrong. Let me share something he wrote."

He paused and put on a pair of reading glasses before reading the passage to me. "'Nothing that is here said can apply, even with the most distant disrespect, to the real character of Jesus Christ. He was a virtuous and an amiable man. The morality that he preached and practiced was of the most benevolent kind; and though similar systems of morality had been preached by Confucius, and by some of the Greek philosophers, many years before, by the Quakers since, and by many good men in all ages, it has not been exceeded by any.'"

"See, I can go that far, if there really was a Jesus. But a God of love who lets us murder, rape, and torture ourselves for His amusement while we struggle and suffer with no help? Evil people get rich and run the world and the good die young on their battlefields."

"Well, I can't argue what is true, and a lot of what you said is truth. Seems like the lie here is this idea preachers collect tithes with: that there's a god that is supposed to be Santa Claus and wants to keep you rich and safe from all dangers in a world we made for ourselves because you are one of the nice boys and girls for believing in him."

"Isn't that what Christianity is?"

"Look, Bodhi, I'm not going to tell you to believe like me. And God knows I'm not perfect. I was at that fork in the road where I had to choose between right at a cost and wrong for a reward. I made my choices, and it hurt and wasn't easy. You've been there, too. And from what I've seen, you do good, and you are a hell of a fighter. Who taught you to fight? Your granddad?"

"No, although I credit him and his example. It was actually some of his students and peers that worked with me when I could spend a little time with them and spar and get pointers to correct my bad habits with. What I learned from my grandad came more from watching him and doing what I saw he did. He didn't want to teach me."

"Hmm, I wouldn't have guessed that. But did you learn by never getting hit?"

"Well, it was mainly soft when we sparred. Pads and protection and low speed. The conditioning for my bones and body was another story."

"So, you learned to take care of yourself by being disciplined and being exposed to pain and being challenged? Why didn't you stay home eating Pop-Tarts and playing video games?"

"Oh, I did for a while when I was a kid. Got picked on for being chubby and having a funny name, too. But I wasn't totally fat and lazy like some I went to school with."

"I feel sorry for those kids, Bodhi. I'm sure their parents love them, but they act like animals in public and get fed candy to the mind and body. But hey, if we got zombies, they may come in handy for bait?"

"Hey, that's not very Christian!" I feigned outrage through my laughter.

"I know," he said, laughing, then got dead serious. "But if anyone had loved them, they would have taught them how to be ready for what this world can do to you. Looks like someone loved you and got you off that couch and made you learn to be tough. If you had been a self-indulgent candy ass, things would have likely turned out different here."

"Yeah, but that was me. No one did that for me. My blood and sweat and bruises were shared by no one else."

"Oh, damn," Hardcastle said with a snort. "I don't know if you're trying to make me into a Democrat or a preacher talking like that when I'm trying to defend the good in others to help you get where you needed to be to survive what you've been up against."

"Nothing like mixing politics and religion in a government institution," I threw in.

"Yeah, but you reminded me of a jackass we had as president, when he got up on TV and preached down at the small business owners, 'You didn't build that on your own. Someone helped you get where you are.'"

"I remember that. Seemed like he had a point, but I think he lost it when he tried using it as an excuse to take from those people."

"Yeah, pretty much. But the thing is, someone shared your blood, sweat, and bruises all alone while nails were driven through Him, to die alone for me and you."

"I didn't ask Him to do that."

"I don't think anyone did, Bodhi. That's kind of why I respect what He did and love Him for it. God sent His own baby down here to be tortured and murdered for us. And we still whine it isn't enough to prove He loves us or is real."

"But it's just a story! There's no proof that it's real."

"Man, back to proof," he said with a chuckle. "I have seen men executed on less proof, and found not guilty when there was more proof. But you are the jury, so it's up to you. But I will say this: You aren't expected to have blind faith. So, I say call God out if you are man enough to challenge Him, and see if He answers."

"Did he ever answer you?"

"I am still here and not locked away in a mental hospital," he said as his eyes bored into mine.

"I have a few favors to ask for now."

"'Least you can do is ask. I will do all I can to return the favors you did for us."

"First, I would like to just be in my cell today, after a real shower."

"I'll make sure you have both."

"I would like to be kept in the loop about Caed. I'm surprised he made it to the hospital, but I don't expect him to make it back."

"Again, no problem there."

"Caed has a Bible and a personal prayer journal that I would like to keep with me until they are claimed by him or his family."

"That would take some serious rule breaking. I can't give what isn't mine. What do you want them for?"

"First, because I think Caed wanted to help me. And I liked the way he put things. I'm thinking about trying to learn for myself what the truth is."

"I will do what I can to help that happen. I think we can work around the Bible as long as I know you'll give it back when it's asked for. Bring the journal to me later and let me see what I can do about it."

I stood up to leave and had another thought. "What about Annie and Las Hermanas?"

"I heard he fell and hit his face on the floor. They took him to the hospital, but it looked like there may have been brain damage from how hard he landed. I'm going to feed the Hermanas a little rope and see if they stay out of solitary confinement for the rest of their prison sentences. Otherwise, I'll lock them up and throw the keys away when I go deep-sea fishing later this summer."

"Never been deep-sea fishing. It looks like a blast, though."

"I regret that I waited so long to try it. Don't make that mistake. Got any plans to enjoy your freedom when you get out?"

"Yeah, staying away from people as much as possible. It's like being a new dog wherever I go—everyone wants to put their nose in my business, except we talk and share feelings."

That made Hardcastle laugh. "Well, back to your cage, Fido."

Damn! Burned me good there.

"And enjoy your day of peace," he added as I opened the door to be escorted to a shower and my cell.

CHAPTER 17

I actually wasn't joking about wanting to stay away from people for a while. Contrary to how things may seem, I am not a chatty Cathy. But being imprisoned confines you with people that have nothing better to do than gossip about each other and share their feelings. Sucks to be you if you're at all as introverted as I am. It isn't so much that I hate people or anything of the sort; I am just more of a doer and a watcher than a talker and pleaser.

Funny how every time I met someone new, though, I wound up getting the third degree and seldom asked anything about the person putting me under the spotlight. *Maybe I should start putting them on defense and see how they like it?* However, that would likely require more interest in the other person than I actually had.

But Hardcastle had made a lot of valid points. Why had my grandad not invested anything much in teaching me how to defend myself in the world? Had I not rebelled against his wishes, I would have been a victim at the mercy of others while imprisoned. But had I respected his wishes, I would have stayed home and gotten a simple nine-to-five job and never gotten myself in such a mess trying to play hero, as he had accused me of once before he passed away.

My grandad and I hadn't seen eye to eye before he passed away and fought a lot. But he was more of a dad to me than the man that sent child support checks to my mom once a month from his Texas cattle ranch.

Right then, I realized why my grandad had done what he did.

The memories I had of my grandad were of a man that had worked harder after retirement age than anyone else I knew for the oil companies in Oklahoma. By the time I came along, he was in upper field management, and on occasion he would let me tag along and open gates to properties and fetch tools for him. Those days slowed down when I hit school age, and came to a bitter halt when the economy went south and his company got bought out by an overseas corporation that "trimmed the fat" to increase profit margins and then looted all the assets, leaving my grandad with no job or pension to show for all the work he had put in.

What I'd picked up about him before I came along was that he was one of the elders of the tribes in our area after the Korean War, a member of the school board, and he'd constantly turned down demands to run for city mayor while he held a seat on the tribal council board. Things he could do while still in the military, taking a role in training new recruits.

Then, after we got ourselves sucked into the police action in a country no one had heard of in South East Asia thanks to our helpless allies in France who thought they still owned what wasn't theirs, my grandad started getting into more arguments with members of the tribe.

Being a member of the military suddenly lost prestige and respect as the hippie movement won over the hearts and minds of the tribal youth—or the "commie pinkos," as my grandad affectionately called them in between cuss words and mentions of treason.

Apparently, revisionist history that fuels hate is more appetizing than even the truth recorded by our tribal lore keepers.

Not that guilt-free sex and mind-altering substances didn't play a part in people calling my grandfather a baby killer, a traitor to his people, and worse while spitting on his uniform.

Did he respect their first amendment rights being used to treat him like that? Of course he did. Did they learn to respect his calloused hands that left their skin split, sore, and stung from a little slap and tickle? No doubt.

However, the policies of the military did not condone such actions in uniform, and he was made an example of.

The American flag would still hang off our front porch every day, except during inclement weather, and in the evening. If it was quiet, you could hear the faint notes of "Taps" from the army base over the community, and my grandad would always stop to turn his attention and give his respect to the colors.

I learned from him that it wasn't about the government, but the people, our freedom, and our family. Even when that government and your family no longer returned that belief in you.

Back in reality, my cell door slammed and the guard told me to enjoy my rest, snapping me out of my thoughts and memories. *I forgot to remind the guard to take a detour to the showers, damn it.*

I ran my fingers over my face and combed through my hair, which was still … wet? I took a deep breath and didn't even have to sniff my armpits to smell the soap all over me. But I had no memory of showering. *Great, there's legit something not right in my head.* I turned and caught the guard before he got far. "Hey, mind making sure I get a chance to go to the yard when it's time? I'm dying for a smoke break."

"You and me both, bro. Tell you what, first one is on me. Thanks for standing up and doing what you did."

I gave a smile and a nod and said thanks, no more and no less. I was nobody's hero. I didn't need a smoke; I just wanted to make sure I was checked on. I know a smart person would've gotten a trip to the ER, but no thanks. First of all, because I used to live out of hospital ERs, and second, I just wanted to relax and recharge. That wouldn't happen for me in an ER. I knew I would just go into hyperalert mode and get stressed out.

I thought back on the epiphany that led to my reverie. Here I was, outcast from all but the closest members of my family, and after being convicted of manslaughter, I would never be allowed to set foot in the rescue service and wear a uniform again. I was finally coming to terms with that and realizing that despite that, I had put in my time serving my community. No one could take that from me. Not even the members of my family on both sides that called me a baby killer, just like my grandad after he'd popped a card-carrying Communist working as a community organizer. My grandad had even found out the man was on a student visa and was responsible for arranging the travel tour of a certain Hollywood starlet that earned her infamy. Don't feel bad if you've never heard of her—Hanoi Jane never was in any movie worth watching before she took a tour through POW camps and tormented and tried to tempt our soldiers into betraying their country, and she damn sure hadn't been in any since then.

If my grandad had wanted me to be a functioning member of my family and pick up where he had left off, there was no way he could've raised me in the ways of military and war that he had learned. And besides, was it not the role of my *actual* father to raise me to be a man?

I didn't know much about whatever had happened with my mom and dad before I came along. I knew my dad's family owned mineral-rich property in Oklahoma—where my grandad managed, in fact.

I had a hunch it was through my grandad that my mom and dad met. I knew my dad had had a reputation as a rodeo playboy, and I figured that played a part in Mom going after him. They divorced within weeks of my birth, and if he ever slowed down from his playboy ways of playing around in outlaw country and chasing buckle bunnies, I never heard of it. He made a few passes at trying to be a dad to me, but I was nearly five when I was told I had a dad and that he wanted to see me and have occasional visits.

I knew my grandad was someone he'd had a lot of deep respect for. Which, now that I was thinking of him, I could see why he was so hands-off and had dumped me and Mom back in the lap of my grandad. I had a hunch Mom was hard to put up with from the screaming and cussing she'd aimed at me when I was growing up. I never was physically abused. Although I'm sure swats with a belt would count as abuse to someone else, I'd no doubt earned them back-talking and rebelling against her authority when I was a child.

On the other hand, nearly every child therapist would still call it what I would when I saw an adult losing their temper and letting their mouth run out of control at a child like that. My dad, though, he was one of those people that had power and enough wealth to make or break you depending on if he liked you. But he would have never given my grandad anything short of a "Yes, sir."

He had recognized good people and admired them, even if he couldn't corrupt them into his party lifestyle. Which was probably why he and my grandad eventually had a falling out, influencing my mom more than the other way around.

Looking at things from that angle showed me a lot more truth behind what Caed had said before he'd gotten shived. I knew at heart I was essentially a good person, in spite of how many tried to make me not be good or prove my guilt—which wasn't hard with the blood of a child on your hands that made you drown in guilt already.

I knew that the angry people that had yelled and spit on my grandad were misguided. But swallowing lies from a Marxist professor claiming one sixteenth or one thirty-second or one sixty-fourth and two halves of tribal blood to promote your screwed-up political ideas fueling culture wars did not change the fact that most people were essentially good at heart. We have it in ourselves to become greater, if only we can surrender our own egos and misunderstandings and give that credibility to the ones we are told to be angry at.

It is ridiculously easy to demean and belittle someone, but the challenge is believing enough in the good to claim redemption. My ultimate challenge when I got released in a few more days was going to be giving that to myself and proving it to others, while the law and society condemned me as guilty for the rest of my life without a trial.

"Ok, God, I guess I don't know you, but what I hear from others is either unbelievable or just bad. But I would like to have something to believe in, and I'd take anything large or small as a gift. Caed back on his feet would be nice. In the meantime, I would like to read about you for myself and see how hard this book is of yours to understand. I guess we'll go from there and see where I'm at when I'm done reading."

You are going to have to confront Topaz when you see him. Would you like to know how to defeat him?

Gotta love an inner dialogue that wants to help out. *Sure, dazzle me with what you got.*

To know where someone is coming from, you have to first see into their heart. Topaz is sneaky and fast. His first attacks will always try to catch you where you aren't looking before he gives a strong attack. He does not ever see the truth in front of him because he is blind to it and expects others to be sneaky like him. Give him brutal honesty and you will defeat his courage. In panic, he will lash out and harm himself. Now, prepare yourself.

My inner dialogue obviously thought he had all the answers. Maybe he did, but I wasn't sure about the question. What I was sure about right now was … I was feeling pretty good about life at the moment. Getting a second wind, I stood up to stretch my kinks out, especially since I couldn't sleep. I went through a light and brief series of exercises Caed had just shown me. *Have I slept since then?*

I cooled off with a little shadowboxing and then felt my feet moving in rhythm to dance steps. *Hell with it*—I danced a little and felt the beat in my head. The beat stretched rawhide drums, the jingle of hawk bells, and I was daydreaming of the days of dancing in the powwows when I was a little kid.

My eyes closed and my feet moved with the fast rhythm of the drum. My arms stretched wide, my palms turning back and my shoulders dipping to increase the reach of my span as I dipped and circled and remembered the wind across my face, the smell of the sweet grass.

Unshackled from the tethers of my present. Earth below me and heaven's endless reach above, I moved in between and raced to confront an oncoming wave that came from the distance and called to me. Growing in force, the earth trembling in the wake of the crackle and rumble of thunder growing as we raced to meet each other. Rolling hills below me were dotted with cedar and oak, and every animal that claimed its home in my domain turned to face the storm, but would not confront the rising tidal forces that came from the beyond.

My focus turned to the towering clouds covering the land as I embraced the shockwave, letting its power wash over me in a baptism of nature's force that stripped away what I once was. I danced and became less of myself as I let go of all the hurts that weighed down my spirit. I saw the dark clouds of the sky send spear after jagged spear of lightning that stabbed into the ground and drew power from the land. The hills covered in cedar before me, the scent a crisp reminder of the purifying life of the Spirit in the land under the gaze of the Great Father. I watched below, the young at play of the deer and the buffalo and the horse. And near the colt, I saw a snake ready to strike at the innocent, and I dived in anger to strike first. I became a streak of fury that raced across the distance, striking from above and spoiling the ambush and robbing the snake of its easy prey, digging into its scales as I carried it away with me. It struck at me and I spun and glared at it and gave back more than it gave to me. I fed on the blood and meat of my prey and heard—a tap, tap, tapping at my door.

I came to myself and snapped my attention to my cell door to see Carls. "You ok, man?"

There is blood on my hands; I will never be ok. I looked at my hands. Expecting the blood of the snake to be there, instead I saw only naked skin, my stiffened fingers curled into grasping talons.

"Yes, I was only meditating and exercising."

"At the same time? Because that looked weird."

"Hey, do I pick on you for staring into space and drooling? What do you want now?" I flexed my fingers and stretched my arms, shoulders, and back as I turned to step over to Carls.

"You asked to be checked on so you wouldn't miss yard time. Jimmy left you a smoke. I had to move him to cover a lunch break, so I thought I would be the good guy I am and take you out ahead of everyone by a few minutes."

"How could it be nearly time to go out? What time is it?"

"Five till eleven. Bodhi, seriously, I know I restrained you pretty hard earlier—"

"When you curb-stomped my head into the wall—"

"Yeah, I actually feel pretty shitty about that, but you're acting a little off. You sure you don't want to go to the hospital and get it checked out?"

"Oh, good lord, if you only knew how many times I heard a patient want to go to the ER saying those four words—'get it checked out.'" I hooked my fingers in the air, making mock quotation marks, while shaking my head. "I knew those were the magic words a doctor wanted to hear from someone with more insurance than sense, because that was really them saying they had nothing really wrong with them and didn't mind clogging the symptom and letting a hospital rack up a bill that starts in the four-digit range and climbs with every order and test they write for what amounts to is this: 'You ain't dying, but these medications will help your discomforts until you see a specialist that will charge your insurance enough money to live on for a year since you can't cope with the suck that is life.' Open my cage. Let's get some fresh air and chemical smoke into my lungs."

"Damn, you sound jaded. Someone, I'm sure, went in with something serious and got the treatment they needed." He opened the cell and escorted me to the yard while we kept the banter going.

"Sounds like the same kind of argument I hear cops make to justify pulling over old farm trucks that belong to old farmers for a taillight out or grannies on Social Security income and giving them a stack of tickets for not being able to afford insurance and repairs to keep the government off their backs. 'Well, every so often we pull over a wanted felon and take a rapist off the street.' Anyway, thanks for the concern. You make me feel like an older brother that needs to take you in a headlock and give your brain a shampoo. But honestly, I know the only thing they'll do is lecture me to watch out for worsening symptoms and diagnose me with a concussion, which would fall back on *you* unless everyone lies to blame me … again. I know the routine and just saved taxpayers a few dimes and me, the headache of listening to a life I once knew a few feet away. Besides, you know this isn't over yet, right?"

"Between me and you?" he asked with raised eyebrows. "Bodhi, look, I—"

"No, dummy. Topaz is not going to let bygones be bygones, especially after what I did to his little Orphan Annie. And I don't suppose any of them died or got locked up in solitary, huh?"

"No," Carls said with a sigh. "Inmate Rudolf was transported, alive, but you really did a number on him, worse than I did by restraining you."

"You guys have your own words for kicking someone's lights out, huh?"

"And Topaz was treated in the clinic for a fractured bone in his hand and is out and about," Carls said without hesitation over my observation at their obvious misuse of "restraining."

"So, are y'all going to let them get away with what they did as long as they swearsies this time to really behave and cross their hearts?"

"Warden wants to let the law do its job. We feed them a little rope and let them hang themselves, and hopefully any of my people helping them, too."

"Sounds like the marketing model for law enforcement to me."

"Now what do you mean by that?" He handed me the smoke and a lighter.

"The only way politicians sweet-talk more money out of voters is by fighting the rising crime, right? Budget gets approved, raises for everyone—manpower, equipment, training. No wonder police departments would rather extort revenue by taxation through citation instead of actually taking a trip to the wrong side of town. Y'all can't afford to work yourselves out of a job going after people likely to shoot at you when they aren't murdering their neighbors." I lit up after my rant and took a deep drag before letting it out through my nose. I watched the gate to see who would be coming out to play.

"I suppose you would like the world better if there were no cops and doctors?"

"Nah, just get rid of the politicians."

"Can't argue there."

"So how about you play for the other team today, then?"

"Are you hitting on me?"

"You ain't curvy enough ... yet."

He fidgeted and sighed, and I smoked and watched the inmates trickle out. One went to the ball court, followed by others. A few went to tables to smoke and play checkers, chess, and cards. Someone started knuckleball. I was getting a few looks thrown my way, no doubt for having a guard on my shoulder. Eventually I saw members of my crew and Reggie come out. Later I would think more about that vision I had in my cell; right now, my mind was on business.

"So, spell it out. What do you want?"

"A date with Topaz, and no chaperones."

"Why not? Beats their deal."

"Yeah? So what did they offer you, anyway?"

"Topaz sent word, said if I didn't get the response team and escort them to breakfast and deal with you ourselves that by lunch,

Officer Becky's daughters would be raped in front of her grandparents and her grandparents, murdered. I had to reply in five minutes, with the team, or the order would have been sent."

"Just keep your people out of the way until the dust settles."

"Just don't get killed."

"Stop bossing me around," I huffed, taking a final drag on my cigarette and putting it out under the toe of my shoe. I blew the smoke out, took a clean lungful in, and began breathing deep, hyper-oxygenating my body to clear all the toxins from my mind and spirit.

"I'm not playing around. I know you're good in a fight—I heard stories about what happened in Beaumont, but that man is horrific in a fight. He bit through the neck of more than one inmate and has used his fingers to fishhook through the faces of others."

"How the hell is it he never got transferred out of here?"

"State board keeps saying he isn't dangerous enough to displace in case he's more violent in overcrowded maximum security centers. No one has ever beat him in a fight that I know of."

"Yeah? Only time I ever lose is when I get restrained by a boot to the head by an army of guards." I spotted Topaz. He was focused on Reggie's back and separated himself from his crew. I walked across the yard, walking at as quick a pace as I could while trying to be casual as I cut through inmates at an angle. I wanted to flank Topaz in his blind spot, keeping a small cluster of inmates between us to screen me from his peripheral vision. I came around the group just as Topaz tensed up and suddenly darted toward Reggie. I did my own dart maneuver and threw a kick at his trailing foot.

"Look out, dummy!" I said as I sent his foot back around his other leg and totally destroyed his stride and balance, making him tumble in a windmill of limbs before skidding face-first on the asphalt.

Several members of Las Hermanas tried to make a run at me but were cut off by members of the other gangs as a solid ring began to form, putting me and Topaz in the middle. I glanced around before giving my focus to Topaz. King and the bosses of every gang were present. As funny as it was to see Topaz crash, no one was laughing after this morning.

Topaz climbed to his feet and glared at everyone, then turned to me. "Bodhi, I should have finished you this morning."

"Between being put in your place by a priest and eating some-one's foot, you were a little distracted to dance with me. Now we're alone—your little sisters can't fight for you, and you get me all to yourself."

"After I teach you what daddies do to bad boys, I'm going to take Reggie and have a black wedding. You think it ended this morning, but this is just the beginning. You are marked for what you did to our *brujo*, and everyone that helps you will suffer in your name."

"Gee, and this morning y'all were talking about love and peace—now it's all death and weddings. You queers sure got your panties in a wad, huh?" I slowly paced around him, keeping him in the middle as I moved like a shark in the water.

"It is love we have for our own people. We protect ourselves from the frauds and the hypocrites that are no better, like you. You could join us and forget about the guilt and sin from murdering a child and telling lies to save your ass. I would take you in and give you my love. But you think you're so much better than us."

"Love? You have a queer idea of it. I watched you single out the newest and youngest to come into this prison and watched them become stupid animals with no sense of honor. I want to know some-thing—and no lies from someone that keeps calling me a liar, but answer me this: In loving one of those boys, did you ever love any one of them for their own sake and not your selfish, corrupt sense of pleasure? Who taught you that way?"

Nailed him! Now you will see his true nature!

I honestly did not plan to get as deep a reaction as I got. His in-stant and uncontrollable rage was obvious—Topaz was frozen with it. His fists and teeth clenched. I had never seen anyone so animated with mindless anger. He was so red-faced, I honestly would not have been surprised if smoke came out of his ears and nose.

"Hey, are you ok, little guy? You look like you are going to cry. Why are you so sad?" I asked condescendingly, like a parent talk-ing to their three-year-old. That seemed to send Topaz over the edge as he started doing something I had never seen an adult do before. Stamping up and down on the ground, he had both feet and both arms pumping as he yelled F-bombs in between incoherent, raving monosyllabic threats and grunts, complete with spittle flying from his lips.

A heart twisted from corrupt desires is impossible for the undisciplined mind to control.

Ok, my inner dialogue was starting to talk nearly over my head and make me think harder than I was used to.

Topaz suddenly bolted at me and crossed the distance quickly as he raised his left fist, wrapped in bandages with his fingers bound around a roll of foam to fix the hand in a position much like he was holding a can of beer to both protect from further injury and promote healing. Probably not a smart idea to use your injured hand as a club, but clearly Topaz was totally out of smart ideas.

I turned my upper body to the right, left arm up in a high guard to catch the blow along the ridge of bone near my elbow, and shifted my stance enough to keep my left foot in his path. He tripped and went down in a rolling heap after I felt a thump and sting on my arm. I looked down and realized he wasn't totally dumb—he had hidden a shiv or razor in the bandages and had gashed me pretty good. Blood flowed down my arm to my hand, but not so much that I was in any immediate danger.

Now witness his fear, a coward's tool and tactic. No honor. Give him no respect in return!

I wiped the blood off my arm with three fingers and then reached up to my face, dragging my fingertips down from my forehead over my eyes and nose before I put them in my mouth, tasting my own blood on my tongue. The salt and copper taste came, and peace came to my mind as my senses flooded with an overload of environmental knowledge. The inmates were cheering and jeering. Bets were being made, and I could faintly smell earth and ozone in the air along with water. Rain would soon come, and the sound of rolling thunder across the land confirmed that fact. A storm was coming as the temperature dipped just a few degrees.

I began to lightly hop on the balls of my feet, my balance shifting in rhythm. I spread my arms high and reached for the sky, bringing down fistfuls of blood and bone bound in the hide of toughened flesh ready for battle.

Topaz rushed to his feet as soon as he got his hands and legs under him and I closed the distance, bringing a snapping left roundhouse kick to one of his knees. He jumped back and brought his hands up, ready to box with me, but I was ready for war, not a fight.

He came at me, but my eyes were no longer focused on him, yet still on him. My focus and perspective had become ... more, greater. I knew from the stance and balance of his body what was coming before he had even committed himself to the act.

I slapped the back of his hand with mine, sending his left away before his fast jab came near my face, then stepped left while he tried to keep track of my moves. He shifted and kicked at me, but my foot was on his knee, jamming him and throwing him off balance as I skipped and moved to the side again, my guard high with my right and low with my left. He swung, and I blocked with my right. My knuckles crushed his lips with my left, and then I was gone and making him spin to keep up. Another heavy right and I slipped under and brought my left fist up in a hook just under the right side of his chest. I had disappeared again as he gasped in pain, trying to keep up.

Again he sent a fast left, and I answered with a back knuckle block on the inside of his forearm and a right fist straight to the forehead, right between the eyes and on the nose of the abomination he'd tattooed on his face. I instantly moved back while his knees wobbled. He shook it off fast, opened his hands, and screamed, diving low to shoot for a takedown. Reaching for the backs of my legs and aiming his shoulder for my waist, I saw his plan coming a mile off and dropped over him, shoving him face-first into the pavement and rolling away instantly as a foot went whistling by my nose. I hooked my arm behind a leg and sent the offender flying in the air to land with an ugly thud on his extreme lower back. I would say it was his butt, but not quite, though I was sure his ass was broken from that fall.

I looked around, moving to do a rapid scene size-up. Las Hermanas members were being "restrained"—one of them was "restrained" as in unconscious and being further "restrained" with kicks to the head.

"ENOUGH!" My voice cracked across the yard with a thunder of its own, making everyone stop in surprise. I pointed at Topaz as he climbed to his feet. "Leave them to witness. This one has no power over them anymore."

The only sound came from Broken Butt, who was reaching around to try to hold his ... ego and was in enough pain that tears were coming down his face between cries of "Ow!" and "Oh, God, this hurts!"

Had I been stupid enough to let myself get suckered into a ground fight, that—cough—*tail* of woe would be mine. Get it? Tail? I am a crack-up!

I was laughing, a belly-rolling laugh that soon became contagious as one, then a few others picked it up. It was like wildfire from that point. Even King was cackling! I had never even seen him give a chuckle at Copper's jokes.

"*Bastardos*! Y'all stop laughing this minute!" Topaz was stamping up and down in a tantrum again. Now his own members started giggling.

"Jefe, you shouldn't act like a baby in front of everyone! You are embarrassing us!" Butthurt said in a whine while still keeping his sore ego in cheek—I mean check! That poor guy was going to be the butt of our jokes for a while.

Topaz reached down and snapped the boy's neck in front of all of us with a scream, then ran at me with his left hand held out like a spear aimed at my face.

The cacophonous boom of a twelve gauge ended that. Topaz ran straight into a dozen rubber balls of attitude adjustment that sent him down onto the ground.

Everyone went to the ground as the response team reclaimed control, except me. I was in a daze as I stared at the open eyes of a dead boy on the ground. I stared at Topaz on the ground near my feet and just felt overwhelming sadness at what I saw.

"You stupid, poor son of a bitch, you just destroyed yourself." I felt a hand on my shoulder dragging me back. I knew it was Carls without looking. I had nothing left for Topaz, aka Ascension, who had climbed so high to power and was now less than nothing by his own hand. Only sorrow and pity remained for a wretched creature that had no hope.

"It was my stepdad." Tears were coming down his face and he choked back a sob and crossed his arms over his chest, clutching himself in pain. "They said I was damned because my mother got pregnant from being raped. She would not get me aborted because she did not want to be damned. Everyone says it's ok to abort rape babies, but she wouldn't and she let him rape me, and she would beat me because I was a *dirty bastardito*." Two of the guards rolled him onto his belly and put his hands in cuffs as he continued with his testimony. "I was thirteen when *mi tio* caught me loving my little cousin and had the cops arrest me. I would see therapists who told me that being gay is natural and not to feel guilty for genetics. My psychiatrist told me being psychotic was probably passed down to me from my father, and there was nothing to make me better except taking pills the rest of my life to be normal. God put me here damned and made me the way I am. Why do I have to suffer and be damned? Why did I have to be born damned?" By the end, he sounded like little more than a wounded animal, tears and snot freely flowing. And I had no answer to give him as he was dragged to his feet, utterly broken.

No one deserves a life without a chance at redemption.

I looked down at this wretch of a man sobbing his story. I had seen cons manipulate others with their stories of endless woe, of the unfairness of life driving them to commit their acts. Most of it was all made-up BS to manipulate you, but their stories always drew the conclusion that they were forced to do a wrong that they recognized as a wrong. Ascension had no concept that what he had done to people was actually wrong.

I stepped out from Carl's reach before he had a solid grip on me and came close to Ascension. I met him eye to eye and saw the hurt heavy brow and tormented anguish in his eyes.

"I do not believe you had anyone to raise you to be a man, to know the difference between love and hate. I was raised to know those differences and stay true to them at all costs. Love does not damn, and hate does not forgive. You saw a man today who gave all of us that example, and you saw what he got in return. We can be good and turn away from what others try to twist us into and follow a better example to become better ourselves."

"How?!" he screamed at me in frustrated anger. "I have no one to follow that would lead me."

"I will follow that example. And I will be a brother to you and lead you to the other path if you will surrender your way and seek mine." I knew with my words, I was committing myself to a road I had never traveled before, but I had been taught by my grandad not to ask of others what I would not do myself. Tears were coming down my face now, too.

Ascension fell to his knees as though someone had cut the strings holding him up. The guards had their arms hooked under his shoulders and kept him upright, dragging him out of the yard and away from all of us.

"Trying to switch from life saving to soul saving? Don't hurt yourself trying for that one. He will never change his nature," Carls commented.

"Maybe not, but I never gave up on someone without a fight. Like you said, it's a nature thing. I can't change."

"You're all heart, Bodhi. I'm proud to know you. Let me know if you need anything." Carls walked away looking like he was rubbing a little dust out of his eye.

I reached up to wipe the tears and dried remnants of blood from my face and finally looked down at the gash on my arm. It was bad enough that I would need to tape it up. No stitches, but thanks for asking. The bleeding had nearly come to a stop on its own.

King, Copper, Reggie, and a handful of others from the Diamondbacks came to surround me. Then Cherry Bomb broke away from the Tribe and ran over to give me a hug.

"Hey! Respect the PREA boundaries!" I said with a laugh, taking the hug.

"Man, Booty baby, that was some fight! Muhammad Ali would even be dancing if he coulda seen the way you got in Topaz's head and danced circles around him! You sure you ain't got any Black in you?"

"Yeah, I know your next line, and I walk funny enough without going there!" I said with a laugh that got sent back from those near me.

"Yeah, Bodhi is all tease and no please, as Topaz found out. Damn, I never thought I would see him taken down. That was epic!"

"Copper, don't use that word. You sound enough like a dork without proving it," King ordered while taking a pack of smokes from Copper's pocket. He pulled out a few, replaced the pack, and handed me one before lighting his and passing the lighter to me.

"Anyway, Bodhi, my Tribe made a killing on side bets, and Big Nas told me to let you know we're cutting you in on the action. Just let us know where to send it."

"I still haven't figured that out yet, where I'm heading when I get out of here. I have family that can put me up and put me to work, but looks like felons aren't wanted."

"Cherry, just tell them to send it down to Gunther Donovan, DBMC prez down in San Antonio. He'll make sure Bodhi gets his winnings. If Bodhi's family won't take him, we will."

I almost said something about my family, but things got real dark on me. Before I knew it, I had people reaching under my arms to help me stand.

"Hey, Bodhi." Copper and King were both in my face. "You with us, man?"

"Just promise you won't let Copper give me mouth to mouth and I'll be fine."

"Don't worry, Booty baby, if he comes near you I'll scratch and hiss at him," Cherry stood up for me.

I looked at the person that was Terrell, saw the good that was there in spite of him being a walking hot mess.

"Do you think a person like Topaz is damned because of how screwed up their parents are? Or do you think he can ever learn to grow past that?"

I don't know why the word "damned" popped out instead of anything along the lines of saying Topaz was crazy nuts, but the question went from my thoughts straight to my mouth with no filter or impulse control to consider that I was asking this of an arsonist who was mentally trapped in a memory of abuse.

"It is what it is; people don't change who they wanna be. Now tell me how many fingers I'm holding up."

"One. I'm fine, I just need a nap since I haven't slept like I got used to in nearly two days."

"You ain't acting like you."

"Guess the guards tap-dancing on my head gave me an alternate perspective on everything. If I became a product of how I was raised, I would've been Topaz's bitch from day one. But I went against that and didn't settle for being a victim controlled by everyone around me."

"Strong stuff, right there. Let's get you into the clinic and get your arm bandaged, then get your head checked out, Bodhi," King said as a command rather than a suggestion.

"Getting it checked out is why 'It is what it is' ain't fair. That's three things people say that irritate the snot out of me. Fine, let's get

Band-Aids for our boo-boos before someone calls me a wahmbulance."

I caught them giving each other looks from the corner of my eye as I stood up. *No one gets my humor.* I felt fine, other than nearly almost dizzy, but yet not … and it really felt like everything I saw was kinda being witnessed through the eyes of someone else.

I was handed off to a guard and taken to the clinic. Luckily, everyone else stayed behind, and real lucky for me, I was passed along to another guard before I made it into the clinic. My cut was cleaned out with betadine and soapy water before glue and Steri-Strips took care of the rest. No stitches—yay!

And no one asked me about my head.

I could understand why people that knew me—and knew I had been "restrained" in the head *numerous* times by the guards—would be concerned for me by the way I was acting. That was fine to a point, but it was starting to get irritating. If you didn't know me, you wouldn't suspect a thing was going on, even if you knew I got kicked in the head sometime during the night.

And yeah, obviously a few things were different. I was seeing zombies and body-snatching demons and turning into some kind of warrior philosopher. All I needed was to start growing bonsai trees and writing haiku, which appealed to me the more I thought about spending my days in a tea garden getting my bushido on.

I made it back to my cell only to find the warden waiting there for me.

"Hey, sir, any news on Caed?"

"Last word I had about fifteen minutes ago was that he died three times before they got him to the operating room, and he died another three times on the table and has been in surgery for three hours. Three, threes," he said thoughtfully. "Apparently, an artery between the lung and heart got nicked. I thought I would come by and let you know and see about that journal."

I picked up the journal from where I had laid it on my bed and handed it to him with Caed's Bible.

"I think you better make sure you're giving me the right Bible, Bodhi. But I'm sure if you ever found out anyone from his family wanted it that you would get it to them if you had it," he said, handing the Bible back.

"Yes, sir." I sat down on my bunk and waited to see if he had any other business. Hardcastle flipped open the book and scanned the pages.

"You didn't strike me as someone that knew Gaelic."

"I wondered if that was Gaelic. Wonder what it says?"

"I'm just guessing that it's Gaelic. Maybe notes for sermons, daily thoughts, secret family recipes for haggis?"

"I heard Topaz got himself into an altercation in the yard. He's going to solitary until he can be transferred to maximum security, along with a few others. I've been dealing with Texas Rangers and calling the families of my people that died all morning. I am fed up with all this. I think it's time to retire and dump this all in someone else's lap. Oh, and Topaz asked for a priest. The prison chaplain is on the way to see him. You must have beat the hell out of him," he said with a laugh.

"Yeah, I guess I did. Warden, I hope you don't think I'm rude, and I appreciate you trying to give me a chance to help, but I am out of steam. Can you let me stay in here for the rest of the day and tomorrow, too? I'm kinda tired of getting into trouble around here."

"Yeah, I'll come by to check on you after a while. Get some rest."

"Thanks." Almost as soon as my face landed on my pillow, I was out like a light.

There were only parts of one dream I remembered when I woke up, but the only words to describe the way that dream made me feel were peace and joy. I rubbed the sleep from my eyes and looked at the time. It was a little after two, and the lights were low for all the inmates to sleep by. I had lost a day.

I stood up and went to the toilet. While I answered nature's call, I thought once more about the dream I'd had. I had been walking across a prairie. The grass was knee-high and lush brown on rolling hills. I approached a stand of trees where there were a few tents, and I turned to the sound of a voice asking what I was doing there. I remember only a few things about the man. He had long brown hair, his arms were open to embrace me, and his smile made me glad he was pleased to see me. I greeted him like a lost brother I'd never known and felt so glad to finally find him.

That was when I woke. I finished taking care of business and turned the sink on and washed my hands and face, drying my hands by running my fingers through my hair. I went back to my bunk to try to get more sleep but before I passed out, I placed Caed's Bible over my chest.

CHAPTER 18

DAY 3

"For in the state of nature, to omit the liberty he has of innocent delights, a man has two powers.

"The first is to do whatsoever he thinks fit for the preservation of himself and others within the permission of the law of nature: by which law, common to them all, he and all the rest of mankind are one community, make up one society, distinct from all other creatures. And, were it not for the corruption and viciousness of degenerate men, there would be no need of any other; no necessity that men should separate from this great and natural community, and by positive agreements combine into smaller and divided associations.

"The other power a man has in the state of nature, is the power to punish the crimes committed against that law. Both these he gives up, when he joins in a private, if I may so call it, or particular politic society, and incorporates into any commonwealth, separate from the rest of mankind."

–John Locke

woke up the next morning with no other funny dreams, just a guard calling my name and offering me a breakfast meal tray. I retrieved it with a thanks and enjoyed a rare, for me, breakfast in bed. I pulled out my notebook and pen and started drawing a picture of an open-mouthed viper in mid-strike with its neck trapped in a set of talons. I was feeling pretty good, and deeply appreciative I'd had the foresight to request time alone in my cell to process everything I had been through in the last few days.

For instance, apparently there were evil spirits running amok in this world. On the other hand, apparently I fought best with a little brain damage. So, was there really a God? I had seen precious little proof in my life, and my mom really hadn't pushed a belief in God down my throat, although she went through spells where she would get deeply involved in some churches. My grandad had never gone to church that I knew of, and I'd never heard him talk about it. My grandmother, on the other hand, she would often sing gospel songs with Elvis and Johnny Cash on her old eight-tracks when I was young.

My dad? I knew he had a family Bible resting on the fireplace mantel, but there had been no other presence of belief in his rodeo playboy life.

Yet, I'd stared evil in the eye and kicked its ass. What did that prove other than evil was real? *Maybe the good needs its butt kicked to prove it still has a pulse in this world, too?* Ok, maybe I was being too harsh. I had seen good in this world at work. A lot of workers of good were my brothers in the fire and rescue services. People that chased into hell to bring life from the flames, and people that went into direct battle against death itself knowing the encounter was going to haunt you if it claimed the life of another from under you. We suffered and did it time and time again, driven to stand in that gap and fight an overwhelming tide rising to bring suffering on any that it tried to drag down in its dark embrace.

It wasn't that there wasn't a force driving good against evil, but that good was the definite underdog in this fight and seemed to be getting its teeth kicked in.

Where were the angels of legend? *I guess people like Caed coming into our lives is the closest we get to having an angel looking out for us.* What he'd said, that he walked around with a God in him, nearly made me laugh remembering it. *But what if he was being sincere and believed it?* The way he'd handled Topaz before being stabbed was unreal, but not totally unheard of. I'd heard stories of people that possessed strength like that in his stature. I think some of them were called Pocket ... Hercules? Herculeses ... Herculi? Whatever. Anyway, short, wiry strongmen that had disproportionate and nearly phenomenal strength. Those people were not like the biblical Samson—as far as I knew, Samson hadn't needed to work his butt off to make himself into a superhuman strongman. The Bible just claimed he came packaged that way because God, of course. The one-size-fits-all answer to every challenge you give a Christian who doesn't have a real answer.

How did that mother lift a car off a baby? *God.* How did that person survive being shot in the heart? *God.* Who made the universe? *God.* Ok, so who made cancer, made babies get thrown into dumpsters, made good men die in fires and go insane trying to stop death from claiming a life, et cetera? *Oh ... well, that other guy, of course!* And why is that other guy allowed to do these things? *God, the apple . . . ummm ...*

Yeah, that is about as far as anyone can explain from what I've seen of the blind trying to lead the blind.

I looked at Caed's Bible. About two inches thick, with thousands of pages of contradictions, parables, and heavy words all over the place. The spine had been creased and worn from heavy use, the leather worn and frayed at the edges.

I ran my thumb down the edges of the pages and picked a place at random close to the front to open to. I wanted to see just how big the mountain in front of me was to climb. Of course, it was the King James Version—so not just heavy words, but heavy Shakespearian words. I scanned over the page, full of highlighted passages and some scribbled notes in the margins and even between the lines. Luckily, Caed's notes were in tiny letters but very legible, made with a fine-point ink pen. I happened to be at a book called Numbers, and my eyes were drawn to the notes made in chapter 22 in verse 30 where the portion highlighted read "Am not I thine ass, upon which thou hast ridden ever since I was thine unto this day?"

In the margin, Caed had written "Funniest lesson in the whole Bible: Your ass will get beaten and you will feel mocked for working against God."

I read back over the verse itself and a few verses before and found myself laughing. Verse 32 made me laugh even more. Caed's note: "Being smitten with your own ass will blind you to truth."

Well, maybe Caed can help me understand this easier than I thought.

I looked up as Carls came to my cell door. Man, I was feeling special with all the attention I was getting from the warden and the head guard over the last few days. Frankly, I could've lived without it.

"The warden was wondering if you would like to join him for coffee. He just got news about Caed."

"Bad news?" I asked, fearing that Caed could live without me having had their attention over the last few days too.

"Probably best I do what he says and just tell you what he told me, and let him tell you the rest."

I guess some people didn't appreciate spoilers to movies and books and finding out what was in the birthday and Christmas packages. Not me—secrets were meant to be discovered while they were still secret. Or what was the point of the challenge? But I didn't feel mean enough to torment Carls. He looked pretty beaten down for the moment.

"Are you going to join us?"

"Nope, I am going out to the yard after you're dropped off to make sure the grounds are secured."

"Ahh, well, we all must do our penance." I guess Carls was going to be picking up cigarette butts for a while to atone for his judgement. I was ok with that, but I had to acknowledge they were right; in his shoes and in those circumstances, I would've thrown me under the bus too. I put away the Bible and notepad and followed him out.

"Guess you're looking forward to your release date. Make any plans yet?"

"Nothing more specific than getting out of here and doing whatever it takes to get on my feet and never come back again."

"Really? After five years, you haven't made any plans or had any ideas?"

"Well, I got offers from friends … not sure what that could lead to. I would rather depend on family than owe friends. But the family that can afford to help won't, and the family that can't afford to would if I let them."

"Well, if you go with the friend route and they turn out to be a bad bunch, maybe we get to look forward to having you stay with us again as a repeat offender, huh?" Carls added cheerfully.

"I think you've 'restrained' me in the head enough for that not to be too likely."

"Guess I'll have to help knock sense into someone else when you leave, then." He opened the door to the warden's office and let me walk in first.

"I'll try to get you a teddy bear to cuddle with so you can transfer that aggression into a positive outlet."

"You two act worse than my daughters. And they haven't even hit puberty! That'll be all for now, Carls, thank you," Hardcastle greeted us as we walked in. Across his desk was a man that stood to his feet. I had seen the prison chaplain around a few times but had never personally spoke to him or attended his services.

"Bodhi, this is Father Goodson. I hope you don't mind him being here. Take a seat."

"You didn't have to bring a pastor in to tell me Caed died. I knew he was going to need a miracle to make it in the shape I saw him in." I sunk into the chair, looking across a tray with a coffee pot, packets of sugar, cream, and stir sticks. I reached over to pour myself a cup and let it sit to cool off. Those men that I had seen take sips straight from a hot, steaming cup must have had too much scar tissue from burning all the nerves right off their tongue to even notice. I still had all mine, and I didn't need to try to melt them by not letting my coffee cool off.

"Oh, sorry, I didn't even think about that! Father Goodson is here because Topaz requested a priest, and with your interest in the Bible, I thought the timing was good if you wanted to ask him anything or talk to someone about witnessing a friend of yours kill the clinic staff. But Caed pulled through surgery—report I have is that he was admitted into ICU during the early morning and is in good hands."

I felt relief from tension I hadn't known I was holding being taken from me. I took a sip of coffee without thinking. It burned, damn it! . . . I hid my pain stoically while I screamed like a girl inside. Yeah, I'm sure some girls out there can drink coffee hotter than I can handle. Bite me.

"Well, I'm glad to hear that news. If he's still in the hospital when I get out, maybe I can go by and see him?"

"Yeah, we can probably help you do that." The warden poured himself a fresh cup and took a solid drink straight from the scalding lava java. I swear he did it just to punk me.

"Mr. Hardcastle tells me you have a new interest in being a

Christian?" Father Goodson also poured and drank immediately.

Ok, I'm calling conspiracy here. I put the cup of evil and sin within far away from me and crossed my arms over my chest, nearly glaring at the brew of torment.

"I don't even know where to start. I was raised in a broken home. Everyone around me believed, but I think it was taken for granted without question. I didn't have any real curiosity until my job kept making me confront the question over and over every time some-one died in front of me. It was worse when I was the one that killed them."

"Oh, dear, that is tragic to hear. What did you do? Drug dealer?"

"I guess that was one part of what I did," I said, giving Hard-castle a look. "I was a medic. I'm here on involuntary manslaughter charges for killing a child patient."

"Oh ... that will teach me to assume, won't it?" His laugh kinda hit a nerve with me. I was getting a bad vibe off this guy ... but I figured it was probably no different than I would get if I dragged myself into a church.

"Well, I decided after all this mess and talking to Caed, before he was stabbed, maybe I should give myself a chance to get to know God firsthand instead of through all the crap I have heard. Where in the Bible is a good place to start?"

"Well, I happen to believe that God does things for a reason, even if we may not understand it. I would say the beginning is the best place to start—why are we here and learning God's laws so we can be good people. You know, Jesus came here to show us that example and show us to live by those laws, telling us he came not to abolish but to fulfill them. The New Testament is good for people to learn how to love each other, but we already know that."

"So, you had a chance to talk to Topaz," I asked, and he nodded. "I won't ask you to tell me anything he confessed or anything ... but do people like him get to go to heaven by becoming Christian after everything they've done?"

"Well, like you said, I can't talk about anything he shared in confidence with me. And it isn't my place to judge, but I do have my own opinions. We serve a God of righteous judgement that has destroyed civilizations for practicing evil. In Egypt, God killed the firstborn of each house. This isn't the first time Topaz has met with clergy members. He generally does this every time he gets himself in trouble and will act like a Christian to the authorities. We have all seen this before. We hope this time he can stay with it, though.

"But I believe what the Bible says in Second Peter chapter two applies here. It basically tells us at the end of the chapter that for someone to have learned the truth of Jesus, and rejected it ... their punishment is worse because they are proving the proverb that dogs will return to their vomit. And I believe this is what Paul also meant in the book of Romans when he wrote that God would give these people over to their reprobate mind."

"Yeah, I can kinda see that. Caed even brought up that reprobate mind issue to Topaz the first time they confronted each other. So, can you tell me why bad things happen to good people, then? Caed seemed like he was one of your guys—why would God let one of his saints fall like that?"

"Oh, son, there aren't any saints. We are all sinners. The only saints are the people accepted into heaven. But we have to keep being good and asking God to forgive our sins and never reject him. I think Job is the best lesson for why bad things happen to us. The Bible says Job was a God-fearing man that obeyed all of God's commands. But he came under a season of testing when God made a bet with Satan that Job could not be tempted away. Job stayed faithful, even when his wife and children died and he was struck with disease, and was greatly rewarded at the end of the story. Through it all, he never stopped believing and continued to repent and ask forgiveness."

"Wait, God let Satan do all that? Why? What did he do to deserve God do that to him?"

"See, this is why I say the Bible should be read from the beginning, and even then it can be very difficult to understand! I recommend a good Bible course in theology if you would be interested. You can even become ordained if you dedicate yourself to a higher calling. But Job did nothing wrong; his story is ours. We all fall under a season of testing, and we must endeavor to persevere through it for our rewards and pray God will be merciful to us in our testing. Job went through a lot because God favored him greatly and let Job prove his worth. We must all do this because of the fall of man at the garden of Eden and the surrender of this world to Satan, who now is the god of this world and runs among us, a ravenous beast preying on the weak. Even Jesus was tested, and look how much He had to give for His love for us to save us from damnation."

"So basically, we are caught in this war between good and evil where God surrenders us to be tested and claims only the faithful, and there's no way out of being tested like that?"

"Sure, turn to God. He doesn't want us to go through that. But when we have sin on us and we aren't living every day according to His laws—ignoring the Bible, not going to church, not tithing our first fruits—we make ourselves uninvited wedding crashers, getting drunk on the wine and stealing from the bridegroom. At that point, as it says in Matthew chapter twenty-two that we will be bound and dragged off to be cast into hell. You see why I suggest people know the law now?"

"Yeah, a lot of this I pretty much heard growing up. I went to church some when I was a kid, even went to Vacation Bible School a few times and church camp. Guess I need to find a good church when I get out of here and start studying. You sure know your Bible. How long did it take you to remember all the chapters and books like that?"

"Well, I've studied most of my life. I knew in high school I wanted to be a minister and went to Bible college and studied for four years to get my PhD. Not everyone wants to study for a living, but for living, we have to study. Trust me, going to church is the most rewarding experience you can learn to love, and it will make you a better person. If you like, I would be honored to lead you in the sinner's prayer so you can accept Jesus right now."

"I appreciate that, and as much as I would like to tell you go ahead so you can feel like you won someone, I still have a lot of questions I need answers for first."

"Well, I have a few more minutes before I need to leave. Can you share those questions with me? I may know where you can find the answers in the Bible."

"Well, that's actually part of one of them. If you didn't have the Bible, how would you know God exists or that you are even worshipping the right god the right way? Seems like it's just one more religious text among others, so not just how do you know you have the right translation, but the right book at all? The other question I'm wondering is if you have ever encountered any proof, like angels or God himself, or demons … and how do you fight a demon?"

"Well, I have obviously encountered enough humans that could be thought of as demonic. And the Bible teaches that angels walk among us and we aren't aware of it. So, stands to reason demons can do the same trick. But as far as the Bible goes, I will say if you seek, you will find. Hang on to that Bible and just believe and pray. You will get answers. God reveals Himself to the faithful."

"Ah, well, looks like I have some reading and waiting ahead of me, then. Warden, is there anything else you need from me?" I reached for my cup of coffee, blew across the surface of the threatening brew, and tentatively took a sip while I considered what Father Goodson had told me, which really wasn't anything I had not heard already. Essentially, "go to church, read your Bible, and don't sin" would have covered everything he had to offer me as advice.

"Actually, yeah, I need to talk about your final evaluations before you can be released in a few days."

"Well, I can hear the calling of the lost needing my guidance. Mr. Bodhi, I will pray for your soul, that when you leave here, God will put your feet on the righteous path so that you can avoid the temptations that led you here in the first place. And Mr. Hardcastle, you may leave him my contact information should he need someone to pray with him or help him study the Bible when he is released." The minister was standing to his feet as he finished his sales pitch.

I can't say I was sad to see him go. He talked a lot but hadn't really given me the answers I was hoping to hear. God sounded like He wanted you to endlessly work to keep proving you loved him while He didn't do much for you in return until all the work was done. Kinda reminded me of my own dad, come to think of it. My dad once told me in every relationship, you have to give eighty percent, and don't expect twenty back. It wasn't anything I hadn't pretty much heard before, but Father Goodson did make a good point in studying the law. I'd learned the hard way you will be at the mercy of those that do if you do not. Funny how that rule applies to nearly everything, ain't it?

I finished off the coffee now that it posed no danger to my tongue and refrained from getting another cup. Hardcastle reclaimed his seat after showing the father out the door.

"Here's the copy of Caed's journal for you. I also went looking for a Gaelic dictionary. Good luck there … I couldn't find one in any store." Warden Hardcastle placed the items on the desk for me. The journal was bound in a leather cover and when I flipped it open, the handwritten notes were copied on very thick, sturdy paper. Don't ask me what type; I wouldn't know vellum from hemp if I smoked it.

"Warden, you didn't have to go this far. Can I pay you back?"

"Nope, it is a gift. My way of saying thanks and supporting you in the direction you are trying to go in. I would offer just one suggestion in your journey through religion, though."

"What's that?"

"Take Thomas Jefferson's advice and question with boldness even the existence of a God, because if there be one, He must more approve of the homage of reason than that of blindfolded fear."

"I thought you said all those Founders were big on religion? Well, come to think of it, they wanted separation from church and state, huh?"

"Well, there is a big debate on all that. Lots of people, coincidentally liberal atheists, try to claim the Founders were not Christians at all, and that is one piece of their argument. They make it pretty obvious that they never really study the Founders' beliefs beyond getting a random quote they can take out of context. For instance, the letter Thomas Jefferson wrote to the Danbury Baptists assuring them he had no intention of using the government to meddle in the church, leading up to his often misquoted stance of a 'solid wall separating church from state.' But Thomas also said something else that really hits home with me when he said, 'God who gave us life gave us liberty. Can the liberties of a nation be secure when we have removed a conviction that these liberties are the gift of God?'"

"You seem to study the Founders like that preacher man studies his Bible. I noticed you had a lot of books about them in your private room."

"Well, every two to four years, a lot of people start talking about, supporting, and defending the Constitution by the choices of the politicians they support. Lot of people on news radio, TV, authors, and comedians do it. And lot of soldiers and flag-wavers do the same. Thing is, a lot of people talk about what they know little about. I got started when I got into debates over gun rights against liberal-leaning

cop friends that didn't support Texans being allowed to carry hand-
guns, even with a license. But we all took the same oath our military
and politicians have to take, too. I guess for too many our oath, like
the Constitution, is just a bunch of words until it's convenient to fish
wrap an argument with. But as far as their belief in God goes, I think
any person that wants to try to argue in that day and age that our
Founders were not Christian is out of their damned mind, and not
just ignorant of what they wrote and fought for."

"Guess it would do me some good to offset the Bible with some
of their writings. Got any recommendations?"

"Well … hmm. Yeah, let me go you one further back, though."
He went into his private room and came back with a hardback book.
"One more gift for you. This is one of the major influences of Thomas Jefferson, and where he got most of the inspiration for what he
wrote in the Declaration of Independence."

"*The Treatise of Two Governments* by John Locke," I read off
the cover.

"There are tons of writings from the Founders themselves. But to
me, that bridges the gap and shows that they did not just make it all
up themselves for the sake of hearing themselves say pretty words.
Lots of people that bother scratching the surface don't go further
back than the Federalist papers and don't read the Anti-Federalist
Papers or the Kentucky and Virginia Resolutions or their letters to
each other or half a hundred other things I can name. What's real sad
is, we have this thing now called the internet. And instead of looking this stuff up and reading it for free, people go online to look at
porn and videos of cats and people making themselves into attention
whores by being stupid to try to get a reaction."

I nodded my head in agreement. I'd served time with a lot of
those idiots he just mentioned—some of whom were busted because
they had updated their social media in mid-crime.

"Bodhi, the real reason I needed to speak with you, aside from
giving you an update on Caed, is I had to make a call to a Texas
Ranger about the murders the night before last. He is on the case
and will be investigating and is going to talk to you. I think the best
way to spin this is as close to the truth as possible, and run along
the lines you have been using. That Spider had been tortured, and
his actions and behavior were from being driven insane, and in his

attempt to retaliate, he killed anyone that got in his way. Leave out all that supernatural crap. If any of us start talking demonic possession and demons, we are both likely to end up in the banana factory. *Comprende?*"

"Yeah, I think I can do that. Besides, from an objective standpoint, that is how it would have appeared, had he not been speaking in demonic rhymes and body switched to Jaime and made him crawl up the wall like a spider. Irony in him doing that and Spider being the victim in all this makes me wonder ... "

"Wonder what?"

"I don't know. Maybe I'm trying to think too hard after taking a few too many hits to the head. Just that we called him Spider, and Jaime suddenly started acting like a spider. Guess it was something to jack with my mind and I need to let it go."

"I certainly hope you can," the warden continued. "You are a good man, Bodhi. I don't think you deserved being locked up, but the law has to be upheld." Hardcastle stood up, his tone making it clear we were about to conclude our business.

"Do you by any chance know where in the Bible I can find scripture giving a list defining what love is? I didn't think of it when Father Goodson was here—he had me distracted over the law in the Bible. But I remember one passage saying something about 'love is patient, love is kind' ... I can't remember anything else, but it was a list of details like that."

"I'm pretty sure that is in Corinthians. Funny, when I was coming to the chow hall yesterday, I could hear Caed talking, and what I caught reminded me of those verses. I nearly didn't intervene because I stopped to listen. Didn't snap out of it until Caed stopped talking and I came in like a bull in a china shop. I don't think that man would have been stabbed if I hadn't distracted him. He was holding his own against Topaz. I don't think I ever met a man with a grip that strong."

"Yeah, Caed showed me better workout techniques. I wish I could've known him better. You think I can get a ride back to my cell? I'd like to get a start on reading and try to finish sleeping, too."

"Sure, I'll take you part of the way back myself. I want to go by and check on Topaz after his visit with the father."

"Any chance I could tag along and speak to him? Yesterday he seemed to have tamed down a lot. We nearly had a come-to-Jesus moment together."

"I don't see any good coming from letting you do that." Hardcastle led us out of his office and back toward my cell as we talked.

"When I interfered in his attempt to kill Reggie, I'm wondering if I made enough of an impression on Topaz yet to tell me why he has been trying to take Reggie out."

"The child molester that is now hanging around the Diamondbacks instead of Las Hermanas? I can think of about half a dozen reasons Topaz would try to kill him by that alone."

"Yeah, problem with all that is Reggie has been telling us a story that sounds plausible about being set up. Claims his lawyer was killed the day I stopped Slippy from shanking him in the clinic. Seems to me too much happened in that time frame to send everything to hell, and I really want to know if it was all just destructive chaos or if there was a method to the madness."

"Well, as much as I like your idea, I think we've pushed our luck bending rules and using you as our workhorse around here. But I'll see what I can get out of him, even if I have to negotiate favors for him if he can give anything to make it worth it. Besides, you are out of here in just a few days now. You don't need to be involved in anything that would put you in a position to stay longer."

"I almost let my release sneak up on me. I stopped trying to count the days to see if it would help make the time pass faster … I don't even know the date today. But I guess you're right that I need to mind my own."

"No good deed goes unpunished, especially around here. Let's get you back to your cell and keep you out of trouble, ok?" He turned to look at me as we came to a checkpoint and put his hand out to shake.

"Few days of reading and having a chance to get my head on straight to get out of here is probably the best thing. If you don't mind, just let me stay in my cell except for meals and yard time? I can't handle being cooped up all day." I accepted the handshake and gave a grip as good as I had.

"Yeah, no need to try to fit you into another work detail, and I don't want you back in the clinic anyway. Looks like you have enough to read to keep you out of trouble for a few days, at least."

"As long as I don't have to mop. Every time I do, I wind up getting Carls's neck deep in paperwork." I was handed off to another guard to take me the rest of the way while the warden went the other way, laughing.

CHAPTER 19

I was enjoying the alone time in my cell, catching up on my drawings. I finished the picture of the snake caught in the talons of an eagle and had given it the secret name of "The Snake Eater." The picture was drawn from the perspective of the eye of the eagle, its talons clenched around the snake under its head. It was some of the best work I had done with freehand sketch. I enjoyed looking at it, seeing the cold-blooded evil I envisioned in the slitted eye of the snake, its fanged maw gaping in a strike that was denied. The lines of its eye were sharp and clear, while the features of the scaled visage became increasingly blurred the further away from the eye you looked. The snake did not have any regard for its looming death; its nature and working was revealed and it would stay true to that nature to the end. The more I looked at the eye of that snake, the less evil I saw in it and the more I understood. Cold-blooded, yes. It was not panicked and not scared, but resolved and unrelenting to face the consequences of its actions. It was a creature unafraid of judgement, because it was already judged and aware of its worth and role in nature.

Down the alley of the cellblock, the strumming tune of a six-string filtered from an inmate I seldom saw but often heard in this way. George had stayed in voluntary isolation in his cell the entire time I had been incarcerated here. I didn't know much about him except he wanted people to think he was crazy, and the story was, he was here for attempted murder of his wife and infant son.

George had a hell of a voice for mixing blues with country. I normally hated thinking about him at all; I had no use at all for someone that would abuse a woman or harm a kid, and God have mercy on them if I caught them in the act, because I would not. Except after watching Topaz break in front of me and looking at the picture I drew, now I wondered if there was more to the story of George and how he had come to dishonor himself in such a way, and if maybe there was a road back for such a person. Father Goodson seemed to believe these people were already condemned by their very nature. The Bible seemed to confirm that from what he said, too, but then so did Topaz's parents, from the little I got from Topaz. On the other hand, Topaz was suffering under the complicated medical term called "batshit crazy" and may have hallucinated his entire upbringing.

I was trying to figure out a good piece of the Bible to start taking a bite from. Looked like the books that pertained to the subjects I had discussed with the good father were in the books of Job, Romans, and Second Peter.

I picked up Caed's Bible and went to the index of books to see where they were. Job was in the Old Testament and the first of the three, which Father Goodson had said was a good starting place. Seemed like this was the worst story in the Bible, too. I knew a lot of Christians didn't like to talk about the fact that God seemed to gamble with Satan and play eternal games with the souls of men, leaving us to face those tests alone. *Somewhere in this book had better be a reason why, if God is good and just and kind.* Because if there was no reason given, then either this book was a lie or God was. And wouldn't that be the same thing?

"Ok, King James, don't make my brain hurt too much trying to keep up with your funny accent," I said, not missing the irony of my Texas-Sooner drawl behind my words. Don't think for a minute that because I'm a mix of redneck and redskin that I wasn't edumacated, either. I might only have a GED, aka a Good Enough Degree, but I'd earned that after dropping out of high school in three years, determined to go to college and set the world on fire in the footsteps of my grandfather through the oil field as a mechanic, come to find out that I was totally not geared for a corporate world.

But as far as my reading skill goes, I was raised reading Westerns. Louis L'Amour, of course, but also Elmer Kelton, David Robbins, and my personal favorite, William Johnstone and his gunfighter and mountain man books that were jam-packed with unrealistic levels of mayhem and action and men of iron codes of honor that never backed down from a fight, no matter how impossible the odds. Now THOSE were some good reads. Those were men I could admire, and those I saw in my granddad and one of my uncles that earned his living building fences and shoeing horses. My unc was a good man— loved to rope in rodeos and train horses in an age and day when the American cowboy should have been dead over a hundred years ago. Now, here I was leaving the world of the cowboy and Indian and traveling through the Bible to navigate a world of science fiction. No doubt smart-assed atheists had a thing or two to add about that line of logic, but you let me know which ones had just been through a near-death experience with the demonic and where they would rather find their answers from.

Luckily, Caed had notes in Job, too, and of course I had to read them first, but having an answer did not give me the question that Caed had answered. So, I read through the first chapter and saw what he meant when he wrote in the margin of verse 5 that "Job does not know that only the Son of God can atone for the Sons of Man. Man cannot take that relationship with us away from God without consequence."

My brows raised. I could see what Caed was talking about and wondered why Job did not do a better job teaching his children to be as upright and fearful of God as he was. After all, this was nearly what had happened to me over my granddad not taking a more active role in raising me than he had. But then, I was not his son, and my dad had taken next to no role at all in my raising ... so who was really to blame for my own lack of preparation?

Next to verse 9, Caed made a note saying "A play on Satan's words makes the truth known: that Job fears what he does not know, God. Job is upright and fears God—this does not mean he knows and understands God. See Jer 9:24."

I was just about to flip across to read that citation when I heard steps approaching my cell and looked up to see Warden Hardcastle standing there. The only description I could think of to describe his expression was haunted.

"Oh, what now?" I bet my face was as twisted in a grimace as my guts felt.

"Bodhi, I'm sure you've probably seen as bad or worse as what I just did ... I have seen a lot of bad things that men have done to each other here. Some of it was more gruesome than what I just saw … "

I stood up and walked over to the door to look at the warden while he cast his eyes down and just shook his head back and forth. I knew that look. I had seen it in others often enough.

"I went through my first medic class with the son of a doctor that couldn't stand to look at the medical pictures in our textbook if they had blood. He would cover the pictures up with sticky notes. Every slide of an injury, he would squeal in class. It was funny to watch—we all laughed. Thank God he washed out. But I never get into those discussions of who has seen worse. I think I've been spared a lot of that, or my brain just doesn't focus on it. I guess it's that lizard brain some people talk about taking over when someone is suffering, but I just act and lose all awareness of thought. Just assess the situation rapidly, make a plan that instant as I recognize each element needing response, and then respond.

"The things that haunt me are the regrets, the what-ifs and what-should-have-beens. I had to learn to stop letting those tear me apart and just carry enough with me to learn from my mistakes, and never repeat the same ones again. But if you saw something that is tearing you up, don't focus on what you saw. Let it go if you can, but don't beat yourself up with it and tell yourself you're weak for letting it bother you. It isn't weakness to be bothered—it's human.

"My rescue squad was called to the home of a mother who had called 911 because her baby wouldn't shut up. When they got there, that woman was covered in blood and she was . . ." I had to take a breath before finishing the sentence. "She was *eating* her baby. That was my shift, but not me. It was another crew that got the call right before we cleared from the ER. Had we cleared thirty seconds earlier, it would've been me. Those two medics never worked another shift after that call. So whether you're the son of a doctor or hard-assed medics that think you've seen everything, we haven't seen it all until we see the one thing we can't get past. And I hope I never see that."

"Yeah, that might be worse. But why he did what he did … that is going to stick with me." Hardcastle took a deep breath and wiped his hands on his face. I waited to see if he could tell me what happened. Remember how I hate being left curious?

"Somehow Topaz had a razor blade, slashed both sides of his

neck pretty deep. Cut the jugulars, and then he ran the blade around his head to the bone and shoved his fingers under the skin. I guess to scalp himself, but he bled out before he could do more than just leave his fingers stuck in his head."

"Whoa." I took a deep breath, but I felt like I needed a smoke after hearing that. I had a bunch of questions, but I bet the warden had even more, and I didn't think me pestering him was going to help what he had on his plate.

"As much of a walking shit stain as he was, I was kinda hoping he was going to turn around after yesterday."

"I think you were the only one left that had any glimmer of hope left in him finding his way back. I try not to give up on the men here. Most of them have no one to believe in them reforming, and when you get out, it only gets worse. Society won't let you forget your sins until you can expunge your record and pretend it never happened. You will always be punished until it makes you come back here, or you find a way to make yourself better for it. And those failures … I take it personally, because when they leave here and hurt someone, I know I had a part in not weeding out the bad in them." He paused and took a deep breath. "Anyway, you are probably the last person I should unload all that on, but I would rather talk to someone with experience than someone with a degree. Know what I mean?"

"Yeah, I should probably tell you that I don't have experience in counseling and therapy, but that's just about all we do every day in this place with each other anyway. If people on the outside knew prison was more of a social club and we got to bond with each other, sharing our feelings more than inciting riots and sodomy, Hollywood might go out of business."

"Is that what it was like over in Beaumont Correctional, too?" the warden wisecracked at me.

"Well, there we had more of an audience for our therapy sessions where people gambled on who would hug who the most until the other guy tapped or chewed the other guy's ear off. Hey, let me give you something."

I went over to my sketch pad and signed my name on "The Snake Eater." I thought for a moment before deciding to leave the title off of it.

I offered it to Hardcastle and let him look at it.

"Your snake looks like he's in trouble."

"Yeah, and maybe he deserves it, but I don't think he has any shits left to give and has no regrets. I have a name for that drawing, but I left it off to keep it a secret. I call it 'The Snake Eater.'"

"Watch your potty mouth, dammit." He was grinning when he chastised me. "I like this. Maybe there's more snake in me than I thought. Might even look good as a tattoo—what do you think?" he asked as he held the picture up high on his arm.

"Well, I can probably help you out with that. At Beaumont I was earning some pretty good cash slinging prison ink."

"Yeah, we aren't going to do that here."

"Nope. Wouldn't dream of breaking your rules here," I said while laughing. "But if you're interested, we might can set up something after I get out of here. I won't do it free, but I will do it right and use what I earn from it toward getting me on my feet."

"Are you thinking about starting a tattoo shop?"

"Ehh, I think that's a pipe dream. My only experience is in prison ink. I would be setting myself up to compete against people that have years and years of experience and portfolios to show for it. I think my best bet is just start with a paying job first, and maybe do tattoos on the side for friends and family until I can prove a client base."

"Sounds like a solid plan. I may be interested in helping if we can get you out of here in one piece. Your friend Slippy, as you call him, is coming back later today and will probably be released into gen pop tomorrow."

"Boy, won't he be coming back to a world he won't recognize. Any news on Rudolph?"

"Apparently when he fell and hit his head, he managed to crack the front part of his skull and damaged his frontal lobe. He's going to be gone for a while and likely moved into a prison hospital permanently if there is serious damage."

"Wow."

"Yeah, I think that floor and his slippery shoes did us a lot of favors with that accident. Too bad they can't get a medal."

"Yeah, he was an evil son of a bitch. That floor has nothing to regret."

"Well, I gotta get to work. We'll pull you out when the Ranger gets here to see you."

"Oh, boy, I can't wait for that," I said sarcastically to hide my stomach turning in knots.

"Don't let it worry you. The records show any involvement you had was in defense of yourself or others. He's just coming in as a formality to make it all official, close the case, and help us give closure to the families. Thanks for the ear, and the drawing." The warden left after giving my fist a bump and my cell door a smack. I decided Hardcastle was good people.

I went back to my bunk, stretched out, and decided to give John Locke's treatise a shot.

Man, and I thought the Bible was going to be a heavy read.

CHAPTER 20

had spent most of my day being lazy in my cell. As fun as it sounded to get away from everyone, and as much as I probably needed it just to stay out of more trouble and mayhem, I was getting bored.

I had read through John Locke, but I knew I would have to read it another time or two to really grasp it and probably keep it close to study with other works. But I had learned a lot about these things we call "rights" that we take for granted and hold no meaning of anymore.

Between reading from Locke, napping, and doing a little exercise to fill in the space in between, I was feeling almost perky, ready to rejoin the herd of offenders in the yard when it was time in about ten minutes.

Hate it all you want, but when you're not in the routine of daily life in the slam, time drags.

I decided to take a leak rather than try to hold it and wait till I got back. You probably didn't want to know that, but this thing you enjoy called privacy? That would be a natural right according to Locke, but in here, there's almost always someone sticking their nose in your business.

CLANG CLANG CLANG!!!! "Hands up! Hands up! Hands up!"

Holy crap! I threw a glare over my shoulder at a chuckling Carls. My cell was still ringing after he had beaten on the bars like a war drum.

"Did I scare the pee out of you, or do you have Tourette's? If you paint the wall, you'll have to clean it up."

"How many older siblings did you have, Carls?" I asked as I flushed and moved to the sink to wash my hands.

"None, I was the oldest."

"They must have made you wear dresses and picked on you, and you miss the abuse. I can give you a wet willy now, if that will help?"

"No, I'm fine, just came to fetch you for the warden's office. You have a special visitor from the state."

"Great timing. I was going to go to the yard this evening."

"Well, the sooner we get you there, the sooner we can get you out. Hopefully you won't miss much yard time."

I ran the numbers in my head—time to walk there, walk to the yard, minus time for the meet and greet before we got down to business, minus the business at hand with questions back and forth, conclusions with well-intentioned advice I likely needed but couldn't use … if it all went as smooth as Hardcastle claimed. *Yeah, no time in the yard for me.*

Carls led me to that familiar office and led me in. I was facing the warden and a man I would not have guessed was a Ranger due to his age, and you'll have to indulge me while I explain that better before I give you the wrong impression about me.

Even though I spent a chunk of my life in Oklahoma, I was born Texan. In fact, I was born in San Antonio, which was one of the reasons that the idea of running down there and being part of the Diamondback family was appealing stronger than I wanted to admit.

So, Texas is actually a bigger part of my heritage than most might think of someone who was raised on an Oklahoma reservation in the shadow of the army base of Fort Sill. But when you consider the fact that my father's family had immigrated to Texas when it was still Mexico and had to become good Catholics to earn a Mexican land grant from Steven F. Austin—along with about 299 other families that, along with my Hall family name, became part of the Old 300—it makes sense. Outside of that particular obscure Texas history, the Lipan Apache Nation was originally from part of Texas known as the Nueces Strip located between the Rio Grande and upper Nueces Rivers. According to members of my mom's family, one of our great-grandfathers rode with the Rangers in the days of the young republic and helped fight Comanche and Mexican troops that didn't like Texicans tossing them out of our Great State.

I know, some bleeding hearts think a bunch of greedy white farmers stole land from poor Mexicans. Got a few points to make on that issue, first being the obvious: that Mexico was barely a nation itself and, over the course of a few decades before and after Texas Independence, couldn't decide which dictators it loved the most between Spain, France, and Santa Anna. About the time one blood-sucking leech would be deposed, another would take its spot. And the *Indios* and *peones* that came later were greedy land-grabbers too.

Needless to say, coming face-to-face with a Ranger was an honor for me. The fact that this guy had seen some years was a credit to him in an age where Texas politics had ravaged the integrity and gravitas of being a Texas Ranger.

Once, they had recruited only from among the best of the best—Special Forces military or very seasoned and experienced law enforcement. Affirmative action and PC-friendly politicians had since bent the Rangers over and forced them to open up to being more inclusive of people who were disadvantaged by culture and gender.

"Inmate Bodhi Hall, meet Rex Huntsman, Texas Ranger."

"Bodhi? That's a hell of a name to carry to prison. Guess it isn't as bad for you as being a boy named Sue, though, huh?" Rex said while extending his hand and an easy smile.

Ranger Huntsman was wearing a white Stetson with a Texas Ranger badge pinned to the center of the crown, his hair that had gone gray going long past his shoulders in shades of steel, and it looked like he had either a bone or piece of antler in a pretty large hole in his left ear. His beard was trimmed, and the power in his grip was nothing to take lightly, one only to be returned in a grip of respect.

"My mom was a little bit of a hippie and liked the meaning. Too bad I wasn't smart enough to live up to it, though. But yeah, I'm not sure Johnny Cash couldn't make a better song from my story than 'A Boy Named Sue.'"

"Well, you got good humor, and good taste in music, I see. Not sure about the hair, though—that's a little wild." Nope, that did not make me blink in irony.

"Well, my grandad was army. So I nearly went high and tight, but he was also half Indian, so I left out the 'tight' part and kept it long. Besides, these days I'm more heavy metal than country." I did not share that the Mohawk was in memory of the child I had killed with anyone. It wasn't anyone else's business.

"Well, I think I take back what I said about your taste in music. Only thing worse than screeching crap is rap crap."

"I agree, but I haven't heard anything I recognize as country in ages. I think pop and club singers should have stayed in the city and left the country to the outlaws and cowboys."

"Amen! Hardcastle, I may like this kid. Why don't you give us some privacy for a while? I'll make sure everything is handled as we discussed, as long as you take care of your end of business."

Having a Texas Ranger say they like you and want to be alone in a room with you sounds great—until you consider the time and place. My gut clenched. I hoped I was ready to answer to this man, because the last person I ever wanted to tell a lie to was a man like this. I wasn't even sure I was capable of it, regardless of if it was a lie for the "right reasons."

"Bodhi, I want to know what kind of a man you are. Can you tell me that, and let no lies be said between us?" Ranger Huntsman asked, looking me straight in the eye.

"You would be one of the last people in this world I would want to tell any lie to, sir. I don't know how to answer that question in my position and not sound like I'm lying, but I think my record is my best witness … " I paused to think back over my life full of mistakes and failures.

"And what would your record tell me, then?"

"That when I did the wrong thing, I did it for the right reasons. I didn't get in here because of drugs. I never touched them, never been high on anything but adrenaline when I worked, beer when I could dance, and tequila to relax. I only smoke tobacco, and only when I'm stressed about crap and have to work it out internally. I don't take my anger out on others. Never assaulted anyone until I got to prison, and then it was only in self-defense."

"So, basically you're telling me you're a prison saint. Wrong place, right time for the worst to happen to you. Misunderstood by the law, and got a hero complex that holds you back from being a star in your own movie, huh?"

"I am no hero," I said after thinking on what he had accused me of and giving my best honest response. "I learned my lesson. All I want to do is do my time, cause as little trouble as I can, stay off the radar of the law, and try to have a life again."

"That is what I hoped to find out about you," the Ranger said with a nod. "That is the best thing you can do, and I want to make sure you do just that. So, I am going to be as honest as I have to be about what happened here. Most Rangers are assigned a company and handle the major crimes in the Great State of Texas. I am not one of them. I am more off the books and into the black ... ops branch. I am not part of the state budget, but I carry the full weight of my authority as a Ranger, meaning not even the goddamned FBI can tell me to do anything. They have to beg me for permission to operate any investigation that I'm concerned with, which is lucky for you and others in this prison."

Ok, this was going out into left field, and not what I expected. But I kept my mouth shut and followed the advice of my granddad: to be seen, not heard, and let the man continue without interruption.

"Had the FBI been involved in this mess, you, the warden, that idiot guard, and some of your fellow offenders likely would have been institutionalized and drugged on a cocktail of big pharma's best. Some combination of hallucinogens and tranqs to make you think you were Napoleon's pink elephant tooth fairy on a grassy knoll in Dallas in the fall of sixty-three."

"Shit, the FBI is doing that to people?" If anyone but a Ranger had tried to tell me this, I would've thought they were sniffing chem trails and licking snozberries.

"Well, technically—not exactly. The law gets real shady over this, and the puppet masters tend to shuffle personnel around behind closed doors as they need to. We're talking about an alphabet branch of regulatory law enforcement under the umbrella of 'homeland se- curity.'" Instead of rabbit ears for quotes, he was using only the mid- dle digits of both hands. "When they show you credentials, it's all FBI, but when you track down the personnel, well, your clearance level better start at the same level as the jackass occupying the White House, because otherwise, you'll get a visit from people in black suits that get their humor from reading Nazi Gestapo torture notes. Yes, this is the land of the free, where you can murder unwanted children in the womb and unwanted elderly in the nursing homes, but if you're the victim of zombies and hoodoos summoned by left-handed jackoffs, you will be institutionalized and given a chemical lobotomy."

"So a reject from a Ren faire gets to summon demons, and I'm the one destroyed by the law over it? What about them?"

"Oh, they get *really* lobotomized. Like your boy Rudolph Vera did after you gave him a good assbeating. Or if I find them, I execute them on the spot—no trial, no paperwork, no remains or witnesses. Law enforcement may be on different pages as far as dealing with witnesses and victims, but we agree with being extreme in our prejudice against evil. See, the problem is, we're trying to keep a lid on everything to prevent people from finding out how disgustingly easy it is to traffic with the infernal. People are stupid, and I blame Hollywood and politicians over that. We took the Bible out of schools, but we watch sad, lonely vampire pedophiles on the big screen, and teenagers and video gamers who never experience the real world at its worst think evil is just misunderstood and needs a hug."

I suppressed my laugh. This was surreal. Where did I make a wrong turn at Albuquerque last week and land in this sci-fi horror comedy film?

"I can see you haven't left your idea of what the real world is yet, son. And I nearly left you there but for the warden here vouching for you to me. It would be very easy to chalk all this up to some misunderstandings and imaginations so far. Gee, did you really see a gang member spider crawling across a wall and ceiling, or were you dealing with too much over seeing your mutilated fellow gang member murder people with his bare hands? There has to a logical and natural explanation for the supernatural, right?" He snorted and clenched his fist. "I've seen this and heard that delusion too many times to count. You think you're a badass and can handle trouble? Look at these hands." He held them up to my face, and I did my best to make sure there was no sign of humor in my heart or on my face to make him think I did not take him seriously. He reminded me of the best parts of my grandad, and more than that, I respected him too much not to take him stone-cold serious. I just wished I could wake up back in the world I had lived in before I was a child killer and convict in a world of horror.

"Yes, sir?"

"Boy, I have had to kill more men with my bare hands than you have tried to heal with yours." I took that as gospel and kept my mouth shut and ears open. "And the only reason I'm here running my mouth at you is because what you did here earned you respect, at a price. That price is a scrubby little gang of left-handed jackoffs who want to nail your hide to a wall. And that's fine—that's your business, not mine. As long as they do it with flesh and blood, then I'm not involved. The real flesh-and-blood law is, and they can do the fighting for you the way the system is supposed to work. When they don't and it's bad enough, maybe I'll have time away from slaying dragons to bail your sorry butt out of the fire you wandered into like a lost sheep."

"I am no lost sheep to be saved." Ok, the old man was starting to get under my skin—not unlike how my granddad used to when he went about trying to light a fire under me to amount to something in my life in the wrong way. Accusing me of something I'm not never went down easy.

"And I am no damn sheepdog, or even a shepherd. I am a hunter of men and a killer of monsters. But here you are in my world, and there are only two places you fit in: as a victim or a predator. And no matter which one you *think* you might be, you are trouble for me."

"So what am I, then, if I don't want to be trouble, and don't want to be a victim or predator?"

"You are smart, is what you are, and you are listening to me. Stay out of this world at all costs, because it will only cost and give you no peace. You would just be a pawn for someone to use, at best. And damned if I don't think you have potential to be more than that, if you had some knowledge to use those smarts with. But you are too dumb and full of your ego to let go and become greater than you are, to be more than just a pawn. Maybe someone's predator, but likely just a victim before it ends for you, probably when I have to be the one to put you down. Better me than the FBI turning you into a drooling retard in a nuthouse the rest of your life."

I winced at his word choice but didn't have to think twice about trying to correct him to not use the R-word. Hopefully he wouldn't go totally right-wing and throw the N-word around like that.

"Aww, did I say something that hurt your ears, boy? Don't like retards, then don't be retarded."

"Wow … ok, sir, I will do my best. Can you tell me anything that might help me get more knowledge so I can avoid all that?"

"Yeah, learn what truth really is first. Without it, you have no judgement, and your intentions don't mean crap because you'll just get people hurt doing the 'wrong thing for the right reasons.'"

Hey, I earned two fingers this time. I wasn't sure that was really a good thing.

"That motto us Texan Ranges have of 'One Riot, One Ranger' wasn't because we are badasses—ok, well, that is a big part of it, but more than that, it says we will do what is right, no matter the odds or the risk and cost we pay to do it. And let's face it, you wouldn't be here if that was you. You would have turned your EMS company into the state the first time you saw them operating with expired equipment and trying to make a buck at the expense of a patient by cutting corners."

"Yes, sir, but lot of those rules are ridiculous for EMS companies to try to keep up with, stay in business, and afford to employ us."

"How is that your problem, though? Ever think that those companies that can't afford the cost of being squared away are the last ones you want to work for, because they'll throw you under the bus when shit hits the fan?"

"So I play by all the rules when no one else does? No disrespect meant, sir, but how does a judge, jury, and executioner get by all that while protecting the Constitution?"

"See, I knew you were smart for a dummy." He gave me a nod and a wink. "I am a friend of the truth, and I use it to judge what matters the most. No one can live under every rule our government, our laws, our employers, and our families push down on us. You *will* break some along the way. But what guides your judgement, boy? What do you use to determine wrong from right when you have to make a judgement call between the 'good' for you and the 'good' for others?"

"I learned from being an EMT to do no harm, and to triage. I may have to put myself first if the worst should happen, but only so I can continue to help those in need. I didn't really expect a philosophy debate, sir. I was hoping more for a suggestion to an idiot's guide for what I'm going through."

"Those tools … " he said, shaking his head in thought. "Yeah, that works fine, boy. Those tools, do no harm and triage, can help you figure out the truth and the path to follow. But for an idiot's guide, I say you pick up a Bible and learn to be a good man, a man of peace, and stop being an idiot. Get a steady job, find a good woman to provide for and that will take care of you, and raise a family of good people. You do that, and you'll be a great man one day—maybe even better man than your old man. True principles and convictions work better than any gun for settling disputes, and they stop evil better than picking up a spell book and trying to fight fire with fire. Any sociopath can pick up a gun and try to cast curses and summon principalities for their will, but can you see right from wrong? Can you tell your right hand from your left and avoid becoming a left-handed jackoff that I'll have to put down?"

"You know about my dad?"

"Yes, but I'm not talking about him—I mean your grandad. He had a bigger hand in raising you, from what I read about your life story, and my two cents about your dad is you have to learn to be a man yourself and not look to him to teach you his ways. Drop the dead weight you're carrying around. I knew about your granddad from when I served. Sherwood Forest Hackberry, Army Ranger, Green Beret, Snake Eater, and one hell of a man from what I know of the people he trained. I read his grandfather was one of the Indian Rangers under Lipan Chief Flacco, who rode with Captain Jack Hays. I came along just a few years after your paps got out of the army and stayed until a few years ago, and now here I am. Small world, huh?"

"I actually just started reading the Bible. My celly left it behind after he got himself stabbed defending me." I actually didn't know half of the history behind my grandad that this man knew. It was indeed a small world full of coincidences.

"Caedmon Murphy. Yeah, I would have liked to have met him. He sounded like a good shepherd from what I read. The enemy wants to destroy men like that so lost sheep like you can't figure out if they are coming or going. I bet Caed would have been handy for me to use. Maybe he will pull through, but from what I read in his medical file, it doesn't look good for him. His white cells are climbing—they're trying to kill out all the infection and losing the battle. If he goes septic, you know what can happen then under the best circumstances."

"Yeah, it will be a small mercy if he never wakes for all that."

"Sometimes a little mercy is all you get in this world, and I would say you've been lucky for what you've had. By this time day after tomorrow, you should be opening your first beer in over five years, hopefully with friends and good food around you. Life doesn't get better than those moments. Don't play hero when you get out of here. I know Las Hermanas got you marked, but they're a little gang of punks spread thin with bigger worries than you. Walk away—walk away, and don't look back. I don't ever want to see you again unless it's to congratulate you on having made something of yourself after all this, you hear me, boy?"

Damn, it was like hearing a younger version of my grandad in every word he said.

"I hear you, sir. I will do my best."

"That's all a man can do if he wants to be able to look in the mirror at the end of his life and have no regrets. Now, I gotta saddle up. This night is young for me, and I got evil to put the fear of God into. You take care of yourself and mind what I told you. I don't normally waste my breath on people anymore these days. Don't make me regret it."

"I won't, sir." I shook the hand he offered.

"That's what I wanted to hear, boy," he said with a big Texas grin. He clapped me on the shoulder with his other hand before walking to the door, leading me outside and into the clutches of Carls.

"Carleton, did you get all those bottle caps and cigarette butts picked up outside?"

"It's Carls, and yes I did."

"Oh, excuse me … " He paused and turned to eyeball the guard before continuing, "*Carols*. I didn't think enough of you to remember your name. It's a good thing you corrected my mistake before I made a bigger one. Take this man out for a smoke and fresh air, and don't let me hear about you stepping out of line ever again, you hear me, boy?"

I think my mouth was hanging open. I shut it before a fly came around. *Holy crap, that burned me just from standing this close. Poor Carls.* I tried to keep my snicker on the inside. I still had a pretty decent goose egg, so I didn't feel too sorry for him.

"Yes, Ranger."

"Need a hug?" I insincerely offered after Ranger Huntsman tipped his Stetson and swaggered off.

"Only if you grow tits first," he shot back and started leading me to the yard.

"Oh, if that's all that's stopping you, I know a Jenny here that used to go by the name Jimmy?" I snickered as I followed behind.

Carls mumbled and grumbled something I couldn't quite hear as we made our way to the yard gate and he turned me loose. I scanned the faces over the yard, knowing I had at most maybe five minutes left until we went back inside and hit the showers before hitting the racks.

I got a mix of looks from the dogs and the wolves in the yard. There were even a few yapping Chihuahuas. My thoughts kinda unfocused, I made my way to where the Diamondbacks were as I thought of a *coyote with three legs loping up the trail. Fire came chasing behind it, eating the gap and gaining as the coyote loped on its three legs, a lucky scavenger that obviously had had to chew its paw off to get out of a trap. It ran straight into a snare that closed around its throat and began thrashing and fighting with no escape as the fire raced over it.*

I shook off the daydream just as I made it to the gathering of Diamondbacks. I reached for the pack of smokes Copper had in his pocket and lit one up with a nod of thanks to him.

"Wasn't sure we would see you again, Bodhi. How are you feeling?"

"I just needed the day to rest up. I'm feeling pretty good after getting smacked in the head. But yeah, I think y'all better get used to me staying with the family. King, if you don't mind," I raised my voice and turned to face him where he was playing chess with Reggie, "I would like to accept that offer for a place in San Antonio."

My announcement earned me some attaboys and hugs from Copper and the gang.

"Glad to hear it, brother. You'll fit right in, and I'll be glad to know someone like you is around to help the old man like you've helped me here."

Even though I was facing King and watching him play chess against Reggie, I didn't see it until it was all over. Somehow Slippy had moved through the crowd without me even seeing him in the yard and came up behind Reggie, running a razor from one ear around his neck to the other. Then he came running straight at me with a grin across his face flashing his chrome teeth.

I smashed into him.

He had tried lunging with his hand slashing through the air to cut me across the face with the bloodied hand, but I brought one arm up to guard and block at the same time. I came straight across with a right elbow into his face as I stepped forward, bringing all hundred and eighty plus pounds of charging muscle and instant fury behind the blow.

Slippy apparently celebrated getting his face smashed by trying to do a spinning cartwheel backflip and only got far enough to smash his face straight into the ground. I stepped over the punk and came down over Reggie, reaching for his neck as I took a knee beside him.

I put my hands around his throat—it took both, and it wasn't good enough. Blood was shooting through my grip along with air bubbles and Reggie reached up to hold my arms in his hands, the look of panic in his eyes as he tried to speak. That only made it worse as I struggled to keep his life behind my hands.

"My daughter" were the only words he tried to say over and over, but no sound came from his mouth.

"I will try to help—hang in there! You'll see her soon!" The words were out of my mouth without a thought behind them. I knew this was a battle I would lose on my knees with Reggie's life escaping from my grip.

The response team was there, trying to pull me away and help Reggie. I had no choice but to let go, and so did he as he lost consciousness.

"This is for Nancy, *puta*!" I turned just in time to see Cherry empty a cup over Slippy and use my lit cigarette that had fallen to light Slippy on fire. He went up like a torch, and the ERT boys went crazy.

Shotgun blasts and whistles sent us all to the ground. The smell of burning hair, something that used to nauseate me, mixed with burning flesh went into my nose and caught in my throat like a fist, nearly making me wretch. I was close enough to feel the heat from the flames as the members of the ERT tried putting Slippy out. Someone came up with a fire extinguisher and doused him, but the burning and the screams continued even when the extinguisher went empty.

Another ERT member came running up with another fire extinguisher and was able to finally put out the flames. The ERT member with Reggie stood up and shook his head when we were all on the ground. Reggie had stopped bleeding on his own after he took his last breath. I was covered in blood from elbows to knees, and I knew I would be smelling barbequed punk for days. *Just something else to add to my stack of memories I try to avoid thinking about.*

CHAPTER 21

DAY 2

"Now prepare yourself like a man; I will question you, and you shall answer Me."

–Job 38:3

I was one of the first people in the yard today, and I brought Caed's Bible with me. Last night I had made it back to my cell and started reading from where I had left off. I was nearly through the book of Job and still not really close to having answers to my challenge. Caed's notes had been helping, pointing out that Job's religious friends were using a lot of the same flawed logic to condemn Job and justify themselves as many sanctimonious people still did today. But now I didn't want to put it down—I was reading it nearly nonstop and had almost finished the book today.

I took over our usual table, the same one we had been sitting at last evening. The bloodstains had been powerwashed out of the ground. *Like Reggie was never here, right?*

I couldn't get over those last moments with him, the plea in his eyes and on his face as he struggled to speak of his daughter. And I'd had no peace to give the man in his final moments except a promise to try to help. Hadn't I already done that as far as I could?

I saw King and Copper coming out. Other members of our club were either doing their jobs or taking classes. Sure made me feel like we were spread then. But Spike was almost back on his feet, just in time to take my spot when I left. I put the Bible down on the table next to the chess board.

"Hey, Bodhi, didn't see you at breakfast this morning."

"Yeah, it took a while for me to get to sleep. I decided to skip breakfast and sleep in this morning. Not like I'm doing anything much around here but watching the clock anyway, Copper."

"Did you tell your family about your decision to move to San Antonio with us?"

"Not yet. I guess I should make time to get a phone call to them and let them know. I was thinking about waiting till I get out of here so I can save them the collect call."

"Well, I talked with Pappa Gun this morning," King said before snatching Copper's pack of smokes and passing them to me after taking one for himself.

"How did that go?"

"Pretty good for you, for the most part. Pappa Gun has a bunk for you with Diesel, our Sergeant at Arms. They'll help you get on your feet and help you find work. The Tribe handed off your money to him, so it's safe. He said it will be waiting for you."

"Hell, I never even asked how much they gave me. I still can't believe all that happened in the last few days. So what's the bad news?"

"Well, there is a little disagreement over how much rank you'll get when you get down there. I suggested they patch you straight in. Pappa Gun was fine with that, but the VP and Diesel say you need to earn it, especially since you waited till the last minute to commit."

"Who's the VP down there again? Pappa Gun's son, right?"

"Yeah, Steven. He's the club attorney and tries to keep us out of jail. He was also looking into everything Reggie claimed. But anyway, it looks like it would take an argument and hurt some feelings if you came in with a full patch like that. To me, you earned at least that busting skulls and keeping Spike from bleeding out."

"So basically I am prospect, and a club bitch to get pushed around until I earn respect by taking crap off everyone?" I shook my head and took a deep breath to calm down, thinking of a plan *B* to my plan *C*.

"I wouldn't take crap from anyone, if I was you, unless you ask for it. Diesel may push you around a little and size you up, but I'm pretty sure Pappa Gun is in your corner."

"Great, and I get to bunk with Diesel? Is he tough in a fight?"

"That's why he's the Sergeant at Arms and not the treasurer or the secretary, man."

I decided it was best to keep my mouth shut and just nod my head. I flicked my ashes and picked up the Bible to start reading.

"Did you ever hear if they found anything out about Reggie's kid?"

"From what Steven said, Reggie copped a plea. The DA on the case had eyewitness testimony from the mother and arresting officer, and the victim was prepared to take the stand and point the finger at Reggie. Sure don't look like he was anything but what he was convicted of. I would cut that weight loose and let it go, bro."

"It was Caed's weight. I just can't stop thinking about the last thing he was trying to say to me when he died … no physical evidence, huh?"

"No need when you were caught in the act by the police and everyone is pointing the finger at you. The case was slammed shut—no way Reggie was going to last through a jury trial. What was the last thing he said?"

"He was trying to say something about his daughter but couldn't talk. It was his eyes, too—they were desperate."

"Maybe he was trying to apologize for what he did and realized he was going to burn in hell and wanted that last confession on the way out?" Copper said with a nod toward the Bible in my hand when he mentioned hell.

"Could be. But he had Caed convinced, and Caed seemed pretty sure. And I feel like I owe Caed."

"Bodhi, Caed's gone, and Reggie is dead. His daughter is probably sleeping better at night. Let this go, bro. You ain't no hero, and you have no way to do anything but get yourself in deeper crap than anyone can pull you out of either way if that mess hits the fan." King was giving good advice, and taking my idle curiosity way too far.

"Funny, the Ranger I met last night investigating everything told me pretty much exactly the same thing you did. Told me best thing I could do is read the Bible and get an honest day job and work on being a John Q. citizen. Trust me, after the last five years of paying for playing hero when I didn't think I was, last thing I am going to do is run around in loud colored tights and save kittens falling from trees."

"Las Hermanas would really be trying to chase you down dressed like that," Copper threw in his two cents.

"I think their day is over now. May have to get some dress-up tips from you, Copper, and get the Tribe ladyboys to chase after me."

"Hey, that ain't happening, ok?!" Copper was trying to play chess, but it was more like watching him donate all his pieces to King.

"Uh-huh. Ok, Copper, have them all to yourself, then, you greedy bastard," I teased him as I stole a smoke from his pack and chain lit.

"Anyway, Bodhi, you heading down to San Antone is a weight off my mind; the old man needs good people around him. Some of the dirtbags we pick up on the side of the road take advantage, like Copper here." King took another smoke from Copper's dwindling pack of cigarettes.

"Yeah, I'm just worried about what I'm going to do to pull my weight so I don't mess up another family."

"Don't worry about that. It's family—we help each other when we can. And that is what's expected from you, to pull your weight and help out where you can."

"Only family I ever had like that couldn't hardly afford to help themselves, much less anyone else. But I will do what I can. Guess any other questions I have will answer themselves, huh?" I flipped open the Bible to where I had bookmarked. Copper and King were trading moves and swapping pawns for rooks.

"Worst case scenario, you don't like the setup and decide Mexican food, river tubing, barbecuing, and rodeos aren't your thing and you get a bus ticket back to your family," Copper offered as he made another move in their game.

"Man, shut the hell up, Copper! You're going to make me

homesick talking like that." King made his move. "You getting anything out of that, Bodhi?"

"Well, Caed left it behind. I figured I would give it a shot, but if it can't answer a question I'm looking for, I'll probably leave it behind."

"What question?"

"Why did God gamble with Satan over Job?"

"I can answer that," Copper said and made a move. "Because your fairy sky god is a psycho and punishes sinners."

"Bet you're glad Caed isn't around to slap ya for talking like that, huh?" King asked as he took a pawn from Copper.

"Well, actually, from what I read—which is basically Job wailing and moaning his butt off after his family was all killed and his body was covered in boils and all his property was stolen or destroyed—his friends showed up and pretty much preached the same thing Copper just said, minus the fairy part. Copper sure has a fixation on fairies, huh?"

"No joke, you should have seen him checking out some of the ladyboys the Tribe has. Guess he likes chocolate-flavored ones."

"Hey! Not true, y'all are just making things up!"

Copper was sounding a little panicked there ... hmm.

"So anyway, I was getting to the part where God finally shows up in the story and tells Job, 'Stand like a man. I will question you and you will answer.' Can you imagine what Copper would do in Job's shoes there?"

"I think we would see Copper literally poop a kitten right there."

"Ha! You would see me ask Odin for a ride on one of his Valkyries to Valhalla, is what you would see."

My eyes rolled, and soon I went back to reading and smoking while time ticked by in the early summer breeze. Today felt pretty good. Hopefully, this summer I would even be able to spend a little time in a river on a tube drinking a few beers.

As I was reading through the last chapters of the book of Job, I noticed two things. First, God sure seemed to like to brag about himself, and the other ... apparently God had made a dragon?

"Whoa ... " I closed the Bible and sat it down, pulling a long drag on my smoke to consider what I'd just learned.

"Share?" King requested.

"Well, in other interesting news, apparently if there is a God, He made dragons, and from what I read, there apparently is scientific proof that there is a God."

"What proof does science have of dragons?"

"Proof of God, not dragons. Clean your ears, Viking wannabe."

"Ok, so share what you got out of Job. I never read it because it sounded like the worst story of God making someone miserable for shits and grins."

"I know, right? That's what I heard, and maybe I would've missed all that if Caed's notes didn't point out what is really there, like how thousands of years before man discovered springs and rivers under the ocean, God was bragging to Job that He had been there, done that where no one else could. Also that air has weight, and several other things proven by science to be true. But anyway, so God is bragging about creating this dragon and how magnificent it is and asking Job if he could wine and dine with it and pal around, go to town, and chase down chicks with it like a bro, right?"

"Uh, that would be cool to have a pet dragon to party with," Copper answered

"After some Satanists turned my bro into a zombie, I'm not sure I wanna see a dragon next," King replied.

"Spider weren't no zombie. That's just a bunch of crap those Hermies wanted to scare us with."

"Right," I said, interrupting before we got into that debate, "so that's when Job understands, he actually never knew God at all. He had only heard about Him, and God can't really claim us as His until after we know the real Him and accept Him. But now that they know each other, God gets to hang out with someone more cool than a dragon: us. We are His favored creation, above even dragons."

"Bodhi said it was true, though. You gonna argue with the expert?" King said to Copper.

"Yeah, but they had a gun to Bodhi's head and made him say what they wanted."

Oh boy. Ranger Huntsman had nailed it, not that I could blame them. They hadn't been there. They hadn't seen Slippy's body-snatcher crab crawl up a wall onto the ceiling and make an offer I wasn't supposed to refuse.

I had compartmentalized it and put it in a file box marked "Can't do nothing but worry—best left alone" the way I had with all the other emotional trauma I'd picked up along the way from family and occupational hazards that go with this thing we call life. That's how we keep functioning, right? I knew King would ask me to go over what I had really seen, and here was the big choice: be honest, tell the truth, and claim my honor for the sake of how someone perceives my sanity, or go with the flow?

"Ok, Bodhi. For the record, what was the deal with the way Spider died?"

I looked up from the Bible, closed it, and quickly thought of a good story. It was way too plausible that what happened to Spider was some kind of psychotic break from being tortured, leaving his mind in a "zombie"-like state, right? Yeah, I could totally spin that and make it totally believable, and maybe even convince myself. *No blood spilled here, man.*

"I know what I saw, and I am fed up with sparing people's feelings at the cost of my own honor. What I saw chased me to this"—I held up the Bible—"for answers. Because evil was proven real to me, and I once heard that a man named Edmund Burke wrote that all it takes for evil to triumph is for good men to do nothing. Apparently, that quote got real popular after Nazi Germany."

"Ok, so was it zombies, then?" Copper pushed.

"Copper, I don't know for sure if it was a demon or a zombie, but whatever it was, it wasn't Spider. That thing knew too much about me and it was possessing Spider's body, then it left Spider, jumped to Slippy, made Slippy crawl around on the wall and ceiling like a spider, and spoke in the same voice that it was using through Spider. Then Spider's body rose up and came after me. But the one that did all the killing was that body-jumping spirit. Spider, whatever he was at that point, just knocked the crap out of me. So call it whatever you want—it wasn't natural, and I got no rational explanation for what happened. But if it helps you sleep at night, call me crazy and tell yourself it was all psychological trauma from seeing Spider tortured and killing people."

Good choice! Welcome to the family, bro! We are gonna rock this world together!

"After what I saw Bodhi do to Topaz, I wanna be ringside if you're stupid enough to call that man crazy to his face." King moved a piece to put Copper in check.

"No thanks. In fact, I think I would like to find me a Bible, too. Got any suggestions what book to start with, Bodhi?"

"Man, I'm new at this, but a lot of the notes that Caed scribbled down here lead to Romans and First Corinthians."

"Oh, those are in the New Testament—that's cool, I got an old Gideon New Testament Bible with psalms and proverbs that has been haunting my cell. I can't ever make myself throw it away."

"Copper, you have a Bible? I thought you were all into Viking gods."

"Hey, man, if you saw something that legit scared you that bad and made it all real, then I'm going to play it safe and not ask for more proof than that. Last thing I want is to have my junk chopped off and get turned into a demon zombie for King to brain-stomp."

We all laughed at that, and Copper was put in a checkmate.

"Guys, I think I'm going to go ahead and use the last of my free time to try to call home, talk to my mom and grandmother, and let them know I'm heading down to San Antonio and will have to put off seeing them until later."

"Yeah, they were probably planning to get down here to pick you up, I bet."

"Last I checked on them, King, they didn't have a running vehicle and had to use my aunt to get around."

"That's tough, man. I know what it's like to be that broke, but we'll get you up on your feet again and help you get money sent their way. They are our family now, too."

"Man, y'all help me with my family, you got me whether you want me or not."

"Glad to hear it, man." King stood up and gave me a bro hug, and Copper joined in. Then it got uncomfortable.

I toed out the smoke, grabbed the Bible, and went out of the yard toward the commissary and phone bank.

CHAPTER 22

DAY 1

"And be not conformed to this world: but be you transformed by the renewing of your mind, that you may prove what is that good, and acceptable, and perfect, will of God."

–Romans 12:2

So, there I was, as we all are with the worst part of our lives behind us: knowing things will get better, and trying to use experience as a learning tool to guide others in the right direction, away from the destruction we leave behind.

The prison gate closed behind me. I looked around the parking lot at the few cars there that day and a bus that was loading. I had the clothes on my back that I had been wearing five years ago—one of the few pairs of denim pants I owned, a white tee undershirt tucked in, and an ugly plaid overshirt. *No convict here, right?*

I didn't see my ride here yet, and the bus driver was looking at me and waving a hand. Looked like I was going to be in for a long walk or a long wait—no ticket for the bus on me. I waved back and sent him on his way.

I had my few possessions in the meager storage box wrapped in my arms plus Caed's Bible, a copy of his journal, and the books that Warden Hardcastle had given me. Hardcastle had even given me his business card to contact him if I needed someone to talk to, or maybe to look him up for that tattoo gig down the road.

Life had hit the biggest reset button on me I'd ever experienced, and the reverberations were still a present echo that gave me a whole new perspective on how to deal with my life ahead.

Yeah, I was at rock bottom, but I had a little cash and some people around me that were willing to give me a hand up, but not a handout. That was all I needed to work myself out of the pit my life had turned into. I had a chance at a life again—maybe not the one I'd thought I wanted, but maybe this would be better?

If you think my positive attitude comes from becoming a Jesus freak, hold your horses. I still wasn't convinced. What little I had read in the Bible was good, and made sense with Caed putting a spin on it and showing other scriptures … but it was still, at the end of the day, just an old book written by some old guys thousands of years ago. And yeah, with no help from the *Good Father,* it survived my challenge of Job. So, I was going to keep it around and see what I could learn from it. Too many people in my life that I respected kept pointing to that book as their answer, and I couldn't ignore that. Especially when what I needed most was answers.

But right now, I was most looking forward to beer, burgers, and boobs, and maybe tubes this summer. Five years stuck in prison looking at a bunch of other offenders, all working out their emotional baggage on each other … yeah, it was way past time to let the bull buck.

Give that up for the sinless life of a monk—are you kidding? I gave my penance and learned my lessons, and yeah I planned on being as good as I could, but where I was no hero, I was by no means a saint, either. I hadn't even got any answers to that "turn the other cheek" crap that would get you cut ear to ear or taken from the rear—pardon my French—in prison. Caed seemed to have a handle on all that, but I was named Bodhi, and I may be smart to some point, but I was not as enlightened as Caed.

In prison, I kept my inner pit bull caged and muzzled up. Last thing I needed on my mind was any curvy bombshells where I had nowhere but men to turn to for comfort. *GAH!*

San Antonio had some good rivers around it and was known for its *señoritas.* Maybe I would get to see some in hot bikinis this summer and bring one home named Lupita, huh?

Luckily, my daydreams were disturbed before they got out of hand by the low rumble of a classic mid-eighties Chevy short-bed truck. It was low and dark silver and cutting through the parking lot straight to me.

"Mr. Bodry?" Hey, don't ask me how to spell what he called me; I am edumacationally challenged enough getting through my own name.

"Must be the guy that just left. I'm Bodhi," I cracked the ice and extended my hand.

"Oh, my bad, bro! Pappa Gun sent me down here, but I guess your name passed through two or three people before I got it—you know how it goes," he laughed and shook hands with me.

"No problem, brother. I just spent five years getting called way worse than that. I answer to just about anything now, as long as you say it with a grin."

"Name's Rooster. Go ahead and put your stuff in the back and hop in. Let's get this show on the road!"

Rooster was, of course, stereotypical ruddy-skinned, red-haired, and freckled all over. He was around my age. I could tell from his voice he was a heavy smoker, and he was wearing a mechanic shop shirt thrown over a white tee with a name patch that read Billy.

I hopped in my side, shut the door, and belted myself in as he turned up the cassette player jamming Def Leppard.

"So who is Billy?"

"Me for today," he said with a laugh and reached for a smoke. "I pick these shirts up at thrift stores all the time, so when I wear one, I get to be someone else for the day, and when I mess up and someone tries to say I did it, I tell them they got the wrong red-headed step-child." He finished with maniacal laugh.

Rooster was a hoot. When I asked him about his truck, he started with "386 stroker" and I heard "Edelbrock" a lot with a bunch of other noise, and some "blah, blah" before he finally finished giving me a detailed verbal tour under the hood set to the tune of "Armageddon It."

I learned about an hour down the road he only had the one tape and the radio didn't work, so it was that one tape, over and over, the whole ride to San Antonio.

We made it to the outer limits of the east side of San Antonio by midafternoon when Rooster suggested pulling into a gas station where gas was more affordable than deeper in the city, and hey, guess what was playing? "Armageddon It," again … imagine that.

"The office of your PO doesn't close for another hour and a half. We should be able to get there in time to have you check in and head home in time for dinner."

Oh yeah, apparently Friday evenings were reserved for the gathering of the Diamondbacks at Pappa Gun's house. Every Friday, families brought potluck platters and roasted some dead critters over barbecue pits, drank beer, and enjoyed the night. The next day was for family or work, but Sundays if you didn't have work, all parolees like me were expected to find a church to get into and learn to be good model citizens of the community to represent the DBMC patch. Last thing the club needed was to be labeled a one-percenter gang by federal task force officials. That might get you a lot of street cred, but that was a commodity that only had value in prison, which was the last place Pappa Gun wanted his members.

You would think the law would be happy with this approach to bad boy motorcycle clubs, and you would be wrong. How do you justify a gang task force with no presence of gang activity? Go after career criminal gangs? What, and get shot when you can pick low-hanging fruit for trumped-up petty charges? Copper and King were both serving for assembling an AK47 and an AR15 for someone that just needed experience putting the parts together. Oh, and that somebody turned out to be the ATF, so you just got a nickel for manufacturing firearms without a license. Others were busted for charges of public dueling that should have been self-defense and other nonsense. Not that the law didn't catch some Diamondbacks riding dirty and selling pot and worse in the streets for easy cash. Hey, not saints—just angels with dirty faces, ok?

Rooster pulled next to a pump and I got out to go pay inside. I left cash with the clerk at the front and stepped back out of line for the customers just as two officers walked in. I nodded and ducked my eyes as they walked by me in the narrow aisle. After they were behind me, I let out a breath I'd been holding and looked around to see a rack of homemade fried pies. Sure enough, they had my grandad's favorite: fried pineapple. I'd never have that next fishing trip he had promised me, but I went ahead and picked up the pie and went to the back of the store to grab a carton of milk too. I got back in line just in time for the two officers to get in behind me, and man I could feel the lip whiskers of a cop 'stache on the back of my neck from how close they felt.

I paid out the gas and my purchases and went out of the store without any trouble. Rooster passed by me to go inside as I walked to the truck.

"Hey, did you forget to pay for everything you got?" said the Voice of Authority behind me.

They couldn't be talking to me—I'd paid for everything I had. Whoever they were after was none of my business. I kept walking and didn't look back.

"Hey, I'm talking to you!"

I looked over my shoulder. Both cops were walking toward me with their hands on their guns. *Whoa!*

"Me?" I asked in stupid confusion. Not my brightest moment. I should've known better than to act stupid with cops, I know ... but hell, I had just been released from prison! Didn't I get to enjoy being a free bird instead of treated like a jailbird?

"Yes, you, Mr. Innocent. You act like you're in a hurry to get out of there and don't want to be around members of the law enforcement community. I call that suspicious behavior for someone not committing any crimes. I think you got something that you don't want us to know about."

"No, sir, you can search me. I got nothing on me."

"Thanks for the invite," the one closest said. His name plate read Det. Andrew Franklyn. He was several inches taller than me and a few weight classes above me as well, putting him in the neighborhood of six foot two and north of 250 pounds, stretching that uniform shirt over a vest. His partner was similar in height and build, but I didn't get a glance at his nameplate. Both had short cropped hair, cop 'staches—think a porn 'stache but on a cop—and dark Oakley shooter glasses.

I followed their orders to put my milk and pie on the hood of the truck and turn and spread. I got patted down inside and out, up and down while I was catching some rough looks from customers going in and out of the gas station. I was hoping Rooster would just stay inside rather than come out and join the party. It was probably a safe bet he would.

"Here is his wallet, Richards. Why don't you run him while I question him, see if he has any priors?" Officer Richards and Franks—sounded like a sitcom waiting to happen. He turned me around to eyeball me and kept me pressed back against the truck. "What's your name there, buddy?"

I rattled off my name and date of birth and offered my old expired driver's license number or social. They had me up on their computer in no time.

"Oh, he's a convicted felon. Just released hours ago."

"Oh, welcome to the Land of the Free! You know all law enforcement has the authority to stop and question you anytime, anywhere for any reason, and there really isn't anything you can say about it, right?"

"Wouldn't want to be accused of not cooperating with the law, sir," I answered and reclaimed my wallet. My heart rate was hammering. I could feel blood rushing to my face the more looks that were cast my way.

"So what were you convicted of?"

"Involuntary manslaughter, due to negligence on the job."

"Says he killed a ten-year-old patient of his. He was an EMT."

"Oh, so you were playing hero and got sloppy with a baby, huh? You know, I have a kid around that age. Glad you aren't on the streets and a threat to him."

"Yes, sir, I learned my lessons."

"Yeah, too bad it came at the cost of someone's kid. But here you are, back on the streets enjoying the good life, while a child is dead and their parents are still mourning, I bet. You think you can walk away from that clean and easy, huh?"

"I don't know if I can ever make up for that loss. But I was given a chance to try, so I will do my best and hope it will be good enough at the end."

"Alright, I suppose that is as good an answer as anyone can give. You stay out of trouble now, Mr. Bodhi. Hopefully we won't run into you again."

"Do my best, officer. Y'all have a good day, too."

They got back in their squad car and sat there while I reclaimed my warmed milk and pie. The milk went into the trash, and Rooster came out about that time to unlock the truck for us to get in.

"Man, I feel bad leaving you alone on a limb like that to be hassled. But Steven gave us all the talk not to crowd cops when they question us. We're supposed to give them space, and if anyone gets booked, stay out of the mess so we can call him to bail us out of the tank."

"Makes a lot of sense. Nothing you can do to help the situation by getting yourself tangled in it, and there comes a time when everyone has to stand on their own feet."

"Yeah, but just because you think you're out there by yourself doesn't mean one of us isn't far behind watching your back." He offered me a fresh milk.

"Man, you just made my day, Rooster. You let me know if I can ever be any help to you, and I'll do what I can."

"That's the way it is with our brotherhood, man. Ain't no thing— we got each other's backs."

We pulled away from the gas station and got back on the interstate to head downtown and put all that drama behind us. I felt like a huge weight was gone from my shoulders the instant we made the onramp.

We made good time getting to the office of my parole officer. Along the way I enjoyed my pineapple pie, thinking of my grandad. I wondered if this camaraderie was what he'd had when he was serving in the military, and what I had never experienced from family or even colleagues in the civilian world.

We pulled into the parking lot and Rooster stayed with the truck to avoid paying for parking. I had a very rough idea what to expect as I rode the elevator up in the building to the office of Stanley Parker, PO.

I made it into the office. Some of the lights were turning off, which I took as a good sign. Maybe if he was ready to leave, we could hurry through all this.

The receptionist had me sign in and detail the purpose of my visit. I was instructed to wait and told it wouldn't be long.

I turned around and got eyeballed by a taxidermy whitetail deer hanging out on the wall. I decided to take a seat near a stack of outdoor and fishing magazines and just chill and enjoy the quiet. I nearly expected to wake up back in prison. The last five years felt like one long, bad dream. You would think the fear of prison rape would be the worst thing, but what was worse than that was the long periods of boredom broken by social circles and drama, drama, drama. If the drama didn't lead to a fistfight or shanking and lockdown, it would be good viewing for a woman's reality show.

Now all I had to worry about was getting a solid job to get my feet under me, staying out of trouble, and figuring out where to put my roots down at. I could spend another five to ten working on that here in San Antone as long as everyone I was around was as cool as Rooster.

"Mr. Parker will see you now, Mr. Hall."

I went through the open door and followed the hall until I came to another office door that was open with a man behind a desk busy banging away at a computer.

"Come on in, Mr. Bodhi. Before you take a seat, let's take a pee test," he said as he slapped a final command at the keyboard and stood up.

"Luckily I know how to pee, so it's pretty hard for me to fail one of those tests."

"That's good to hear. Some of the people that come through here make a career out of failing everyday tasks." He ignored my lame joke and handed me a cup in a sealed package.

"Take this with you, fill it to the first line, set it on the sink, don't shut the door, don't flush, and don't wash your hands until after I have collected the sample."

Stanley left me to follow the instructions, and while I was making a deposit, I heard him tell his receptionist to start a file on me.

"Bodhi, I haven't looked at your folder yet," he said after processing the lab and showing me clean and clear. I was seated in front of his desk after having washed my hands. "Why don't you save us time and tell me what kind of record you have and what you learned from your prison experience, and what your game plan is now that you're out?"

"Well, sir, I never did drugs, never stole anything or hurt anyone until I killed a boy through negligence on the job as an EMT. I had a hard time dealing with the responsibility of my actions for a long time. It was easy to use excuses and blame others, but ultimately it was my responsibility to make sure the truck I was on had no expired drugs or equipment and that I was following all protocols. I followed my protocols, but I got complacent and sloppy checking off equipment, and I let the company I was working for push us out on a call without taking time to make sure the job was done right."

"Any violence inside prison?"

"I had to defend myself a few times, but I was cleared of instigating each time." *Boy, if you only knew how many times.* Including my stint at Beaumont, where violence was mandatory and sanctioned by the warden and guards in a cage with another inmate. I had no doubt there was underground film out there on those fights. Good luck ever getting that evidence to court to use against me, though—too many politicians from on high along with lobbyists and corporate barons controlled that action. "I learned the easiest way not to ever lose a fight is to never get in one in the first place. I see trouble starting, I try to get out of the whole area before it catches me."

"Glad to hear that. You look like you are a rough customer. You might try to tame that outlaw look down and get a clean haircut, keep those whiskers off your face. I know in prison you had to look a little tough, but out here you will get further looking like a fine young Republican than a fine young parolee."

"Well, the people taking me in expect me to go to church, and I plan to grab the first job I can to carry my weight. So the next time you see me, you may not recognize me when I clean up."

"Glad to hear that, Mr. Bodhi," he said, standing up and extending his hand. "Make sure you contact us if your address or phone changes from our records or if you plan to travel to visit relatives. I will schedule you to come in three weeks from now and see how things are going for you. I don't have to tell you not to be stupid and stay away from drugs, firearms, and any criminals or breaking the law, right?

"I can avoid those things. I'm pretty challenged, so it's been hard not to be stupid, but I will do my best." I shook the man's hand and stood to leave.

"It's easier to avoid being stupid if you can avoid girls. If not, look out." The man deadpanned so hard, I wasn't able to tell if that was a joke. "My job is to keep you out of prison and honest, so you keep in touch. And if anything starts making it hard for you to stay out of trouble, you call me and I'll help you get on the right side of it."

"Well, I plan to make your job as easy as possible. Usually, smart, pretty girls run from me, so hopefully I can avoid being frequently stupid."

"Those are the ones that will keep you out of trouble by challenging you to be a better man. You have to have a job and go to church to keep up with them. The low-hanging fruit will drag you down to their level and run you over looking for trouble to get into. See Wendy on your way out for your next check-in."

I made it down to the truck just in time for us to pick up where we left off in the Def Leppard marathon. It was close, but luckily Rooster had the truck turned off and was taking a nap, so I didn't miss a single power chord. I honestly felt scared my hair would turn bottled blond and grow into a mullet by the time we made it to my new home.

I had enough metal head in me that the experience of a four-plus-hour road trip of one album of Def Leppard wasn't an end-of-the-world experience. Give me classic rock any day over half the crap coming out that was a mix of pop-hop and rap singing about going to the club.

Not to get on a soapbox rant, but what the hell was happening in the world when a bunch of losers had nothing better to sing about in any genre but life in the club getting drunk?

Ok, maybe that was a little preachy for someone that would love to go to a club and find some "low-hanging fruit" to nibble on. But hopefully I wouldn't find myself in a dance club, chasing girls and getting tipsy, while listening to music about going to a club chasing girls and getting tipsy. That made me dizzy just thinking about it.

"Is your first day out of the pen everything you thought it would be so far?" Rooster helped me shift gears.

"Honestly, I thought my first day would be spent further away from having interaction with law enforcement. But yeah, I figured it would take me a minute for it to be real."

"Ha, yeah, don't worry about it. A few beers and some grill burgers and chicken and you'll remember where home is after tonight."

"Sounds like music to my belly," I said with a smile. It sounded like a better homecoming than I would have had with my own family, too. The best reception I would have had would have been with my mom and grandmother, who were barely getting by on government aid and occasional help from other family who were barely getting by themselves.

But I could never think of my mom's family without being reminded of the stark contrast on my dad's side and my failures to live up to everyone's expectations and be the provider my grandad had needed me to be. Seemed like every time I found a path up that mountain, it only led me to a hard landing as a reward for a hard climb.

Rooster took us south of San Antonio where the land was somewhat flat and the dirt turned to red clay, very similar to land around where I was raised in Oklahoma, except with occasional palm trees.

We turned off the main road and took a county road that turned to a farm road and finally turned into a property gate with a dirt road that led through half a dozen trailer houses set in rows facing each other. Behind that was a stand of oak trees throwing shade across a picnic area beside the dirt road that kept going deeper into the property.

"Looks like we got here in time to help set up and start the grills." We parked next to several other late-model trucks. Rooster got out and I shadowed him for a while until I could figure out how to not act like a lost pup. I was introduced to the people already busy unloading ice chests, chairs, and other supplies before I got busy putting up chairs and tables.

I got to a place when all the chairs had been set up and all the tables placed alongside ice chests of food and drinks brought out as people showed up that I couldn't do much else but stand around like a sore thumb. So, I went over to Rooster's truck and went into my box of personal items. I picked up the book the warden had gifted to me by John Locke, found a Coke looking for a thirsty person, and sat myself in an empty chair out of everyone's way.

I was just about to open the book when I took a deep breath and just looked around for a minute. The Texas sun would be setting soon, and the skies were deepening to red in the west as a breeze kicked in. Not bad for midsummer, when being outside at all could bring misery for a working man, even at leisure.

Already more than a dozen people had showed up, close-knit and related by blood or bond through the MC. There were still over a dozen more chairs laid out, and one custom grill mounted on a trailer was being fired up along with a couple of smaller ones. Most of the men that I had briefly been introduced to were congregated around the beer and fire there while the women were at the tables, both sets catching up on gossip I would be totally lost at.

The only thing obstructing my view of the area around me was the live oaks, brush, and houses around the property. No concrete, no guards, no iron bars and fences and concertina wire, and no clock ticking away the free time I had left.

I saw a red-tailed hawk swoop through the area in a low glide and took a deep breath, relaxed, and let it out. I people watched, sipped my Coke, and nibbled at *The Two Treatises of Government*.

CHAPTER 23

It actually didn't quite go like I thought it would. Instead of staying out of the way and being able to people watch, it wasn't long before Rooster came over and asked what I was reading. And by twos and threes, everyone else did, too, until I was suddenly the center of attention and catching everyone up on how King, Copper, Spike, and the rest of the members of DBMC were doing when I had left. More vehicles started showing up, and then I heard the thunder of V-twins on two wheels.

My experience on a motorcycle had been limited prior to my incarceration. I had free use of a friend's bike when my truck broke down for a while when I was working in the hospital ER, and I enjoyed any time I could put miles on it out of the city. My family, of course, did not approve, but what really stopped me from getting uncaged was a tight budget between the ongoing training and education and the need to have enough room to haul gear, books, and equipment around.

I had an addiction but was always denied the fix.

Half a dozen bikes and a few more trucks and an SUV rolled in. I recognized a Harley Dyna, and after that everything looked custom except for the lead bike. That one actually reminded me of Steve McQueen's Harley from *The Great Escape*. Most of the bikes had "get back" whips dangling nearly all the way to the ground from the handle bars in braided leather colors of the club, black on brown.

Everyone migrated to where the bikes were for a new round of hugs, greetings, and introductions. Pretty much all the men and some of the women were wearing the club colors or kutte, vests carrying patches, insignias, and ranks and no shortage of personality. Most of the men were wearing brown pants and black shirts or vice versa, while the women were dressed to stay cool in summer-weight pants and shorts and shirts. The few dressed in heavier clothing were riding also.

I was totally losing track of who was who, but some names and faces stood out, and others I made sure stayed printed. Tugger, who looked like a six-foot Wookie under all the hair and beard, had huge pierced gauges I could stick my thumbs through in both ears and an easy smile. Geezer, a grinning baby-faced silver-haired man that looked anywhere from forty to sixty, was close to my height and less weight with a handshake that nearly crushed my knuckles. Steven, the club VP and attorney, looked like he spent too much time working in an office and not enough time enjoying life and was there with his wife and daughter. Don't ask me their names—I was doing my best to forget and stay dumb. I saw enough curly long blonde hair and curves on the daughter to get in trouble if I didn't keep my eyes and attention elsewhere.

Then Blonde and Curves turned to a fireplug wearing a steel-colored goatee and matching hair with a working man's tan named Gunther Womack, the Prez—or Pappa Gun, as he told me to call him after telling me to knock off the "sir," crushed me in a hug, and pounded my back.

Among all the details I took in, Pappa Gun had a billy club attached to a dog choker chain that wrapped around his waist. Nasty little weapon to use in a fight. I was under the impression state laws would frown at something like that, but kept my mouth shut.

Then Diesel came through the well-wishers and stuck his hand out to shake. He looked about six foot six and 245, and if you know the song, you knew this wasn't a man to give any lip to. He looked like the wet dream of every football or military recruiter: clean shaven with short blond hair and pale blue eyes. Probably had a black book of names for every Saturday night for ten years. How he got the nickname Diesel and not Hollywood or Kowabunga was beyond me.

Was I going on about his looks too much? Maybe. Did that make me attracted to him? Hell no. Threatened? Ehh. I guess if you're going to feel insecure about someone, it would probably be the next Thor or He-Man come to life to make you feel like the short, fat, ugly kid in the shadow.

"Hello, Bodhi," he said as his mitt engulfed my paw. I looked up at the man as he pulled me close to him with a grin on his face and didn't let go after a simple shake. "Heard our new prospect thought prison was a shortcut around getting to earn our colors."

Tread light and be honest. This is the day to leave all ego behind and learn to be humble.

"Well, that was before I was told how much you wanted to let me earn it." I was well aware of how many looks we had drawn; everyone was trying to have their own conversations with each other and play catch-up.

"Oh, that's good to hear … " Blondie seemed at a loss for words while still holding my hand. I was honestly expecting him to keep trying to push my buttons, but instead I was starting to feel uncomfortable watching his gears grind till Pappa Gun rescued us from a socially awkward moment.

"Bodhi, we had a visitor come by the other day. I got a story from King about everything that happened, but I would appreciate you telling your side of it here to the family before dinner."

So, I spent the next thirty minutes telling how things pretty much went down during the last seven days of my incarceration, starting when Spike was shanked, while the smell of sweet meats cooked over wood smoke and coals and we all enjoyed company and drinks. I fielded odd questions here and there as the story unraveled, and I left out a lot of the gory details I would normally have shared with people in the medical field. Public speaking was something I'd had to do when I was a medic and taught training classes on the side to new EMTs and expanded to giving public awareness speeches to public schools. I'd even taught first aid classes to everyone from teens getting summer jobs at local pools as lifeguards to physicians who were required to continue training after spending a chunk of their lives in school already before embarking in a field where the hours are long, the debt from learning is high, and the appreciation seldom outweighs the stress.

I don't begrudge a doctor that finds time for a golf outing or vacation. A politician that tries to dictate how doctors are allowed to deliver care? Now that's a whole other can of worms.

"We were told Spider murdered several people and you had to kill Spider in self-defense. We've known Spider for years—he never would have hurt anyone except in self-defense." Steven's wife seemed be the prosecutor of the family and picked up on a big gap I had left in the story because of how sticky this issue was. "Did that really happen?"

"I'm not going to lie about what happened, ma'am. But I will ask to wait till a better time than before dinner to get deeper into the details than what I am fixing to say, because it's pretty bad … " I had to take a second to take a breath and gather my thoughts on how to word this without coming off sounding psychologically deranged myself.

"Before Spider did anything to anyone, he had already been tortured by Las Hermanas. The person that did those things wasn't Spider. There was nothing left of the man I knew and would have fought like hell to protect."

"So what did they do to him that you had to put him down for, then?" That accusation came at me from Diesel. I had really hoped that King had done a better job informing DBMC what happened so I wouldn't be left trying to explain this to everyone.

"Evil" was as much as I was willing to answer until I had talked with Pappa Gun one on one.

"All right. Food's hot off the grill, and I think we need to spend the rest of the evening giving thanks and celebrate the life of our brother, Spider, and not mourn and be angry," Pappa Gun stepped in with a voice of authority that easily tamed the moment. "I've talked with King about a lot of this, and some of it, as Bodhi said, is not fit to discuss right now. We know enough: that Spider was a victim, and the people responsible for what happened to him have been dealt with, mostly by Bodhi. Now, all of you bow your heads while I give grace."

And that ended the group entertainment provided by yours truly. I was impressed by the way Pappa Gun said the prayer for the meal. It was short, to the point, but covered a lot of ground, which was good since my stomach was letting me know it was going to eat me if it didn't get some meat pretty quick.

I made it through the food table and selected pork spare ribs that looked like they had only been teased with a sauce glaze and a kiss of salt before being slow cooked to perfection and a grill burger. I sat my drink down at my feet as I reclaimed my seat from earlier and placed the book I had been reading down to the side and my plate in my lap.

I had a nose full of the smell of sweet meat and nearly had a spare rib to my lips when Diesel walked up and kicked my foot, knocking over my drink.

"Up and at 'em, squirt, you're in my seat."

My heel cracked into the inside of his right knee, half spinning him off balance as I shot out of my chair without a thought and he turned back to square up against me. I came inside high and tight and sent the crown of my head smashing into the bottom of his jaw.

"Briggs! Go grab me a beer and step off before I send you home."

Diesel froze, but I wasn't sure if it was because the birdies and whistles had him entertained or if Pappa Gun had stopped us from being bigger asshats. To be honest, I felt like the asshat, and my face was stinging with embarrassment that I'd reacted the way I did. I took a deep breath and let it out as I stepped back, and Diesel stepped back and turned away to follow orders. I made a note to catch him one-on-one and make it right.

Steven's daughter walked up and leaned down to pick my book up, reading the spine. I tried not to let the blonde curls and firm curves lower my IQ further.

This was probably a situation that would've made my ancestors say something overly intellectual, like, 'Ugh, me Bodhi … how do,' at the white girl.

Pappa Gun came up to join her. "Bodhi, looks like you tripped trying to stand up and do what my Sergeant at Arms asked you to do and knocked over your drink. Are you ok?"

I know I didn't get caught staring … Any second, my brain would give me the right words to say to Pappa Guns to apologize for my actions. Did I mention she was wearing shorts that showed off a generous portion of tanned thigh?

"Yes, sir. Only thing worse than my clumsiness is my bad manners. I been locked in a cage too long and act like I was born in a barn. Let me clean this up and get out of the way."

"Eh, belay that nonsense. What are you reading there, Reba?" he asked the white girl with curls and curves. A sunny smile lit her face as she handed the book to Pappa Gun.

"It isn't my book, Pappa," she answered before I could figure out if I was coming or going. I saw Diesel coming back with one hand loaded with food and another holding two bottles of beer. Reba took my spilled Coke and walked off to throw it in the trash. Pappa Gun took his beer from Diesel and handed it straight to me.

"Those ribs go better with a cold Lone Star. Trust me." That earned me an unpleasant look from Diesel before he walked off to go join Steven and some other members of the club.

"Have a seat and eat and talk to me. This your book, Bodhi?"

"Yes, sir. The warden gifted it to me one of the last days at prison after the dust started settling down."

"Pretty heavy reading. Not many people these days ever hear the names of our Founders much anymore, much less the people that inspired the Founders like John Locke. Are you reading anything for fun, or is this your idea of entertaining?"

"I used to read Westerns, but they just make me homesick now. I started reading some old science fiction books, like the Conan series from R. E. Howard. I didn't know before I got locked up that they were into fantasy and science fiction like they were a hundred years ago. Blew my mind that they were casting spells at orcs in Tolkien's books and creating tales of high adventure with barbarians back then."

"Do you read any vampire books?"

"No, those last movies killed me on vampires. Since when do they sparkle and go to high school? Give me cursed monsters over toothy drama queens any day."

"A drama queen *is* a cursed monster in my book." Pappa Gun picked up where I was going and I nodded my head, putting my plate back in my lap and reclaiming my seat.

Oh yeah, when I got up earlier, my plate went into my seat neat as you please without spilling. I was a little impressed with that, myself, since my caveman brain was the one in control at the time. 'Least I didn't pie face Diesel with my food, because … oh my, this meat was the best thing I could remember ever having. 'Course, maybe if I'd shoved food in his face, he would have accepted it as a gift instead of an assault?

"King told me you were a medic, told me that it was a bad rap from the job that landed you in jail. I won't ask about that, but I was wondering about your skill level. King told me enough that it sounds like you were a good hand in the field."

"I was an intermediate level, just a cert level down from paramedic. All the skills, just not as many drugs to play with."

"Oh? What stopped you from making the red patch?"

"Well, I enjoyed playing with skills as a basic too much, and all the old-timers had advised me to take my time and not go from zero to hero. Kinda wish I'd stayed a basic now."

"You have regrets, I see."

"Hard not to, sir. They do a pretty good job driving home reasons to have remorse in prison."

"Well, you probably heard from King I was a marine chaplain once upon a time. But what you don't hear much of is that I enlisted navy and became a corpsman." My brows shot up as my respect went up yet another notch for the man.

What a lot of people may not know about the marines is that while the USMC was among the greatest fighting force in history, they did not designate combat medics. There's no such thing as a marine medic. I may be wrong—it happens on rare occasion, so I tend to keep my mouth shut about what I'm not certain on, and I am a civilian—but from what I understand, you could technically enlist in the marines to become a medic, but you got shipped out to the navy to become one.

Consequently, when a sap got suckered by the navy to enlist to become a corpsman to pass out drugs and hang around nurses all day, they got shipped out to the marines and learned how to handle a rifle, ruck, and got sent to the front lines of any combat theater and worked twice the load of a marine infantryman.

"So let me tell you something now that you're back out in the real world and you have the option of accepting God's truth over incarceration indoctrination."

I see what he did there.

"The hard truth medics learn," he continued after swallowing a bite of delicious grilled goodness, "if they stay in the field long enough is that it isn't a matter of if, but when you kill one of your patients." Pappa Gun both repeated and confirmed what I'd been told would be likely to happen. It didn't make what had happened any easier; in fact, it only made me question how stupid I was for trying to answer a higher calling.

I swallowed some beer down and hoped he could tell he had my full attention and respect and would speak more.

"Maybe it'll be from something you miss and you give the wrong drug. Maybe you give the wrong dose. Maybe you have your head up your butt because you been running from one patient to the next for more hours than any sane person stays awake before they go to a soft bed and climb under cool sheets and blankets to sleep without the nightmares of the crying, bleeding, and dying keeping them going nonstop. And long before all that, you've been setting yourself up for burning out because you saddle up for a fight every day and set yourself up for failure with the promise 'Not on my watch, not on my bus, not on my shift.' And you cling to that vow in clenched blood-drenched hands so tight that when you break that vow, it breaks you."

All I could see now was a ten-year-old boy. A tube shoved into his mouth, covered in oxygen lines and IVs stabbed into both arms, my hands over the center of his chest, pushing down one and two and three and four …

"Yeah, I see it in your eyes, Bodhi. I saw it when I first hugged you to me. I been there and back from that, and I am here to tell you there is life after that still. There is hope, there is daylight. You don't have to let it drag you down and destroy you. You can get back up, you can be stronger than death, and you can continue to be the man that can be healed and be a healer. I am done preaching unless I see you making wrong choices, but you come to me when you're ready to talk, you hear me, boy?"

"Yes, sir. I will try to take you up on that."

"Good man. Now, in the meantime, I suggest you fill your belly, enjoy the night, and don't worry about anything. Make sure to take a plate home with you for breakfast in the morning. Tomorrow, if you don't have any other plans, I want you to come by my place for lunch. I have your package, and I have some other things for you, too." And with that, I got a slap on the knee and Pappa Gun stood up and swaggered off to get a second helping, getting hugs and kisses from family every step of the way,

"This book doesn't look like much fun to read." Hazel eyes and a teasing smile aimed themselves at me. Self-preservation kicked in and I looked around, but her mom and dad were talking to another couple by one of the grills.

"Uh, well … " Yeah, remember, no matter what someone says, I am a smooth public speaker. "It's kind of been a while since I did anything for fun. I did my best to make prison an experience to better myself in spite of how far down I've fallen below good people now."

"Looks like you did a good job of it in spite of how much you kick yourself while you're down. So, what does a Bodhi do for fun?"

She made me smile. I didn't know the last time I'd felt that, but it felt good, and I did my best to curb my thoughts from spilling replies that would get me nothing but trouble. Time to be a gentleman, especially since she looked too young to buy a drink. *Yup, that's Coke and not beer in her hand.*

"Well, I was looking forward to seeing if the rivers around here are anything like I've been hearing. I used to enjoy hunting and shooting sports, but felon, so no guns. Back when I was in high school and I lived on the rez, we would go camping a lot. Some friends had trucks we would take off-road and go mudding and enjoy getting stupid, riding horses and being a wild Indian—excuse me, Native Aboriginal American, or whatever they're calling us in universities these days."

"Oh, look out, are you the PC police?" I had her laughing.

"Eh, I guess I can respect everyone to be what they want. But I was raised on the rez, had a white father, and a quarter-blood mom under a half-blood grandfather. And not once do I ever remember those protestors and their lobby groups coming to us and asking us what we call ourselves. They are all no better than what they preach against and just want to put us down in a column with a checkmark to divide us from other groups."

"So what are you, then?"

"Generally confused. It's probably a good thing I got a GED and stopped getting smarter and just got a job, shut up, and went to work."

I had her laughing again, and I enjoyed that.

"What about you? Are you with the PC police?"

"With a name like mine? I think my parents plotted against me to make half the nation hate me before I got out of diapers."

"What's wrong with Reba?"

"Reba isn't my name; everyone calls me that as a nickname. My full name is Rebel Helen Womack. My parents loved the song 'Rebel Yell' and nearly named me after it. Pap calls me Rebel Hellion."

"Guess it was a good thing they weren't Damn Yankees fans. Wonder what name you would have caught then."

"Oh, I am a huge fan of the Nuge. I probably would have named her Stranglehold if I had thought about it," her dad said from behind me, nearly making me spill my beer. I got to my feet nearly as fast, and probably not as smooth as Diesel got me up earlier.

"Oh, go ahead and take my seat, sir! I was just about to go see if there was more food left if everyone got a plate."

"Well, I'm not going to fight you for your seat, that's for sure," he said with a laugh.

Oops, guess people saw and are talking.

"Go fill your plate. Everyone will have enough to take home leftovers, I'm sure. We usually have plenty left for family that can't always make it. I'll keep your seat empty so you can come back and talk to us."

Well, crud. I was honestly hoping to sneak off and find Diesel to apologize, but I didn't see him around, and now with the VP watching to see that I did what I said, I was stuck. Especially since I was still under the belief he was in charge of me and I was staying at his place.

Again, it was a serious moral dilemma I was faced with. *What to do, what to do?* I elected to go with ribs, of course, figuring the grill burger would be best for my breakfast in the morning. That left me with another difficult choice: sweet tea, coke, or beer. My prison figure was going to hell with these options being forced on me. I went with another beer since I wasn't feeling anything from the first I'd had.

"So, Bodhi, I take it you're into politics?" Steven's wife asked when I returned to my seat. I finally remembered her name—Melissa.

"Not really, ma'am. I never even voted. Seems like whoever gets into office does stuff for their own interests most of the time and don't really care much about who they step on. I nearly voted for the last guy we just got rid of. Then I found out his dad was an illegal alien that got deported and he had too many shady questions about what citizenship he may or didn't have. Ain't it funny how many people on both sides just play stupid with things like that? But he was right that this country needs to change. Looking back, he was totally wrong about healthcare, and I watched the government's idea of making something affordable totally backfire."

"Well, I'm glad to hear you aren't into politics," Melissa said with a laugh. "You and my husband should have a lot to talk about."

"Well, you got me. I think I better lay off the beers since this is only my second in over five years. I guess I should have said I don't care about party politics, but there are issues that I care a lot about. When I see people being harmed rather than protected by the government, I'll say something. I might not know what to do about it, and maybe that's why I should probably just shut up, especially since I may never be able to vote again with my record."

Yeah, I definitely needed to follow my grandad's advice and be seen and not heard. I was blaming the beer, though. It was that or the ribs, and it couldn't be the ribs—those ribs were sweet, innocent, and pure and needed to be in my mouth and fill my belly.

"Well you sound like a conservative, if you don't mind me saying. Especially reading John Locke. Liberals don't have a clue what natural rights are," Steven chimed in.

"Well, maybe there is a little of everything in me, I guess. I should probably shut up about politics. Someone made it a rule not to bring up politics and religion when you're enjoying the company you're in." Maybe I could dig myself out of the hole my mouth had gotten me in?

"Oh, don't worry about it. I get into political arguments all the time. Goes with the territory of being a criminal defense attorney, plus running for office on occasion. I think it's good to see what people are made of. I don't care for someone flying false colors and hiding their feelings. Some of what you said I can go along with, and I am totally with you on that healthcare nonsense. The government has no business in welfare. But I never considered voting for a democrat, even if they promised all kinds of 'hopey changey' nonsense, especially when they were promising to change a lot of the things that were good for our country, like lower taxes, less welfare, more defense."

"Well, see, that is what I mean, though, about not getting into it. We have some things we agree and disagree on. I am not totally against welfare. The government is taking all these taxes from people. Funding defense sounds good until you have a standing military doing nothing and decide it's a good idea to send them to war to either colonize other parts of the world, stick our nose where it doesn't belong, or get your corporate buddies rich on government contracts. I watched a lot of starving people on the rez and in the military, too, that need welfare and help from the government just to get by."

"So you support government handouts?" Steven asked me with a raised brow. Great, my mouth was digging me deeper instead of staying busy on delicious rib goodness.

"Well, to a point, doesn't everyone? I mean, I don't expect you to say the elderly and indigent should get locked out in the cold while politicians get rich on tax money and collect from lobby's and make corporate fat cats above the law."

"No, I agree to a point there. I do think if the government kept its hands out of everybody's wallets, though, there wouldn't be as many indigent, and families could afford to care for their own elderly better. But you do see there is rampant abuse in the system, right?"

"Oh, absolutely. I saw that all the time with people treating the EMS service like a taxi service. I will never forget transporting this one patient. He wasn't old enough to buy a beer legally, but he was already on food stamps, welfare, and Medicaid. He had headaches and depression, and that was enough for him to claim disability and stay at home playing video games on a fifty-inch plasma and drink energy drinks, eat pizza, and suck a bong all day, every day."

That made Steven laugh. *Good, a laughing boss is a happy boss.* I started stuffing my face.

"Better watch it, Mr. Bodhi. My husband will make you a conservative monster the more you talk to him, sounds like."

"That's funny. My mom used to call me her little Bodhi monster when I was a little kid," I said before taking a drink from my beer to hide the smile from the few good memories I had as a kid. Don't get me wrong here, I was not abused; I was cared for by a lot of great people, and this world is full of people that have it worse than me every day. I just wish I could have been better and not disappointed so many so much.

"Oh, I bet you were a little handful for her to keep up with," Melissa said.

"No, ma'am. I was sweet and innocent—my grandmother will vouch to anyone for me."

More laughs, and we all relaxed and enjoyed a pretty good visit where they started talking and let me step away from the spotlight. I finished my plate and my drink, then decided it would be a good idea to fix a plate for taking home and grab another drink.

My elbow got bumped at the food table and I cut a glance at Rebel. After telling me her real name, I couldn't bring myself to think of her as Reba. That name really didn't fit well, especially since she was trying to get me in trouble here standing next to me when I hadn't been around any ladies my age in years. Now, I was around one that was likely just shy of old enough, and way too easy to stare at.

"You trying to make yourself fat your first day out?" she teased me with a smirk.

I tried avoiding the dancing glimmer in her eyes and told myself, *She's just like a pesky little sister. Best to friendzone her.* "It would be easy with this food. Luckily, it's mostly protein and flavor instead of carbs and fat. But I figured I better do as Pappa Gun said and make a plate to go and set it aside, then try to find Diesel and figure out where I'm staying at."

"That sounds like a good idea. Anyway, I was going to tell you, Sunday me and some friends are going to go tubing. You can come along if you want."

"Wow, um, thanks. I want to say yes, but I think I better wait to talk to Pappa Gun tomorrow and see what all I can get done to get settled in. But if I'm able, I'll have a hard time saying no."

"Good, you look like you could use a little fun in the sun. Can I ask you something about what happened to you in prison?"

"No, I never married or kissed on the first date," I said sincerely.

"What?!" Her eyes got big.

"I'm joking. Go ahead and ask." I had a plate with a burger, 'tater salad, and two more ribs. I was going to eat like a champ in the morning. I sealed it in plastic wrap and put it in a sack with a can of Dr. Pepper. I was set.

"Oh, you're funny. I figured you were property of Copper, though, so I know you're hands-off."

"Ha ha, yeah, King owns Copper, Copper claims me—it was a reality TV show in the making." I had her laughing. *Just a little sister—off-limits. Oh, I might see her in a bathing suit? Seriously, off-limits.* Hopefully older, cuter friends would be there if I was stupid enough to go Sunday. I really wanted to go, too, and that was before I'd been invited by this little troublemaker.

"Well, um. No, I was wondering if you could tell me something about this person that the club tried to look after. Reggie was his name? I think you left out some things from what I heard my dad and mom talk about."

"Well, yeah, I left out some things I figured were best left buried. What did you want to know?"

"Well, my dad said you brought that other man to the club, and both of you kinda got Reggie protected, but that Reggie was accused of awful things he did to his daughter. Why did you guys try to help him?"

"Well . . . we may not have, had it not been for Caed. The first time I stepped in was kind of an accident. I happened to be in the clinic when he was there for treatment, and a punk from Las Hermanas came in and tried to kill everyone there and frame me for it. I made him ride a mop handle around the clinic and named him Slippy for getting lippy."

"You're a poet, too?" she said after I earned a giggle.

"Not exactly. But apparently I got hit in the head too much and it's given me brain damage." I was being serious there, but I knew she would think I was joking still. But honestly, ever since that night Carls had curb-stomped me into a wall and the following day ... the inner dialogue, the visions, the insight that made fighting Topaz a cakewalk? I didn't know exactly if this was all internal, all organic within me, or something ... more, and what "more" that could be. On the other hand, if it was organic and internal, I was obviously walking on the razor edge of psychosis at some level. I was not sure which was scarier there.

"So what did Caed have to do with it? He wasn't a member of the club, right? I got the impression King didn't know Caed until sometime this last week."

"Well, that morning after I dealt with Slippy, they moved Caed into my cell. He was a very interesting person. I kinda wish I had been able to get to know him better. He was a little guy, about your height and hardly any weight on him. But he was like a big brother to me ... and I think to Reggie, too. Anyway, Reggie came out to the yard that morning and came to where me, King, Caed, Copper, and everyone was at to thank me. Caed took one look at him and was convinced he was getting framed after hearing his story and talked King into trying to look into it. Caed promised Reggie he would look out for him. That was outside the club, but King had me looking out for Caed, so the club kinda got roped into that. But they got Reggie anyway, and all that is one long, sad story. I don't know who did what to his daughter; if Reggie was right, then he was framed and someone else was abusing her. But if everyone else is right, then she won't ever be hurt by him again."

"Oh. Well, I wondered because I heard my dad say it was fishy that Reggie's attorney died, and apparently there's been rumors of corruption from the sheriff's department of that county. But nothing else."

"Yeah, and apparently the daughter was in line to testify against her dad in court if Reggie didn't plead guilty. So looks like Caed was wrong and it's best to just let the issue bury itself and move on, huh?"

"Yeah, it's sad things like that happen. But thanks for telling me. I couldn't see how we got involved in the first place since it wasn't club business, but when I heard Dad say the attorney was run off the road, I had to get your side, too, because I was so curious."

"You heard someone ran the attorney off the road? I thought it was just an accident."

"Well, at first that was what Dad found out. The sheriff's department originally filed it that way. But state troopers followed up, found black pant from another vehicle on the back side where another vehicle pushed him to spin out and fly off the road into trees. Airbag didn't save him, and his head was smashed in."

Now, I had seen airbags cause trauma to people I pulled out of wrecks. I'd seen them break noses, even break arms, but to smash your skull in after being shoved off the road? I would ask Pappa and Steven about all this later. I didn't like the idea of Las Hermanas getting away with killing Spider, Reggie, and Caed *and* being connected to this crooked sheriff's department.

"Anyway, I'll probably run into you tomorrow at my Pop's house. Hopefully you can figure out Sunday by then and let me know."

"Thanks. Do you know who all will be going?"

"Me, Tugger, Geezer, Diesel, and some of my friends from school."

"Oh, I don't know if I can handle seeing Diesel in a speedo. I'll try to keep my hands to myself and my thoughts pure," I said with mock flamboyance, the way I used to tease Cherry Bomb.

"Ack! No banana hammocks allowed! No one needs to see Geezer's white self in one—we would all go blind."

"Hey, you're too young to know what a banana hammock is!"

"Oh, please, I turn eighteen soon and am already out of high school! This is the internet age and everyone knows too much."

"Uh-huh, that means nothing from someone that would have big X marks on their hands and probably a huge letter M on their forehead if they could find a club to go dancing at."

"Yeah, makes me not even want to go, if my parents would even allow it."

"That's probably the best thing for this world. No telling how many fights you would cause if you went to a club."

"Why do you say that?"

"Some pretty boy would come up and say all the right words to sweep you off your feet—"

"I don't much care for pretty boys."

"And then some ugly man like me would have to run the pretty boy off. He would run crying to his friends, and the ugly guy would have to kick all their butts. The pretty boy would go to a hospital and come out looking like Frankenstein, then the ugly man would wind up in prison after the bar got burned down. The mayor would have to call the governor to get the National Guard involved. There would be riots. Taxes would inflate, new laws instituted, politicians would lose their jobs, and they would have to put a bunch of public service announcements on the radio and local airwaves to stop it all from happening again. So, yes, it's all your fault, and your parents should keep you locked away until you're fifty-three and get your first gray hair."

"Wow, that escalated quickly."

"Sure did. And speaking of pretty boys … " I saw Diesel heading out toward where all the bikes were parked. "Let me see if I can catch that man and get lined out."

"Ok, it was good to meet you."

"You, too, Miss Rebel. Talk to you soon."

I hurried off to catch up with Diesel. I was feeling pretty good from the way everyone had treated me, but I knew I needed to patch fences with Diesel. This was probably not going to be fun, but I deserved to eat some crow for the way I'd handled things.

Food sack clenched in one hand, I jogged away from the tables and tents and sweet smells of cooked meat.

"Yo, Diesel!" He wasn't too far off that I needed to call the cows home, and I got his attention well enough that he turned his head to glare at me. *Yeah, this is going to be fun.*

"What do you want?"

"Uh, well . . " Smooth public speaker alert. "I'm still trying to get oriented to where everything is and what is expected out of me. I was told by King you were going to be keeping an eye on me? I understood that there was a bunk for me somewhere that you might know about."

"Hmpf. Yeah, we can walk there. I sure ain't letting you ride bitch with me. Get your crap and let's go."

"Ok, it's in the back of Rooster's truck. I'll be right back."

I fast stepped over to go grab all the belongings I had with me that fit in a small box. My food sack rested on top of everything. I didn't have far to go since Diesel was parked near Rooster's truck, but Diesel was obviously not waiting. He had started back down the road without me, leaving me to hustle to catch up. I realized after I started after him that I was leaving my book behind at the gathering. Hopefully I would be able to drop off my stuff and come back to get it, though.

"Hey, Diesel, I really wa—" As I got near, Diesel turned when I called to him and blindsided me with a haymaker straight into the side of my jaw under my ear, putting me down on the ground before I knew I was even hit. My first clue was the ringing in my head, the world spinning, and sometime after that registering, the feeling of my face trying to plow into the dirt.

Now you will listen, and so you know, I will make sure this is well heard.

"Listen up, punk. I am only going to say this to you once. You don't know anything about loyalty, and it showed when you waited till the last minute to come here. You waited for one obvious reason: you hoped your rich daddy would come and offer you the easy way."

"I didn't ask for this … " My perception of time and motion felt … off, as if everything around me was moving too fast, making me struggle to keep up while the world tilted and tried to spin. I put my hands on the earth and pushed myself up, my eyes on Diesel for any sudden moves.

"Are you kidding? You went to King and you asked him for a chance to prove you're a man on your own. This is it, your one shot. And how do you act? Like a damn feral animal that should have stayed in a cage away from decent people!"

These are the conditions you placed on the author of your destiny. One chance to meet the demands you placed for proof in the Bible and to be real to you, to come to your level and prove Himself to you. He chose you for a purpose greater than any normal person has ever realized because every person before you that was given a choice wanted to satisfy their own selfish desires instead of serve a greater purpose, to become greater than themselves. Were you grateful? Were you humbled? Do you wish to forsake Him who sacrifices and favors you, only to watch you reject Him and return to your own path and see how that will work out for you?

"Yeah, you may have me nearly figured out." I climbed to one knee and looked up at Diesel through narrowed eyes. "But it wasn't disloyalty that made me hesitate to take this offer. My first loyalty is to family and to make right my screwups to them." My box of belongings was scattered, and the food sack looked like it had kept my food from being scattered on the red sandy trail we were on.

"You're here with us and made your choice, but if you don't want to man up and earn here, don't unpack. I will get you a bus ticket from my own pocket and ship your feral ass out first thing."

This is your last chance to take the easy way out. If you stay, you will face tests and trials few ever face, and even fewer have ever passed. To become your best by doing what is Right with a capital R on it. Choose wisely your next words, and with eyes wide open, accept the consequences of your decision.

I rose to my feet and squared up to Diesel. I stood within striking distance, looking into the darkened shadows of his brow where his eyes were hidden from visibility by the growing twilight. I took a breath. In the distance I could hear the laughter of members of the families gathered, and on my face I could feel the cooling breeze coming across the rolling Texas flatlands south of San Antonio. There were no concrete walls, no fences topped with concertina razor wire. Here, there was opportunity for me to grow to be the man

I wanted to be for the people I cared for.

"The first thing I wanted to do when I could talk to you alone after you tried to kick me out of my seat," I started and raised my hand, "was apologize for what I did to you. This is your home, and I have not earned my place yet. But I want the chance to see what I am really made of." I offered him my hand on it.

"You talk real pretty. Let's see you walk it." He took my hand in a strong grip.

"'Least you didn't tell me I have pretty lips, but should I be worried you want me to walk pretty for you?"

"Only if you want me to make you walk funny."

You understand your path will be full of hardship in the days ahead. I suggest you begin to make a habit, starting this night, of reading the Bible when you get a chance. It will be one of the few things you have to consistently guide you the Right way, but only if you want to go the Right way. Use it any other way, and like a double-edged sword, it can swing back to destroy you.

"You know how awkward you just made it for me to ask you to show me where my bed is now?"

CHAPTER 24

DAY 2

"Well, you may throw your rock and hide your hand
Workin' in the dark against your fellow man
But as sure as God made black and white,
What's done in the dark will be brought to the light."

–"God's Gonna Cut You Down"
by Johnny Cash

I woke up with no idea what time it was, and it took me a minute to orient myself and figure out where I was at. I felt rested, but the world wanted to tilt and whirl. I sat up and ran my fingers through my mane of hair and took a deep breath as everything came back.

Not in prison. What a hell of a first day out.

After Diesel had shown me the points of interest in the trailer house we were now sharing, I learned there was a master bedroom on one end past the kitchen and in the opposite direction, through the living area, was a guest bathroom and two rooms equal in size and accommodations with two sets of bunk beds in each room. All unoccupied, all with a sleeping bag rolled up at the foot and pillow at the head. No other furniture, no lamps—just the light fixtures in the ceilings and bare mattresses.

But, for the first time in so long, there was privacy. I had no change of clothes, no toiletries, either. I went to the guest bathroom. Luckily, there were towels, bar soap, and a half-used bottle of shampoo. I considered running the bath but decided there would be time for that after today, maybe tonight before bed.

I cranked on the heat and stripped out of my clothes that I had slept in. Last night I made it to my room in a mild funk—a little disappointed in myself for the way I had acted, and unsure of my standing with Diesel since I'd really jacked up my first impression. I wondered if I had set myself up to be his punching bag until I earned respect from him, if that was even at all possible.

I had stayed up for hours, but actually not stewing and stressing over everything. I had picked up Caed's Bible and started reading the Gospels of Christ. I finally started getting sleepy toward the end of the book of John, but through all of the reading Caed's notes were guiding me, helping me understand what I never really knew before.

Everything I was reading was a great story, and great philosophy, but I was unsure how it fit in today's world and how I could live by much of it. The more I read, the more I realized I had even more to learn. Some of the things that stuck with me the most were from the Book of John, showing that Jesus was the Good Shepherd. While I was reading that, I remembered the conversation I had with Ranger Huntsman about Caed.

Among things I was struggling with, did I really have to live by this impossible set of standards in order to appease a God for rewards in the hereafter while struggling every day here? What I'd read that Jesus said was a little hard to follow with what Caed said and had a lot of cross-references to other books in the New Testament.

I had nearly spent all night going back and forth on what I was trying to read and what Caed was trying to show me till I decided to try reading through the Bible once. After that, I'd come back to chase down all the trails Caed was trying to send me down on any given topic.

After being locked up in prison, all I could think about was what I had missed doing and what I could look forward to when I got out. Beer, babes, and tubes, right? Well, I had some beer; I'd met an off-limits, barely legal babe that I was doing my best to think of as a little sister, which wouldn't be hard once I found another babe to focus my energy on; and it looked like the tubes were happening tomorrow.

Or was I going to lose all that by picking up the Bible life? Ugh!

The experience I'd had last night was a stark reminder that just because I was free from prison didn't mean I could afford to play fast and loose. I needed to tighten up and get my business straight or I would screw up with the MC and likely wind back up in prison or, at best, shipped off to my family to screw up with them too.

I shut everything off and squeezed the water out of my hair, wiping it off my body before picking up the towel and drying off. I could find no comb or brush. There was toothpaste, though, and I used that on my finger and washed my mouth out before putting my clothes back on and stepping out. Luckily, the clock on the box above the TV and the stove were showing the same time—after nine a.m.—and the rest of the house sounded dead empty.

I opened the fridge to get my food, which was all by itself except for rows of Beck's beer in cans. At least Diesel didn't have to worry about me taking his beer. *Yuck.*

I put my food in the microwave, wishing Diesel had at least foil to cook with, but no such luck. From all appearances, he spent little, if any, time here. His room probably told another story, or just confirmed that all he used this house for was to sleep in and grab beer from.

The timer dinged, and my food was warm enough. I sat at the table and scarfed the meat down. I tossed out the trash and went to the back door, interested to see what all there was around the house.

A raised deck overlooked a fenced yard that was coming due for a mowing. Guess I knew what I would be doing around here to help earn my keep. There was an outdoor grill and picnic table on the deck and a few trees in the backyard. There was also a stack of cedar posts piled against a corner of fence, but nothing else I could use for exercise.

That was going to have to change. Diesel was in pretty good shape; he probably had a gym membership. I had no intention of spending money on a membership when I could go to a hardware store and a used tire shop and get just about everything I needed to stay in shape. Not that I planned to get into any more fights, but obviously Diesel wasn't shy about laying hands on me, and I had a feeling that club and chain Pappa Gun wore was not just a fashion accessory.

And, knowing all that, I was still a recently paroled felon. It was highly doubtful I could allow myself to get involved in any kind of public dueling, aka disturbing the peace. I had no faith in the justice system being on my side if I allowed myself to get into any fight for any reason. Responding law enforcement would detain and arrest me for anything they could hang on me and take me to holding to let the attorneys decide my fate based on proving guilt, regardless of if I was innocent or not.

Luckily, I had no prison ink, and I could simply cut my hair shorter so it would easily be presentable for any interviews for jobs or dealing with cops.

I know people will say I was being paranoid. Here I was, released, and should have been able to relax about badges pushing me round. But I'd already found out I couldn't even walk into a store to get a cheap pie without instigating an encounter. I know it may sound superstitious to some people, but I'd been around enough officers of the law to know that seasoned ones could smell "offender" on you once you got a record. Obviously, Beans and/or his partner, Franks, had smelled it and didn't mind pushing me around and likely would again.

Being affiliated with an MC, even one that worked at staying legit and legal, was not going to help any of that at all. But since I likely had a green light on me for Las Hermanas to take me out when they saw me, having the MC at my back was essential.

I considered going back into the house, but the only reason would be to watch TV or read. Which reminded me—I had left my book behind at the picnic area. Guess the best thing to do was to go see if it was left there, seeing as I had nothing else productive to do here.

I was on foot, I had no exercise equipment, and I was basically trapped at the house until I could figure out where Pappa Gun lived and go to his house for lunch. I went back inside the house after considering what I needed from the hardware store to set up my own outdoor gym in the backyard.

Today, you will realize your purpose and why you have been chosen.

I took a deep breath with my eyes closed and placed my hands on my face, rubbing my eyes and cheeks before giving the rest of my skull a short but vigorous message.

When I opened my eyes, it didn't help any. I still felt mild dizziness and slightly disconnected from the flow of time.

I went to the bathroom, turned the shower on cold, and put my head under the water for a minute. I came out after toweling somewhat dry and combing my hair back with my fingers to look somewhat presentable. Diesel was also coming out of his room, shirtless and wearing Jockey undies. The guy didn't have much spare flesh on him and was beefy enough that his stature would easily compensate for technique with just brute force and his speed on nearly anyone else.

"Morning, sunshine."

"Ungmf," he replied at me. Gee, either he wasn't a morning person, or someone had blindsided him onto his butt with a haymaker last night. Oh, wait, that was me! He was just a wuss when it came to waking up motivated.

"I was about to go down to where we had dinner and see if I left a book there. How do I get to Pappa Gun's house for lunch?"

"You don't. Steven's wife is on her way here to get you now and take you shopping for groceries. We don't let our family go anywhere alone, so it's your job to look out for them and carry anything they need."

"No problem. But why the high alert? Has there been trouble?"

"Man, this is San Antonio. It isn't like it used to be. Drug cartels have been moving across the border, and no one is stopping them from operating. Cops don't go where gangs claim until they have to write crime reports on bodies being discovered, and that only happens during the day. We're left alone because we don't let anyone go anywhere alone and we don't look for trouble. So, Steven is going to talk to you about how to handle yourself when you encounter police, which is basically just keep your mouth shut and let him do all the talking for you. Your job is keeping the families safe, my job is keeping you on task. *Comprende?*"

"So far, sounds like what I was doing for the last year with King." As I answered, I heard a vehicle pull up.

"You have any colors?"

"I got nothing but the clothes on my back."

Diesel snorted and walked back into his bedroom. I could hear the vehicle still running; no one had got out yet. Melissa had no idea the show she was missing out on with Diesel in his Fruity Looms. "This will do until we get you geared. Put the bandana in a pocket or through a belt loop, and don't jack the bill on my cap. Make sure the bandana can be seen."

I slipped the black cap on, tucked a third of the brown bandana into my hip pocket, and turned to go.

"One more thing: Your job is to keep them safe, not get into trouble. Bring anything down on the family, and you and me will have a date at the woodshed."

That reminded me too much of the rules I'd had to live under when I was in grade school. Defend myself, but don't get into trouble with the teachers and principal, or I would get into more when I got home. I was left with no option but being bait for bullies under those rules. "I hear ya."

"Good, because saying what you should already know once is too many times. But until I see you acting like a man instead of a feral, I guess I got to train you."

Swallow my ego? I can do that to a point. I nodded and kept my eyes away as I turned to leave. If there was going to be a trip to the woodshed, teaching manners and respect would definitely go both ways.

Let it go and just do your best. As long as you are doing that, then don't worry if anyone else is pleased when you can look in the mirror and know you did the right thing.

I took a breath and let it out, letting go of the tension as I stepped outside and shut the door behind me. A silver Porsche Cayenne was in the drive, and Melissa waved from the driver's seat with a big smile.

Wow, I was coming up in the world. The only vehicles I had ever been in that cost as much as this ride had lights and sirens. My grandmother always tried to stay in a Cadillac, but other than a few times my grandad had bought her a new one back when he was in the oil field, they were usually second-, third-, or even fourth-hand. Of course, my dad was another story; he usually stayed in a truck that never got over thirty thousand miles and was always the top-of-the-line deluxe edition, usually worth as much or more than the little trailer house my mom and I had lived out of when we lived under my grandfather at the rez.

I got into the Porsche, carefully, and gingerly shut the door. This thing was loaded with more features than I was smart enough to know anything about. I felt like I was going to smudge it if I wiggled wrong. I put on my seatbelt while Melissa greeted me and asked how my day was so far.

"I slept late, ate like a king for breakfast, and got a disturbing visual of Diesel in his undies. You know he wears Incredible Hulk whitey-tighties?"

"What?! I never heard that, but I know he is on his computer all the time. We always get invites to play games with him."

"Oh, lord, my roommate is a gamer geek? King did not prepare me for this." I put my face in my hands, groaning.

"Did you play video games, Bodhi?" She was driving this Porsche like a blue-hair going to Sunday social, but I wasn't going to say anything. It felt like we were doing fifty-five in a sixty-five with traffic going eighty around us. I peeked over—sixty-two miles an hour. *Ok, I was wrong.*

"Yes, then I turned twelve and discovered girls and little things like the sky and fresh air."

I had her giggling. "Well, Nathan does go out on Saturday nights to clubs and is always posting selfies of himself in the gym working out. Every time my husband goes to the gun range, Nathan is there, too, so maybe there's hope for him."

"Oh, your husband likes guns?"

"Oh, you don't approve of guns? That's ok. Steven is a gun nut. I have my own, too, but I would rather go shopping than to the gun range."

"No, I am a gun nut, too." I was laughing. "Both my dad and

grandad loved guns, so it came natural to me, especially growing up near an army base. I used to go with my grandad and his friends shooting all the time. But I can't be near a gun now. Looks like that part of my life has to die for a while."

"Oh, yeah, I keep forgetting when I'm around you that you're just out of prison! I never heard anything but good stories about you, and I don't see any bad in you. You know your manners and give respect. That is growing rare these days, even here in Texas."

"My grandad and uncle taught me to show respect by having manners. So, where all are we going?"

"Well, I have some groceries to pick up at the store for lunch at Pappa Gun's house. Do you need to go anywhere while we are out?"

"Well, if you wouldn't mind, I would like to go by a Goodwill and pick up some clothes to get by until I start earning a paycheck. Right now all I have is what I am wearing. Anything else I need for now, I can get at the store while we're there."

"Oh, perfect! I know where one is next to a candle and bath shop I love to sneak into. We can split up and meet when you're done. Do you have any money, though? I would be glad to help you get some clothes."

"I have some on me. And I think Pappa Gun is hanging onto some that I earned in prison, too, but I'm not sure how much. I just figured I better grab what I can while I have a ride to town."

"Oh! So no one has told you how you can get around, huh? We must plan on keeping you chained to the yard so you can't run off!" She laughed. "I'm joking with you. Don't worry, we'll help you get on your feet and get established."

"I don't know if I can ever thank y'all enough for the help. The only other place I could go was to my mom and grandmother's, and I know I would have been a burden on them if I did."

"You never talk about your father. Is that a touchy topic?"

"Ehh, not really. I just don't know how to talk about it without sounding like I have daddy issues," I replied with a loaded smirk.

"Oh? Why is that?"

"Probably because I have daddy issues, like any good TV therapist would claim," I said with a snort. "He divorced my mom within weeks of my birth, from what I was told. I didn't meet him until after I started school. He came one day and told my mom he wanted to take me to visit him. Day trips turned into weekends. I thought we were good until this all happened. I haven't heard from him since he told me I was disowned and never to speak to him or darken his land again."

"Sounds like your dad is the issue."

"Yeah, but I brought all this on myself. Guess in his shoes, it doesn't help to let people know your son is a convicted felon and child killer."

"How did you bring it on yourself?"

"Dad wanted me to follow in his footsteps, I think. Be a football star and rodeo king with buckle bunnies chasing me down, living like the bull of the ranch. But I also think he wanted me to follow my grandad's example, too, and be a man that cares for his country and family above everything. I think my dad likes people like my grandad and wants to reward them by giving them the best he enjoyed from life. First thing I think I did wrong was not kiss my dad's butt to live like that.

"My dad's first rule was follow his orders without question. My grandad's first rule was do what is right, always. Dad put me in a place where I could do one, but not both. I made my choice and things were never the same between us because, as he put it, I was not helping him with the ranch, and I was undermining his authority and defying him. We didn't talk much after that. I went from being a volunteer EMT to full-time, killed a child, and got disowned. Now, here I am. I'm sure my dad would really blow a gasket if he knew I was a member of a biker gang after getting out of prison."

Luckily, we were pulling into the parking lot of a shopping center with the Goodwill and several clothing and boutique outlets. Like Melissa said, the candle and bath shop was just a few doors down from the Goodwill.

"So, are we going to your shop or the Goodwill first?" I asked because she had seemed to imply that we would split up, and that seemed like a good way to get myself in trouble if anything happened.

"Nope, divide and conquer. You don't need me to hold your hand, and I know you don't want to go into a woman's foo-foo shop and come out smelling like you were rolled in powder, bathed in perfume, and slathered in lotion."

"Gah! Well, maybe Diesel would appreciate having me around

more if I smelled pretty for him?" Melissa giggled at that. "I was told to stay close to you, though."

"Oh, don't worry. I'm going to be easy to find, and you'll want to look around and probably try on clothes. Besides, I feel guilty pulling up in *this* and going in there."

"Ahh, well, I understand that. Maybe I better put off shopping there till the next trip, then. I'll just hang out with you."

"Nonsense. You are a grown man and free to go where you please, same as me. Now you go take care of your business and I will do the same. From here, I can peek out and see whenever you come out of the store, or you can peek in the door and yell at me there. We are fine, trust me." She got out without waiting for an answer from me. I felt some trepidation, but she was the boss's boss, right?

"Yes, ma'am," I said after getting out and looking after her. "I should be pretty quick. I'm only looking for a few shirts and maybe a pair of pants and shorts to swim in."

"Good idea, my daughter said she invited you out to go tubing tomorrow. I'll see you in a few minutes," she said with a wave over her shoulder.

I glanced over the parking area. Only a few people were going in and out of the stores and shops, none of them setting off any of my alarms.

I went into the Goodwill and glanced over the store's layout to orient myself.

Racks and racks of used clothes were pretty well organized by size and color. I went over to the men's side and started combing through the shorts. I wasn't a big fan of wild colors, but luckily I found a pair of navy swim trunks close enough to my size to be a little on the baggy side. Last thing I wanted to do was print my junk around the guys and Rebel. I spotted a pair of boots I made a mental note to check on last and went to the pants, scored a black pair, and then went to the shirts. I laughed and thought of Rooster when I found a mechanic work shirt belonging to "Mike" and grabbed that and a black button-down that looked like it ran for an easy fifty dollars new off the rack and hadn't been worn enough to be discarded for two dollars. I added up the total—still under ten bucks, *way* under where I thought I would be with this much. *Damn, I should have been shopping in Goodwill a lot more when I was on my own trying to live off the paycheck of an EMT!*

With a black polo shirt and a few T-shirts added to the pile, I stepped in front of a section of paperback books. I looked through the Westerns, thinking of my grandad, and got a little homesick for the life I would never have back. One stood out to me more than others: the autobiography of Geronimo. Fifty cents and in good condition—how could I turn that down? This book was a part of history and belonged in a collection. Mine!

I thought of how eclectic my library was going to be: John Locke on one side, then the Bible and Geronimo. I was sure to violate the boundaries of social justice just placing such tomes together on the same shelf, much less reading all of them.

I went back and priced the boots. That was going to be the purchase that would nearly break me. I tried them on and liked how they felt, since someone had been gracious enough to break them in for me. The soles had a good tread that didn't slip. So not so much for dancing or even riding a saddle, but more for everyday wear, which was fine. I was pretty certain I couldn't go to any of the clubs around here anyway and doubted I would be able to cowboy again for a very long time, if ever.

I walked out of the store with less than ten bucks to my name. I was pretty sure I could get cheap deodorant, toothbrush, and toothpaste on that. That left me short a razor, which would probably run me as much as the boots had, unless I bought something cheap to peel my face with.

I cringed at that thought as I sat down on the curb where Melissa could see me near her Porsche.

I dug the book out of one of the bags and thumbed it open just in time to hear a very angry buzz of four banger Jap fury in the air. I'd never understood why anyone tried to run huge exhaust pipes on a tiny engine like that, but the answer came dressed in orange stripes over Christmas-tree green paint flecked with enough metal flake to probably add another fifty pounds to the fiberglass skate on the twenty-inch rims coming my way.

I watched them crawl one wheel at a time over a speed bump and park across two spots not far from where I was sitting. Three homies got out of what I thought was a two-seater—no idea where that little guy was crammed at.

Maybe a floorboard?

I had no idea what kind of car it was, but I knew the colors of the gang these three jokers were representing. My buddies from Las Hermanas. And from the way they were dressed in oversized pants and hiking boots, I had no doubt they were concealing machetes down their pants legs stuffed through pockets that had been cut out for quick grabs. This was going to get worse before it got better. Hopefully Melissa wouldn't come out and get in the middle of this.

And seriously? There were over a million and a half people in San Antonio, and God knows how many other places they could have been at. But here they were, and here I was.

I stood up and stepped up as they came ... swaggering? No, this was too comical and effeminate—definitely sashaying, each with one hand on their crotch, making duck lip sneers with their lips and flashing gang signs with their other hands while talking shit. Maybe diplomacy would work to de-escalate this situation?

"The hell is a Diamondback doing on our turf?! You better pack up, vato, and get out of town."

"Your turf? This is San Antonio. Since when did little runts like you lost girls think you owned any turf here?"

"Wrong play, homie. You're new blood, so looks like you're our bitch now, *cabrón*."

"Yeah, I am new here. Where I was at, you Las Hermies couldn't handle me and got destroyed. Now here I am, just a DBMC prospect telling you to mind your manners in public before you three get yourselves in trouble."

"Oh, you going to step up, homie? You're talking a lot and saying nothing!"

"Do you dummies really think this is going to go far before some cop shows up to bust all of us? That really the way you want this to go, right before we all get cuffed, is to feel your teeth being knocked out or swallowed? You know what that will feel like when you try to poop, right? Especially with all that metal on your grill, you're probably going to tear yourself a new one."

"Well, ain't you just funny. Too bad you aren't going to live long enough to see a cop come to the rescue. What's your name, so we can tell your wife where to find your headless corpse?"

Well, I tried diplomacy. Now it was time for pain compliance.

"The name's Bodhi. Y'all want beef? You got it, or you can step off before I break pieces off you for keepsakes."

"Yo, this is the *pinche* that took down Topaz."

"Our lucky day! Let's take his head back to show Chupi."

I was shaking my head in disbelief at the level of brazen stupidity here. Sure enough, a squad car was coming up behind them when they reached into their pockets. Two whipped out machetes, and the third that had been doing most of the talking let them make the first moves just as the police siren squawked and lights came on.

The first two ran for their car while the third ran up and snatched my cap. I let him rather than assaulting him right in front of the cops, hoping they would do their jobs since it was pretty obvious they had witnessed attempted murder and would stop them if I demonstrated no threat. Right?

"You're dead, *pinche gringo*. We are gonna burn your house down and piss on you while you scream!" Gotta appreciate the balls someone has to taunt while running away like their ass is on fire. But seriously, the cops were parking right beside them as he got in threw it in gear and drove off. "Thanks for the hat! We'll be at Seven Sisters if you want to save us the trouble of coming to you."

I managed to close my mouth before a fly came in. The cops did nothing, and when they got out, I knew why. Ok, God was seriously monkeying with the script of my life here. Remember my buddies, Beans and Franks, who were on hand to stop me from stealing the pie I paid for?

"Well, if it isn't our friend from yesterday. Fresh out of prison and trying to duel in public? Looks like your taste of freedom is going to come to an end, my friend," Officer Richardson said after drawing his gun and aiming it at my head. I raised my hands, palms out, without prompting and finally caught his nameplate. Det. Ben Richardson. *Oh, good lord, it really is Beans and Franks.* I did my best to keep my face straight, which was easier than you might think considering how pissed off I was.

"Are you kidding? They pulled machetes on me in public and you let them drive off?"

"Oh, we didn't see that. And all I got here is a gang member that keeps getting into trouble. You need to be kept off the streets, punk. Put your hands on the hood of the car," Franks—excuse me, Det.

Andrew Franklyn said as he came behind me and pushed me toward the hood of their squad car. I was shoved down across the push bumper and my hands came down on a scalding hot hood. I kept my mouth shut and did what I was told.

I was getting patted down top to bottom, inside to outside. When Franks got to my crotch, I got a pat, another pat ... an exploratory squeeze on the inside of my thigh, where I was pretty sure state weapon laws had not codified that particular instrument and where his hands had no business at, and a quick pat elsewhere. I shook my head and rolled my eyes. I bit my tongue before I could fire off one of a dozen comments, figuring that would just get me in more trouble since these idiots would likely take me serious.

"Were you trying to score drugs and the deal went bad?" Richardson asked.

"He's clean," Franks announced.

Yeah, just a little violated. I kept my mouth shut and didn't answer.

"Answer him!" I got slapped on the back of the head. I shut my eyes and took a deep breath. Hopefully tomorrow, I would be enjoying tubes and burgers and beers with babes and laughing at being *manhandled.*

Now you are starting to see what is happening here. There is no justice for the guilty, only oppression against the innocent. But there is more to show you—just keep your peace.

"Excuse me, officers. My husband would like to talk to one of you." Melissa came out of the store, holding her phone out toward both the cops. I turned to look at her, real sorry she was getting dragged into this, and hoped they wouldn't treat her the way they were me.

"Ma'am, you need to stay back. This is a dangerous felon with a record for manslaughter involved in gang activity. We will be taking him into custody and don't have time to talk to your husband."

"I am the one who called 911 because of that gang of punks coming here and trying to threaten us. My husband is this man's attorney and wants to hear why you are harassing this man, who is a victim here, before he talks to your supervisor and hands the film of the incident I took to the press that includes your assault on him."

Richardson walked over, took the phone from Melissa and tersely stated, "There is an obvious misunderstanding and your client is not going to be detained further." He handed the phone back without waiting to hear a reply and walked back to the driver side of the car I was still pressed on. "Let's go get some lunch. We can eat free at the hospital down the street."

It didn't seem like that long ago I probably would have been sitting at the same table with them, eating free hospital food. I stood up and gingerly rubbed my hands against each other.

"I thought I was supposed to watch your back. Thanks, Melissa, that was getting ugly fast."

"Which part, the wusses that wanted to murder you or the clowns that wanted to arrest you?"

"Yeah, the part where I used to be ignorant of this kind of life."

"You poor child. Life must have been so boring for you." She got a smile out of me at that and I started laughing. What the hell, no one was dead and it was a good day.

I put my purchases in the back seat and we got back on the road. Melissa asked about my purchases and what else I needed to get settled in. By the time we made it to the supermarket, I was starting to breathe normally again and my nerves were settling.

Now, let me explain the experience of going to the *local* supermarket in this part of Texas. I have been to other chain markets in North Texas and Oklahoma, and they don't compare. Luckily, this local chain was spreading out and even had one back in Lawton the last time I visited. But what you were in for as far as produce is the next best thing to a farmers market, and here in SA, these stores put "SUPER" into a higher class of its own. This store had a section for electronics, some clothing, and indoor furniture. I was a little taken back; I didn't know these stores had grown so … SUPER, and so crowded. Good lord, the aisles were choked with people.

I had about ten bucks on me and needed around thirty dollars' worth of supplies. And no, the thought of asking Melissa for any kind of loan or help was off the table; it was embarrassing and would shame me. I said nothing and picked up a small box of baking soda, a cheap toothbrush, a cheap comb, and a bag of socks. If I had any money waiting for me with Pappa Gun, then I could go a few days between shaves and make do on the shampoo at the house. Food might be an issue, though, but at least I had lunch waiting for us.

Maybe I could take some leftovers home for dinner since I was going to be on foot for a while?

Melissa looked over the handful of purchases as we cut through the crowds to get to the checkout line, then looked at me while I tried to be busy looking elsewhere. And there was a lot to look at, especially trying to make sure I saw no one who appeared to be a threat.

"Bodhi, you didn't get any food, unless you're going to eat that baking soda. Do you have deodorant and shaving stuff?"

"Oh, ha, yeah … no. The baking soda is to brush my teeth with. I believe Pappa Gun has a little money for me. I figured I would just get what I could with what I had on me and try to hang on till I got another ride into town to get the rest."

"Bodhi, I asked for you to come with me today so I could make sure you got what you needed. You are part of the family now! We knew you didn't come here with everything you needed, and God knows Diesel doesn't know how to keep food around the house. He either goes out to eat or to someone's house for dinners. Now, let's get you some food and whatever else you need to smell and look human, and don't argue or I will tell my husband you gave me a hard time, and he'll have to take you shopping from now on."

"Ack! You aren't leaving me anything to argue with, ma'am."

"I didn't plan on it. That's why Steven is the defender, and I am the persecutor."

"Uh, you mean 'prosecutor'?" I had a feeling she probably meant I would be persecuted if I didn't do what she said.

"I can do that, too." She smirked at me and took me back through the store.

By the time we got out of there, I was done with the shopping experience. I was glad we had perishable goods that needed to go to the fridge, because I wasn't looking forward to going to any more stores crowded with weekend shoppers.

Melissa took me first to Diesel's place and waited in her Porsche while checking her phone. I ran inside and put up the groceries, then took everything else to my room and laid it out on the bed.

First thing I did was rip open the bag of socks, put on a fresh pair, and put on my new boots. The running shoes I had could stay under my bed out of the way for now and would get more use when I was working out. I went back outside without running into Diesel, but I could hear music from his bedroom and his bike was in the driveway, so I knew he was around.

"So how far away does Pappa Gun live from here?" I asked while being very careful to close the door on the Porsche. I had no idea how delicate this thing was and didn't want to find out.

"Oh, he has his house at the far back of this property. The picnic area is halfway. You could walk it, but I'm going there anyway."

I nearly asked if we could stop at the cookout area to see if my book was still laying around, but since I could walk back to where I was staying, I figured it could wait. I had put Melissa out too much already.

"I didn't know Texas had so many palm trees in it."

"Yeah, they are popular down this way and as you get closer to the coast. Everything north and northwest of San Antonio is the Hill Country; you see more oak and cedar in that direction. It isn't fun for allergy sufferers like me, but sure is pretty. We try to head out that way for campouts, and Steven and all the hunters in the MC go deer hunting on property we have when hunting season starts."

We pulled up to a ranch-style home put together with yellow limestone, a tin roof, and an attached two-car garage.

"Do you hunt, Bodhi?"

"I used to, but I doubt I can now with my record and not being allowed near firearms."

"Oh, well, that sucks. What about bow hunting, though? Do they count that against you, too?"

"You know, I don't think anyone ever said no to me, and I never asked. Good question, though. Sure would be nice if I could hunt, if they let me have a license."

"Wow, sure sucks if you can't even go hunting and self-sustain. Good thing you told me that without Steven around; he would get on a soapbox about daring to kill the king's deer."

"Good to know. I like hunting, but I can't argue against trying to limit it. Hunting for food is one thing, but as a sport, it doesn't seem very sporting."

"Oh, Steven is going to enjoy showing off his trophies to you, then," Melissa said with a laugh as we got out of the SUV.

Ok, first of all, I really needed to learn to keep my mouth shut and opinions to myself. Second, it may have had a Porsche name on it, but this was an SUV any soccer mom would love to take shopping. I gingerly closed the door while red dust settled on it from being kicked up as we passed down the road.

I collected as many bags of groceries from the back as I could handle, leaving Melissa with one after I got out of her path and waited for her to lead the way.

"There's my ugly son's pretty wife!" Pappa Gun called as he came out of the door of the house to greet us.

That earned him giggles and hugs.

"Bodhi, come on in and put that stuff on the table. Meli will take care of it while we go into the backyard. I want to show you my hobby."

I followed my orders. Melissa was already putting stuff away as I was led through the dining and living room and through a backyard door.

I stepped into a Japanese tea garden.

I had only seen them in movies and read about them in books, but here Pappa Gun had a koi fish pond laid out with a stream under a short wooden bridge. The trail wound through a landscaped yard that included one area with a large rock in the middle of a bed of sand and a smaller rock nearby. The sand had been carefully manicured so that it had ripples, representing ocean waves beating against the islands of Japan and Okinawa.

"Wow … " A lot of work had gone into this place. There were two other buildings of traditional Japanese architecture set side by side. Pagodas? I wasn't sure of their proper name and felt very ignorant to be looking at so much culture and history and know very little about it.

"King said you knew a little martial arts. I thought you might appreciate this."

I followed Guns along the path. We went to one building and as he pushed open the sliding doors, I tapped on one of the panes in the door to see if it was real rice paper. Frosted glass rang beneath my fingernail.

"No rice paper. I needed something a little more climate controlled for my health. When I was serving, I had a series of heat strokes in the jungle. It didn't bother me much when I was younger, but now at my age, it hurts if I'm in the sun too much or try to sweat."

"Oh, I'm sorry to hear you went through that, but very grateful for your service, sir. I don't know if you heard, my grandad served in the Korean and early Vietnam Wars. He would have loved all this. He was a combatives instructor. Most of what I know came by way of him and what he taught to people that helped me learn." This first building, I wasn't going to think of as a pagoda until I was sure that was the right name for it, and I didn't want to ask and look as stupid as I felt. Pagoda was probably the name of those take-out boxes, but that might get a laugh from Pappa Gun.

Right now I was looking over his collection of bonsai trees lined out on shelves on either side of a Buddha in front of smoking incense. I was about to ask him about being a Christian and having a Buddha when I noticed Pappa Gun was barefoot and the wood floors had a very high-gloss shine.

"Oh, crap, I should have taken off my shoes, sir. I'm sorry!" I quickly sat down to take off my boots. Pappa Guns laughed and waved me down.

"Don't worry about it. These floors are concrete, not wood. This is just stained and lacquered to look like wood."

"What?!" I felt the floor, and the cold stone made my eyes liars. "Wow. This is all amazing. What made you do this in the middle of Texas?"

"Well, I actually reconfirmed my faith in God in a little Buddhist temple when I was stationed in Okinawa."

"You found God through Buddhism? That sounds like a story that belongs in a book. I would sure like to hear some of it if you ever feel like talking about it."

"Yeah, one day I need to sit down and write it all out. But I have a hard time sitting still; I need to be doing something with my hands. But no, I don't think you can rightfully say I found God there. I had already been raised Christian and planned to go into the seminary when my service was up. I was sick to death of death, Bodhi. I went from Vietnam at the end of that mess and was shipped out to jungles in South America to fight drug lords down there. Half of my team was out of action with malaria, and one of my boys had some kind of parasitic worm that got in his eye and ate its way from one eye to the next before we got him to the States. And we were going to villages not really different from what I saw in Southeast Asia.

"We got to this one drug lord's village … and the things he had been doing, Bodhi, it's classified, and even if I gave much of a damn about opsec for something that happened over thirty years ago, I don't want to relive those nightmares. But we Charlie Miked until there were only a few of us that made it out of the original platoon I had been assigned over, and I just didn't see how there could be a God anymore. I believed everything I grew up hearing as a Christian was just a lie we told ourselves to sleep at night."

"Yeah, I can kinda relate to some of that. I didn't grow up with a lot of religion to fall back on, though, so I didn't really see much to make me believe in more than what we see until the last week I was in prison. Now, I know there's more, I just don't know how much."

"Oh? Now that sounds like it should be in a book, too."

"Ha, yeah, or a Hollywood horror film. I was already warned against speaking about it, and to be honest it sounds nuts to try, so it's probably for the best I don't try to write a book about it."

"Ok, now you got me too curious—I love crazy stories. And my pay grade is higher than yours, so debrief, son. What happened?"

"Aww, crap. I need to learn to keep my mouth shut. I never used to get into so many conversations with people, even in prison where all everyone wanted to do was share and express feelings."

Better get used to it. Everyone loves new shiny people to rub on, and you are all kinds of shiny after we had our hands on you.

My inner dialogue was seriously disturbing me now. I was starting to think I was going psychotic. Hearing voices? Check. Do they ask you to kill people?

Be patient. We will get there before you know it.

"Uhh … well … " Mentally deranged, I needed to talk to someone about this, and it was either Pappa Gun or a shrink. I probably need a shrink. So, I said hell with it and didn't hold anything back, starting with how Spider had really died, the demon body-swapping zombie experience, and the seemingly alien thoughts and visions.

"Hmm. Well, I guess you know more about what I went through than both of us thought," Pappa Gun responded cryptically. About then, we both heard the rumble of a V-twin coming down the drive.

"What do you mean, sir?"

"We'll have to talk later. That's my boy and grandkid coming for lunch, and probably to talk to you about the mess you got into with

Melissa this morning. I was hoping to talk to you about that alone first, but I think some things more important were discussed."

"Oh, great. Yeah, basically Las Hermanas already found me. There is trouble brewing, sir."

"Yeah, I see that now. Don't worry, though. Here, let's go inside. I got stuff to show you, and me, you, and Steve can talk while the ladies cook our meal."

We left the tea garden behind and I followed Pappa Gun like a shadow to meet and greet Steven and Rebel.

"I saved your book for you, Bodhi."

Those curls and curves. I made sure I kept my gaze at eye level when I had to answer her, but I seriously needed to train myself not to look at all. "Oh, thank you so much. I didn't get a chance to go back after I realized I didn't get home with it."

"You're just lucky it wasn't a vampire romance novel or you would have had to fight her over it," Steven busted on her. I caught her blush out of the corner of my laugh as I laughed.

"Yeah, prison would have been another experience if I got caught reading books like that."

"Would that put you in She-Hulk whitey-tighties, then?" Melissa added her two pennies.

"Oh, man, if you tell Diesel I told y'all I caught him in his Hulk undies, he is liable to choke me," I said with eyes wide and face serious. Ok, you have to know a little something about first responder humor—pranking and ribbing is part of the bread and butter of being an EMT or fireman. We do it to ourselves and put red Kool-Aid in the shower heads and other such pranks that are borderline felonious on each other. If you aren't being pranked, that meant no one loves you. And we seriously love cops. They make such cute couples with blow-up dolls in their passenger seats when we catch them napping at speed traps.

Obviously, my friends Beans and Franks needed some love, but I hoped I wouldn't see them again.

Steven, Rebel, and Pappa Gun were laughing at the mental picture of Diesel stomping around in Hulk undies when the devil himself pulled up on his bike. Luckily, Pappa Gun had a long dinner table that could fit all of us.

"Let's go to the garage. I want to give Bodhi his gear and give you ladies room to cook," Pappa Gun announced.

Guns stepped into his garage and flipped a few switches. The automatic door started rising and the lights came on. Pappa Gun had a couple of nice vehicles anyone with any taste would give body parts to have. The first to catch my eye was a Chevelle. I wasn't sure on the year, but it appeared to be a '70. I wondered if the short-bed Chevy truck was the same year. Both were golden brown with black race stripes.

"Wow."

"You've been saying that a lot since you got here, Bodhi."

"I admire your taste, sir. A seventy Chevelle?"

"Yup, just a little modified. A 454 with a race shifter. All engine, none of that nitrous crap or superchargers. Same year and setup with the truck, too."

"Wow."

"And I got you a backpack for your gear. There is a disposable drop phone inside with the numbers programed for me, Steve, and Diesel.

I unzipped the muddy-brown backpack. It felt pretty nice and looked military-issue with no brand labels on it. Inside, the spacious main compartment was a brown sack. I pulled it out and looked inside to find the phone and a stack of money.

"Oh, this is nice—I appreciate the backpack. I can put my books in it and keep them safe."

"Yeah, well, since you're inheriting Spider's bike, you'll probably need it if you go shopping or anything."

"Uh, what?" *Did he say I'm getting a bike?*

"His family wanted you to have it for what you did. It's parked on the other side of the truck behind my bike."

I went around the truck. If I wasn't already feeling a little dizzy before, I knew I would now. This was too much, and I had not even counted out the money the Tribe had given me for taking down Topaz.

"You sure we can let him have it? He can't even stop skank punks from taking his colors," Diesel finally chimed in.

"News sure travels fast around here, huh?" I observed dryly and looked at him. Truth was, I didn't know how to accept the bike as a gift and was about to say so.

"It's club business, so yeah, the VP knew to spread it around."

"Oh, that's good to know. I was feeling guilty about telling everyone about seeing you in your undies this morning."

"You think you're a smart-ass? Get serious, you let those punks push you around and dropped your colors."

"Are you kidding me?" I looked from Pappa Gun to Steven before asking, "Can I tell the Incredible Hulk, or do you want to?"

"You can if you want to. I was curious how you would handle this."

"Thanks, I prefer taking care of my own business before unloading it on someone else." Steven raised his hands in compliance and leaned back against the front fender of the truck.

"First of all, I let him have your hat without a fight because the cops were already on scene. I expected them to actually do their jobs, but they didn't. As it is, if I stomped them, I would now be in jail and Steven would be dealing with that headache."

"That don't matter. They pulled machetes on you and took your colors! You should have taken care of business first thing and put them down if you weren't chickenshit."

"That the way you want it handled?" I asked, looking at Steven and Pappa Gun.

"You do have a right to defend yourself, always. And I am ready to take that to court if I have to," Steven gave me a mild chastising.

"Really?" I was mildly shocked, after all the talk about not getting in trouble and keeping things legit.

"I still haven't seen the video or heard what all happened, so I don't have an informed opinion yet like these two," Pappa Gun responded.

"It doesn't matter. He dropped the flag to scraggly beaners over a hat. And you want to trust him with Spider's bike and to watch out for our families?" Diesel was sticking his finger in my face at this point, and I was trying to remember why I wasn't breaking it off and feeding it to him.

"Here you go, Pops." Steven had a big smartphone out with a video of the episode. I knew there would be no sound, but I hoped the picture should say a thousand words.

"Nah, not with those dickheads right there. Bodhi did right by turning the cheek. Issue settled," Guns announced after watching the whole thing.

"Oh, come on, Pop! This is Texas law, not Bible law."

"See, Bodhi? They want a prez until they don't want a prez. They want to be legit until they don't want to be legit."

Oh crap, I could see this opened up a standing argument. *And I'm caught in the middle on this.*

"Oh, come on, Pop, you know it isn't like that. But we can't let these assclowns push us around! They're already trying to cut into our remodeling business by stealing our customers from under us."

"Bodhi, what would have happened if you fought them?"

"It wouldn't have been much of a fight. Bones would have broken, blood would have spilled, and I'm sure the cops would have been caught in the middle. And as stupid as those two are, all four of us may have been shot in the back in self-defense."

Steven actually nodded his head, conceding that last point.

"Oh, whatever, tough guy. I swatted you down last night without breaking a sweat and had you kissing my ass. You would have cried and run away if the cops weren't there to save you."

Ok, I'd had enough lip. I turned to square up on Diesel but got cut off by the prez.

"You did what?" Pappa Gun put his hand on my chest and pushed me back.

"I put him in his place for sucker punching me last night. He deserved it."

"Is that true, Bodhi?"

"Yeah, when we were going back to his place last night. It happened before I could apologize, so I felt I owed him one."

"Wait, you *let* this lug hit you?"

"*Let* me? He couldn't stop me if he wanted."

"Ok, Diesel, I have to admit my first impression of you was pretty high. I mean, you're like a ten when it comes to looks and appearance. But the more you open your mouth, the lower your score goes for being a dumbass. You want to dance with me, then let's—"

"Both of you, shut up, or I will kick all of your asses!" Pappa Gun's voice cracked through the garage.

Steve's eyes were wide and his mouth hung open at that. Diesel looked embarrassed and shamefaced. I chilled, but I really wanted to bang my knuckles on his face.

"Nathan, next time you hit Bodhi and he doesn't kick your ass,

I will. Bodhi, Nathan may be a dumb brute, but he is your brother. And I expect you to both act like brothers and always have each other's backs, no matter what the play is."

"Yes, sir," I answered automatically, Diesel right behind me. We traded looks at each other. I wasn't sure what he was thinking, but I knew I would have to teach him respect. Guys like Nathan "Call Me Diesel Because I Want to Be That Much More Cool" Briggs didn't give respect until it was impressed into them, usually by pressing their face into the dirt while stomping a mudhole in them and walking it dry. But out of respect for Pappa Gun and the club, and how much everyone was doing for me, I would bend over as far backwards as I could and let him be the one to make the first move.

"Alright, then. Men will stay here and shake hands. Boys will go inside and set at the table while the mommas feed them. Come on, boy," Guns said as he reached out to Steve, clamping a hand down on his shoulder and dragging him off.

"Aww, do we have to?"

Watching the father and son joke with each other helped me relax a bit. This was a true family, even with people that weren't bonded by blood, opening their arms to welcome me, and I was causing nothing but grief for it. I needed to do better. I *would* do better.

"You know," I started first after Poppa Guns and his son left us there alone, "I'm not afraid of a fight. Never was and I don't think I ever will be, even if I get my ass kicked or worse. But I am afraid of letting people down and making their life worse because I couldn't see the big picture."

"Well, that probably was harsh for me to say what I did," he said after chewing over what I said. "Since this is your first real day of being free, I can see why you did what you did this time. But you are going to have to step up from now on and not drop any flags."

"You think I dropped the flag, huh?"

"Where's my hat?" he retorted.

"Probably getting STDs by now. Want me to get you another one?"

"Dude, I don't give a crap about the hat. It's the principle of it."

"Yup, I see that it is, and I won't forget it."

"As long as you do, we should have no problems." He stuck his hand out. I shook, and we went in some type of peace to have a good meal and visit with family.

CHAPTER 25

After lunch, Steve and his wife took off on his bike, leaving Rebel to clean up after everyone. Diesel took off, but I hung around because I really had nowhere else to go, and I wanted to get situated with Pappa Gun and see more of his Tea Garden.

"Oh, boy, that was a good lunch. Bodhi, it sounds like you had a hell of a day already. I hope we can keep you out of trouble. I like having you around to keep Diesel on his toes."

"I don't think I've done that yet. But I sure feel like I am causing more trouble than I'm worth."

"I don't want to hear that nonsense," he said with a wave of his hand. "I saw Diesel try to push you around at dinner last night. You shouldn't have clobbered him, but he shouldn't have tested you after what King already told us about you. And today, I think you did the right thing. The law was out of line, but my boy is going to do something about that, if I know him."

"Yeah, my lucky day. It just so happened to be the same two jackasses that harassed me yesterday on my way here with Rooster. I need to buy a lottery ticket."

"Well, life is kinda funny like that. I don't believe in coincidences at all. I used to, but not after what I experienced when I was in South America and then coming back to God in front of a statue of Buddha. That anyone wants to try to claim creation happened out of random coincidence, perfectly, is madness to me. But if makes them happy to believe their life is without meaning, far be it from me to take away their bliss."

"Yeah, I still want to hear some of that. How do you get to God from Buddha?"

"Well, in the first place, I don't really consider Buddhism as a religion and more of a lifestyle of discipline. If it is a religion, it is an atheistic one since they believe in no god at all. But I never bought that lie. I always believed there was a God, but never felt sure I was … facing the right direction to see Him, I guess you could say. Do Baptists go to the same place Catholics do, for example, was a question that worried at me. I just needed a quiet place when I came to that temple. I watched those monks for a few days and started spending all my free time there. They taught me how to meditate and fast, which all conforms to Judeo-Christian teaching. I had run my wife off by that time, and really had nothing left except my service to my country keeping me going while I sent her all the money I could from my paychecks to take care of her and Steven, who was a young boy at that time. I remember I wanted more than anything to be the man I needed to be for him to have a good father.

"See, from Vietnam to South America, I cheated on my wife while she was left behind to raise our boy. I couldn't tell you how many prostitutes I had been with. But I got sent home on leave and gave my wife an STD I had. Man, I can't tell you how humiliated and ashamed I was when she confronted me. When I was overseas in combat, I thought I was hot shit, cock of the walk, alpha to the corps, heartbreaker, and a life taker. Even when I was pretending to be a Christian and act like a chaplain whenever it was needed. I knew the words to say when I was asked, but I guess somewhere along the way I'd convinced myself it wasn't really that important to walk what you talk. Nobody's perfect, right? But that is what the most important thing for any man of God? To be the example, not the excuse."

We were standing near the Buddha in the … pagoda … thing—I seriously needed to ask what the name of this kind of building was, but I figured it could wait. I had learned a long time ago when someone opened up to show you their soul, sometimes saying anything to them was not needed and seldom wanted, so if you cut in, it better be with something important and helpful. I kept my mouth shut, ears open, and eyes on his while he taught me lessons from his life.

"She left me, and I didn't fight it. Whatever I had is probably what gave me prostate cancer, and that had to be removed. That was the last time I have ever been with a woman. She remarried a good man and moved on with her life. So, there I was in Japan, and I think it was the winter of eighty-six or eighty-seven. My life was a blur of depression in those days, but I remember Texas had the most snow anyone remembers that year I found God again."

"Can you tell me what happened when you found Him?"

"Some of it, yes. But you need to know the most important part. The most important part is not my personal experience. Everyone will hopefully have their own, and from what I can tell, I think He is knocking on your door to be let in. And that is what is important:

to know that there is a true God who wants a personal and direct relationship with you with nothing getting in the way, especially your own self. But for everyone else who doesn't want to believe in that kind of transcendence, you are crazy. Especially if you tell them about hearing voices and body-snatching demons.

"So, this is what I'll tell you about what happened to me. Somewhere between Texas and Antarctica, there has been at least one place where true evil was witnessed. The people there were enslaved by it since after World War Two and offered the lives of their own children in sacrifice to it. Torture, experimentation, and worse and more that defies all imagination and horror happened there. So when you tell me how Spider really died, yeah, I can confirm that it is real. Now, as to your voices and visions, I can't confirm what's in your head or heart. But I know from reading the Bible that such things were extremely common in the Old Testament, and somewhat spoken of in the new also. You being part Indian, too, you probably have heard of such things in the history of your ancestors and ceremonies."

"Ok, so how do I know what the truth is in all of that?"

"What, like are you going psychotic? Or if it's an Indian thing, or a Christian thing?"

"Exactly." I nodded and waited for him to tell me the magic answer to the riddle I was facing.

"Bible says to test everything," he answered with a shrug. "I didn't need much convincing after what I experienced in that temple. I knew God was real, and I remember the scripture where Jesus quoted the law 'Thou shalt not tempt the Lord your God.' I didn't push my luck any further after that day. I got back in line, and I started following the commands of Jesus to give love and mercy to everyone. That is what I want for this club—a place to give people that second chance to get on the right path. I learned being a man is about more than your anatomy. It's about honor. No one can take that from you by cutting off a piece of you, but you can sure throw it away when you don't treat it with respect."

"Yes, sir. That was something I learned pretty quick in prison. There were a lot of people there who all had some history as a sex offender to one degree or another. Some of it was harmless, but it dragged them down the rest of their life. Others definitely went too far, and they were reminded of it every day in every way you don't want to know in prison. I learned in that environment, the best way to get by was with cold showers, lots of cardio, and weight lifting, and to abstain, abstain, abstain from thoughts, pictures, books, anything that made you want—" And of course Rebel came out about that time. Luckily, I saw the door open and was at a good stopping point anyway.

"Ah, well that explains why you look as jacked as you do. Being locked away and abstaining for over five years increased your testosterone. Don't worry, though, we will get you into church and find you a good woman to take care of you," he said, without a care in the world, right in front of Rebel. I wasn't sure what color red I was, but it was made worse by her raising a brow.

"Is that the only reason single men go to churches, Pop?"

"Of course it is! Where else do you expect men to find someone that will overfeed them and turn them into nice guys like your daddy?" Pappa Gun teased with a laugh and hugged his granddaughter. "You just do your part, and don't let any single men pick you up at church. That way, everyone stays honest and keeps going back."

"So where am I supposed to find mine, then?" Rebel asked, acting coy. I was starting to get uncomfortable.

"Your daddy and me will find you one. The rest of my boys in the MC will put the fear of God in everyone else that chases you." Pappa Gun was laughing and kissing the top of her head. His smile was infectious; it was hard to believe this man had ever done wrong by his family in any way. "You gonna leave me all by myself?"

"You have Bodhi here to keep you honest. I just wanted to see if he was going to be able to go tubin' with us tomorrow or if he was busy."

"Oh, I'm still not sure yet. I would like to, but if I can find work, I better make sure I'm able to take care of that first. What time are y'all going tomorrow?"

"I'll make sure he goes, hon." Pappa Gun became my favorite person in the whole world at that moment. "You make sure you drive that Porsche thing of your momma's safe, now, you hear? And wear your seatbelt."

"Yes, sir." She gave him a hug, then turned to me with a smile. "Looks like we'll see you here tomorrow at two."

"Thanks for the invite. I'm looking forward to it already." I returned the smile and watched her leave. This all still didn't feel real to me. Yesterday morning, I had started my day off inside a prison cell; tomorrow, I was going to be enjoying Texas rivers around a bunch of very cool people. And oh yeah—I got a motorcycle to run around on and backpack full of cash!

"You like my granddaughter, Bodhi?"

"I like all of you, sir. Even Diesel isn't a bad person. Maybe not so bright, but I see his heart is in the right place for the club."

"Eh, I really don't much care for all the club jargon, to be honest. In my mind this is a clan, not a club. Most of us may have different last names, and we may not be blood kin, but we are family. This nonsense with colors, kuttes, patches, ranks, and turf is all fodder for ego. I used to be into that back when I was younger. I hung around a lot of rough people and knew some rough ways. I don't want people to experience the consequences I went through to be where I am today. If that's what they want, then maybe I can be there to put them back together when they've had enough, but for anyone that wants to learn how to be a better man, there is a much easier way without all the scar tissue I have on me."

"I'm trying to figure out the easy way, if you mean God. But it sure don't seem easy, like today. I'm pretty tangled up right now on this 'turn the other cheek, do unto others, give someone that stole my coat my shirt, too' part. I always tried to help people when I could, but what do you do when a gangbanging Satanist comes after your heart and soul?"

"Oh, you need self-defense lessons? I can teach you a few things," Pappa Gun said in surprise.

"No, I don't mean—" I said in exasperation as he started chuckling and waved a hand to cut me off.

"First, let me ask you this. If you saw those three jackasses attack Melissa, would you tell her to turn the other cheek, or would you throw them a beating?"

"Without hesitating ... but?"

"As far as the Bible goes and what Christ was teaching, you have to look at the entire context of the Bible. Jesus was proving that following Mosaic law by itself doesn't make you a good person—that it's what is in your heart that matters. That if you think you are good because someone did you wrong, and you let the law repay them tooth for tooth, well, you aren't as good a person on the inside as someone that"—he looked me in the eyes and thumped me on the chest—"forgives the debt. But you look later on and Jesus also said, 'If you have no sword, sell your cloak and buy one.' So in situations where it comes time to protect and be the peacemaker, you do what you know is the right thing to do. And letting people hurt others, even yourself, is never right."

"And if the law happens to be standing right there?"

"Use good common sense, like you did. If you didn't, then like you said, either the cops would have shot you or we would be trying to get your butt out of jail. I'm thankful you have a better temper than Nathan. I would probably tell Steven to let him cool down in county for a few days."

"So I take it that isn't just for decoration with you?" I gestured to his chained billy club on his waist.

"This?" He unsnapped the leather band and held it up. "This is my compliance appliance for catching stray dogs for a friend of mine that runs a rescue shelter."

"Oh, so you don't use it on people, then?" Of course, I had intentionally baited my own trap and walked into it with a smile and was not disappointed.

Pappa Gun had been holding the club in his hand so the chain was held in an open noose in the lower two fingers of his hand. If being old enough to be my young granddad had slowed him down any, it would have been scary to meet him at my age. He had the noose around my wrist and put a foot down on the inside of my knee, taking me to the ground, and was behind me in a flash, using my own arm to give myself a rear naked choke with a knee behind my back. When I reached up with my free hand to gain space around my neck to keep from passing out, he jammed a thumb into my armpit with just enough pressure to let me know what a pickle I would be in if we were going full speed and I let myself get in such a position.

"Uncle! Uncle!" I let out quick before I started giggling. Yes, I'm sometimes ticklish—sue me.

"I expected a little more fight from you from what King had said." Pappa Gun laughed and released me.

"Ehh, I already know what I can do," I said as I got back to my feet. "I wanted to see what you could teach me. I like the way you use it, but I don't think I could get away with carrying that the way you do. A cop wouldn't think twice before running me in for an illegal weapon, even with a cover story."

"Yeah, there is a reason why we're cop-friendly when we can be. There are some that have bad attitudes, no doubt. But I wouldn't care if there was nine bad for every one good. That one good one is gold, in my book, and worth giving everything to help." Hearing Pappa Gun say that reminded me of Ranger Huntsman. that man was definitely in a class of his own. "But this definitely has more than one trick in it, for me at least. I studied a little Japanese jujitsu and Filipino martial arts when I was bouncing around in the Pacific."

I'd had very little exposure to Filipino martial arts and asked him if he could show me a little. He turned out to be a better teacher than I was a student and taught me how to use his compliance appliance, which I decided to start calling a "choke stick."

What he showed me in the first lessons was how every attack flowed into the motion of the next hit at angles. It was all another tool to add to the box, and as far as using it with the choke stick, it turned me into a human buzz saw once I got it down. After that, he brought out two escrima sticks and taught me a few *sinawali* drills. Even as I got better at it, I didn't particularly care for all of it as a style. It seemed to depend too much on attacking in a set pattern, although some of the sinawali was too easy to not use if I ever picked up a pair of sticks to whack someone around with.

"You're clumsy out of the gate, but you learn very fast, and I see you don't repeat mistakes. Very good."

I noticed Pappa was breaking a sweat and wasn't complaining, but I remembered what he said about having problems with the heat and called for a water break. I expressed the need to use his restroom so he wouldn't take it personally.

He met me with a stainless bottle full of chilled water after I came out of the bathroom. I noticed the logo of a remodeling company on the bottle and asked if that was his, and that led to him making me a job offer if I wanted to work for the club. The terms seemed fair—as long as I was living on his property and eating under his roof, I was a salaried employee. And in between remodeling jobs, I could help out with odd jobs between his friend's dog rescue or whatever work

I could do on the side for myself.

"We're all caught up on business for the moment, though. We had a job lined up with this old motel out at Seven Sisters, but a new commercial developer came in and took it from the owners and have their own people fixing it up."

"Seven Sisters? Is that like a subdivision or something?" My short hairs were standing on end. I wasn't going to mention the threat from the gangbangers, but too much was lining up into a pattern around for me to think it was a coincidence.

"Not exactly. It's a recently renamed offshoot of a road from old Highway Ninety on the east side. They're talking about opening up some new manufacturing not far from there and cutting new roads. That old motel may be on a gold mine if it all goes through, and it probably will, as big as San Antonio is trying to grow. Anyone with a mountain of money and any good sense is buying up all the empty land they can right now."

I took a deep breath and started thinking about everything I had been through in the last week leading up to today.

All at once, I envisioned *a German shepherd, pestilential green foam continuously flowing from its gaping maw while it herded sheep far away and beneath me in a green fertile land. Where the virulent saliva landed, the ground withered and the grass blew away as ash on the breeze. At the command of its master, a man in robes holding a staff with his face turned from me as he tended the flock before him, it mauled one of the ewes, pulling it down and tearing open the flank of the sheep in a viciously senseless attack. The muzzle of the dog thrashed and tore through the snow-white spotless fleece until it was bloodied and the sheep was bawling. All the other sheep milled around, only one coming near, and yet did nothing to protect one of their own. Finally, the master called to the dog and it heeled, coming to the man and getting petted and scratched behind the ears for being obedient and faithful to the master, who was laughing. The lame sheep was left on its side, dirt and blood staining its once pure-white fleece. I felt rage well in my chest, expanding my lungs in a shrill battle cry that pierced the tableau below as I swooped down. The land must be defended, innocence must be guarded, justice must be done! My vision focused through the wind rushing across my visage, intent only upon the diseased predator. It had spread its suffering enough.*

"Hey, where did you go?"

"I don't know yet," I answered with a trace of a laugh to hide my own confusion. "It happened again, though. I don't know if it's bullshit or not. If it is, then it's a hell of a daydream that I could make into an art rendering, but if it is real, I don't know how … "

To be honest, I was a little scared, whether or not it was real. Was this what psychiatry called a hallucination? That didn't feel right, because this was obviously just my own inner imagination working. Everyone daydreams, right? But in such a vivid manner that takes you away from your present environment … ?

I had a million and one questions, but at the moment, I was actually feeling pretty clearheaded for once today. I took a deep breath, and even inside the house of my host, I could smell weather trying to build, the first hint of rain being carried across the land.

"Bodhi, do you mind telling me what you saw? I give you my word I won't judge you."

I looked at him and decided to go for broke. I had been running without any landmarks to navigate by for so long, just doing my best to do what was right without knowing for certain what the meaning of "right" really was. But this man seemed to be one of the few men I believed had a good understanding of it, and maybe I could hang on to that until I understood it better for myself and made it mine too.

I told him of my vision, and then I told him what I believed it all meant. Saying it out loud made it sound like describing a fantasy of a pipe dream through a hall of mirrors.

"Well, I don't think there's any harm at all in going down there to check it out."

Did I ever mention how much I love that phrase?

CHAPTER 26

Spider's brown leather chaps fit me nearly as well as his hog. It had started life as a Dyna, but it got a little rake to the forks to stretch out the front wheel and give it a wider rear wheel, and it now had a V-twin power plant that had been to a machine shop for a few aftermarket parts and machining. I had to be careful not to shred pavement when I dropped the clutch. The idle of the bike thundered from the pipes and begged for the hammer to fall.

I had Spider's brain catcher strapped to my head, goggles on, and stuffed my rolled backpack into one of the saddlebags, enjoying the Texas summer air across my face.

Pappa Gun was ahead and on my left by a bike length, and we ate the road into town. I don't think I remember grinning so much since my early days running lights and sirens through the blood and tears.

The years of being stuffed behind concrete and bars, packed with offenders of society, all poured away as we rode. I had been locked in my own head for most of those years, escape from my environment only coming from pain-filled memories and daydreams of guilt.

I climbed through the gears and kept in tune with the traffic around us, but we stayed agile and hostile around the rolling cages that lumbered at a snail's pace around us. In the meantime, I was keeping track of landmarks and road names. I knew a little about San Antonio, but I had a decent memory for figuring our city layouts from having to memorize neighborhoods and hospitals in the cities I had worked in as a medic.

We finally took an exit somewhere in the middle of town for Texas Highway 90 East, then another exit, and finally we turned under the bridge, following the signs to Old Highway 90.

"Your first day in town, we should be going downtown to the Riverwalk or up north to the Hill Country for a ride! This is a seedy side of town we are going to. Won't be no fun," Pappa Gun learned over to shout in my ear at a red light before it went green. We took off with no reply from me.

I was good; there would be time to play when the work was done. Hopefully, we would get to Seven Sisters and find out these daydreams were just my imagination trying to inspire my artistic talents.

Not that I had forgotten my three amigos from Las Hermanas. They had said that was where to find them. We had a good chance of finding a little trouble from them alone, but the question was how many of their friends would be along for the ride, and how ugly would this get if I was actually playing with a full deck. Granted, my deck seemed to be all wild cards lately.

Eventually we went far enough east that businesses began to spread further apart, and traffic wasn't much of an issue. We had gone several miles between red lights when Pappa Gun took a turn on a chewed-up road full of potholes and misery. I never would have spotted the side of the building facing the highway as part of the motel until we turned down the road. The grass was overgrown, the curbs had crumbled, and the fences were dilapidated. There was nothing on this road except the old motel, its signs torn down and its facade covered in construction black plastic. The road we were on continued into an industrial park.

Work trucks, cargo vans, and personal vehicles cluttered around where the main office was, crowding the horseshoe parking area around an empty swimming pool. Luckily, no activity was outside, and sure enough, one car stood out. I'd never liked those little foreign sports cars, especially when someone shoved an oversize tailpipe up its rear, making it an offense to the eyes and ears.

We cruised by without seeming to draw attention and continued into the industrial park. I followed my prez as we turned down another road, taking us out of sight around a long manufacturing building. Everything appeared closed for the day with no traffic and no vehicles parked anywhere else. After we got out of sight, Pappa Gun found a spot in the shade of a building for us to park and turn off the bikes.

"They're here," I said after the last echo faded. I was craving a smoke for the first time since prison. I took a deep breath instead and flexed the muscles from my neck and shoulders to my upper back.

"What do you think we'll find there?"

"Maybe Diesel's hat. Definitely trouble, if we stop by to see if they have any coffee."

"We can go back home and forget this, if you want."

"Yeah, that would be the smart thing," I said, really wishing I had a smoke now. "But I don't think they're going to let me go that easy. And if they can do what they did in prison out here, someone is going to get in a world of hurt. So I'm going to stop by there, see if they come out shooting or poke their heads out and are willing to talk. Maybe we can settle this without anyone else getting hurt. I'm willing to give them that backpack full of cash if they leave us alone."

"Maybe that will work." He appeared to be in thought. "How do you want to play this?"

"I'm thinking we ride in, sit on our bikes to see who comes out and if they'll talk. If they come out and make any moves for guns, we get the hell out of dodge. If they'll talk, I'll get off and talk to them. You stay on your bike, ready to run for the cavalry if they get nasty."

"Hmm, well, we can see if it goes that way," he said before sweeping his vest to the side to show a 1911 holstered with the hammer back at his right side. "But I don't plan to just run off and leave you behind, so you make sure you're ready to keep up with this old man if this goes sideways."

Before I could voice any concerns, he had already started his bike and had a grin on his face.

I knew this wasn't smart, but I figured the odds of Las Hermanas shooting at us on sight, if they had any guns, were small. They would know we would just go straight to the police and turn them in.

I led the way back and came around a corner to see a stretch hummer limo had parked. A driver was opening the rear most door of the thirty-some-odd-foot-long vehicle and a very elegantly dressed Hispanic lady was stepping out. Oh, now *this* was going to be interesting. *The odds of a violent outcome just evaporated.*

The entourage was walking around the back of the limo toward the office of the motel when we pulled up to a crowd. We sat on our bikes, letting the engines do the talking while hostile faces glared at me. I was pretty sure Pappa Gun wasn't getting any heat. Almost two dozen people were there, most of them in work clothes except for the lady in charge, a young girl with her dressed in a similar dark dress, and her driver, who was pulling double as her guard.

The three punks from this morning were grinning big, getting excited.

I shut off the bike and kicked the stand down before climbing off and facing all of them, picking out the shot-caller that was just coming out of the office.

"May we help you?" the lady asked me with a slow smile. Her long dark hair framed her face and poured over her shoulders with blue highlights, her eyebrows, her nails, and her skin all carefully pampered and trimmed to perfection. She had come from champagne and caviar on high, down to cow patty earth.

"I was invited by those three dummies."

"Oh, you must be the famous Bodhi they told me of." This was from the shot-caller. He was wearing orange ostrich boots that were probably worth as much as my bike, per boot. His slacks and shirt weren't off the rack, and his watch was probably the real deal too. But the face—that was all comic book villain. Tattoos adorned every bare inch of his head devoid of a single follicle of hair. "I'm Chupi."

"They mentioned you. Said you would like my face around here. If I had known you wanted to see me, I would have stopped by when I had time. As it was, those idiots nearly got us all put in jail."

"Oh, I sincerely doubt that my employees would have done anything to go to jail over. We have a very good relationship with all of the local law enforcement in the area." The lady surprised me by stepping up to confront me.

"That's good to hear, ma'am. The machetes they pulled out with the death threats right in front of the cops had me worried they were mentally impaired and unemployable. Our welfare state suffers enough without idiots like that dragging down the system."

"You have a very intriguing aura … Bodhi?" she asked as she sashayed closer to me. I held my ground, but got a little creeped when she reached up to run the backs of her knuckles down the side of my face. "An interesting name, too. It means 'the enlightened one,' and you do not appear to be too *estupido*. I am Contessa Serena."

"No, I try not to be that stupid. I came to see if we could act like adults and settle differences so no one has to worry about winding up back in jail, or worse. Jail sucks—I would rather not go there. Hospitals suck—I would rather not send anyone else there, either. I know I've pissed off some people, but I don't know if you're a part of that world."

"Tell me, Mr. Bodhi, do you walk the path of the left hand?"

"I saw enough of it to try to avoid it. I want to stay out of trouble, ma'am." I kept my emotions in check and stayed relaxed, my eyes unfocused as I faced her, keeping as much of my attention as I was able on the thugs behind her.

"So polite, too." The Contessa demurred and cocked a hip as she stepped back a pace, obviously considering me the way a buyer might consider stock for breeding, or for hamburger meat. "Chupi, darling, why would your little flock trouble such a delicious morsel as this and not recruit him into the family?"

"Obviously eager to please without any restraint, Contessa Serena." Under all that ink was a working brain, and it was homed in on me with the gaze and intelligence of a predator, not a scavenger the way his underlings leered at me.

"Do not be offended in what I say to you, Mr. Bodhi, but you have a very peculiar aura, unlike any I have seen before. I am not sure what to make of it, but may I be so bold as to make you an offer?"

"I didn't come here to fight, or for war, but to seek peace. I actually came here to make an offer myself," I said after taking a moment to carefully choose my words. Judging by the smile I got in reaction, I was advancing on somewhat better than thin ice.

"Consider a position … under me. You have hidden talents that should be explored and encouraged. I would hate to see them wasted for naught. Of course, I would tempt you with materialistic means— wealth, women—but I can see enough to know that you are not impressed with materialistic comforts, which, of course, are enjoyed by any under my employ. You have a hidden potential that should be explored and defined. And that is what I wish to bring out in you, should you accept."

"Do you want an immediate answer from me?"

"I would not expect one for such a level of commitment from you that I desire. Consider it a standing invitation."

"That is good, because I came here to attempt to settle business and accounts. I would hate to give an answer to you when the balance is tipped in your favor. I might mistake your sincerity for an attempt at extorting me."

"Interesting. In spite of your Southern drawl, I see a sharp intellect at work. What is it you would like settled before you could seriously consider my offer?"

"First of all, members of Las Hermanas have started serious beef with me and the Diamondbacks. One of our family has been killed, and several have been attacked. And it appears y'all have a green light on me, the way those three dummies acted this morning and from what another banger bragged about in prison."

"Are you asking to execute one of our people as payment for the debt?" she asked with a brow raised.

"No," I said after considering her reply. I decided to push a little and see how far I could go. "But the least I am owed is my hat back by those three. We can go from there."

"Hey, pinche gringo," the one who had taken Diesel's hat and threatened me said, "we pissed all over your hat and threw it away. You want anything from us, you can start by taking this first." Predictably, he started grabbing his crotch.

"Stop making me laugh. I never saw anything there a Las Hermanas had to give, much less take. Just keep your mouth shut while the adults talk, Spanky."

"We can call off the hit, and order a cease-fire if there are any open hostilities against your organization. As to the blood debt for the dead, we can offer a wergild depending on how much Mr. Gunther Womack, your *presidente,* deems fair?" She started raising her voice and looking over my shoulder, surprising me by knowing who Pappa Gun was. I had never heard "wergild" before—it sounded very old, and the way she used it, I knew what she meant anyway. Hey, just because I had a GED didn't mean I wasn't smart—I read a book a time or two. Ok, I tended to be a bookworm, in fact, but don't let that get out.

"We're fine without your money," Pappa Gun replied evenly. I kept my face without expression. There are some things money can't buy, and I figured that was why I respected the man as much as I did and never would be able to live with myself if I went with these people.

"So there you are. What more can we offer you to settle accounts besides a hat?"

"You know, I'm pretty happy with the hit being called off, and the cease-fire and the offer you made. But that guy," I said and pointed at Spanky, "he came at me this morning and took from me. Granted, I let him, so I guess some people might say that's my fault for letting him have it. But I think I need a very sincere and heartfelt apology from him for what he did."

He started spewing vulgarities at me in Spanish and reached into the waistband of his baggy pants, pulling a Glock out and stepping forward as he lifted it high and turned it to the side to try to get an angle for a shot at me.

That was what he tried, at least. What he did was hand me his pistol with his finger trapped in the guard for me to nearly snap off as I brought him down to his knees and gave a twist and a yank and raked the guard from his mangled finger, sending a rising knee into his chin with a lunge as he started. It is a little-known medical fact that a human finger is not meant to bend in that direction without experiencing discomfort, and my knee crashing into his jaw shut him up before he could compliment my technique.

I gave the gun a blind toss over my shoulder behind me to Pappa Gun. Spanky was stretched out cold and I stepped up and to the side, placing the Contessa at my back in line with Pappa, who had caught the Glock about the time Spanky was using broken pavement for a pillow. Pappa Gun pulled out his 1911 just as every member of Las Hermanas pulled out machetes, knives, Glocks, and kitchen sinks to try to use on me.

I was face-to-face with Chupi while his boys were reaching and grabbing for their weapons, and that little girl was looking at me with the eyes of a doll. I don't mean big, wide-eyed innocence, either. The line from *Jaws* where that old sailor was talking about a shark's eyes fit about right—no signs of life or innocence.

Chupi was raising his hands in the air and screaming for everyone to stop in every language he knew.

I glanced from Chupi to the girl and back, turning my face to the side with a near smile as I watched him for his next move and kept the Contessa between me and Pappa Gun. I kept my arms spread wide, hands open, and appeared to shield her while posturing for peace. She probably thought I was being foolishly gallant. Pappa Gun had an open field of fire around her, and all I had to do was jump to the side and she would be killed by her own people if this dance started.

"If your people start shooting, I may not be able to accept your offer," I said over my shoulder.

"We wouldn't want that, now, would we?" she answered, placing a hand on my shoulder and stroking my neck as she came around me like a tango dancer. "And I owe you for protecting me. Such a gentleman as you are is certainly rare," she added as everyone lowered their weapons.

"I think we should leave before we have any more

misunderstandings. I'm glad I didn't ask for a kiss after that reaction," I said with a devil-may-care smile.

"Maybe I owe you more than that," she breathed as she leaned in. Her breath smelled, but I didn't let it show. I just stepped back and kept my eyes on her for a moment before glancing back at Chupi and backed up to my bike. Spanky started moaning from the ground.

"I would say a Glock for a hat is a good trade. Tell Spanky thanks for the dance when he wakes up." I mounted up and Pappa Gun shoved the Glock into his pants, keeping the 1911 casually covering all of them, and started his bike right before I started mine.

"I'll talk to Chupi if I take your offer."

"Try not to keep me waiting, Mr. Bodhi."

"I'd hate to be a disappointment." I dropped the clutch and led Pappa out of that crap hole.

I kept a close eye on my rear mirrors, watching out for Pappa Gun and to see if any of that bunch ran for their cars to come chase us. We turned back onto 90 going west, and at the first gas station I pulled in and parked on the far side. We faced back at the road, using the building to block us from passing westbound traffic.

"I need a smoke, and I owe you a Coke, Gunny. Keep an eye out to see if any of them come out to follow us?" I asked as soon as we cut the engines and I kicked the stand down.

"Copy that," he said, pulling his 1911 from where he had crammed it under his crotch against his seat and holstered it. He pulled the hammer back, cocked, locked, and ready to rock again. I got my first good look at him. His face was flushed and he was sweating under the Texas sun, but any discomfort he felt under the layers of biker leather and street clothes was belied by the ghost of a smile on his face.

He had his eyes on the road ahead and was relaxed in the saddle of his bike, the picture of cool as I turned to go inside the store. One customer at the pumps was oblivious to us, tapping away at his cell phone with earbuds in both ears. Another was leaving the store as I entered and glanced around. I went to the cooler and got a glass bottle of Coke for the Gunny and a tall bottle of water for myself before going to the counter and paying out, adding a box of mini cigars to the purchases.

"Anything?" I asked Pappa Gun when I came out and handed

him his open bottle of Coke.

"Clear so far. That situation could have gone worse than it did," he observed.

"Yeah, when I saw that limo there, I knew somebody was right when they told me there's no such thing as coincidences." I pulled out my bandana, opened the bottle, and soaked the cloth in the chilled water. I shook the bandana out in the air and laid it on the back of Gunny's neck.

"Oh, wow, that hits the spot. Thanks, bro," he said with a sigh.

"No problem. Hand me your bandana and I'll soak it, too, so you can cool off a little. I think we better sit here just a few minutes to make sure they aren't going to come after us."

"Sounds like a smart idea. You don't seem to trust them, after sounding like you were interested in that offer the Contessa gave you."

"Oh, I have complete trust in them. They taught me enough in prison. I know their nature, and I am not going to forget it." I handed him his bandana back. A trick that went back no telling how far—people in hot climates had scarfs to get them wet, snap them in the air, and let evaporation work to drop the temperature of the cloth down dramatically. It was in the high nineties now, which was mild as far as Texas Summers go, but then we had another four months or better to go where the sun would just get hotter before fall finally arrived. The bandanas were both cooled down to somewhere around sixty degrees and did wonders to cool a person down that was over-heating, as Pappa was on the verge of doing.

Me, I wasn't that smart. I put a death stick in my mouth and held an open flame to it until my mouth got a good taste of cheap cigar tobacco.

"I won't say anything about Clint Eastwood right now, but you sure handled yourself pretty smooth back there."

"You can't make the man with no name blush," I replied back, running my fingers through my hair while I took a drag from the little cigar. Come to think of it, they looked about like what Clint smoked in those spaghetti Westerns. *Crap, I'm turning into a cliché.* But what the hell, they weren't bad for the price—way better than those other cheap cigars with the funky filtered tips.

"So, I won't comment on your skin being a little red, either," he offered, and I grunted in response. "Mind explaining, though, what you mean about trusting them?"

"I had a pretty good conversation with their brujo when he had a metaphorical gun to my head." I cut a glance at him to see if I could tell if he was testing me or just wondering what kind of people Las Hermanas really were made of. He should've known the answer to both by now. "They don't have a good concept of moral good and evil, right and wrong."

"So how do you trust that?"

"Most people that I've seen react with how I understand human nature to be. Look out and take care of yourself first, then those you care about. After that, maybe you try to do right by others if you are a good person, or maybe you look for how you can take advantage of and use for your ends if you have an excuse. I grew up around people like that. I went to jail with people like that. Hell, I guess I *was* that person when it comes down to it, but I never wanted to hurt anyone. But these people? It is a nature, but not human." I stopped there to smoke and think about it more if he asked me to explain further. I wasn't sure I could, and I hoped he got it and could actually explain it to me.

"So what happened in prison that showed you what they act like?"

"Topaz ... " I handed the Gunny my bottle of water so he could rinse and repeat with the bandanas again. "I don't know what all King told you about him. But that poor son of a bitch was actually a victim. What his parents did to him—that was evil. They twisted him up, and he came away with a perverted understanding of how to love people he cared about, but he still cared for others." I shook my head, remembering his face when I had broken him. "Even if it was wrong, unhealthy, hell, it was totally psychotic. But he might have had a chance had he been in a better environment and had a better education. I don't know how to reach someone like that, Gunny. How to heal like that. But I was always told that is what Jesus could do, what being a Christian meant. But these people, they take that and make it ... natural to be that way. And if they hurt anyone in their way, oh well."

"I think I see what you mean. It reminds me of African lions. A male will find a female with cubs, kill all the cubs, and then mate with the female right there. We would call that murder, and rape. But in the animal kingdom, it's just nature taking its course."

"You think people like that can ever be reached?"

"When it's their nature like that? I don't know. The Bible speaks of God letting people have their hearts hardened from making choices that led them to that point, so they led themselves to their own destruction. I don't know if you read about the reprobate mind yet." I gave him a look. I was starting to get dizzy from all the not-so-coincidences I seemed to keep running into. "But I believe, or hope, there are very few who ever get to that point. The ones that do … maybe that's what happened to Hitler?"

"So who judges and who destroys them when they're like that?"

"Not us. God judges, always. All we can do is try to show them mercy and forgiveness."

"Yeah?" I tossed my cigar down under my boot and ground it out, shredding the remnants, then reclaimed my bottle, took a long drink, and put it in the saddle bag. Pappa Gun handed me my bandana back. "So, how much forgiveness is in that old forty-five of yours?" I asked with a laugh.

"About seven, plus one for mercy. This is Texas—don't forget, we been teaching the gospel from the barrel of a gun since 1836 when we told some tyrant land-stealing Mexicans to 'come and take it.'"

I smirked at that last part. I knew of some politically correct-minded people that would try to argue we stole land from the Mexicans. As if the Mexicans got their land without bloody conquest and were so sweet and innocent?

"Think the coast is clear to head home, Pappa Gun?"

"You were calling me 'Gunny' a minute ago. First time in many years I've heard that. Yeah, let's hit the road."

On the way back, I stayed close to Pappa, but even if you thought my mind would be laser focused on the road and environment around me, it wasn't. I kept going back to that vision I had at Gunny's house and thinking about that girl I saw. The pieces seemed to fit if that girl was the mauled lamb, Spanky was the diseased dog, and Chupi was the psycho shepherd. But it was off—Contessa had to be the shepherd since she was obviously higher rank than Chupi, but that young girl didn't have the look of a victim. A shark was a good call, especially considering the behavior of lions that Pappa Gun mentioned. No, there was something cold, and off, about that girl. Not that Contessa Serena was a peach.

No, there were no victims present in our visit, but plenty of corruption against the land and its people. But I was off their hit list, and they would leave us alone now, right? *Sure, as long as they can keep taking business from Pappa Gun and as long as I give them whatever they wanted.*

That aura crap nearly jived with what I had been experiencing. Auras have been observed by seizure patients, and obviously a lot of people claiming psychic ability play off all that. How real it was for me, though, was a wild card, since it was entirely possible auras could be a way of observing someone's spirit. Mine was definitely off lately, and if I was experiencing some form of psychotic episodes over the visions, voices, and whatnot, then a psychic telling me my aura was special just meant I needed to be wearing a helmet and ride the short bus, not a Harley. Come to think of it, my mom had been into that new age spiritual crap too. *Duh, that's how she cooked up my name.*

Just one little problem with the theory that this was all in my head, though: There should be other observable signs and symptoms of impairment, especially with my motor skills. I was totally on point for disarming that punk and feeding Pappa Gun a blind hand-off.

I cleared my head with a shake and enjoyed the ride. But seriously, I needed to get some ear protection. I thought maybe I could make a shopping trip after we got back and pick up a few things with the cash I had on me and talk to Pappa Gun about getting a trip to the hardware store too, and maybe check out his friend's animal rescue for a steady job.

There was a lot of daylight left when we made it back to Rancho Del Diamondback, as I was internally calling the property owned by Pappa Gun. Maybe Rattlers' Roost was a better name? I parked in front of Pappa Gun's house and followed him through his garage inside, wanting to make sure he had cooled down before I left to go roam.

"Can I get you a drink?" he asked as we stepped into the air-conditioned house.

"I'm good right now. But I wanted to poke at your brain a little before I sneak off to go explore a little, if that's ok?"

"Sure, what do you need to know?"

I wound up getting scratch paper in preparation and taking notes. I needed to know the address of where I was living and asked him if he could tell me how to locate his friend's animal rescue. Pappa Gun told me he would call ahead after I left so they would be expecting me, and he let me know the dinner plans.

I told him my ideas for the backyard of the house I was staying at, got his approval, and we made plans to go shopping Monday since today I was going to roam around and do a little personal shopping. Sunday looked like a go for the river, since I didn't have any other commitments for jobs and wasn't getting hospitalized or killed to death by psycho lefty demon lovers.

And seriously, what was the deal with the left hand crap? I needed to do some serious research.

CHAPTER 27

B ack on the bike, my ears had not stopped ringing, and the vibrations going through my hands was beginning to sting. Oh, the price of freedom! I could make myself go deaf and dip my hands in fire and still fight a mob to get back on two wheels.

Of course, keeping it at or below the speed limit and observing all the traffic laws was somewhat of a challenge when my inner outlaw was screaming to rampage the road. I was hoping if I somehow gave an excuse to get pulled over, I could get a little grace and understanding to get a warning until I could get into the first riders class and get my driver's license all set. This next week was going to be busy without even having a job yet, and I was on my way to try to pile more onto it.

After five years of watching a chunk of my life be lost that I could never get back, I was not just anxious to make up for lost ground and get legit again; I was driven and determined to make it happen by taking advantage of any open door that presented itself to me until I could find a way as a felon to be a productive member of society, someone that people respected and did not shun. Needless to say, getting caught up in any kind of gang war or hanging around demon-loving pieces of human trash was not even a consideration. Staying as far from them as I could, on the other hand … see what I did there?

If they were left, I wanted to be so far right that there never would be any relationship between me and people like Rudolph, Chupi, and Serena.

I found "This Place Is the Pits," where Pappa Gun had told me the rescue shelter was. He didn't give me the name of the place or tell me who my point of contact was. Maybe I should have asked, since this looked like a place that handled pit bulls.

Now, let me back up and tell you a little about me and animals. I am not what you would call an animal lover. I like some animals, especially when they're in their natural environment and I can just observe them in action in the wild. Horses, I love to ride; cattle, I love to chase around; dogs are ok; cats, I don't care for. My experience with dogs was from working at my dad's ranch. He had border collies that herded the sheep he ran as a hobby, but he was a cattleman, and Black Angus had been the family business for generations, from my understanding.

I really knew very little of my dad's side of the family. He tended to get irritated when I was young and barraged him with endless questions. As I grew older, I learned to keep my mouth shut and ears open and soak up any knowledge he let out without asking him. If he wanted me to know something, he would tell me. And if he didn't, then it was best if I was seen and not heard.

That being said, I didn't trust dogs that had reputations for attacking people, and trusted cats even less. I have treated more people for injuries from cats than dogs. True story.

I walked into the office, which was more of a trailer you might see on a construction site. The property was surrounded by privacy wood fencing that was at least six feet tall, so coming in I didn't get to see what was behind the scenes. But there were closed-circuit monitors high on the walls that showed a pretty large open yard with what looked like tubes for running through, ramps for running over, and an above-ground pool you might expect small children to play in. I could also see a large barn and a storage shed. The cameras inside the barn showed all empty kennels, as all the dogs were running around in the yard.

A lady at least a few years older than me came in from the back door of the office trailer. She was red-haired and freckled with ridiculously green eyes.

"Howdy, I'm Trish! You must be the help Gunther thought I might can put to work?"

"Glad to meet ya," I said, taking her hand in a friendly shake. "Yeah, I'm Bodhi."

"Oh, that's an interesting name. I like it."

"Oh, then you can't be nearly as bad a person as Pappa Gun told me," I said, straight-faced.

"What?! Oh my gosh, what did he tell you about me?" she said in wide-eyed shock.

"I'm teasing. He said you were a friend, and I know he wouldn't say that lightly about anyone."

"Oh my goodness," she said with a belly laugh, "you gave me a start. He is a sweet man! I would have cried if you said he thought badly of me."

"I'm sorry if I offended you." I kept an easy smile on my face and raised my hands in peace. "I tend to have a pretty mean sense of humor I picked up from my last career field."

"Oh, what were you?"

"I was a medic for about five years."

"Oh, I see. Come on, let's walk around and show you our operation here while you talk to me. Have you ever worked with dogs?"

"No, ma'am," I said as we stepped out the back. I stuck close to her while we walked through the yard. Luckily, all the dogs were on the other of the play area, chasing after a college-aged guy who was leading them from tables to tubes and across ramps. Some of the dogs were running ahead, some around, and some were going through the obstacles. We were heading for the barn. "But I learn quick and adapt to my surroundings. I know how to apply myself and not repeat mistakes."

"That's good to hear. Are you a dog lover?"

"Well, I'm sure not a dog hater, but I haven't really had a lot of time to ever be around them a lot."

"Ahh, well, what made you decide to work for a rescue shelter? I hope it wasn't the money. Did you get burned out being a medic?"

"Well, not exactly," I said as we stepped into the barn and walked by row after row of stalls where the dogs were kept. Each stall had a pad to sleep on and their food and water dishes. "I guess Pappa Gun didn't tell you a lot about me. I was just released from jail. I won't ever be able to work as a medic again with my record, so I need to start over and figure out what I can do to earn an honest living."

"Well, Mr. Bodhi, I'll be honest with you. This shelter is more of a labor of love than a path to wealth. We can't afford to pay for all the help we need, and we rely on donations for dog food and any volunteer help we can get."

"Yes, ma'am. I have put in time as a volunteer for EMS. And I have an arrangement with Pappa Gun, so I'm not really counting on any money from you. Not that I would turn down any money bags falling from trucks! My main goal is to earn credibility so that I can present myself to the public as an honest man that can be trusted, and not a convicted felon that should have been left behind bars."

"I can respect that. But I'll tell you what I try to do for people that don't have a lot of experience before I turn them loose out here. I have a working relationship with the city shelter down the road. I can get you a paying job with them, and they have city benefits and decent wages and will train you how to handle dogs. Why don't you let me give them call and get you started there, and anything else you have leftover, you come here to help out when you have time for me?"

"Well, I feel like Pappa Gun wants me to help out here when I'm not working for him," I said, considering the job lead she was handing me. A city job with benefits for a freshly released felon was not going to come around that often, and maybe I could figure out how to juggle work for the Gunny, Trish, and a good-paying honest job, too.

"I know Pappa Gun; he wouldn't want to hold you back from a good job. But it's up to you and what you have going on."

"I guess I can't turn down offers for honest work right now. If they'll hire me, sure, but if not, think we can figure out how I can help here?"

"Let's see what we can make happen! Hang on just a minute

while I call them." She pulled out her cell phone and hit speed dial. I heard her talking to someone named Cody, and it sounded good from her end.

"Perfect. I will send him right over."

My attention perked up and I glanced at her. I kinda liked this place, but I was a little leery of working with pit bulls. But if she was doing it, and that other kid, I figured the risks were minimal.

"They are so shorthanded, they said you can start on the clock as soon as you get there and they'll worry about paperwork as you get settled. Can you go ahead and head over?"

"I don't have anything else planned for today, but I am kinda new around here. Can you give me good directions?"

"We can do better than that," she laughed and led me inside the office trailer again.

She went to her computer and printed out a map from the internet with directions straight there. "Ask for Cody when you get there. He's a big corn-fed hick, and let me know how it goes when you have time to swing by here again. Just make sure you take off those chaps and colors. Any dummy city officials see gang colors, they may fire you before you get hired."

"I will, ma'am. I sure thank you for your help. My biggest worry was that my life was over when I went to jail and I would never be able to have an honest job or chance to get on my feet. I wasn't sure if I could get a second chance."

"Oh, this place is all about second chances! Tell Pappa he owes me a dinner out sometime and we'll call it even," she said with a twinkle in her eye and a grin on her lips.

"I'll twist his arm for you, but I bet I won't have to that hard. Thanks again."

I looked over the map to make sure I knew where I was going before I got on the bike. I was giving serious thought to investing some money in enough technology to handle navigating around the city. I started the bike, dropped the clutch, and was shifting gears as I left the rescue behind. I pulled into the first gas station I came to and went inside to change out of the chaps and put ten bucks down to fill up the gas tank. I had forgotten to ask if anyone knew how much Spider's bike got in fuel consumption, and there was no fuel gauge. I reset the trip meter, filled the tank up, and went back inside for change—and to change. The chaps went into the backpack, and now I didn't mind keeping it strapped to my back since it had more than that prepaid phone and a stack of cash that I still had not counted yet.

Gee, where are my priorities?

Back on the road, the city pound was only about five minutes from the rescue shelter and was within an easy thirty minutes from Rattlers' Roost. I pulled into the pound, found employee parking in the back, and kicked the stand down. I took off the goggles and helmet and looked at myself.

Crap, I really need a hat. Luckily, my hair was lying down and back, and you wouldn't know it was cut in a near Mohawk unless I pulled my long bangs back tight and showed it off.

I went around to the front entrance and walked inside. A very overweight lady was behind the reception desk. Not to be rude, but she looked like she stayed off her feet and only moved when God commanded, or when she had to chase down a Happy Meal.

Am I fat shaming? Ok, look, I used to have a gut on me, even when I was working as a medic. It kinda went with the territory of working more hours than any sane person would consider and never having the energy to go to the gym on the few days off between work, school, work, sleep, work, eat on the run in the truck before the tones go off, and so on. Needless to say, when I got laid off and started facing trial for homicide, I crash dieted and got my butt in shape like my life depended on it. I still hit prison soft in the middle, but that went away fast, and luckily the ten years of martial arts and conditioning of my shins and fists from my early teens had saved my butt when the first prison I was sent to was one of the most corrupt in the nation.

I'm not saying that to brag; I had to do a lot in that first prison I'm not proud of to stay alive. I am just pointing out what motivation to live can do. Now, I try to eat to feed my body and not please my face. Just don't put Pappa's spare ribs in front of me. Oh, but those ribs were sinless, pure, and so innocent, there was no way they could ever corrupt me. *I must save those ribs from being corrupted.*

Ok, anyway—yes, ribs could seriously throw me down a rabbit trail, and this receptionist was looking at imminent and catastrophic health problems in her near future, in addition to all the psychological depression issues she was probably perpetuating.

"Can I help you?"

Luckily, she had a very abrupt and near hostile attitude or I would nearly feel guilty. And yes, I realize it was probably reflexive on her part. *Paging Dr. Phil, someone has worse daddy issues than me here.*

"Hey, I was told to ask for Cody? Trish from the rescue shelter sent me over to see if y'all we're hiring."

She pointed at doors beside her and said nothing else.

"Thanks. I bet I can find him. You look very busy." I noticed she had her cell phone going with her social media running a mile a minute. *Hashtag "someone feed me attention with a side of fries."*

Yes, I know about social media, twits and hashtags and selfies. It is twits, right? I get confused what you call people that spend their day taking selfies during everything they do to feel important.

I went through the door and down a hall of cages. Dogs were stacked in cages on top of each other three high, every two feet. The floor of each cage was a grate. The noises … mind-numbing whimpers, whines, barks, yelps, and yaps. Some faces pushed against the doors, trying to lick at the air as I moved by; others were huddled in the darkness in the back of their cages. Each had one empty bowl, and I couldn't tell if it was for food or water. Urine and feces drained down from the top cage to the middle and down to the bottom.

The air was stagnant, fetid, and above warm. I was already sweating and had not gone halfway down the hall where another hall intersected. I looked either way. Down the hall to my left, the painted cement was clawed up leading to a thick heavy door. Another door to my left was marked STAFF. I had a feeling this was a kill shelter and that's probably what happened behind the heavy door on my right.

I swallowed, wiped my brow on my shirt sleeve, and turned left, knocking on the door when I came to it.

I entered an anteroom, and the symphony of misery dimmed behind me as the door closed and I could feel a hint of cool air through the next door. I entered to find two men watching TV in what looked like a lounge area. There was a couch on one side, a dining table in the middle, and a kitchen area on the other side of the room.

"Cody?" I asked as they turned to look at me. I was looking at two overweight guys who looked like they really didn't want to get up.

"Hey, you the man that Trish called me about hiring?" one said and surprised me by standing up to lean over the table and shake my hand before sitting back down.

"Hey, yeah, she said y'all could use a hand here."

"Oh, man, you got here in time. Yeah, we could use help—we're short three people on the roster, so there's lots of work around here not getting done. Go ahead and put your bag down and I'll show you where to get started."

He said it *almost* like he was going to get right on getting up and showing me around.

"So, go back out all the way to the other end of the hall, and through that first door you'll find the hose for washing down. Just use it and give all those cages a good shower, and leave water in the dishes when you are done. Make sure everything goes to the drains in the middle of the halls."

"Ok. With the dogs in their kennels?"

"Yeah, they need their daily bath. This way, everything gets done at once. After that, come back and see me. Then the real fun starts."

Yeah, this is already shaping up to be a circus. I went back out to follow the directions I was given.

I went through the heavy door to find another area with bigger cages, and bigger dogs barking more hysterically. Some were foaming, and the smell of urine and dung about knocked me over. I found a heavy hose tight with pressure with a nozzle already leaking water from its tip. I hauled it out of that room back into the hallway and gave it a test squirt. Pressure nearly hard enough to chip paint came out. I went back and turned the spigot down and tried again.

I came back down the hall of cages with the hose. Now the dogs were all in total freak-out mode. I considered what I was about to do. Obviously, these animals needed clean cages, needed to be cleaned off themselves, and needed water ... but this didn't seem right at all to do to these animals.

I started spraying the cages first. dirty water poured down on the dogs underneath, raining over them until I had cleaned the top cage, the dog, and filled its bowl, then moved down to the next. I turned off the part of my brain I used when I went to work on patients, focusing on the job and task at hand to make sure I was thorough and did what I was told to do. Nearly an hour later, I was almost finished when the two men came out of the lounge area.

"Oh, no wonder you're taking so long! Someone must have turned the sprayer down. Oh well, we'll show you how to do it faster next time. Go ahead and stop there. Let's get these other dogs dealt with, and we can finish this later."

I kept my mouth shut, for now, but my temper was starting to rise. This was day one, not even the first hour on the first job since getting out of prison. Hopefully this was the worst it got. But I had a feeling if this was a kill shelter, I was doing the easy stuff right now.

We went back into the room where the larger dogs were. "All these dogs are either deemed a danger or have been here too long and are unwanted. Any dog you see that shows any sign of aggression comes here, man. So if you see a dog growl at you, bark mean, or especially if they try to bite, that's it—they come here. So feel free to kick at their cages, yank on leashes, yell at them, slap them, whatever. They respond with aggression, they come here. Got it?"

I nodded.

"End of the week, every Saturday at the end of the business day, we load them in the box and get rid of them. Today, just hold the door for us—we'll haul them in there and show you how for next time. So go ahead and open that door there." He pointed at a part of the wall that had a thick, heavy door on it.

I was feeling sick. *How much was this supposed to pay, again?*

Cody and the other man took noose sticks off the wall and I opened the door. This was turning into the worst job I'd ever heard of, and I was feeling like a pile of steaming crap being a part of it. Even when I was in the first prison I got sent to, making the guards rich by beating other prisoners they put in front of me in the fight cage didn't make me feel this bad. But not as bad as I felt when the world crashed down on me for killing a boy on the job. Those were the blackest days of my life I nearly didn't survive from. This was a job that had to be done, right?

I held the door open. Cody and the other guy slipped nooses over two dogs and jerked, dragged, kicked, and whipped the dogs down the hall to me. The dogs tried fighting back, but as each came near the door, they slung them through the opening and released the noose and then beat them back with the sticks until the door was slammed shut.

"We gotta fill that room up before we can stop. Two more, and then let's see what you can do, buddy." I looked him and nodded my head, saying nothing still.

Two more dogs were on the way, only one of them was just yelping piteously. Now it was my turn. "Go ahead and get that bitch pit. She doesn't have any fight in her, so you won't get hurt."

"I thought you said all these dogs were aggressive?"

"Well, she's a pit—that's strike one—and she's carrying a litter. Pits need to be cleaned off the streets. They turn on people and kill kids, man."

I looked at the dog. She was dark and huddled in the back, her nose down, tail between her legs, eyes hauntingly sad. I don't remember ever looking at a dog and seeing such a vivid expression on their features—this was too much.

"Can I adopt her?"

"What the hell?! No, she isn't adoptable. She goes in here with all the others. Don't tell me you're a bleeding heart. Look, dude, even PETA members bring dogs turned over to them for us to kill. We are over quota, and overworked and underpaid. We gotta kill these dogs to keep the streets clean and keep people from being attacked all the time."

"That dog has a collar on her, though. Did y'all look for the owner?"

"Man, there are no tags on that collar, and we aren't going to keep a pit here to drop a litter. Let's get with the show! Come on and noose her and throw her in with the rest."

"No, this job isn't for me. To be honest, I don't know how anyone can do it."

"Yeah, it takes a real man for this kind of work. Go ahead and get your crap and go—maybe you can get a job washing dishes or cleaning hotel rooms. This ain't no place for pussies."

"I bet Nazis were saying something like that, too, huh?"

"You asshole, go to hell. Get out of here before I shove this pole in that pie hole!"

"Maybe one day you'll get a chance to try that." I was doing my best to keep my cool, but I was seriously rattled and really wanted to bounce him from wall to wall.

I stepped back and walked through the door, shutting it on them. As fast as I could, I got my gear and left.

Did I say goodbye to the lovely receptionist? Hell no. I didn't flip her off, either, though. Anyone working in that hellhole didn't need me to tell them their life sucked; she could look in a mirror.

I made it to my bike and sat for just a second with the keys in the ignition, trying to calm myself. Did Trish know how much of a shithole this place was? Hell, did the rest of the city know, for that matter?

I started the engine, dropped the clutch, and put this place behind me, receiving instant therapy from the wind in my face and ground racing by beneath my feet. I got on the road and explored a little until I found the shopping center that Melissa had taken me to ages ago. *Oh, wait, that was this morning. Gadget shopping should help clear my head.*

So, I had a secret guilty pleasure.

A vanilla Frappuccino with a pump of peppermint. Yeah, on the pricey side, and probably not that healthy, especially if you have a habit of indulging in one more than every five years or so.   I was enjoying a frozen one at the coffee shop in the same shopping center where I scored several hundred in tech gadgets.

At the moment I was chilling outside, enjoying a smoke and a sip while freaking out whoever monitored the Wi-Fi network with the areas of the internet I was using to test-drive a little tablet I'd bought.

I nearly went with a laptop, and that would have been a simple one-and-done purchase, but I was going for mobility and portability.

A small tablet, an external hard drive, and oh yeah, Bluetooth earphones were among my purchases.

No doubt, anyone looking over my shoulder would likely have a few words to say to me.

But I was learning.

What I first learned was what exactly was down the left path. We are talking some dark and morbid questing for power here through arts such as sorcery, necromancy, satanic worship, Luciferianism, and the list just goes on. On the other hand—ahem—the right path is more of your white magic and healing arts. Many of the same disciplines claim to offer both paths, such as witchcraft and even Satanism and Luciferianism.

Where some of it had an argument based on the perspective of the practitioner, everything on the left was bad juju. Calling this stuff "magic" did not give it the gravitas it seemed to deserve, but that's what we were talking about, whether the power was derived from sacrifice to channel power from the demonic as sorcery did, or some of the powers over the dead that came from necromancy.

Judging from what I had witnessed and overheard in prison, Las Hermanas Del Muerte was playing with a hybrid of left-handed arts. Santeria popped up on the radar here because of some of the tattoos I had seen regarding the worship of Saint Death and other things.

But I had a nagging question that was obscure in all this, and my threshold for being creeped out was reaching its limit. Topaz first had a swastika tattooed on his forehead and seemed to regard Hector James as a prophet of the apocalypse. A swastika was the last thing I would expect any ethnic person to tattoo on themselves.

I started a file on the tablet for all the information I dug up and simply named it Left. Then I enjoyed the rest of my smoke and beverage, looking up information on Thomas Jefferson, while the back of my mind cruised on what I had experienced today and what I'd just learned.

I knew I was going to have a few bad nights over what I had witnessed at the kill shelter. Not kicking Cody's ass hard enough to give him a permanent fur collar was going to stress me out, too. But with him being a civil servant, I know I would have gone straight to jail, and nothing Steven could have done would have gotten me out of that mess. Not smart.

But doing nothing was not going to help me sleep better, or help me look in the mirror. I didn't need the ghost of a dog and her litter of pups haunting my sleep with a child I already had back there.

If there was any happiness in the eternities, that dog and her litter were being welcomed by the boy and would forgive me for not doing more to stop what was coming to claim them.

"There is a good place for them after this life, right, God?"

The suffering of children grieves and angers the Almighty. It is His delight when they are provided for and protected. You would not be a good man if torment and suffering did not weigh on your conscience and spur you to act to prevent such misery. Now what will you do?

I snubbed out my cigar and tossed my empty cup. The tablet

went into its case and everything went in my backpack. I mounted up and started the bike. A Beamer on one side and a Mercedes on the other started squealing and screeching when my bike coughed to life. That got a grin from me as I dropped the clutch and geared up.

Not to rub it in, but if you've never felt the wind on your face, nature pouring through your senses on a bike, you are missing out. My ears were enjoying heavy metal tunes, thanks to the tablet, and the rumble of the pipes was a dim growl in the background.

I arrived back at This Place Is the Pits a little after office hours had officially closed. But did a place like this ever really close? I had left here barely two hours ago, and I was back now after having officially failed my first job out of prison.

"Well, you didn't last too long, I see. Come in and tell me what happened," Trish greeted me after answering the after-hours door-bell. I sat at her desk, put my pack and gear down, and ran my fingers through my hair. I knew I needed a shower, and deodorant had not been an option this morning.

"I guess it's a good thing I got out of there before I committed another felony. Do you know how that place operates?"

"I can't imagine, and honestly don't want to know. If you had landed a job and enjoyed the work, I would have wished you well but would not have wanted you to work around here."

"I don't try to claim people owe me anything, but if you want me to talk Pappa Gun into taking you to dinner, I would like an explanation."

"Well, I honestly hoped we could have this conversation! Because we do need help here, but I only want the right kind of help."

"You want someone that actually cares about the dogs and not making a buck," I observed while watching her face.

"Exactly. But even just a dog lover sometimes isn't enough for pit bulls. Public perception has put a bullseye on them and made them public enemy."

"Yeah, so how much of that was earned by their natural behavior?"

"You asked that in an interesting way. Can I get you a water while we talk? I'm thirsty." She got up and went to another room, and I followed behind to keep the conversation flowing.

"I actually just had a drink, but thank you. Why was it interesting?

Labs and retrievers aren't known for being attack dogs, right?"

"Right," she said as she got her water from the fridge. "So, we're talking about dogs that are bred and used for jobs they are naturally good at. Some are great for herding stock animals, some are bred for hunting. Guess what pit bulls were bred for?"

"Uh … " I felt like this was a trap. I was going to get it wrong with the obvious answer, but what the hell. "Are you going to say 'not pit fighting'?"

"They were nanny dogs who minded infants and small children. As far as I know, they were the first actual service dog. And in that job capacity, they are in their element. They make some of the best therapy dogs for vets with PTSD, and I know nursing homes that have used them as the dog for therapy for the elderly."

"Well that is good to hear, but we're still talking about trained behavior versus natural, right?"

"Now, see, that is why I tripped over your question. If we're talking nature and dogs, we are talking about behavior and habits they learn through environment. With me so far?"

"So far, I have heard this argument to explain human behavior and claim that we are a product of our environment."

"Let's go outside. I want to introduce you to my best worker here." She led the way out and I started to grab my gear. "You can leave that there. It's safe, and I won't let you forget it."

"Thanks, I just didn't want my gear cluttering your office."

"Oh, you aren't any trouble. So, do you believe humans can change their nature? That tigers can change their stripes? Oh, gosh, I'm asking this of someone that was released from prison, and I didn't even ask what you were there for."

"It's a little complicated, but basically I was found guilty of negligence in the death of one of my patients."

"I see. But it wasn't intentional, right? I don't think you would be out if you were one of those 'angels of death' serial killers."

"No, it was not intentional on my part. I was sloppy with my check-offs and inventory and did not start my shift after first ensuring I had everything I needed, and that all of it was working correctly. Too many balls dropped, and when the blame game started, I was the man that had care of the little boy that died in my hands."

"I didn't mean to drag up painful memories like that—I'm sorry.

I don't see how you wound up in jail for that, but this is an unforgiving world, isn't it?"

"My partner told me, when I asked him why he was making it worse by throwing me under the bus, 'Live by the sword, man.'"

"Was his name Cody?" she asked with a laugh.

"That guy is a serious douchebag. Hitler would have put him in charge of one of his death camps."

"Yeah, but he knows how to two-step and party at the dance halls. I dated him for a while, but you're right. Small men, small ways."

That caught me off guard for a minute, since Cody was a head taller and several weight classes above me.

"You must have liked him for the laughs," I played off her double entendre.

"Oh, yeah, there was that." She laughed. "But anyway, back to the question I asked you. Do you think people can drastically do a one-eighty?"

"You know, the last few days I have been seriously confronting that question. I don't have a good answer for it."

"But you haven't seen it often, I take it?"

"I actually have not seen it at all. For the most part, I think people just learn to grow in the direction they're already going. If they are good, for better; but if they're bad, for worse."

"Yeah, I can agree with that. So, let me introduce you to Uncle Ted." She brought me to the barn and one of her dogs was out of its stall, lying on his side. He was a brindle tiger-striped pit with ears cut to points. When he picked his head up, half the hide on his face was torn off, exposing scarred pink flesh and an eye that was sewn shut. His mouth opened and his tongue lolled out, or rather half a tongue. The more I looked, the more scars I saw across his chest and shoulders. Half a paw was also torn off, and he sat up on his hind haunches and reached up to shake with his good one.

"Oh, my, what happened to you, buddy?"

"He was rescued from a dog fighting ring with a dozen others. We had to put one dog down out of the bunch that was just being used as a bait dog. Do you know what that means?"

"No, ma'am." I shook Uncle Ted's paw. I swear, that dog had the biggest doggy grin and had me smiling back in spite of the pity I felt for this poor animal.

"A bait dog is basically a harmless dog they command the fight dogs to tear apart and learn to fight on."

"Oh, damn. That is about as sick as what I left behind at that dog pound."

"Ok, you got me now. What did you see?"

I ran her through everything I did when I was there—how the dogs were caged, how they were cleaned—and then told her what happens on Saturdays and the last straw for me.

"I could not tell you, honestly, how many stories like that I've heard. And he wasn't lying about PETA. Those are some of the craziest whack jobs out there. And I wouldn't be surprised if that poor momma was even microchipped."

"Oh, damn, I didn't even think about that. But to not even let me take the animal out of there? I couldn't understand that. I knew you would have come and got her."

"Oh, absolutely. Pappa Gun calls me all the time to get stray pit bulls he catches running the streets. Of course, then he takes me to get a milkshake and a burger at his favorite burger joint with him. I swear, he wants me fat. But he knows the best place in town for old-style burgers I can't say no to."

"Well, I am honestly sorry, but I didn't know what to do. If I had gotten there a day earlier, maybe I could have bribed the son of a bitch into letting the dog go."

"Nope, I tried that already. Cody loves his job and won't risk it. That, or he hates dogs and you can't pay him more than the pleasure he is getting—I'm not sure which, to be honest. I think you have to hate dogs to work in a kill shelter, so maybe I'm biased. But I wanted you to meet Uncle Ted so you could see, these dogs can easily change their nature. The problem, though, is it *is* environmental with them. If I chained you to a yard, never let you be around humans or other dogs, and maybe fed you once a day, eventually you might be a little temperamental, too."

"Yeah, good point. But some working dogs know that life and do ok, right? Like Alaskan sled dogs?"

"See, they have their pack and family, though, and are trained. They don't exist isolated like a typical yard dog that attacks a toddler that wandered too close."

"I follow you."

"So, now we aren't talking cute blue-eyed huskies here. We are talking pit bulls. Who else comes to mind that owns them besides thugs and gangbangers?"

"I think I'm starting to follow you." I was giving ear scratches to Uncle Ted, and he was making sounds that signaled he wanted more.

"These guys are living under death sentences. People that call themselves dog lovers won't always defend pit bulls. Too many stories of them turning on people and attacking. But no one ever looks at how they were trained and treated. Spoiled Chihuahuas and Pomeranians and other foo-foo dogs ankle bite all the time because their owners spoil them. Treat a pit bull the same way, or rather *mistreat* them the same way, and when they bite like that, there's no second chances. They go to the kill shelter and make headlines."

"I got a feeling you have a lot to teach me on this subject," I said as Uncle Ted went belly up for more rubs. I indulged. "I can tell this one doesn't get enough spoiling."

"I'm glad to see you're good with animals. But it really takes a good person to be good for pit bulls. When someone adopts, I interview them and investigate their homes, not much different than the state would do when they interview parents to adopt an orphaned child."

"What can I do to help?"

"Come by whenever you can! There's always work to do. Kennels to clean, dogs to bathe, play time, training, feeding. If you see any stray pits, please call me or Pappa Gun to come and take them off the streets before the city catchers get to them. And if you come across any money bags that fall off bank trucks, don't forget us."

"Well, I was invited to go on the river tomorrow. Is it ok if I come by Monday?"

We made plans, and I told her I was planning to go by the hardware store on Monday but would show up and help out with a chunk of the day. Good thing about being a volunteer is you couldn't be fired for showing up late or be required to keep any kind of schedule! I had loved being a volunteer medic when I first started because of that. Working by a clock and calendar really turns your life into a grind.

I was back on the road and cruising toward Rattlers' Roost when I pulled over at a Walmart to do a little last-minute shopping. I needed gloves and a decent hat to run around with, and while I was there I picked up a pair of brown denim pants. I'd figured out an appropriately

Texan way to represent DBMC without looking like anything out of the ordinary. We would see how well it worked out down the road.

I scored a pair of brown leather work gloves and passed by a rack of comic shirts and couldn't resist one that was cheap, yet pretty badass looking. Hey, don't judge, comics helped a lot of troubled youth develop past those awkward life stages. It was a caterpillar, cocoon, butterfly kind of thing. I got a brown ball cap too, and I was set to get back to Rattlers' Roost and shower and clean up for dinner.

I made it back to the trailer without further incidents. Looked like the rest of my night would be quiet.

Oh man, I remembered when I hated that word. It was like throwing a red flag at a bull and shaking your butt at the horns coming at you in the emergency field. The worst was when we worked in the ER and patients would come in at *just* the right time to say, "Gee, sure is quiet around here."

Occasionally you would get a psycho nurse who had been in the field too long or was off their meds that would tempt the gods of chaos by making such unforgivable statements.

Burning at the stake or ritual sacrifices had been known to occur after such events.

I got inside and luckily Diesel was there. I needed to ask about a key. *Hopefully the door is locked when no one's here?*

"Diesel, you home?!" I announced myself after walking in without knocking. He poked his head out of his room. "Oh, hey. I got you something while I was out. Give me a minute."

I left him with a brow raised on his face. Pretty boys like that shouldn't be able to raise a single brow. He must practice that in the mirror.

I went into my room, spread out the purchases from the day, put the toiletries I would need for a shower in one bag, grabbed what I got for Diesel, and went back out.

"Look, I let my temper get me today at Pappa Gun's. I think we both are getting off on the wrong foot and thought you might like this as a peace offering. I nearly got you Captain America, or Thor, but I thought this guy suited your personality better and would remind me to stay on your good side."

"Hmm. Yeah, well, Pappa is right, and you are our new little brother. I need to do a better job looking out for you rather than try to start a fight with you. Thanks for the shirt, I needed a clean one for tonight," he said as he ripped the tag off and pulled it on. Some people have their own ideas about clean clothes. "You going over to dinner at Pappa Gun's house?"

"Yeah, but I figured I would get another shower, actually use deodorant, and shave."

"You going out tonight?"

"I have no plans, but I'm enjoying riding around and getting familiar with where everything is. Did Pappa Gun tell you about our ride earlier?"

"No, I haven't seen him yet. Where did y'all go?"

"Might be better to let him tell it. I figured he might have told you someone gave me a gun and since he didn't want it, we were going to give it to you since I can't have it."

"What do you mean someone *gave* you a gun?"

"Dude just walked up and handed it to me. I'm one of those people that everyone would rather have as a friend than make angry. I'm going to jump in the shower—tell you all about it at dinner."

Wow, taking a shower with your own personal soaps is a *highly* underrated luxury. This was the first time in over five years for me that I'd gotten to use my old deodorant, my old shampoo and conditioner, and my old shaving kit. In other words, I had my old smell back. Before, I was good; now I reeked awesome.

Steamed, cleaned, all my exhaust ports scrubbed, and my face shaved slick, I felt pretty good when I came out of the bathroom and put on new clothes and new—to me—boots. I decided what could go in the backpack, what could stay here, and where was a safe place for the valuables I'd bought. Diesel had left ahead of me, and I totally forgot a key again. But I could bring it up at dinner.

CHAPTER 28

I went over for dinner at Pappa Gun's just in time. By that, I mean Melissa was asking Diesel about his new shirt.

"Yeah, this way everyone knows not to make me angry, or I may let my inner Hulk loose!"

"Oh, we don't need to see your Hulk any more than we have already, big guy," Melissa said with a giggle.

I swear I am sweet and innocent—just ask my grandmother. Oh, yeah, the comic shirt wasn't for me. If I had been able to find Incredible Hulk swim trunks, trust me, I would have got them for Diesel, but this worked better than I had hoped.

I didn't have to get payback on someone that sucker punched me by hitting them back. There are other ways to skin a cat, ways that are far more amusing.

Was it passive-aggressive? Only if I was doing it to get petty payback. No, this was my own inner sadist at play. There was nothing I enjoyed more than tormenting anyone that reminded me of a bully. And siblings torment each other all the time, right?

"Hey, Bodhi, lookin good in the DB colors. I like how it's low-key and under the radar, too, for the public." Pappa Gun greeted me with a hug and a big pat on the back.

"Thanks, I wasn't sure if it was too subtle." I had been wearing tactical EMT BDU pants for years before going to prison and wearing prison scrubs. Brown denim pants and a black Henley shirt said enough for the right people who were looking.

"Hey, Bodhi, looks like you did some more clothes shopping?" Melissa asked in greeting as I unslung my pack and placed it at the door.

"Yeah, I managed to get everything else I needed between meeting Trish at the rescue shelter and avoiding felonies today."

"Yeah, how did it go there?" Pappa Gun asked as he led us into the dining room.

"Well, she tried to sucker me into talking you into taking her to dinner. But I think I got you out of it, because I didn't take the deal she set up for me to get a job at the city animal shelter."

"Oh? That shithole?" Melissa said.

"Hey, is that any way to talk about a girl that wants me to take her to dinner?"

"Oh my God, Pop, you know I didn't mean her!" Melissa said turning beet red and she laughed.

Is it bad that I nearly said the same thing Gunny did to tease my VP's wife? We sat down while dinner was cooking. Steven and Diesel joined us while Rebel stayed busy in the kitchen. She came out about the time I was finishing the telling of my job performance review at the shelter.

"That place should be shut down. How can they operate like that?"

"About the same way some prisons stay open, hon," her dad offered. "It sure is easy to have sympathy for dogs. But there is barely any to be had for humans that essentially get caught up and hauled off to prison to rot or get put in overcrowded cages and wait twenty years on the taxpayers' dime before being put to death."

"I thought I would be the one at the table to say something like that, boss."

"Well, Bodhi, if you take a look at the Sixth Amendment of our Constitution, one of the things you are guaranteed is to have legal counsel. Eighth Amendment protects against excessive fines and cruel and unusual punishment," Steve put in his two cents.

"And not that I'm obviously in any position to disagree with those points. Like I said, I thought I would be the one arguing for advocacy and prison reform."

"Glad to disappoint you there. I still favor the death penalty, and hard punishment for violent offences. But there are obvious abuses in the system. I just want to see a fair fight and the process work as it's supposed to."

"I'm glad there are people like you out there, boss."

Steven favored me with a smile and raised a bottle of beer in salute. Rebel came back with a stack of plates and started setting them out. I was being very careful not to pay any attention to the blonde curls and curves, and the way she smelled. I needed to consider Diesel's idea of going out tonight and meeting other women.

"Oh, Diesel, Bodhi got this for you today, but I would think twice about keeping it," Pappa Gun pulled out the Glock and ejected the mag and round in the tube, catching it in midair with his off hand before putting them all on the table in front of his Sergeant at Arms.

"Damn, I thought Bodhi was kidding. Did he steal it?"

"No, he disarmed that shithead that took your cap this morning and kept the gun."

"Where did y'all find him at?"

Rebel started putting enchiladas on everyone's plate while Pappa Gun told them what happened at the Seven Sisters Motel. I was remembering the way the dogs had looked while they were dragged and beaten from their cages and stuffed in that gas chamber. Did they know they were going to die?

Animals have a better sense of danger than humans. We have to forgive, because they know not what they do.

How many offenders had I run across in the five years I was in prison that got their start when they were a kid that used bad judgement? Maybe it was cousins who played doctor with each other, or siblings that even went further. Or parents who were twisted up and preyed on their children, and those kids grew up and continued the cycle of abuse on others.

I had little doubt that Topaz's mother had been abused, and likely by family. Hell, Topaz may have even been a result of that abuse. And how many times had I always heard the argument over abortion to allow the loophole for rape and incest situations? As if terminating the life of an unborn child that was conceived through such circumstances made the world better?

Oh, if you thought because I tend to straddle the political fence I may be pro-choice, think again. You won't actually find that many in the healthcare field who support abortion. And where I ran across some nurses and medics who might have, I never once found a doctor that did. When the subject came up in my earshot during political season, one doctor straight out called it murder, unethical, and a violation of the first law of medicine to do no harm.

But imagine living in a society on the extreme end where one day, we woke up and some politician pandering to rabid pro-lifers got a law passed to imprison women that have an abortion? How many would find themselves going to jail because they thought it was their right to end a pregnancy, just because they did not look past themselves to see that their actions harmed someone else?

That path to the left sure seduced a lot of people under the false promises of being natural and ok as long as it felt right to you.

Dogs didn't have anyone to tell them not to do what they did or suffer the consequences. Our existence with nature just doesn't work that way where animals have the luxury of choice, and the consequences that accompany it. They were just dragged away for being themselves, and if the excuse to destroy them was there, that made society safer, right? And it was in me to try to save them from that fate if I could. How far would I go for a person who believed they were just doing what was natural to keep them from being dragged away and destroyed?

"So, we have a truce with Las Hermanas now?"

"Only for now," I said, rejoining the world. I took a deep breath as I figured out what I needed to do before the night was over.

"But the reason for that is they want me to join them."

"Why the hell would you want to join those queer fairy farts?" Diesel threw out the question.

"Money, women, power, do anything I want guilt-free. They are bragging in our faces about owning the law here and doing anything they want. In prison, they sure rolled like they owned the world, and I think they make a hard argument."

"Women? I thought they were a queerbait bunch?" Poor Diesel had some confusion over the orientation of others that he was obviously working through.

"In prison, I think a lot of it was an act to throw people off of what they were really about. I think they start off all about no boundaries, no laws, no rules. But I think they quickly make it into breaking every rule, corrupting the law, and having fun while you do it."

"Ok, so, the million-dollar question here is, what power do they broker with?" Steven asked as drinks were served up and a huge bowl of avocado dip was put on the table. Sweet teas all the way around. Good lord, I was breaking every good diet rule I'd lived by to get my butt in shape. I had to learn to put my foot down … after tonight.

"That is where things get … weird." Pappa Gun cut a glance at me and raised a finger to stop me.

"Before we go further, I am going to bless this meal so we can eat Rebel's awesome enchiladas."

Curls, curves, and she could cook. That girl was going to make a lucky man into a king one day. Pappa Gun said grace over the meal and we started digging in.

"So, how weird?" Steven brought up again.

"Well, remember last night I didn't want to talk about what they did to Spider? They seem to be in some kind of mix of Satan worship, ritual sacrifice, and no telling what else."

"Magic? What a load of crap! Someone call me an old priest and a young priest! BA HA HA, huuurrrrrr!" I thought Diesel was going to suck a fly down as he inhaled while trying to laugh. "HAHAHA-HAH!" For the record, Diesel's laugh was one of the worst I had ever heard. How did he not get beaten up as a child with a laugh like that? But he got me laughing, too—just don't ask if it was at him or with him.

"What else did you spend money on today, Bodhi?" Rebel asked, mercifully getting us off the subject of Las Hermanas. I told her about the toy shopping I did.

"Oh, hey, want me to load your hard drive up with music?" she offered, and everyone else started talking around us about plans for their evening and the next week.

"Depends on what kind. You aren't one of those girly girls into boy bands and Disney pop music, are you?" I teased with a grin.

"Maybe I should have asked what you're into first to make sure *you* can handle *my* music," she shot back and had me and the rest of the table laughing.

"With hair like that, you know Bodhi is into rap," Diesel remarked.

"Hey, watch your dirty mouth! No, mainly heavy metal, but I think music died while I was in prison. All I hear these days is country singing like pop stars and metal bands getting older and playing the same music that has been out for the last twenty years."

"I listen to power and symphonic metal and dark country," Rebel informed me.

"Huh, what? I only know classic and heavy metal. I don't much care for speed metal, and any other rock genre they play on the radio doesn't count. And what is dark country?"

"It's where blues, country, and rock collide. Most of my metal comes from overseas. Vikings are some of the most hardcore metal heads."

"Ok, you got me at Viking metal. I'll have to try that, and I'll trust you with the dark country."

"Put your ears in my hands and throw away your fears," she said with a laugh.

"Be gentle. They haven't been used much in the last five years and I scare easy."

"After the day you have had, I bet your poor heart can't handle much of her music, Bodhi," her mom teased me.

"Good metal music relaxes me. I used to play it when I was on the job. Listening to AC/DC while performing CPR on someone made it real easy to keep my pace."

"What song were you listening to?" Pappa Gun asked.

"Well, true story. One time I was listening to 'Highway to Hell' when a code came into the ER I was working at. One of the doctors was watching me and the heart monitors while I worked and asked me how I was keeping such a good rhythm with my chest compressions, and I told her what I was listening to. I am so glad family wasn't around. We brought the guy back, so hail, hail rock and roll!" I said while me and Pappa Gun shared a laugh.

"I'll remind you after we eat to get your drive for me before we go, Bodhi," Rebel offered.

"Well, it's in my backpack if you want to go ahead and get it. I would now, but your enchiladas have me hostage. I have to give in to their demands."

"Ha, don't let the dip get away from you, either." She got up and went to where I'd left my backpack in the living room. I tried a spoonful. Ok, I was hooked. I got about four more and smeared it on my enchiladas, which earned me a stare from Diesel.

"What?! Don't judge me, Hulk!" I fed my face while everyone laughed.

"I'll give your phone a call when I have your drive loaded up, Bodhi," Rebel said while laughing at me, or Diesel, or both. Hard to tell.

"Thanks, Rebel. I can make it up to you by eating your enchiladas and avocado dip any time they threaten to take over the kitchen."

"We call it guacamole down here." She pronounced the first syllable like "wok."

"What, y'all don't say it like Fozzie Bear? Gwaka gwaka?" I joked. Just because I spent time north of the Red River didn't mean I talked like a Yankee and didn't know how to say some words in Mexicish. And yes, "Mexicish" is an actual word. Just ask any Texican.

Steven then had to explain to Diesel who Fozzie was. It didn't make it any easier when Rebel thought I was talking about the rock band helmed by a wrestler.

I managed to stop eating before I got stuffed. The way the day was going and where I was heading, getting overfed was a bad idea, even if the enchiladas a la guacamole came a close second to Pop's ribs.

By the time dishes were cleaned off and leftovers put away, the sun was painting the landscape red and the horizon in purple hues for me to enjoy by dropping the clutch on Spider's bike and putting the wind in my face and the miles behind me.

It didn't take long to get dark. I was questioning my sanity for at least the eleventy hundredth time in a week as I parked in front of the Seven Sisters Motel. A spotter picked me up as soon as I pulled in and had passed the word inside the first room on the bottom floor.

I kicked the stand down and put my gear across the tank, hooking my helmet with goggles on a handle, and dismounted. I waited by my bike while the first four rooms emptied as Las Hermana's vatos gathered. I was pretty sure that was not proper Mexicish, but I hadn't picked the name for this twisted gang.

Chupi stepped out, and he was dressed in—I shit you not—a cloak.

"Mr. Bodhi, our oracle told us to expect you tonight. We have greatly anticipated your arrival."

"Saw me coming a mile away, huh? Who is your oracle?"

"You met the wife of Contessa Serena earlier this day. She is whom I speak of. The Contessa told me to express her regret at not being here to entertain you herself, but she gave us directions, and we have followed them to the letter in order not to disappoint you."

"That was unexpected," I said carefully. "To be honest, when I left here today I didn't plan to come back. So that was Serena's wife? I guess I misjudged her age; she didn't look old enough to drive."

"Oh, you did not guess wrong, my friend." Chupi's smile disturbed my calm. "The Contessa has known her since a very young age, indeed. As you will find, though, we live beyond the laws of man. Please, come inside. Your possessions will be well guarded where they are, I assure you. I would like to give you a tour of our construction efforts here. We are still many hours from the grand festivities, but already the young night is giving birth to many forms of entertainment." He placed an arm along my shoulder and guided me as a confidant to room number one on the bottom floor of the motel.

You are about to enter a world of the profane. Prepare yourself for temptation, and challenge.

"We have prepared these rooms as a gauntlet of pleasure. In each room, we offer sensual pleasures of the mind and the body to enjoy."

Behind the closed door, clothing was obviously optional. This room reminded me of the days when I'd go to drinking parties in high school—everyone had drinks, few had clothes, and the lyrics I could catch from the music were both violent and vulgar on a level I'd never heard even from gangster rap. Insane Clown Posse might even blush if they heard what was being played. I had a feeling this would be the theme of the night, and suddenly had very little curiosity as to what was under Chupi's cloak. The stink of marijuana was nearly overpowering, along with other smells of incense and drugs clouding the air lit with black lights and neon colors.

Needless to say by now, in my life of five years in the medical field and five in prison, I had seen more nudity than I'd really ever wanted to in my life. If you think I was impressed because there were a lot of females here, think again.

Being in the medical field had taken a lot of the thrill out of seeing people without their clothes on. Mainly because they were usually covered in blood, puke, and poop in various stages, or even worse. My brain was not wired the same as it was when I was a young teen, and well before sharing showers in prison I'd developed a near paranoid possessive streak for my soap bars. So forgive me if I'm harder to please than most.

I have come to a place in my life where seeing, and even touching, does nothing for me more than make me miss something I never really had—a connection based on attraction, affection, and something . . . more. Something I had no words for at a much deeper level than the superficial.

You can try to stuff that void with cotton candy and cokes for the heart. But the artificial only rots and corrupts.

And what I was seeing would definitely do at least that. *Bag and double bag needed here, yikes.* I tried not to grimace instead of smiling back at one hoochie mamma. My eyes saw tracks going down both arms, and she tried to get in front of me to give me a dance. I spun her around me and continued following Chupi, who was laughing.

"This is our room of spirits. See anything you would like to sample, just say so. The bar is fully stocked." He gestured carelessly at one wall lined with glass-doored fridges, the shelves lined with everything from tequila to absinthe. I had never personally seen the stuff except in pictures; it looked like it could easily be confused for radiator fluid. *Hell, with this bunch, it might be radiator fluid.*

"Thanks, but I don't drink when I am on a bike."

"Absolutely understandable. Come, the tour continues!"

"What band is that playing?"

"DEF Corpse. They're an underground group. DEF stands for 'dick-eating fag.'"

Wow, wait till I tell Rooster the competition Def Leppard has now! "Corpse as in ... ?" I really shouldn't have asked, but color me curious.

"Oh, they are practicing cannibals. You should catch one of their shows!" He was laughing, and I was very careful to keep the shock I didn't really feel from my face. Seriously, why should I be surprised anymore?

We went through the connecting door into the room number two.

"This is the Room of the Mind. If you are abstaining from spirits, you may want to avoid some of the more trendy experiences here. Although we have meth and other uppers that we can mix up that I'm sure you know won't make navigating on a motorcycle more challenging. If anything, it will be easier for you." He made the offer.

"Sorry to turn you down," I bald-faced lied. "Being recently paroled and with an upcoming appointment with my parole officer, I can't afford to pop positive for anything stronger than sweet tea."

"Oh, I understand your caution. But should you change your mind, we would ensure that Stanley, your parole officer, would not consider ever revoking your parole for any reason he could find."

"I see y'all did your homework on me."

"As Contessa mentioned, you are a very intriguing personality. After what happened last week, a lot of research was conducted. I'm sorry if that offends you, but we have no secrets from each other, and I would not hide this from you. We have copies of all the legal records and medical profile that the state corrections gathered on you."

Of course they did. Welcome to the twenty-first century. If you have enemies, anything the government knows can be learned by anyone who knows how to go through their Swiss cheese-protected databases.

"You know everything about me, and I know so little of y'all other than what I saw in prison. Which, to be honest, I did not like."

"Yes, well, that is understandable. And, in the spirit of honesty, is why I believed you would not be here this evening, but our oracle is never wrong. The front lines of expand and conquest is a very different place for bystanders than behind the front lines. And for people on our side, it is a totally different world altogether. Come, the next room will be easier to explain all this in—much more quiet."

We left through the door of room number two, and outside I looked around at the night sky and took a breath of fresh air. The smell of cannabis was probably going to cling to my clothes bad enough to have to burn them.

"This is the right room," he said with a laugh.

Cheerful psychopath.

"I am doing a study in here until it's time for the ceremony for the left." We entered a room, and some kind of transcendental Eastern meditation music was playing. There was only a handful of people present. Of course, what I had an issue with was that one of them was an obviously underage female who wore a shawl of thin white threads made into a pattern of spiderwebs that left it obvious she wore not a stitch on underneath. I wondered idly how many felonies I was guilty of committing just from taking this tour.

She sat on the floor, legs folded under her in a somewhat discreet manner, in front of a Ouija board she was playing.

I glanced around the room. At a typical motel table with a deck of tarot cards to the side was laid out in front of a young male, thankfully covered in his own cloak, but every square inch of bared skin was marked in foreign lettering with brown-stained brush strokes.

"If you would like a reading, Pablito is actually quite good and learning fast." Chupi provided the introduction as I glanced from face to face and paused at an obviously pregnant woman. She could not have weighed more than a hundred pounds and her belly seemed swollen with a baby elephant due to the disproportionate size. I know she was likely only to be carrying one child, if she was near to term. Small-framed women always looked like they were carrying an army when they got near their due date.

"Right room, right path, I take it? I thought Las Hermanas took the left path?"

"Left, right, these terms honestly hold little meaning except to vanilla tourists. Some people tell themselves what they want to hear, that doing white magic or white witchcraft makes them somehow better than anyone who plays in the darkness. But there is no 'wrong,' as these terms may imply to some. Just purpose."

"So, to the question I asked before: What is the purpose of Las Hermanas, then?"

"Freedom. What else, my friend?" he said with a laugh before taking a seat in front of an art canvas and picking up a brush. I walked through the room and came to his side to look over his shoulder at where he was painting the girl. He had enough talent to make his work look not unlike a photograph.

"You have a talent," I observed, cautious of the felony in progress I was witnessing. Child porn in the name of art was a shady topic—no doubt many would defend what he was doing, maybe even apply the First Amendment to it. But the truth was that a young child was being exploited right in front of me.

"A most appreciated gift, thank you. And like all gifts that come from a transcended origin, it serves a purpose, or it is a waste and will be awarded in the hands of another. That is from the Holy Bible."

"You are the mother of the child, I take it?" I asked of the pregnant woman.

"Oh, you won't get much from Crystal, I'm afraid. And yes, she is the mother. She has a lot of healing to do from what happened to her. Please, let me formally introduce you to the recent Mrs. Reggie Collins. I believe you were somewhat familiar with Reggie from prison, yes?"

I felt cold chills run down my spine. I turned to look at him with a raised brow.

"Oh, please. Reserve your judgement until you hear the truth of what happened. Crystal here is a longtime customer of ours, and also a confidential informant of one of our networked law enforcement officers. He came to us with a story that her husband was abusing the daughter and asked us to make sure he was never heard or seen from again. Both Crystal, and her daughter Jennifer here, corroborated and were prepared to swear under oath and testify against Reggie. This all, I swear to you, is truth and is easily verifiable, as I believe your club vice president discovered.

"But what was not so easy to find out is that apparently, our trusted deputy was also guilty of what he accused the father of. We have taken steps to separate and protect them from him, and take them under our wing. Crystal is being treated and observed for her addiction. Her child she carries is also undergoing medical treatment for heroin addiction since she refused to abort the baby, and now the laws will not allow her to do so. Jennifer has some growing talent for the arts, and I have taken her under my wing to instruct and tutor her. One day she will be a great priestess if she applies herself to study under me and can put the past abuse behind her and realize that her body is merely a vessel for pleasure and purpose and is to be used for that, no different than anyone who eats and shits. It is her mind that is sacred, and no one can hurt that but herself by believing the lies of hypocrites."

It was good to hear that they were seeing to the medical needs of Crystal, but why would they care for a druggie whom they had wanted to make abort her baby? Furthermore, what would have happened had she aborted? I had little doubt she would continue abusing drugs all she could in this environment.

"So the real party starts later, huh?" I asked. I walked over to step in front of Crystal where she sat on the floor, her legs also folded under her. She looked up at me, her eyes glazed, and in the low lighting I could not see how dilated they were, but I saw nothing but a broken spirit beyond torment there, looking back at me. *A bitch pit who existed in the hands of tormentors until her fate was determined. Who would adopt such a creature to rescue?* My eyes began to water as I realized she needed the same savior that I did to adopt me and save me from the hands of torment. A good shepherd that would lay His life down for the both of us.

"Yes, then we open the left room," he replied obliquely as he applied stroke after stroke to the canvas in front of him.

"Well, don't leave me hanging. What will I find in that room?"

"Oh, we will be conducting another black mass. It will be our fourth. Each room will be blasphemed before this establishment is reopened for business. Four masses this month, then eight the next, then sixteen, then sixty-four as more priests at my level of power are drawn in to perform the ceremonies until the grand finale. Have you ever seen a black mass?"

"No, and I don't know much about them other than from listening to some old Ozzy and Black Sabbath songs."

"Hmm, I never cared for rock music, but I may have to try those out sometime. It will be at three a.m., what is known of old as the witching hour. Do you know why this is?"

I shook my head and turned to face him, my arms stacked across my upper abdomen. One was wrapped over the other and holding an elbow as I listened and learned.

"It is said that the Christ died at three in the afternoon. We prove He stayed dead by mocking His sacrifice and gaining power at the opposite hour. There will be a sacrifice, of course, and I will perform the ritual to curse our enemies and give us wealth and pleasure."

"So, is the power you get internal or infernal, then?"

"Oh, clever boy. You know more than you let on. Let's say all the above, and below, and outside."

"A last question?"

"Oh, this must be a good one. Please, by all means, knock me out."

"Other than dying for you, why do you hate Jesus?"

"How can I hate someone that never existed?" Chupi said with a chuckle. "He is a lie told to children to scare them into doing what other people want. He is no different from Santa Claus, used to manipulate the weak of mind. He was conjured by the church, who wrote lies of good and evil when there is no such thing as good and evil. Hypocrites who do what they want, no different than anyone, and subject others to their power for their wealth. We are no different, and that is the truth!

"There is nothing holy or unholy; morals are a lie. We do what we want because that is our nature. It is in our DNA to do so only based on a reaction of hormones. You are a man of science and medicine—you know that all reactions in the brain are based on a balance of chemicals and PH. There is no hell, except on earth, and when we die we all go to the same place and do the same thing. Only when I die, I will get there with more power than anyone else who is too weak-minded to reject the lies of religion."

"Yes, I am a man of medicine and science. But you missed something."

"Oh, please forgive us and educate us. What have we missed, *child*?" he said derisively. Funny how upsetting such a simple question had been for him. I turned from him to look at Jennifer.

"That I am also a man of sacrifice, commitment, and honor. Do you know anything about those principles, or shall I explain?"

"Oh, knock yourself out. Don't mind me while I continue my work here, though."

"As you like," I said, noting that he was going to try to tune me out and dismiss everything I said unless I seriously rattled his cage. I was just a buzzing fly to someone like this.

"You were wrong earlier. You don't know the difference between what is sacred and what is profane. Only someone raised in an environment of sacrifice could understand such meanings of selfless actions. You are inspired to act through petty selfishness, little different than a child who takes from another because a toy caught their attention for a moment."

I had his attention now—I knew it before I even turned to level my gaze at him and let him see what I felt about people such as him. Had I caught him spitting on the uniform of a soldier, it would hardly have been different. My blood was pumping, and I felt the call to battle thundering in my veins and through my heart.

"Every evening where I was raised, the tune of a bugle is heard playing 'Taps.' And everyone who hears it stops what they are doing, turns, and faces the flag of our country raised high on a standard. Higher than any other flag, because it has no equal. When that flag is brought down, it is done in a ceremony where it is not allowed to touch the ground and be soiled. It is reverently folded in crisp corners, tightly and neatly, and presented with a field of blue under the stars for our states. That flag is carried into battle, where our soldiers place their bodies in harm's way to make sure it never falls as long as there is a soldier standing to defend it. That, sir, is sacrifice, and that, sir, is what 'sacred' means."

I took a breath and watched him. I had his full attention, and he could not tear himself from every word I said. I was not finished yet, and he knew it. I turned from him and looked at the mother and daughter as I spoke.

"Our bodies are sacred. In the first room you took me to, sir, how many in there had STDs because they don't have enough common sense to know basic human anatomy and what is meant to go where in a safe manner? How many were challenging the organs of their bodies to carry the weight of the corruption of what they ingested? The mind is also sacred, as you say, yet in the second room, how many were abusing theirs recreationally, destroying brain cells and meddling without any care or concern? Tempting psychosis and the disease of addiction and becoming willing prisoners of their own mind, cutting themselves off even from the worldly pleasures of the first room of corruption you set up?

"The relationship with our Creator is sacred, yet here is a mother who you felt should abort what she had created in the same room with a child, who is also sacred, who you tempt with powers beyond her understanding with total disregard for any consequence of what may come after this world. She exists in an environment that has corrupted and exploited her understanding of what is right. The idea of 'right from wrong' is lost to you, sir. Yet honor is sacred, for without that, we are poo-flinging ape-minded mammals. Without knowing what is right, you have no idea what honor is or how to maintain it, because you sacrificed it for what is profane. Let's face facts, sir." I gestured to his artwork. "Even your talent is twisted. Tell me something, truthfully: If you found pleasure in finger-painting in dog shit, what would stop you from licking your fingers to see if it tasted good?"

Ladies and gentlemen, that is what you call a mic-drop moment. And I took advantage of the dumb, open-mouthed expression he was giving me by turning on my heel and walking out of there before he could answer, and I shut that door behind me.

I know for a fact I can swagger with the best of them when my mind is in a certain mood. I was in that mood right now, and the homies ... homos? Both? The Las Hermanas persons of alternate deviant and queer lifestyles of more genders than made by God and nature were taking the party to the parking lot, saw me coming, and got out of my way. Anyone that could not figure out my body language meant bad medicine for those that got in my way. *May God have mercy on them.*

You are protected! But you are not yet finished here.

"Leaving so soon, sheep?!" Chupi screamed from behind me. So he had found a voice after all.

I turned my bike to face the crowd.

"You're right, I didn't really explain commitment." I reached deep from my diaphragm as I took a breath and continued with a voice that thundered authority across the courtyard, bringing all activity to an instant halt. "But I have committed my life in service to helping others. I can't help people from themselves and the consequences of their choices. But I can warn those who are willing to listen and smart enough to act. So I say this: Anyone here who stays is too deaf and dumb for my help. The sword of justice will swing, and you can either live by doing what is right by God, or you will die by its judgement."

Now, it is time to leave. You have done everything you can. But watch and see what it is worth as you go.

"Now, I say this to you and your dead god: we will prove to you, with you, how protected you are!" Chupi said. He started laughing as each and every person present jeered, cheered, whistled, and cat-called, filling the air with profanity and vulgar suggestions they no doubt carried out on themselves for fun.

I mounted up, watching them with pity as I put on my backpack. I kept watching them while they grabbed their crotches and flipped me off. Putting one glove on at a time, then putting on my helmet and goggles, I started up the bike with a crackle of thunder and revved it up. Drowning out their misery, I watched them all go silent and sullen as they realized they could not even hear themselves over the battle cry of the beast under me echoing through the motel courtyard, amplified by the design of the building in an unintentional amphitheater. Only when they were all silent did I stop and bring it down to a dull roar, kick it in gear, and drop the clutch.

CHAPTER 29

I hit the road and cruised to Rattlers' Roost, realizing as I turned off the road that I had forgotten to ask for a key yet again. Hopefully Diesel would be around, or maybe it was early enough to bother

Pappa Gun if his lights were on.

No such luck, I realized as I came to the house. Lights totally out, doors all locked up. I pulled out my prepaid phone and looked up his speed dial number and tried it. If he was in a club, fat chance of him answering.

Oh! Surprise?

"This is the man, who's this?" I could hear club music in the background nearly drowning him out.

"Bodhi! Can you hear me?" I yelled, my voice carrying across the property. I had no idea who was who in the other houses, or even if they were club members or just rentals for extra revenue. I was considering my options if he didn't want to leave.

"Hey, what's up?" he yelled back.

"Hey, I'm locked out! I forgot to ask for a key, man."

"Oh, yeah, that sucks. I should have given you one. Oh well, remind me tomorrow, ok, probie? I'll see you when I get home around two if I don't score some action." Click.

Damn it! Ugh, guess I can't blame him though. Clock on the phone showed nearly ten. Maybe Pappa Gun was still up, unless he was on a date with Trish.

I was getting back in the saddle again when the phone went off. *I'm saved!*

"Diesel, man, I didn't think you would come through!"

"Do I look like I wear Incredible Hulk tighty-whities?"

"Ack! Well, you don't sound like you would, anyway … Miss Rebel?"

"Good job. Better look before you leap next time."

"I will do my best. What can I do for you?"

"I loaded you up with about ten gigs of music. You're all set."

"That was fast! I thought you would be a day or two at least for a few dozen songs, at best."

"Nope, this thing made it a snap to just move my mp3 folder into yours. It took less time than taking a shower."

Ok, first the undies, then a shower. This girl was trouble. Last thing I needed was to think about what kind of undies she had and her taking a shower. I thought I probably better talk to her dad, and soon, or find myself in trouble if she talked like this to me around anyone else.

"Well, I guess when I see you tomorrow I can get it then. I sure thank you for hooking me up."

"Any time. So, what are you hoping Diesel is going to pull off for you?"

"Well, I'm kinda locked out. I was about to head over to Pappa Gun's house and see if he was awake and maybe had a spare key."

"Oh, good idea, but he took a shower and got dressed up and took his truck out. I'm pretty sure he's out with Trish."

"Guess I can't blame him. Everyone else is having a good night, looks like."

"Aww, not you, though? I figured you would be out with Diesel hitting strip bars."

"Oh, is that what he does? No thanks. I thought about going to a dance club when I got out of prison, but this wasn't a good day for that. Maybe next week, if I don't piss the world off any more than I probably have."

"Wow, don't tell me you found more trouble."

"Ehh, yeah, and everyone should probably know. I'm pretty sure I got a hit back on me, at least. You better tell your dad and tell him I'll explain when I see him. Hey, Miss Rebel, I'm sorry to cut this short, but I don't know how much time is on this phone and I need to make a business call before it gets too late."

"Oh, wow … ok, I'll tell him. We still on for tomorrow?"

"I hope so. You take care, ok? Don't fall for any losers if I'm not around to chase them off for your grandad."

"I don't know. Some of them are pretty cute! Good night, Bodhi."

"Night." Click.

I sat on the porch for a while, replaying the events of the day in my head. Mystery of my vision solved—Reggie's daughter was the wounded lamb, and her mom was one of the milling sheep. But what I went through at the kill shelter today, that was just as much of a living metaphor as you could get for Crystal locked in a cage, waiting to be dragged off. Narco gangs in general had no use for dead weight. An evil left-handed, demon-worshipping, body-stealing cartel? Oh man, how hard would it be to possess Crystal the way they did Spider?

With Spider, his body had been tortured either to death or until his mind broke. The only thing I was never sure of is whether or not

Slippy had offered a hand willingly in whatever ceremony they performed. What little I had read earlier indicated there were varying components and prices that had to be paid depending on what was done.

If I was going to make a guess, I would say everything that they had done was required. Chupi said black masses were done as a blasphemous mockery of the crucifixion of Christ. That meant that all of the torture done to Spider was part of the ceremony, including the offering of his life. Slippy's hand was obviously part of the bargain.

These freaks had a mother and two babies to use any time they wanted.

Was I jumping to a lot of conclusions? Yeah, but I would rather make a mistake that saves a life than dismisses it. If I was wrong, the worst that would happen tonight at this black mass was maybe animal sacrifice, drugs, and an orgy with some card reading and Ouija playing. All harmless fun and games, right?

I had nearly decided against calling Warden Hardcastle, even as the thought came to me while talking to Rebel. I had only conjecture, coincidence, and circumstantial evidence, as any fine lawyer would tell you and have everything thrown out of court. But Hardcastle had something I did: firsthand experience and animosity for any of this crap. Either way, I was planning on taking another trip down there to see what I could do. If I had to, I would report strange smells and smoke to 911 to get the fire department down there just in time to jack up their ceremony. That would be easy to call in anonymous.

Best cover all my bets, though, and at least let Hardcastle know what I ran into my first day out.

I pulled his business card out of my wallet. I never asked how often he gave them out to parolees, or if I was a special case. I sure felt special, at least in the head. Ha ha … yeah, not so funny.

Voice mail. I kind of expected that since it was late and I was using a number he would not know. I left a brief message that covered all the basics. "Ran into old friends first day out, they can't get enough of me and are at a motel here in San Antonio on a road called Seven Sisters. Funny story, looks like they are going to murder me and worship Satan by killing Reggie's wife and possessing her kids, but maybe not in that order. We should do lunch soon, yeah? Maybe I could buy Ranger Huntsman a burger if I ever saw him again. Or, if this all goes to hell, maybe you can keep a cell open for me." Click.

Ok, I confess, I hadn't been that flippant or sarcastic. If I had been, I would have probably come off insane or high. But maybe I was anyway.

I took a whiff of my shirt and kinda wished I hadn't. I was right; the thing needed to be burnt. I peeled out of it and tossed it on the porch, stopping at a sage bush. I crouched down and ran my hands gingerly over the ground under it, gathering dried leaves and sticks, and snapped off a branch. A neighbor had a lavender bush, so I took some sprigs from that as well and then went to a cedar tree. Now, botany wasn't really my thing—don't ask me if leaves grow on cedar limbs. I'm pretty certain they have their own name, just like how pine trees grow pine needles. But under the boughs of the tree was a layer of carpet from dead and dried leaves, berries, and twigs. I gathered the foliage—ha!—then peeled off several handfuls of long wispy bark. I had enough of what I needed.

I didn't know a lot of my own heritage from the Lipan Apache side, just bits and pieces. I had no idea if what I was about to do was even half-assed right, but it felt right … and maybe that was good enough for tonight.

I cleared off a place on the ground near my bike, kicking grass away down to the red sandy dirt, and laid everything in a small pile that could fit inside of a hat. I shredded the cedar bark into wisps, crushed the leaves of sage and lavender, and rubbed the sprigs and sticks between my hands until the fibers were crushed, broken, and pulped. Then I performed a task that was timeless and ancient, one that required great skill and knowledge by the first Indigenous peoples of the land: I made fire.

Taking a BIC lighter out of my pocket, I lit all the dried foliage first and let the flames from the dried stuff eat at the not-so-dead stuff.

Oh, if you thought I was going to sit all night banging sticks and rubbing rocks until I made fire, you are nuts. Or is it banging rocks and rubbing sticks?

I sat downwind from the smoke, letting it wash over me. I knew this was kind of similar to something called smudging. Taking a bath in smoke, I grabbed handfuls of it, pouring the smoke over my hair, dragging it into my face, and rubbing it across my chest, into my armpits, and taking the smells inside with the good medicine.

Funny how popular aromatherapy was becoming when people had been doing this since the beginning. But this was just the first part—I was just about to do the hard part.

I took a deep breath and cleared my thoughts. I felt like I had been on a very long journey just over the last few days. I looked up into the sky. From the position I faced, San Antonio lights were obscured behind the tree line and I could choose to turn south away from that, west, east, or north toward the city and its sins. North seemed right, but the wind tried to pull my smoke away to my side.

I fanned it to me with my hands and looked up into the night sky, finding the Big Dipper and chasing its tail to the North Star. I felt deep in the core of my being this was the direction of Las Hermanas and the Seven Sisters Motel.

"I have heard of You, but never seen You. I believe I feel You around me, but where I face is misery and torment. I never believed You could be found in such a place. But I read that is where You sent Your only Son to die for us in an act that saved us. I don't understand why it had to be that way for someone who has the power to create existence, write the rules of the universe, and could wad it all up like a piece of paper and throw it away and start over with something better at a whim. But I can't deny that if all that is true, You sacrificed for us. You are committed to us, and You are a Man of Honor.

"You give us what is sacred to protect, and we throw it down and let it become soiled, or as I have done … neglect it through careless and selfish acts that harm others. And You offer forgiveness for that if we ask for it. I never felt I deserved forgiveness for what I did to that child, even as I struggled with my own guilt of it and belief that it wasn't really my fault, or that it wasn't fair to be punished. Today, I believe You showed me a number of times where people suffered greater and were punished worse for their choices and did not know the consequences of what they were doing to themselves, and to others. Am I, then, to sit back and do nothing when I see people about to be destroyed? Just pray that You will take care of it and do everything? Or do I have a duty to act, just as I had when I became a medic and saw someone in harm's way that I could help?

"I don't think I can sit aside and do nothing. I do not believe I am placed by You to do nothing and expected to be a silent witness. Does not evil triumph when good men do nothing? I have so many questions, so much doubt, and so little understanding and knowl-edge. I do not want to make things worse than they are. Many times, I have had to act on my best judgement of the situation, to react as soon as I recognize and can make the plan of action. Sometimes I had to act by what I felt was the right thing to do without being able to ask permission first and beg forgiveness later. So, I may be com-ing to You if I find anything I do tonight to be wrong. I will just ask this of You: First, if I can avoid jail, that would be great. So, if You give me a way to end all this and stop what they are doing, I will take it. Second, if I can stay out of jail long enough to enjoy some more ribs, go tubing, and find a good girl, that would be awesome. Be-cause You know this whole virginity thing? It's old. It was old when I was a medic and running from psycho burnt-out medics trying to crawl into my bunk and never had a chance to find a decent girl to take on a date, and it was WAY old when I had to go to prison with it and had psycho offenders trying to crawl into my bunk. God, please don't let me die a virgin, ok? Oh, but thanks for keeping me one in prison. That was very appreciated."

Yes, ladies and gentleman, you now know why I am likely in-sane. I am nearly thirty, haven't looked at porn in over five years, and have only been kissed a few times, not counting what happened with a certain cousin at a family reunion. I swear I didn't know we were related. Anyway, she was way older than me, like twice my age, and had probably learned how to kiss like that from someone older than her, like a tenth grader maybe. I was young and exploited, you gotta believe me. Anyway, my uncles put the fear of God in me about girls over that episode when we got busted. I think she was sent to a convent, or the military.

So, yeah, I was pent up. But I'd learned it builds testosterone, so needless to say, I was a ticking bomb. Porn was certainly not an option in prison; you would get an eager audience of participating offenders if you tried that. So, I'd channeled my thoughts.

No, it wasn't easy. It takes mental discipline and a driven desire not to wind up with stitches where the sun don't shine if you act out.

So, my testosterone went up, my muscles bulked, and my energy and strength climbed. What did I do to vent? If you have a floor, you do push-ups; if you have weights, you lift. Jumping jacks, burpees, shadowboxing. Oh yeah, and the whole "defending my life thing when I was tossed in cage fights in the first prison" and "more defending my life and my friends when I was transferred" thing.

Great therapy for any porn addiction and deviant thinking in prison. I had even helped a celly work through his issues! I once woke up to him standing over me about to perform an act I wish I could forget. I guess looking back, demonic possession and poltergeists were always haunting me and my cell, because that pervert went flying from one wall to the other and then got dribbled against the floor before his groin got stomped by an alleged size twelve foot.

I recommend the easier path, though—don't do crap you know isn't right like your daddy should have taught you, and I won't have to stomp your berries into jam. Oh, excuse me, Carls called that "restraining." I won't "restrain" my boot up your butt.

I heard a vehicle coming down the road of Rattlers' Roost. The embers of my little fire had just about died down, and I was feeling pretty good. I decided to smoke one of my little cigars.

I was considering pulling out my tablet and listening to music when the familiar SUV came into view.

I lit up and stood with one hand in my pocket. No, I wasn't putting that shirt back on. It reeked of recreational abuse, something else I was a total virgin about. I waited for Steven to get out of the Porsche but of course, instead it was blonde curls.

How did I not see this coming?

The VP should've known better than to let his daughter visit a felon at this hour after I just sent word that a gang of psycho lefties wanted to kill me. Come on, man.

"Miss Rebel, I thought I was the troublemaker around here," I said politely, seriously considering throwing my shirt back on. *Well, crud, not like she won't see this and more tomorrow at the river.* I settled into my skin and relaxed.

"I heard there was a dangerous-looking person lurking around and figured I better check it out to make sure the Incredible Hulk's tighty-whities would be safe."

"Nice, but please don't tell me you snuck out just to bring me my drive. Wait! I actually know your dad wouldn't let you out of the house willingly, so tell me you snuck out. No wait, scratch that—I want to know your daddy knows where you are. Ugh! I'm so confused right now!"

"Well of course my daddy knows where I am! I am a good girl. So what are you doing for entertainment out here?" she asked, handing over the drive to me.

"Having a shirt-burning party. You know I am going to totally call your daddy now, right?"

"Oh, I came just in time, then. Call my daddy if you don't believe me."

"It isn't that I think you are a troublemaker. I just think you're trouble for me and want to make sure your daddy knows you are safe."

"Why do you think I'm trouble for you?" she said with a laugh and stepped closer to me. I stepped back.

"Because I'm not as stupid as I wish I was."

"Why do you want to be stupid?" She had a grin I could see in the starlight and stepped closer to me again. I stepped away and stumbled on a rock. She giggled and put her hands on her hips.

"Look, Rebel. I think if you were a little older, I would have a hard time not being that stupid with you. But you are barely old enough to drive legal, and you got the world in the palm of your hand. I am a low-life ex-con that has zero business being alone with you under any circumstances. Half the daddies in Texas would introduce me to their shotguns if they stepped out and saw me with their daughter like this. I like your family, and I don't want to mess up what is probably my only chance to reclaim my life again by falling to temptation."

"Bodhi, you are no lowlife. Why would you think of yourself that way?"

"Because right now, that's all this world sees. And if you have any respect for me, and if you want to be my friend at all, you will see that, too, and help me make my life right. I know I'm a new face, but come on. I ain't no pretty boy, and seriously, you should have zero problem having any boy your age eating from the palm of your hand. I got baggage and scars and am best left alone before you get hurt and my life is wrecked because of it."

"Oh" was all she had to say. I could see she was trying not to let her lower chin tremble, but there was no hiding the look of hurt in her eyes, even in the darkness. Crap, I felt like I'd kicked a puppy that I wanted to take home with me.

She turned to leave. I started to watch her go and all rational thought was totally destroyed.

"Rebel, wait!" I threw away my cigar and put my hand on the driver door of her parents' Porsche. "I don't want you to think I don't like you and can't see what an awesome person you are. I just don't—" I stopped as I heard a high whining buzz on the interstate slowing down to turn into Rattlers' Roost. I knew that asinine car engine sound.

"Crap, call your daddy and get down by this wheel, and be ready to run behind the house. We got trouble."

I stepped backwards from the SUV, keeping the driveway in front of me and the house behind me so I would be in full view of the Jap crap car as its headlights came into view. I watched it get closer until I saw an arm come out, and then I casually stepped forward around the front bumper of the Porsche and used the vehicle for cover as I ducked low. The homie from Las Hermanas slowed down and came forward, shooting blindly through the Porsche, not getting out of his car. I kept track of its speed and movement and darted out when I knew I could cover the ground and intercept it at the driver's door. Sounded like he got another Glock and couldn't shoot for crap left-handed.

I grabbed Spanky by his left shoulder and reached in to snatch a fistful of his shirt in my left fist, then brought my left heel back and spun. Spanky and me did a do-si-do and he went out the window, his car going one way while his ass went flying the other.

"Aaayiiiiiiiiiiiiiiiii!!!!!!" Is it seriously stereotyping to notice that all Mexicans make that same yell when the right music plays?

I chased after my dance partner and caught him after his face had been used to plow the front forty of the yard. I came down with one knee driving into his kidney and flipped him on his back. My fist went down when he tried to pick his head up. His head went down faster and harder and dribbled up into my fist again and again while I held a wad of his shirt in my left fist, pulling him into every punch that landed on his nose and between his eyes.

"Rebel, do you mind turning that clown car off, please? No one else was in it."

"No, Daddy, I was coming back with the milk and decided to see how Pop's date went and drop off the hard drive off at Bodhi's with him. I saw Bodhi first but don't think Pop is back yet."

"Let me talk to your dad. You go deal with the clown car, ok?" I gave her a perturbed look. She handed over the phone with a wide-eyed expression that read "Don't rat me out, bro" all over her face. I shook my head and took the phone.

"Hey, boss, can you come over as quick as you can? There has been trouble and I may need to consult with my attorney before calling the police."

"What the hell happened?! Is my daughter ok?"

"Your daughter is unharmed. Your Porsche may be suffering and need to be put out of its misery, though. Right now I'm sitting on the chest of a trespassing piece of shit that I just beat the crap out of."

"I will be there in less than ten."

"Drive safe, sir, I got this under control. We don't need more emergencies. Just come and stay calm until you get here and decide how bad this is."

"Roger that."

I found and hit the Off button on the mini computer phone, then patted down Spanky. I noticed the trigger finger of his right hand was splinted and bandaged to his middle digit. Good thing his gun hand was taken out of the fight, but why had he not brought some of his friends to do his fighting for him?

I found a cheap knife in one pocket, another mag for his gun, and a folded wad of hundreds thick enough to choke a horse. I thought about giving that to Steven to cover the damages to his Porsche, but hell, maybe the bullet holes added character to it? Temptations.

I heard the crackling rumble of another vehicle coming off the interstate. *Now* that *is the sound of horse power.*

"Hey Rebel, does he have a phone in that car? Careful what you grab and touch in there, these guys are carrying things a tetanus shot won't touch."

"Ack! I don't wanna know!" she said before announcing, "I found an iPhone."

"Is that your grandad coming?"

"Yeah. Are you going to tattle on me, Bodhi?"

"That depends," I said and looked up at her. "How long before I can get some more enchiladas and guacamole dip from you?"

"You wait till you try my chicken fried steak and pan-fried gravy.

Or fried deer backstrap with gravy."

"Good lord, how long before you are legal to date?"

"I am legal, stupid. But we gotta keep you honest, remember?"

"Some days I wish I was stupid instead. How much information does he keep on his phone?"

"Like, a stupid amount. It's loaded with pictures and music and phone contacts. What is DEF Corpse?"

"You don't want to know, and trust me. It sure isn't rock of any sort. It's the worst crap I've ever heard."

"There is a whole section of contacts labeled 'Cops.' He has cops from all over on this. Hey! I know this name—Deputy Richard Burkhardt. He was the guy that arrested that man that went to jail for raping his daughter!"

"It's a small world after all, huh?" Hey, another cop named Dick. What do you know? "Do me a favor and put that phone in my backpack, and don't mention it to your dad or grandad."

She did what I asked without question and came back just as her grandad pulled up.

"What are you kids up to?" he asked cheerfully before he noticed the body under me or the jacked-up clown car trying to park on a tree a little ways down the road.

"Our buddy from this afternoon came looking to ask me on a date, Gunny, but I don't have any shirts for the occasion."

"Oh, hell, was there trouble?" He cut his engine and got out, drawing his 1911 and looking down at my dancing partner.

"He declared war on the Germans and shot the Porsche. No one got hurt, though."

"His face looks like a mule kicked him."

"We danced, but I promise he isn't feeling pain."

"I like your dancing style. Did y'all call Steven?"

"Yes, sir. He should be here in a few minutes."

Spanky groaned and his eyes fluttered. I looked down at him and waited for him to wake enough to grab him by his nose and hold him still, gently.

"Mornin', Spanky. Did you miss me?"

He started to unleash a string of cuss words. I gave his nose a jiggle and a squeeze.

"Shhh, shhh!" I cautioned him while he started squealing. "I said shush!" I flicked his beak with the back of my fingertips in a sudden snap and waited until he was giving me his teary-eyed attention.

"I am going to *essplain* something to you there, Pedro. That man you met with me today you see there"—I gestured with a casual hook of my thumb over my shoulder at Pappa Gun—"was running through the jungles of Vietnam babysitting marines. Comprende marines? They are among the greatest warriors on the planet next to the Apache. He was killing commies with that forty-five in his hand before you were born and keeping ears the way Indians kept scalps. And guess what I am? Apache. And I'm about to ask that man for his knife and show you things the marines don't know an Apache can do with a blade. And if you don't want to talk, well, that is fine. I'll start with your tongue so I'll hear no lies and no cries from someone with no honor to die like a man."

"No, no, tell me what you want! Don't cut me, Hombre!"

"That's better. I have to admit, being called 'Hombre' pleases me. Shows you know what respect means, and I won't have to carve you up like a dumb animal. Why did you come alone?"

"I thought if I kill you for Chupi, he won't kill the *madre* of our young *bruja* tonight."

"You mean Crystal? What is he going to kill her for?"

"*Si, si, es verdad. Yo no sabi* why he no wait like he is supposed to. But he is spoiling the grande mass *por la* Contessa."

"Oh, you are trying to save Crystal for killing later by killing me. I see. You are a good soldier, little guy."

"*Gracias, Hombre.*" He obviously thought I was sincere.

"*De nada,* Spanky. How is your nose?" I asked before slapping it, hard. I stood up off of him while he squalled and twisted and turned on the ground, holding his beak.

"What's in your head, bro?" I turned to look at Pappa Gun, nearly too old to be my dad, nearly too young to be my grandad, and calling me brother. I wanted to hug him for that honor.

"Y'all circle the wagons and try to call in the cavalry. I'll play Injun scout and sneak up on the enemy camp. If they send anyone else after us tonight, we need warning. Could be after they pull off their black mass they try to rush us, or me, anyway."

The thunder of a hog turning off the highway came to us.

"That's my boy's bike. The only thing I don't like about your plan is the lone Injun trying to sneak in there."

"I'm on board if anyone comes up with another plan, but I call dibs on the one horse we have for the job," I said, pointing at the rice burner.

The VP and club lawyer pulled up on his custom chopper. He had a plate carrier vest with mag pouches stuffed with magazines for the AR he had strapped across his back. I could just see a deputy asking if he was carrying a concealed firearm if he got pulled over. No doubt under the vest was a sidearm, and I was sure he had the license to carry for it. Carrying a rifle in Texas openly was legal, but heaven forbid you carry a handgun openly. Oh, and you have a bowie knife? That will land you in jail. But AR15, six mags of thirty? No license needed. Have a nice night and drive safe to war.

Stupid lawmakers.

Steven hugged his daughter and was a father first.

"Geared for war and not even a phone call do I get?" Pappa Gun said, still holding cover on Spanky.

"Goes straight to voicemail on you and Diesel. Melissa is calling everyone—it should start getting crowded here soon. I take it this is the dirtbag?"

"Alleged, councilor," I informed him.

"I'm thinking of *allegedly* putting bullet holes in him like he did to my Porsche. So what's going on? I thought we had a truce."

"That was before pinche gring—" I cut Spanky off with a groin stomp.

"He will get to you when it's your turn, so just be thankful you have a tongue by not using it until you are told," I instructed while he turned over, gagging and puking. "Well, I went back to them for a visit this evening and killed all the peacemaking efforts, I am afraid."

"What, why, and how the hell did you do that?!"

I took a deep breath and spent the next fifteen minutes running down what happened when I had gone back to the motel, skipping over the why.

"But why did you go back in the first place?"

Oh boy, gotta love sharp attorneys that don't miss the small details.

"Boss, we got precious little time," I began as bikes, trucks, and foot traffic continued to trickle in. I was really missing a shirt. "His story is, a woman is going to be ritually sacrificed at three a.m., after or during which they are going to come for me."

"Hey, stop acting like I'm asking you why you're shirtless with my daughter and answer why you went there in the first place!"

What the hell? Was he in my head?

"Fine. Remember at dinner I mentioned I was at a kill shelter and we hauled a bunch of dogs into a gas chamber to be destroyed?" I said, tired, aggravated, and wanting this day to end.

"Yeah, so?"

"The female pregnant pit I tried to adopt, too?"

"Uh-huh. I'm listening."

"I saw one big cosmic metaphor in all that for these jackasses that no one is trying to turn from that path."

"Oh. Well, I understand that."

"You do? Thanks, because I'm not sure I do."

"Oh, I don't approve at all. I think it's stupid and irresponsible, but I understand it. You have endangered our lives for theirs. That's your idea of loyalty?"

Pappa Gun was filling in the newcomers as they came, pretty much staying out of me getting chewed out by his son.

"Betrayal of loyalty would be accepting their offer. Not turning it down."

"Endangering my daughter and family, you shithead!"

"Daddy!"

"Hey, everyone calm down. Bodhi's heart was in the right place—let's figure out how to move ahead."

"Yeah, but his head was up his butt," Steve retorted, "again, in the same day!"

"Maybe so, but he's young and isn't used to being out of prison and looking after other people."

I looked from Steven to Pappa Gun, and I honestly could not say who I was more disappointed at.

I reached into my front pocket and pulled out the roll of hundreds from Spanky. I tossed it to Steven and said nothing as I turned around and went to my backpack by the porch.

"What are you doing?"

"What I told your president I would do," I said lowly, forcing my teeth to unclench to speak. I stooped down to my smudge pit, pulled the ash and embers into my hands, and rubbed it across my chest, feeling a few light stings as the embers were mashed into my skin. I then wiped three fingers each down the sides of my face, stood, and walked to the overgrown kiddie car. No one moved to stop me, and everyone kept their teeth.

One nice thing about the car, it was stick shift.

"Bless my hunt, Father," I spoke as soon as I shut the door. I started the engine and backed out before pulling a one-eighty burn-out. It was not on purpose—the car had a lot more giddyap than I thought it would and sent a red cloud into the night air in my wake. Luckily, this area had sparse rocks on the ground. My tires hit the paved driveway and dug in, trying to launch forward, only to be brought short by my reflexes.

Pappa Gun stood in the middle of the road and came to the driver door.

"Don't do anything stupid, bro. I'll try to get help there, but you keep out of sight and don't stick your neck out, ok?"

"Too late for me not to be stupid. I'll warn you if I see trouble coming for you." I dropped the clutch and shot off.

CHAPTER 30

DAY 3

"O Lord, You brought my soul up from the grave; You have kept me alive, that I should not go down to the pit."

–Psalms 30:3

It would appear I may have owed someone an apology for my attitude. Turns out the little Nissan I was in had some balls to it. It was actually faster than anything else I had ever been in. Maybe I would have hated it less if it didn't have such a horrendous exhaust profile. On the other hand, maybe that helped make it quick. I needed to pull over and make a call.

I went through the contact lists and picked another name to use from what was on it. I turned the radio up on whatever this jackwag-on was listening to until I could barely be heard through the garbage and then called Deputy Burkhardt.

"This is Deputy Burkardt. Who is calling, please?"

"My numero uno in the law enforcement. *Orale, ese?!* How's it hanging, homeslice?" I lowered my voice and increased the strain until it sounded something like trying to drop a deuce.

Think Macho Man Randy Savage with a chulo accent—so, even cheesier and not as cool as the Macho Man.

"Who is this?"

"This is K-raz, man. How could you forget me? Listen, we got this thing happening tonight, and we need some presence, know what I'm sayin'?

"Presents? What are you talking about? Who is this again? I can barely hear you. Can you turn down the music?"

"Is that better, you dumb shit?" I turned up the heat and got abusive in my language. I know, I promised I wouldn't be cursing much, but when you act like a lowlife, your mouth is a reflection of what's inside. "I'm trying to do you a favor and bring you back in the fold even though Chupi thinks you are worthless, mi hermano. Now get the crap out of your ears and listen carefully! We need presence, as in protection, comprende, vato*?"*

"Oh, shit! Anything, yes, thank you!" he gushed over the line. "Anything I can do for Chupi, tell me what you need!"

"Chupi doesn't want you here, but I begged because what we're doin' tonight will be incomplete without you here. Our soldiers are here in force and we got a hell of a party going, know what I mean? So, grab whatever you can to pay homage, and come here to convince him how much he needs you here to make sure that any other cops or nosey neighbors come around, an off-duty cop in uniform working security will make sure everything goes off without a hitch, comprende?"

"I can do that! I got some shit here that—"

"I don't care, ese!" I threw in a giggle. "I don't care what you got. Make it work, homes. And no matter what, don't name-drop. You play this cool, ese. Don't bring up the past, don't bring up anything but what you can do for him on your own. Get here at the motel on Seven Sisters after two. But if you can't get here before three, don't even bother!" I ended the call.

I shut off the stereo, put my headphones in, and got ready to listen to some real music. At least that was what I hoped Rebel had set up for me.

My head started banging on its own. This was a good sign. I put the little Nissan in gear and dropped the clutch, leaving rubber on the road until I was in third gear and shifting to the fourth.

I wasn't too worried about Deputy Burkhardt. I knew the sound of desperation when I heard it, and that man had some serious internal wiring issues that made me think the reason Chupi didn't want him around had nothing to do with protecting Reggie's family and everything to do with the deputy being a liability.

I had obviously found my crazed sheepdog.

Spanky's phone came in handy for this night. Since I had a prepaid flip phone and no internet with it, the only way I could use mapping systems was by finding a Wi-Fi signal for my tablet. Spanky's service gave me a handy way to go to the industrial park behind the motel through a longer route and a short maze of neighborhood backroads.

The poor Nissan had no defense from speed bumps. My inner child was grinning at the destruction to the body. I just hoped I didn't rip off an oil pan.

I didn't know half the music I was listening to, but it had me ready to invade, conquer, and pillage. Viking rockers knew how to seriously metal. I found a good place to park the Nissan—the loading ramp for freight trailers went down and totally concealed it.

I got out and pulled out my gear, put my gloves on, and then went through the car from bumper to bumper. I wasn't sure how many felonies this car had inside of it. I lost count after finding four hidden compartments. A bloodied machete was tucked down between the seats for a quick grab. A cheap snub nose .38 revolver under the dash and two fat bottles of NOS hooked into a fuel delivery system made up the light side of the crimes and misdemeanors.

The trunk had three stacks of cash wrapped tight. Those, I kept and tucked into the backpack. There was also a canvas shopping bag full of cheap revolvers. Funny that whenever you hear politicians talking gun control and the need to make it harder for honest citizens to own guns, they always try to claim criminals will have high-dollar assault rifles with silencers and endless amounts of clips and ammunition to spray down schools and take over cities with. Truth, very seldom do you find them with anything they can't use and throw away. The Glocks these guys had were probably all police-issue and reported "missing" and sold to these gangbangers for half or a quarter of the market price new. Why the surplus on cheap revolvers? Too easy to walk up on someone, unload it, and keep walking without missing a step or worrying about spent casings with fingerprints to pick up. It was a one-and-done gun in the wrong hands. What I did not find, however, was any ARs, AKs, sniper rifles, or shotguns.

There was a brown bag full of prescription bottles, all of them with different names, either stolen or bought up for selling on the street market. I considered keeping the antibiotics and painkillers, but they could've easily been laced with this crowd. The internal back-and-forth debate ended with me leaving everything there along with the bale of weed and bags full of narcotics in pills, rocks, and powders.

Spanky was obviously one of the delivery boys for dealers. Or just loaded for the party.

I slung my backpack over my shoulder and jogged out of the park toward the motel. Within a few minutes, I was creeping through the knee-high grass across the street in an open field that made the vacant lot between the motel and Highway 90. I moved as close as I could and still have cover and sat down, enjoying the music playing from my drive while watching everything happening in the courtyard of the Seven Sisters Motel.

Many of the partygoers were enjoying themselves outside the first two rooms, and I started counting. There were almost two dozen cars and trucks parked wherever the hell they wanted, most of them blocking each other in. Work trucks from earlier were still there. All activity was confined to the first three rooms, with very little happening around the third.

But near as I could count while I waited and watched and listened to my own music, there were at least twenty males and give or take an equal number of female or female-looking people at the party. I knew that wasn't all, either, because Chupi was staying out of sight, along with Pablito, Jennifer, Crystal, and a number of people I saw inside who weren't wearing clothes.

One good thing about smudging myself was that it also worked as a good bug repellent. Sitting in a field shirtless for nearly two hours would have been a minor torment by now otherwise. I'd heard Canada was actually the worst place for mosquitoes, but crazy Texans have been known to proudly argue otherwise.

Seriously, some contests are best lost.

I watched a white sheriff's department SUV drive up. It wasn't Bexar County, but I wasn't really sure where it had come from. I was pretty certain this would be the famous Deputy Burkhardt come to the rescue.

The whole party came to a stop, and I watched as Chupi came out and quickly engaged in an argument with the deputy. I planned to throw the corrupted law dog a bone, though. I pulled out Spanky's phone and called 911.

"911, what is your emergency?"

"Yes, ma'am. I was driving home with my wife after a late dinner date and passed by this old motel on East 90 that's been under construction. I think the road is Seven Sisters? Looks like it has been taken over by vandals. I could smell smoke and it looked like there might be a fire, but I didn't stop to check. Like I said, I have my wife with me and didn't know if it was really dangerous or not. It looked like there was nearly two dozen people there, maybe more."

"Yes, sir, I am dispatching emergency services now. Can I have your name, sir?"

"Well, to be honest, I am off-duty SAPD and I really don't want to get caught in the paperwork with this. But this is Detective Andrew Franklyn."

"Don't worry, officer. Your name is recorded, but if it's nothing, then I doubt you will be stuck with any paperwork. You and your wife have a good evening."

"Thanks, and you do the same." I ended the call, still watching everything that was happening across the street. It looked like Burkhardt was about to lose his appeal until he walked back to the SUV.

I was close enough to overhear them if I wanted … but I didn't badly enough to trade the music I was listening to. There was nothing his crap-sorry bunch had to say I was interested in other than guilty pleas and requests for mercy and forgiveness. And honestly, I wasn't sure that was enough.

But I was not their judge.

That thought crossed my mind as I saw Deputy Burkhardt open the back door of his SUV and pull a boy out who had the same cry as the baby goats I had heard many times at my dad's ranch.

The boy was young and pudgy, maybe a preteen or young teen, and only wearing his white underwear. Even chunkier than I was at his young age, and probably for all the same reasons of playing video games indoors and avoiding other kids when outdoors.

His hands were cuffed behind his back, and the deputy dragged him by a fistful of hair out of the SUV and then slapped him for screaming.

My temper welled while I watched. I shut off my music and pulled out my earphones to listen as closely as I could.

He had Chupi's attention now, or rather the boy did. I felt sick with the rage; my fists and teeth were clenched with it and I sat up in a crouch. Reason was in a battle against emotion internally, and I really wanted to let go. I faintly heard the sound of sirens while Burkhardt was bragging about connections to a pipeline that used his county as a relay point.

The sirens grew louder, and I could see law enforcement leading a lumbering fire truck. Three police cruisers slowed and turned behind me. I turned from watching them back to the pieces of sick trash, watching Chupi leave along with the boy in tow under his arm. Burkhardt was bragging that he could handle this and that was what he was there for.

We would see just how much interdepartmental cooperation and respect there was.

"Ok, God, show me how much control you have in this world. These are your servants, and I know if you want to, you can make them investigate and bring all this to an end and save that boy, save Jennifer and her mother, and no telling who else tonight, besides me."

It finally occurred to me that I had two phones that could take pictures. I felt like such a dumbass for not having it out and ready while I sat on my butt instead, listening to music.

I pulled both out and made myself familiar with the camera functions, setting Spanky's up to film video and my prepaid to snap shots if calling 911 didn't work. I took a few seconds' worth of footage panning from where the fire truck was staged over to the motel with the cops having a meet and greet. It was fifteen after two, but I didn't need to speak or make any note on the film. 911 dispatch would log what time the police were on scene and keep a meticulous record of responses.

Burkhardt's credentials weren't even called in. The cops all shook hands with each other, waved, and called it a night without even being on scene more than five minutes. I watched the lights of the fire truck turn out and the cavalry all mounted their horses and left, probably to the nearest IHOP.

I waited to see if Chupi would come back out with the boy.

After all the heroes left, Chupi did show his face again, but the boy was left in room three. I swallowed down the bile of rage, taking it into my belly, and listened.

"I know it was that damn Bodhi that called 911." Chupi reached up with both hands and placed them on the sides of the head of the deputy, not unlike I wanted to do before bringing his face down to kiss my knee hard enough to make his brain shoot out of his ears. "After tonight, there won't be a family for him to call home. I am going to go scorched earth on that son of a bitch, and everyone around him is going to pay for giving him a home! Stay and do your job, officer, and after tonight, we will put you to work again. I like the possibilities of your resources."

"Thank you, Master Chupacabra. I am your faithful servant!"

Then I nearly hurled when Chupi brought him in for a long, wet, sloppy kiss.

I did not need to have that in my face. My brain was vomiting, and I needed to scrub my eyes with bleach.

Someone might think because I had spent five years in male prisons, saw a lot of ugly man ass—and I mean *ugly* … hairy … ugh— and had a friend or two that played for the other team that I might be more … open-minded?

Get real. I am a raging hetero and consider it a compliment when someone figures out I have no confusion about my orientation by calling me a homophobe. These days, a lot of so-called open-minded people ran around slapping that name on people that had no confusion and knew how basic anatomy worked. Frankly, they were obviously so "open-minded" their brains fell out of the cavity into the clear blue light of day and they acted like the organ was something to kick around, play catch with, and throw into a vat of chemicals until nothing held meaning or definition.

I pulled out the flip phone and saw there was a message from Rebel. I kept her off my mind and didn't open it. I called her dad instead after being briefly entertained over the idea of stealing his daughter.

"Bodhi? What is going on?"

"I called the cops in with a fire report to 911. They did their job for about two minutes and left when the other cop here—you know, the one that set Reggie up for raping his daughter—told them everything here is legit. So they don't know about Reggie's daughter being exploited, they don't know about the drugs, the black mass happening in the next thirty minutes—oh, and they don't know about the child sex pipeline that Officer Burkhardt is involved with. He brought a sample with him tonight for his dark lord and master, Chupacabra. And seriously, what kind of cheesy Satan-worshipping freak calls himself Chupacabra?

"Anyway, they also don't know that thanks to me, the entire DBMC is greenlit and probably going to be wiped out after tonight. But hey, don't feel bad—it wasn't anything you did other than knowing me and offering me a home. Anyone they can hurt to get to me is going to get hit, so you'll have to excuse me while I go to war. You may want to make sure everyone is where you can keep an eye on them, and keep watching out for your own ass. Tell Pappa he makes the best ribs, tell your daughter I can't get enough of her guacamole and I love her music. Nice knowing you, jackass." Click.

I shut everything off—all phones, all electronics, and put it all in the backpack and left it there in the field in the tall grass. Either I would be able to come back to it since you could walk right over the top of it and not see it, or one day some day laborer would plow a mower over it and scatter God knows how many hundreds of hondos through the air for a surprise tip.

I scurried back the way I had come. My heart was pounding in my chest and adrenaline was racing through me. Fear tried to twist my gut into cold knots in its icy grasp, but I wrapped my arms around it like an old brother that had been lost to me and made it mine before turning it into something … else.

"Ok, God. So be it. Maybe we will meet each other in a little bit and I can cuss you out in person for leading me to fail so many."

Dude, the party isn't going to start by itself. Get your butt in gear and crash it!

On my way back to Spanky's car, I was thinking of the boy that had been kidnapped, Jennifer, and the unborn child of Crystal. I could feel the beating of my heart racing as anger began to consume me. *I was in a thicket, racing between trees and bellowing my rage as my claws dug angry wounds into the earth. Ahead of me, my cubs were being attacked by a pack of wolves. One was down, its hind legs cut from fangs, the other was crying and surrounded on all sides. I crashed into the mob like a hurricane, sending bodies flying and chased them down, one by one imposing punishment and righteous wrath on every single one of them. Blinded by rage, I homed in on some that were foaming at the mouth, their saliva falling to the ground and destroying the life from the earth. All others were swatted away, but these diseased animals, they would not run from me and turned to fight in their own crazed bloodlust.*

I shook my head clear and reached the little Nissan, sliding behind the wheel and starting it up. I backed out into a one-eighty again, only this time when I slammed it into first, I didn't need the brake. I came out of the spin and kept the tires smoking as I curved around the building, spinning the wheel one-handed and shifting with the other into second, then accelerating into another turn around the last building that hid the motel from my view. I hit the road leading to the front of the motel and slammed the brakes just in time to come sliding sideways, facing the courtyard, when I came to a smoking stop.

I revved the engine, redlining the high-performance car, and lit one last cigar after shifting out of gear. Taking a nice long drag, I pumped the gas, bringing the engine to its limits and dropping it down over and over, over and over to the tempo of my heart hammering in my chest as the rooms all emptied and Las Hermanas saw me. They raised their fists, their bottles, and their glasses and cheered in the night.

After my second drag, filling the little cabin space with a cloud of smoke, I slammed the stick in gear, dropped the clutch, and spun the wheel. I did a donut in the road, then another, shifted into second, and then did another, cutting tighter than the first until I was spinning the car nearly like a top and a cloud of white smoke from the wheels cycloned in the air. I came to a stop facing the crowd again and nailed the pedal down and held it there, long and loud.

That engine took all the abuse and didn't act like it was about to blow. I was impressed.

"You got heart, but you gotta die, car." I let off the gas and shifted into gear, easing into a parking spot beside the deputy's SUV and pulling out the machete. I had to admit, I had missed driving like a maniac. I had been a pro at it in an ambulance—that car made it too easy.

I shut off the engine and hacked through the fuel lines of the nitrous oxide bottles before climbing out of the car.

I faced the stupid faces of Las Hermanas, total confusion on every single one of them as I got out and not Spanky. I tossed the bloodied machete and my cigar into the Nissan, slammed the door closed, and walked away. My chin was down, fists clenching and unclenching.

The deputy got in my path and telegraphed every move he made to me before the signal from his brain had even traveled to his arm as he reached for his gun. I let him pull it and hand it to me. He tried to eat my elbow but swallowed his teeth instead as I sent him down, still holding his gun hand. I stepped over and twisted around, feeling more than one thing break across my knee, and continued walking without hardly missing a step. I ejected the magazine and racked the slide, sending a round flying through the air, and tossed the gun into the pool.

Rooms one through four were on the bottom floor on one side of the pool after the office to my left. I walked to the right and went to the last door and kicked it open, then walked in after a quick peripheral glance over my shoulder. Every member of Las Hermanas was standing there, watching me with confused and bewildered looks on their faces. Chupi had come out of room three and saw me just as the Nissan blew. A fireball went into the air and green flames spread wide, bathing the other vehicles in fire. I shut the door behind me and flipped on the lights in the room. I crossed over and kicked the door leading to the adjoining motel room and left it open.

I spread my legs wide and went low into a deep squat, stretching the muscles of my thighs, and centered myself, calming my mind and dumping all thought with a hard breath out before standing up straight and facing the door. I stretched both my arms back, flexing the muscle groups through my chest and shoulders to my back and snapping them forward. I started moving from my right foot to my left in rhythm.

"Let's rodeo." Another explosion went off outside. I wondered if it was the SUV belonging to the deputy.

You will find the tools you need to carry on the fight in the next room. Do not leave them behind. You are not alone in this war, but always do what is Right, for that is when you are at your best!

The first to enter oriented himself then rushed me low, reaching for my waist. I saw what he was going to attempt before he ducked and instead of taking me down, he met a flying knee that snapped his head back and flipped him backwards. I stomped his groin and caught the next coming through the door with a roundhouse shin kick over the thigh that crumpled him to the side. I came over with a high left roundhouse that caught him over the ribs, I felt the snap and crackle of at least one pop under my shin and left him down and backed deeper into the room. Gunshots filled the door and peppered the wall as I hit the floor and scooted backwards.

This room had no furniture or bed in it except for an overturned chair against the wall on my right. *No place to hide for cover if they just unload everything in here.*

When the shooting finally stopped, I hopped to my feet and went to the side of the door just as someone tried to hand me another gun, poking the gun and arm in first as they failed to slice the pie. They got the edge of my hand in a slice across the throat instead and I took control of their gun and the rest of their body, flipping them over and snapping their arm across my knee. I curb-stomped his jaw and dropped the mag and ejected the round, tossing it aside.

People may die tonight, but I was going to make it obvious I was defending myself and not intentionally murdering any queer-eyed Satan-worshipping homo … sapien lefty that came at me.

Two more came through the door. One caught a thrust kick that sent him into the wall behind him as the other tackled me from the side. I rolled with him, coming out on top, and smashed an elbow down into his face, then back into the side of his head. His arms went slack around me and I was on my feet, giving him a stomp to the groin as the other guy came out of the hole in the wall, crashing into another thug that was trying to rush through the door with a third behind him.

I gave the first another kick over the diaphragm, sending him airborne through the door and the other two.

"This is all you sonsofbitches got?! You can murder people in their sleep, but in a fight you can't get through a paper bag!" Gunshots answered, and I dropped, crawled, and scurried through the open door behind me. Light from the other room fell on a wrecking bar that looked nearly two feet long, hooked on one end and angled at the other tipped with nail-pulling prongs lying next to a two-pound hand sledgehammer. *This will do.*

I picked both up and kicked the door shut, staying low in the darkness while Las Hermanas unloaded everything they had in the other room. Gunshots started peppering the wall in front of me, cutting through the room at an angle that left me clear for the moment. Shooting stopped, and I hopped up and moved to the corner against the other room and courtyard wall where I could keep an eye on both doors.

Hammer in my left hand, the heavier crowbar was in my right, its hook reversed. The first coming from the room I had already kicked ass in got his forearm shattered as he led with his gun arm. I carried the hit through with the crowbar, coming around to send the hammer into the side of his head way harder than I had meant for nonlethal force.

So far, it had mainly been fun and games and groin kicks. This guy, however, had his brains bashed and was dead before he was on the ground.

Kill or be killed now. They will give you no mercy, and there is no other help coming to stop them. You are running out of time.

So be it unto them! The next through the door caught the bar across the trachea as the door behind me crashed open. I spun around, one foot over the other, and caught the gang member on the forehead with the face of the mallet. I came around again and went low as the next body filled the doorway, hooking him behind an ankle with the crowbar and bringing the hammer down on his knee. I came up as he went down and sent a field goal kick under his chin before racing back to the door to the other motel room.

The next one through the door caught the crowbar down the center of his face, crushing bone and sending him down into the man behind him. I stepped on the body and brought the hammer down over his chest, feeling the crack of bone at the clavicle. I smashed his face with an elbow as I twisted to the right to catch the knee with the hammer of another gangbanger as I went low and came high, sending the crowbar across the side of his neck and jaw. He went down and I sent another blow to his face with the hammer just as I looked up at another being fed to me. I was breathing heavy and covered in the blood of my enemies from belly to face. I stood slowly and felt a grin coming to my face as I took one step, then another toward my next prey.

Mortal fear obviously gripped this one and he turned to run. I was on him sending the crowbar down to his ankle. He crashed down against the door and flipped over to crab crawl away from me, raising his hands in surrender as I raised the hammer high. I stopped myself just before it came down and swallowed the battle lust down. Instead, I spun on my heel and ran to the other room, a gunshot chasing after me as I darted through the door and crashed straight into another thug. I sent my forehead crashing down on his nose and when he staggered back, he caught the bar across the knee, hammer to the hip, bar to the ribs on his right side, and hammer back across the side of his head as heaven and earth crashed back and forth up and down his body.

I ran through the open door, sprinting around the corner. Before anyone in the courtyard could fire any shots, I was back through the door of the first room again, coming up behind three Hermanas.

I threw a flying kick at the center of one's back, sending him face-first through the open door and putting me between the other two. One ate bar cross the mouth. I twisted down low, sending a backhanded hammer blow to the knee of the other, and came back up and offered him a slice of crowbar pie too. He tried to nod his head in thanks, so he got a face full instead across the nose and eyes. I danced from one foot to the other as I spun and brought a roundhouse kick down on the thigh of the other guy. My shin caught him above the knee but the hammer came across his temple, sending him down, and I chased the first guy through the open door. This one I had spared earlier was bringing his gun up to shoot at me. I danced to the side as he pulled the trigger and came down on his gun hand with the crowbar. Bones crunched and the hammer fell on his other shoulder, shattering ball and socket and sending him down screaming.

"I do not believe your friends can hear the sounds of your rewards for your treacherous ways. Let me help you," I offered and placed the heel of my boot on his hand, giving it a grind.

The volume of his screaming really went up then. I beckoned him with a casual wave of the hammer. "Now beg for mercy," I coached. He complied, screaming for mercy.

"Ask for forgiveness." I gave his shoulder a tap with the toes of my boot. Over and over, he begged for forgiveness.

"I will if you say to me, 'Thank you, sir.'"

Oh, he was so grateful!

"Again! Louder!" He did. "Say it again and again unless you want me to break more!"

As loud as he could, he yelled, "Thank you, sir!" repeating himself over and over.

"I will leave now to teach your friends their lesson in manners. But if I hear you stop, I will come back and give you more, so do not stop. Because I am just getting started, *amigo*!"

He shook his head and kept going with his mantra. I left him there, walking out the door and looking at the rest. No more than half a dozen stood facing me in the courtyard.

"Thank you, sir! Thank you, sir! Thank you, sir! Thank you, sir!" rang out behind me as I began walking toward the remaining bunch. One came at me and I met him with a kick to his knee. I felt bones easily shatter under my shin. He went down, cursing me and screaming. I watched the others as I brought the hammer down, permanently ending his pain with a single blow.

I stood and walked to the next, but he ran into room one. The others followed, and I felt no need to run after them. They had nowhere to go, nowhere to hide.

They slammed the door and I stood over Deputy Burkhardt where I had knocked his ass out at the start of the battle.

I looked down at him and flipped him on his belly with a boot to the side. His cuff pouch was empty.

"Well, I guess I do this the easy way. You need to stick around, deputy." I brought the bar down on his right hand—*that* woke him up. He tried to turn over, but I came down with a knee on his back and hammered his left hand.

"You don't know me, but Reggie would want me to say hi to you for him," I said into his ear before standing up. "If he was still alive. Tell me something, did he really rape his daughter?"

"Yes, you son of a bitch. Oh, God, I am going to throw your ass in jail!"

"Maybe we will be cellies, then. Chupi already told me you raped her yourself. I have evidence on you trafficking child sex slaves." I brought the crowbar down on his ankle, shattering it and letting him scream, drowning out the gangbanger that was still chanting his thanks to me.

"Last chance, deputy. Do you swear to uphold the law, to defend the Constitution, to defend the helpless, and to execute the laws of the county you serve in the Great State of Texas, so help you God? ANSWER ME, YOU PILE OF SHIT! Did Reggie really rape his daughter?"

"No, no, it was just me! I hate myself for what I did, but I can't stop it! I am sick and evil and should be killed!"

"Maybe, deputy, but that isn't for me to judge." I crushed his other ankle and left him there screaming while I took his cuff keys and put them in my back pocket for an easy grab. Next, I stood up to walk to the door to room one. I smashed it open and stepped to the side as bullets answered.

"Everyone in there, you may think you don't have a choice, but I am giving it to you. *Leave.* Just run and get out of here and don't look back down this road ever again. I will let anyone that comes through that door get into a car and leave, no questions asked. The police are coming back, and this time they will see what's happening. Everyone will be going to jail that I don't deal with first."

"You'll let us go, Hombre?"

"I give you my word on it. I won't stop anyone but Chupi. All I want is him now."

"Some of us are coming out. Please don't hurt us!" a female called out.

"Twenty seconds! Get out of here." I was glad for the gloves. My hands felt sweaty inside, but they kept a strong grip.

Some of them started cussing at the ones leaving. That was before the bullets started flying. I crouched down and one naked female made it out after being shot in the back and leg, flopping on the ground near me and crying. I ditched the crowbar and reached for her hand as she was shot in the back again. I dragged her clear, but she was beyond help. When the gunfire stopped, wet, meaty whacks started and the screaming never stopped. I reached for the crowbar again and peeked inside to see three Hermanas with machetes going to town on everyone else inside.

"HEY!" I bellowed, and they stopped in mid-swing.

"Shouldn't you be trying that on me instead?" For the first time, I turned the crowbar around so the hook was facing forward and swapped weapon hands, putting the hammer in my right hand.

One beefy vato my size and weight nodded his head, smirked at me, and stepped forward.

"Orale, Hombre, let's see what you got."

"Oodalolly to you, too, punk. Step up and let 'er buck."

The other two went back to work, finishing off everyone else in there. I couldn't do anything about it, because a machete came swinging at my head. I blocked with the hook of the wrecking bar in my left hand and came down with the hammer in my right. He stepped in and headbutted my face.

Damn, that stings!

I danced back out of the door with tears in my eyes and he came after me, swinging again. I jumped back and let it slice by, feeling the tip dig in across my belly. *Not good*—I wasn't chubby there like I used to be. I push kicked with my left foot on his right elbow, sending his swing into a spin as his body went off-balance. I came down with a hammer blow, but he used his spin to roll away from me, coming up to his feet and dancing like a boxer.

"I'm starting to hate you, hermano. Drop the blade and run, or I'm going to have to kill you too." Hate him, I did, but my respect, he had.

He flashed a grin and came in again, swinging low for my legs.

His blade met the crowbar and I swept it back the way he had come from and high around the clock, coming inside with a spin and backing out under his arm as the blade disengaged from my bar. He tried to turn with me, but the hook of the bar caught him on the side of his trachea. The teeth of the nail puller gouged into his flesh and dug into the esophagus as I gave a yank and a twist, tearing through tissue and cartilage and ripping through both jugular veins. He stood there for a second as his brain suddenly lost signals from air and blood flow before falling at my feet, his life pouring across the ground.

I turned as the next guy with a machete rushed out of the door to try to get me from behind, his homie on his heels.

I dropped a knee to the ground, bringing the hammer down over the knee cap of the first, and used the crowbar to block the machete. A shattered knee later, I stood and used the first Hermana as a shield as his partner tried to swing at me. He hit his partner instead, chopping into the upper arm as I darted to the side.

This poor guy.

I shoved the dis*armed*—ha ha—Hermana into his friend. They hugged it out as blood geysered and gushed on them both and they tripped over the severed limb on the ground. I took advantage of the shock and awe to bring the crowbar down over the wrist of the good buddy, breaking bones and sending the last machete to the ground. The hammer came down on the hip of the disarmed, the crowbar on the knee of the armed, hammer on the ribs of the disarmed, crowbar on the face of the armed, hammer on the back of the head of the disarmed, all in one continuous onslaught blow after blow.

They fell in each other's arms in a bloody embrace of death. I finally entered room number one and found nothing but dead and hacked bodies. I went into room two and found half a dozen people in various states of being drugged stupid. I calmly opened the door outside and quietly closed it behind me so as not to disturb them from their high and precious escape from how hard life can be for some people.

I checked the cut on my belly. *It's not too bad*, I thought. And then stopped as I realized … *Crap! God knows what was on that blade.* I was going to need shots. Lots and lots of shots.

Stupid perverts and their STDs!

Room number three. I took a deep breath for the last confrontation and kicked the door open, stepping to the side.

The door smashing open was answered by the yelp of a Nancy boy, but no gunfire. I gave a quick glance inside and ducked back in a blink. Only Pablito and the boy were in there. The card reader had the boy in his arms, and they were huddled down in corner.

I came back through the corner and eyeballed Pablito, but he was disarmed, one hand held up in front of him. "Don't hurt us!"

"Have you harmed that boy?" I asked. Jennifer and her mother had evidently left with Chupi. The door connecting to the fourth room was closed.

"No, I'm a healer! I would never harm another being!"

"Tell me if he is still cuffed and what I am going to find in the next room, Pablito."

"I don't have keys or I would have taken them off." I put the weapons in one hand and tossed him the key from my back pocket while he talked. "Chupi is planning to sacrifice Crystal now, and use Jennifer to perform the ritual."

"Yeah, that ain't happening. Now, you take those cuffs," I ordered him, pointing the bloodied hammer at his face, "and go into the bathroom and cuff yourself to the bottom of the toilet. And leave your phone here."

"I couldn't do anything to stop it—please believe me! The black mass tonight was supposed to only be some bloodletting—no death, or I would not be here."

"Yeah, I want to believe you, so do what I told you so I can do what I gotta do."

He nodded his head, sobbing as he took the cuffs off the boy and scurried into the bathroom. If women learned to do what a man told them that quick and without argument, they would never have trouble finding and keeping a good man.

"Lock 'em tight, Pablito. You wouldn't like me when I am angry." I figured my inner Incredible Hulk had been channeled thoroughly as it was. I turned to the kid. He was shook up and obviously needed someone to help get him out of here.

"Can you talk, kid?"

"Si, *señor.*"

"Good. Can you call 911 on that phone and tell them everything you know to get them here?"

He nodded his head and picked the phone up. When he bent over, I could see red and purple welts and bruise about two inches wide crisscrossing his back down to his lower legs.

"I'm not going to let anyone hurt you while I'm here, kid. Do what you can with them—I gotta go finish this before that bastard can hurt more people."

"*Si*, I can do this for you, *señor*. I prayed to the Virgin Mary to save me, *señor*. Now I will be praying for her to save the others, too."

"Let's hope she tells her boy to get off His butt, then."

I turned and took a big step forward with my left foot and turned into a spin, sending the heel of my right foot into the door above and to the side of the doorknob. I nearly bit into my tongue as the jarring force was sent straight back, reverberating through every bone in my body and nearly bouncing me on my butt.

"Son of HAAAAAA!" I put everything into a heel kick straight at it, reaching down and releasing all the energy in my lower gut in a yell of rage.

The door didn't have to mock me—Chupi already was, laughing loud enough to be heard in the next room.

"You aren't invited into this room, Bodhi. I have warded the doors and the window. No one is coming in here to stop me!"

"Yeah?!" I gave him my best witty retort back. "I am curious about something, Chupi. You said that oracle had you set everything up to greet me. Does that mean you were fed to the lions along with every one of your Satan-worshipping fairy friends, since she sees everything that's about to happen and knew I would come for you?"

"Shut up! You know nothing! Shall I tell you? We have a few minutes before I begin. We don't worship Satan. I don't even know if there ever was such a being, and I don't care! I have real power, and not just from the infernal! But you showed me how to reach for more when you told me how to profane a mother by her children. I never thought of doing this until you showed me the truth!"

"Bodhi!" I heard a desperate whisper from the bathroom.

"I'm a little busy—what?"

"I know how you can get in there! He said he warded the doors and the windows—you won't be able to break them down. But the walls! This place is made like a stack of cards—there isn't anything but drywall keeping you out!"

Yeah, that'll work. I hoped I was smart enough to have figured that out on my own had the little guy not suggested it.

"Now, Jennifer!! We have to do this now—he will be here any second!"

Crap, those walls really *were* thin. I took a few steps back and focused on the wall in front of me. If I plowed into a stud, that would not be good. *Two studs should never collide.*

I took a deep breath and forced it out hard and fast before taking another and launching off my right foot. I had maybe step or two before I crashed into the wall, bringing my forearms up in reflex across my face.

I crashed through drywall, feeling it biting and digging across my arms and missing my face as I ducked my head into the charge. My feet got tangled as I destroyed the wall and I went tumbling end over end into the next room. Before the dust had cleared and I could get to my feet, it felt like someone used a baseball bat on my back and shoulders. I went down as pain made my world light up. I rolled over, catching the end of another swing on the side of my head.

Get your arms up, dummy! Guard, guard, guard. Shake it off and get to your feet! The old lessons I'd learned many years ago, conditioning my mind from fight or flight into pure fight when instinct was all I had to survive by. I rolled backwards over my shoulder, catching the next blow across my legs.

That was fine. The pain there was easy to manage after the countless times I'd spent conditioning them to take punishment.

I got my feet under me and arms up, catching another blow across both forearms. Again, I was ok with that too.

I came to my feet and the fog of near unconsciousness thankfully stayed on the ground.

"My turn," I growled. I had no clever insults, no taunts, no thought other than my drive and focus to inflict catastrophic and overwhelming agony on this human being. And he was a human—there was no other creature or object worthy of that insult. This person deserved to be held on a platform for all of humanity to see and be shamed for tolerating in society. And here he stood in front of me, having used a thick ceremonial staff as a club. One does not poke bears with sticks and not suffer the consequences.

"Now, Jennifer, kill her now!"

I turned to look behind me, my eyes taking in a single glance that told me everything at once. Jennifer was down on her knees above her mother, who was inside of a pentagram marked on the floor surrounded by five candles. Each point of the star had either a skull too small for an adult and too wide for human, a golden chalice filled to the brim with blackened liquid reflecting the light of the candle from its surface, a book, a red crystal the size of a fist that reflected the light of the candles from each facet in display that dazzled the eye, or a chunk of black obsidian rock carved into a shape that made me feel nauseated and darkened the area all around it despite the candle next to it.

Jennifer raised a long, wavy bladed dagger high. Crystal was unbound and awake but just lying there, doing nothing to stop her. I turned to intervene and was rewarded with a blow across my head hard enough to drive me down to my knees. Another and another came down on me as my hands lost their grip on the hammer and crowbar. I brought them up in a cage around my head and got to my feet again only to catch the butt of the staff in the gut. I lost any air in my lungs, and my hands came down just in time to intercept a blow coming at my face. My hands fumbled for the staff and we wrestled. My head cleared and I gave him a wrench, then sent my foot for his crotch. I caught him, and it did something—don't ask me what, because I honestly did not hit what I expected.

It is a medical fact that men are born with additions to the anatomy not found on any of the many other sexes any person may try to claim to be other than female. Females, of course, do not apply to this term because nature made them the way they are. There is a very complicated medical term for a person who was born a man in such a condition after making life choices that led him down the road to do this to himself. It's called being dickless.

Ask any doctor and they will have to agree that for a man to decide to do this to himself makes him dickless.

Now, you may think being dickless could be an advantage against someone such as me, who is putting a size twelve where it is obvious that I am fighting a disabled, maimed, and impaired person who failed at life and could not cope with the titanic struggles of becoming a man that only men can understand once they have graduated into manhood.

However, this so-called "advantage" would not appear to actually be helpful in any way. In fact, since there are less jiggly parts to cushion the trauma, the bone there has even less protection. Breaking that bone is horrendously painful. Don't believe me? Ask the dickless priest in front of me that just ordered a daughter to kill her mother and see if he'll tell you that what Bodhi kicks tends to break.

Chupi went down to his knees, hands clutching where my foot had landed. His mouth was open and he was out of breath from the shock of encountering the boot of a man. I introduced the side of his head to the shin of a man, too, and sent him down for the count.

I turned to see Jennifer clutching the handle of the knife, its blade buried in the chest of her mother, who was still alive. Jennifer yanked the blade out and I came around and sent a kick to her head before she could drive it down again into her mother. It didn't take much, but I wasn't measuring. Jennifer crashed through the circle, sending a candle and other paraphernalia rolling across the room and smearing the white paint of the pentagram.

I brought my hands down over the wound. It wasn't in the heart, but that didn't mean that fat, wavy blade hadn't hit some serious veins or arteries. I was looking down into her eyes. The front of my brain slipped into gear, but I had no words that weren't lies for this. That knife was meant for destroying anything that was put in front of it. Crystal had precious moments of life left, and the baby in her swollen belly was tethered to that life.

"Can you save my baby?"

"I am sure going to try to save both of you, ma'am. The police should be on their way back with EMS. We will get you to the hospital—don't give up the fight." Blood would not stay behind my hands. That knife was an evil thing.

"If it's a boy, I want him named after Reggie, please. Oh, God, I am so sorry for what I've done."

"Hey, I am told God always forgives if you ask. Hang in there, Crystal, I'm not leaving you."

"I prayed, you know. For months, I have prayed—no answers. Help for Reggie, help for my daughter to save them from what I did. This is all my fault. I gave my daughter to them because I was hooked on cocaine. I tried to go clean, and I even called the law for help when the dealer made threats. The deputy raped my daughter and made me get high again."

I felt her body going cold and clammy. I reached for her wrist and could feel no pulse. She was there, but just barely, eyes open and heart fluttering under my hands beyond my reach by inches.

"Crystal, if there is a God, He sent me. I may be too late for a lot of things—I'm sorry, I'm sorry, I'm so sorry I didn't know or I would have done more. I don't believe in accidents anymore. When I first saw you, I knew you and I both needed the same Savior to save both of us. I briefly knew Reggie, and he knew the right person to talk to that got my attention and brought me here. Now I am going to do what I can to make sure your baby lives no matter what. But that Man Above us is waiting to see if you will accept Him and ask forgiveness and change the rest of your life, no matter how much is left."

"If He would have me. I don't know if he would, after all I've done."

"Let it go, darlin'. There was a thief on a cross that asked at the last minute, and Jesus claimed him. If I pray for that for me, will you pray, too, so we can both be saved?"

She reached up to my face, struggling to speak now.

"Just say it in your heart. Father God, I believe, and I am sorry it took so much to make me see that You had to let Your child be murdered for me. Please forgive my sins, please wash all of my guilt in the blood of Your precious Son, and take me for Yours."

Crystal was struggling now, her mouth opening and closing without any breath moving through her lungs. She wrapped a hand around my arm over her chest and her nails dug into my skin with what feeble strength remained.

"I see it," she gasped out finally and fell away.

CHAPTER 31

"Kid, did you call 911 for us?" I yelled into the other room and reached over for the dagger. It was all I had with a blade around here. Yes, I should have had a pocket knife—all men should; it is required equipment for being a man—however, I had decided against getting one because of how many encounters with police I'd had in the last two days. *Oh, God, this is only my third day out of prison ... it feels like it has been decades already.*

"Si, they no wanna come and claimed I was playing a hoax and threatened to arrest me and then hung up. Want me to try again?"

"Ugh, that figures. Go see if you can get a shoelace from that kid handcuffed to the toilet." I said as I laid the knife to the side. I took Crystal's gauzy white dress in both hands around the tear made from the knife and gave it a rip, tearing it wide open down her belly.

"Actually, uncuff him and tell him to get his butt in here and help deliver this baby!" I yelled after the boy. "God, you know I never got the shirt for delivering a baby." More of a complaint than a prayer, since it looked like now was my time for baptizing my skills. "Now I am totally shirtless and going to get seriously messy. This is how you treat me now that I'm not a medic? You better guide me, because I don't know what the hell I'm doing. C-sections weren't covered in any class I took." *Amen!*

I placed my hands on her lower belly, feeling around to try to gauge the anatomy of the child, then pulled off the gloves. I needed more tactile information than I could get through these gloves. Boy, this was going to be messy, and totally going to violate the rules for body substance isolation and infectious disease control. Good news was, the baby was already turned over. If I remembered right, Crystal was near her due date. I felt movement, which was another good sign. The bad news was that where I was going to slice was near the head of the baby. Too deep, and not only could I slice organs that could send the baby into toxic shock, but I could also potentially cut the baby. And this wasn't the only hard part of the whole process.

I clutched the knife by its blade high near the tip, leaving about a fingernail's length, and placed my hand where the baby's head was. I gently tried to push the baby away from where I was going to cut and inserted the knife with a sudden shove until the belly met my fingers, the blade no more than half an inch deep. I would almost rather be too shallow and have to cut again, but I did not want to waste time and make this mess more traumatic than it already was. The tip of the blade went in on one side of the lower belly below where the head felt to be, then I made a slice across nearly from one hip to the other.

Now the fun part. My hands went in as Pablito came into the room behind me.

"Do you know what you're doing?"

"No, but I was a medic and I read the instructions in a coloring book once, so I'm a professional now."

"A coloring book?" he seriously asked while I felt around and reached under shoulders through God only knew what.

"Yes, but I flunked the open-book test because I ate my crayon, so you better get your shirt off in case this gets messy and you have to catch a baby."

"Well, you look like you know what you're doing," he said, pulling his shirt off and holding it open as I dragged a baby in a placenta out of a dead lady's belly. My fingers tore open the bag and fluid gushed over my lap, soaking me from the waist down. The baby slipped, slid, and nearly flew out from my hands as it flopped and nearly flipped before I got my crap in gear and got everything under control. Only he—and it was a boy—was turning blue, getting darker by the second and not breathing.

"Here, hold this." I handed him the baby. He needed both hands to hold the baby for me to do what I had to do next. I pinched my fingers around the umbilical cord a good six inches or more away from the belly of the baby and used the knife to sever his connection to his dead mother, then dropped it to the side and kept my fingers clamped tight on the cord.

I used a corner of the shirt to clear out the baby's mouth and wipe his face clean. I tried flicking my fingers against his feet to shock and startle the baby. Nothing.

I covered the mouth and nose of the baby with my mouth and breathed life from my lungs into his, just enough to see the chest rise before stopping. Again, no response.

I felt the inside of the upper arm of the baby, trying to feel for a pulse in the brachial artery. Nothing.

"Put him down on the ground," I ordered. *This baby was moving just a few moments ago.* I had time—precious little, but I had faith in my skills.

My fingers found the landmark easily over the sternum in the center of the chest and I started making this baby's heart work, whether it wanted to or not. Fast and rapid, I gave thirty chest compressions and then breathed once, then another time. The baby responded, lifting its arms and legs as it squalled into my mouth.

"That's it, Reggie! Give me your war cry, son, and let this world hear your fury!" Tears were racing down my cheeks toward the grin on my face. "Death has no victory over you, little brother." His outrage was fierce from such a small chest, and his fists were clenched as he screamed over and over with every lungful he pulled in. I took a deep breath and held him to me cradled in one arm. I was drained physically and emotionally. "Pablito, we need your shoelace or something to tie down this cord."

"You were awesome. I've never seen anything like that before," he said, pulling off a short shoelace from a loafer. Lucky he wasn't in slippers.

"Well, of course I'm awesome. But I thought you were a healer?" Fingers freed, I let go of the cord and gathered the little man in my arms, wrapped in the shirt, and stood up.

"No, I read tarot and can do séances. But I try to use crystals and herbs to heal sickness of the mind and heart with."

"Ugh. When this is over, get your butt into church, put that crap away, and consider nursing school if you really want to learn to heal. This left hand, right hand crap will get you hurt."

"Oh, but I'm a white witch. I don't do this left stuff."

"Pablito, I am done warning you. Don't make me give you last rites."

His eyes got wide and he shook his head like the fear of God just gotten laid on him. I had doubts, but that wasn't my call.

I turned around and spotted the boy that had been kidnapped.

"Hey, kid, you owe me your name so I can stop calling you 'kid.'"

"My name is Thomas for the saint who walked with the Christ, Jesus."

"You keep walking in that direction. You still have that phone?" He pulled it out as I heard the rumble of V-twins and something else with more horsepower than anyone with good judgment would want to be driving.

I walked through my trail of destruction, leading Thomas and Pablito. "Come on, Pablito, I'm going to introduce you to my attorney. He doesn't have enough work to keep him honest with just me, so I'm going to tell him to represent you, too, and you are going to tell the police and news and anyone who will listen everything you know and saw."

"I can't do that! Las Hermanas Del Muerte will have me killed. This was just a local coven, and not even one of Contessa Serena's main ones in Texas!"

"That's good to know. We will need to know everything else, too," I said over my shoulder as I stepped out into the courtyard. Parking was limited to lining up on the side of the road and most of the bikes were lined up on the other side, which was good, because that was near my backpack.

Pappa Gun was blocking the whole road with his Chevelle. I had a secret love affair in my head for that car.

"Room four has Chupi and a young girl that murdered her mother. Both were knocked out when I left them, but you better put some of the boys on them until we can get the police back here to actually work," I told Pappa Gun by way of greeting as he ran up to me. He nodded his head and started pointing fingers and giving orders. Steven came up calling my name and asking what happened, no plate carrier vest or AR this time. That made him better at holding a baby for me, though. I handed him little Reggie and placed a bloody finger to my lips. The baby had just stopped screaming, and I wanted to keep it that way.

I left Steven in startled silence, holding a baby in a shirt, and kept walking. Pablito and Thomas tried following.

I put a hand on Pablito's chest. "This is Attorney Steven Womack." I looked at Steven. "And this is your new client. You can talk to him before me."

I continued walking toward the line of bikes as Thomas stayed at my heels. I had a shadow, and I didn't mind.

"Thomas, where are your parents?" I asked as we walked through the DBMC, a lot of whom I did not know and had not meet just a few days ago. They looked a little confused when they saw me walking by without speaking to any of them. Gee, I was sure glad the cavalry showed up to rescue me. *That was nearly close.*

"Mexico, señor. I rode the train to the border, but *los coyotes* took me and other kids. They claimed they would take care of us and get us to America and get us jobs to support our families."

"We need to get your hiney home. I don't know what made them try to send you by yourself here, but you have no idea what—" I stopped before walking into the grass and looked at him. "Well, ok, you've probably got a good idea now. But anyway, you need to be home. Stay here a second, I'm just going to get something I dropped here."

"If I go back, *señor*, I'll be killed. All boys my age fight for *Cuchillo del Santa Muerte* or die."

Was the whole damn world on fire? I picked up my backpack and came back to the kid, leading him as I slung the backpack into the back of Pappa's Chevelle after snatching my smokes and a lighter.

I lit up and watched the tableau in front of me. Steven finally came back to confront me, still cradling the baby and gently rocking it. I really wanted to sit down right now. Hell with it—I did, even if that put me at a lower position under Steven psychologically. Whether he felt superior or not, I could care less right now.

"What the hell did you do, Bodhi!?" he somewhat quietly stage-whispered.

"That depends if you are my attorney or if I am persona non grata. Right now, I am only going to talk my attorney. And someone should really be trying to get the police here to do their jobs. I've tried several times already."

"Fine, stand up and talk to me. I'll be your attorney."

"If you want to represent me, Steven, then you get your butt off your high horse and down to my level."

I tried to feel bad for hurting his feelings bad enough to make him cuss at me and stomp off. Maybe he needed to go cry now. I took a drag from my cigar and sat in the middle of the road. I really needed a shower now. I was streaked in blood and gore, little of it mine.

I heard the sound of a loud diesel engine burning up the road of Highway 90. I didn't know what kind of SUV this was; its panels looked welded and riveted, it was all flat black, and it had nothing but angles and armor on the outside with a serious bumper on the front. It came around the corner without slowing, its tires giving cries of torment as the helltruck went into a slide and came straight at us. I turned my head sideways, considering it as I was caught in its headlights. Everyone else scattered, but it pulled into another slide until it came to a smoking stop, engine rumbling as I sat there on my butt about two feet from its fender.

I took a long drag before standing up, hearing the driver door click open and slam closed. I saw the hat first, a silver crisp felt Stetson with a Ranger badge in the center of the crown, then saw the rest of Ranger Huntsman come walking around the helltruck. He was kitted up in a load-bearing vest and an old hogleg single-action cross draw on his left hip in front of a legit battle sword. *Someone should tell him he's breaking the knife laws of the state. I could use the entertainment.*

"I like the way you make an entrance, sir," I greeted him and waited to get my butt kicked in a one-sided fight. "Can I surrender myself to your custody?"

"What the hell makes you think I even want you?" He said it the way someone would talk to a stray dog that wouldn't go away.

"If I was you, I would run from me, too. You are too good to be seen around someone like me, but if I could be anyone I wanted when I grow up, it would be you."

"I thought I told you to stay out of this mess? You have no idea what you've done."

"No, sir, I don't. But I know what I had to do, so I did it. I got no regrets. Put a bullet in me, lock me up, or write me off—I wouldn't blame you no matter what."

Pappa Gun came walking up about that time, along with Steven.

"Bodhi, just shut up and say nothing else to law enforcement. I'll do all the talking."

I turned and gave him a look.

"Long time no see, Gunny."

"Do I know you?" Pappa Gun gave Ranger Huntsman a quizzical look.

"We were in the same place on the same day and time as each other. It was the fifth of November and across the world from here. We were never introduced, but you carried me through hell while I leaked all over your uniform until you got me to the LZ and left me there while you went back for more like me."

"Were you one of those Green Berets that got blown to hell?"

"I'm not able to disclose the nature of where my presence was or was not and what we were doing. Do you know this snot-nosed kid?"

"I do, and I claim him as one of mine. Does that carry any weight for you, Ranger?"

"Damn, small world. I hoped I would never see him again, and when I heard he was in your organization I hoped you would be able to take care of him and keep him honest so I wouldn't have to. He did a lot of good in the prison he was at—not many like him. Most who are get dead or get smart. I see you done got, stupid boy. How many casualties?"

"Well, I'm not honestly sure how many of their own got taken by friendly fire, sir. I think they are all in room one, though. Every person that got hacked with a machete or shot with a gun, they did to each other. I asked the Gunny to put some men in room four on their high priest and priestess. That girl was the daughter of one of the men Las Hermanas killed in prison, sir. She stabbed her pregnant momma to death under the command of the dickless priest. There is a crooked deputy sheriff with his hands and ankles broken. He kidnapped this boy and brought him here to serve up to that dickless priest."

"Must you keep calling the priest 'dickless'?" Steven asked.

"Well, he is a eunuch," I stated the obvious.

"Oh, you're being literal. Either way, Bodhi, I think you should stop here and talk to me before going further."

"Sorry, but I won't do that to the Ranger. He has a need to know, and if he asks anything of me, I will give it to him."

"Just tell me how much trouble you're in, little brother. I don't know if I can help, but I won't hurt you. How many did you shoot?"

"None, sir."

"None? How many did you fight, then?"

"Everyone not shot or cut, sir. I only defended myself against anyone that tried to shoot me or use a machete on me."

"How many was that?"

I started trying to replay the fights in my head, counting on my fingers as I encountered them in my mental feedback.

"Counting the two in room four trying to do the black mass, nearly two dozen, sir. I think close to half are in serious need of a trip to the ER, but none need it more than the baby I delivered from the mother the dickless priest had the daughter murder."

"Hand to hand?" Steven asked, sounding shocked.

"Guns are against the terms of my parole," I again stated the obvious with even more certainty.

"I think if that's the way it went down, I can make a call and make sure he won't see the inside of a cop car, unless he wants me to give him a ride. Are you injured anywhere?"

"That is very tempting, sir. I got cut by a machete that was used on people in room one. Some of those skanks and crapheads looked like walking fungal experiments, so I probably need a lot of testing and shots."

"Oh, I got something for that. Hold your horses a minute." He went into his SUV and came back with a tiny brown jar with an eyedropper cap. "Here you go. Now put a drop of this under your tongue. The way, you'll know if you got something if this tastes good. If it tastes good, go ahead and apply this to any wounds you have once every three days. It may sizzle and pop, but that's just from killing any bacteria or diseases in your blood. This medicine will cure zombie bites, so keep it handy."

"Zombies? Those are real?" Steven asked.

"Hell yeah, they're real. They tend to vote in elections. They even voted a Canadian citizen for Texas senator once. Dummies. Some creatures a double tap can't cure."

Steven looked like he couldn't tell if he was having his chain yanked. I was considering the bottle thoughtfully.

"So what if it doesn't taste good?"

"You will projectile poop and vomit your butt off."

"I had a Singapore Sally do that to me once. I paid two dollars for it, though," Pappa Gun said.

"Better than a Singapore Johnny, huh? Bodhi, hang out here while I go do my job for a few minutes."

"I will be right here until you say different. I know you'll want to handle Chupi yourself. I'm not sure what to tell you about the daughter, sir. She has been pretty badly traumatized by all this—I think brainwashed, and no telling what else. Pablito over there should give you a lot of intel, too, and confirm what I said. Oh, wait a minute."

I walked over to the right side of the courtyard.

"Someone isn't sounding grateful!" I yelled at one of the rooms. "Do I need to come back and check on you?!"

"Thank you, sir! Thank you, sir! Thank you, sir! Thank you, sir!" answered back.

"There, now I feel like I did a good deed for someone," I said as

I walked back to the group. I hopped my butt up on the front bumper of the Ranger's helltruck and waited while he got on the phone and walked to the motel to survey the carnage I left for him to have fun with.

"You know," Pappa Gun said as he came up alongside me, "one of the best things about family is when you say or do something stupid, they have to forgive you, or they aren't family and aren't worth wasting your time on."

I nodded my agreement with that, not looking at him, just watching the Ranger go to room four first, try the door, and go back to three.

"But when one of them asks forgiveness anyway, you know that means they want to be a part of the family with you, right?"

"I don't have much family. But that's how I would want it to be with those I call family."

"So, I try to make sure I don't do much to need forgiveness to be the one to ask. But I am sorry for what I said about you to my son earlier, Bodhi. I hope you can let that go and know I had my heart in the right place, just not my head."

"You are cool with me, Gunny," I said. I was so drained. I thought what I'd went through with Crystal and her baby had taken everything out of me, but I still had more to wring out. I wondered where it all came from, where the bottom was, and just how bad it was going to hurt to find it. "I just hope I'm half as cool with you."

"That depends if you can drag yourself to go tubing today or not. If you can, you're awesome. If you can't, well, you might not be as cool as I think you are."

CHAPTER 32

So there I was, as we all are at the worst parts of our lives where we must define what we're made of. To be at our best while going through our worst, hoping that we will still survive with enough humanity to help others and learn to do good without constantly failing from bad judgement.

Our lives are all interconnected in a tapestry that weaves the story of human history. We all begin at one point and move in the same direction, crossing intersecting relationships that shove us down or lift us up as we wind and weave our ways ahead. Maybe humanity is reaching the end of the story told by that tapestry, or maybe we are just getting the party started. Like the song says, "The wheel in the sky keeps on turning."

Seldom do we attempt to lift ourselves up high enough to see where we're going and what we do to get there, much less to gain a bigger perspective to see the whole picture. I doubt there has ever been anyone able to do that this side of life.

I had blood on my hands, blood washed all over my body. It covered me from head to toe along with all of my guilt. I had failed one son in this life, saved another son, and asked to be saved by a Third. It was the Son of God that I gave myself to and begged salvation from.

No other son could give that to me.

I was shirtless still. I was probably blinding a lot of people on the river, but I was enjoying the cold beer in my hand, the water under my butt, and the girls in bikinis around me.

Rebel had her feet hooked under my tube, and the ice chest on a raft with a waterproof speaker was cranking out music that made everyone else's ears bleed and my head bang. She had brought along a gang of her girlfriends. I didn't know how many were legal drinking age, but all were either starting college in the fall or older siblings and friends of friends. They had Diesel for eye candy, Geezer for laughs, Rooster to make me look tan, and Tugger because everyone needs to see a wet Wookie at least once in their life. I totally envied Tugger and his beard. It was epic.

One of the girls was playing with his hair and giving him a manbun. Which is totally an oxymoron, but Tugger had lost that war to a dark-haired Cajun queen that had transferred to the university Rebel would be going to in the fall with some of her friends. They had it all planned out, and the world was in the palm of their hands.

I didn't know if I was going to have more visions and voices, but I figured if they came when trouble was around, that would be good.

The people I had the highest respect for in my life had taken an oath to defend the Constitution and put their lives on the line, and I would never be among them. But I knew what separated the greatest of them wasn't just that they served their enlistment and did what they were paid for. It was that they saddled up when trouble hit and settled accounts without asking for repayment.

Now I was a dreg of society, a felon who was struggling in a sub-citizen class to have rights and be a man.

Regardless of how you may judge me, I know what is right, and I know how people should be treated. Respect given is a reflection of the honor you possess. Honor could only be possessed as long as you continue to do what is Right. Not by yourself, but doing right by others as you would have them do to you.

It was biblical, a concept that laid a universal foundation for achieving the best conduct from anyone regardless of their religion.

Could I ever be redeemed for the death of one son, no matter how many others I could save? That was for my God to judge, but I would do my best to make it impossible for anyone else to condemn me by doing what was Right, with a heavy emphasis and gravitas on that word. Rebel had texted me before I kicked off the dance this morning to tell me she couldn't keep me honest if I didn't come back.

I still wasn't sure giving her the chance was in anyone's best interest.

It's sad how easy it is in this world to turn from what is Right. Many people can't see the difference between right or wrong to understand it for themselves or teach it to their own children.

Yet somehow, in the founding of this great country of ours at the darkest hours of the birth of this nation, the greatest of men managed to unite on such principles under the same banner.

Could I do less than they and consider myself at all a patriot, or even a good man?

That is the example of the good that I would become, shown to me by my grandfather who loved his family and sacrificed for this country. All I had to do was see, through his eyes, the direction he was facing and orient myself on where my life should be going.

Just because my grandfather was not a churchgoer or big on religion did not mean he did not deeply respect God. I knew at the end of his life he had recommitted himself.

It wasn't an eleventh-hour conversion, either, such as I had experienced last night with a dying mother in my arms just before I brought her child into this world. Giving her child a chance to continue a legacy, to hopefully break the cycle of death and destruction in spite of all the sins of the parents that went into the DNA of that little person. He could find redemption, just as I could if I wanted it bad enough to earn it and keep it.

PROLOGUE

The following is the final encrypted and still unread entry in the Journal of Caedmon Murphy, presently waiting for discovery and understanding.

Brother Bodhi!

I knew when I was brought to this place and first saw you why I was needed. I do not believe I will be able to personally explain this to you, so it is my hope that one day you will find this and learn for yourself.

I have asked my God that my Bible with its notes and my journal both be found in hands worthy, that should I be taken away, they would be of use to the Right people, because I will be surprised if I walk out of this place. If my tools should fall into your hands, please care for them for me. I would like them returned if I am able to continue the good fight, but I hope they may be of some use to you. If they should fall into your hands, that truly would be a sign from God, wouldn't it?

There is something I will confess to you that I share with few people, and that is that our Father has given me a prophetic gift. But one unlike any I have known ever to exist. However, I believe I have rarely, or perhaps never, actually met a true prophet of God. Most I meet who claim such a gift run around telling people they will become rich and glorified through ministry.

They look to the heavens for signs and cast predictions, without encountering The True Face of Our Lord and hearing His direct message to them.

I have such a message for you, and I doubt you will take it seriously unless I prove it to you externally, so bear with me and please keep an open mind, for what I say comes as a burden to bear with a warning.

Time belongs to God. No other can claim control over the future. God's word is His, and no one else can claim it for their word without suffering the curse from it. God will use law to reach you, for all good law is God's law. And do not be surprised if He allows it to be corrupted by man to reach you all the more conveniently, for there are consequences of violating the law that He can exploit, as I am well paying myself to bring me to you, my brother.

The numbers of 7 and 3 come strongly into my heart for you, and I believe these to be measurements of days of trial for you. 7 and then 3, with the 3rd day being the single most personally defining for you, and I am guessing the dates began when you lost your last celly for me to take his spot. So, you can see 7 and 3 plus the 1 and get 11 there, or just see the two 3s to make 33, and not just see that I am totally randomly, accidently, for no reason showing you 33, 7, and 11. Though it may be madness, there be method behind it.

So, read from the book of the Prophet Ezekiel chapter 33, verses 7 and 11. These speak of your calling.

Math has laws and even a language of its own that can speak for itself. As far as I am aware, I am the only person such a talent for dividing the word into prophetic message since the age of Babylon in a mathematically coherent (to me) message to prove by has been granted to. I know not why, because I suck at math, and when this first happened to me I had yet to read the whole Bible a single time. Perhaps this is my penance for cheating (violated a law or two meself) on so many math test papers in school and believing I would NEVER need math in the real world?

So hang on, because I am showing you God owns time and can use any law to teach us His Will and Way.

Though I was lead to Ez 33 and 7 and 11, maybe you question if it should not be 30, because 7 and 3 equal 10 and times 3 comes to 30. Well, so be it. We can do that, and I will show you the difference is your relationship.

But I will also show you why this is your personal calling and why not anyone can assume it onto them, because of the difference in you, your calling, and your relationship, and no one else's.

The difference in 7 and 11 is a verse 4.

The difference in 30 and 33 is one 3, so 13.

Or we can argue between the 2 of us over 30 and call it 15, and take your 2 again from that division between the 2 of us.

So, 13 and 4 with 15 and 4.

The difference in your calling AND relationship from everyone else is in both those chapters and verses.

Romans 13:4 for God's apostle where he covers law the most, and John 15:4 who witnesses the relationship of Christ the most.

These four verses found in Ez 33:7 and 11, John 15:4, and Romans 13:4 are all the inheritance of anointing and blessings and burdens from the Lord our God to you and you alone, Bodhi, should you accept and not reject your calling and your anointing and BE THE DIFFERENCE in this world.

Now, my word of caution in rejecting this calling and relationship. Take the difference away, and you have just two 33s and have taken the difference from 7 and 11 and are left with the words of caution from the prophet Isaiah in 66:4 that apply to EVERY PERSON who rejects their calling and their relationship with our Lord and Savior.

So, do us a favor and look up those 4 verses I showed you, challenge yourself to learn what true liberty from our Lord is and means, and seek first the kingdom of the Lord.

We have only just met, and I watch you sleep after baring your soul to me and the God that is within me. But I will watch over you while you rest as long as my God will allow me to help protect His servant.

I pray your path brings you to that relationship, and I pray that we meet again one day. I pray God does not take me from the war, because the battles ahead for you should be a hell of a fight I would not want to miss!

Ezekiel 33:7
"So thou, O son of man, I have set thee a watchman unto the house of Israel; therefore thou shalt hear the word at my mouth, and warn them from me."

Ezekiel 33:11
"Say unto them, As I live, saith the Lord God, I have no pleasure in the death of the wicked; but that the wicked turn from his way and live: turn ye, turn ye from your evil ways; for why will ye die, O house of Israel?"

Romans 13:4
"For he is the minister of God to thee for good. But if thou do that which is evil, be afraid; for he beareth not the sword in vain: for he is the minister of God, a revenger to execute wrath upon him that doeth evil."

John 15:4
"Abide in me, and I in you. As the branch cannot bear fruit of itself, except it abide in the vine; no more can ye, except ye abide in me."

Isaiah 66:4
"I also will choose their delusions, and will bring their fears upon them; because when I called, none did answer; when I spake, they did not hear: but they did evil before mine eyes, and chose that in which I delighted not."

www.ingramcontent.com/pod-product-compliance
Lightning Source LLC
Chambersburg PA
CBHW051136030726
47504CB00004B/901